IN THE SHADOW OF SHAKESPEARE

A Novel

Ellen Wilson

Four Clover Press
Jennifer Luitwieler editor

His pen was sharp-pointed like a poignard. No leaf he wrote on, but was like a burning-glass to set on fire all his readers.

Thomas Nashe – playwright

When a man's verses cannot be understood...it strikes a man more dead than a great reckoning in a little room.

As You Like It - Shakespeare

Chapter 1

It was dark, except for a single soft spotlight in the middle of the stage. Contained in the spotlight was a woman curled in a fetal position. She was quiet and unmoving, simply dreaming of how everything had developed. She had been a woman with child.

The experience had left her drained, as birthing a new dream would. She stirred, yawned, and stretched her arms and legs; unfolding in spread eagle fashion like da Vinci's Vitruvian Man. Alice had written the play at night, after teaching. When it was done she had put down her pencil and cried. It had been that much a part of her. Now it had to live without her.

She thought of how they had bonded like a family during the course of this production. It was closing night, and the theatre was still packed after a continuous eight-week run. They had all received standing ovations, so they held hands onstage, bowing deeply, laughing. The audience finally let them go. Backstage Derrin brought out the champagne, opened it, and promptly dumped it over Sonia's head. Alice was to say that her theatre family was more real than her family of origin–certainly more genuine.

If someone were to open the door to the theatre, they would see this image. They would see Alice on the stage, as a sacrifice to her art. They would wonder about this writer, director, actor–what was she thinking? Or perhaps, given the whims and eccentricities often attributed to the artist, they might think this woman was giving herself over to some artistic method—some sort of meditative muse.

The door creaked open and a small sliver of light appeared on the dark red carpet. Alice waited, expecting to hear the voice of Sonia or Derrin. Nothing. Her irritation grew, and she felt the red flush of blood rise from her neck to her face.

"Yes?" She sat up.

Alice peered through the dimness to the crack of light and waited for her eyes to adjust. The light illuminated a shadow of a man with dark, shoulder length hair. Alice shielded her eyes with her hand. He wore a doublet adorned with little red slashes. A costume, she thought, something from the Renaissance. She worked her memory, running through the plays that were scheduled, but there was certainly nothing of that period, nothing Shakespearean.

"Can I help you?" she said.

For a moment, she thought he was going to come through the door and down to her on the stage, and she was afraid. He had hated the play—it was too feminist, too radical…her mind trailed into the possibilities of what someone could do with a knife, and she scrambled to her knees.

After gazing at her a moment, he silently turned and shut the door quietly behind him. Alice sat back on her haunches, perplexed. *Who was that? Somebody playing a trick on me.*

"Wait!" She ran up the aisle, passing the hundreds of seats that just a few hours before had been filled with people.

Grabbing the door handle she flung it open. Passing into the hall she looked both ways but saw nothing. It was completely quiet. No one. She went to the main doors and opened the door to the street, looking up and down for the man in the doublet.

He was gone.

Chapter 2

Mary held his hand as they walked down the lane. He was only three, but his legs were sturdy, and he was used to walking along with his sister. Kate had shooed them out of the house when she had begun sweeping. They were getting underfoot and she was an exhausted five months pregnant.

He patiently plodded along beside her, feeling safe and warm. The day was sunny and the breeze was soft. A laugh escaped him, and he was overcome with joy—eyes rolled back, head lolling. It was a laugh caught in blissful merriment, and it would also be characteristic of him when he was older.

At the Mermaid, playwrights Jonson and Kyd would turn their heads expectantly, knowing there was only one owner to a laugh like that – Kit Marlowe.

"Look what the cat dragged in. Marlowe!" Jonson pulled a chair next to him.

Kit motioned to the hostess. "A round for my fair play makers." He sat next to Jonson.

"You'll never for the likes of you guess who I've got for a patron." Kit said.

"I know, " Kyd said, taking a long drink of ale. "The young Walsingham, cousin of Sir Francis, the spymaster. I have seen him making eyes at you."

Kit smiled, stretching his hands before him. Hands dirty and stained with ink. He took a shilling out of his pocket and pressed it into Kyd's hand. "Never Tom, never, do we need to go hungry again," *and kissed him on the cheek.*

The dust clung to their clothes, to their hands. It got in their eyes. It couldn't be helped. All the streets in Canterbury were like this. A fly landed on Christopher's face, tickling him. He rubbed his eye and then immediately took Mary's hand again.

"Go?" He said, looking up at her face.

She pointed towards the end of the lane where the road turned out of the city and headed towards London. He strained his eyes looking. There was nothing but pasture and a few gardens the townspeople had planted. The air was fresher here away from the stench of the city. Mary took a deep breath and coughed. Her face turned red as the spasm clutched her, pressing her lungs to wheezing gasps.

The trees stood out along the road and Christopher remembered when he saw them. He ran ahead and picked up an apple, taking a bite. Mary came along side him, examining his apple.

"No. Rotten." She grabbed the apple from him and he cried. He was hungry for fruit; something fresh, beyond day old bread and salted meat.

She circled the tree looking for a fresh fallen apple. Finding one, she handed it to him and looked for another. A coughing spasm gripped her and she covered her mouth. Lifting her hand away, she looked at it. It was covered in blood and grime.

There was some movement across the lane in the tall grass by some rocks. A figure stirred and rose. It was a man dressed in dirty rags with a filthy hood over his head. He was rooted to the spot next to the rocks, staring at them. Stretching, he put his arms over his head, then on his hips, and continued staring at them. Mary watched him as she held her skirt open and Christopher filled it with the apples.

The man was a beggar, someone not to be trusted. The beggars sat outside the taverns and inns, waiting for handouts or money. Her mother had warned her about these kinds of people, calling them hobgoblins and snary spites. Mary watched.

He started walking towards them and she grabbed Christopher's hand. The apples tumbled to the ground.

"Come." She firmly gripped his hand and walked briskly towards home.

The beggar watched them leave as he stood next to the trees. He bent over and picked up an apple, gnawing on it with the few teeth he had left.

Chapter 3

Alice lay against the pillows reading and the side lamp softly illuminated her side of the bed. Next to her, Albert slept. He snored softly and then rolled over, grunting.

"Will you turn that bloody light out and come to bed?" He propped himself up on an elbow. "I can't sleep with that thing on. I just had the most horrid dream."

"Oh?" Alice examined the newspaper clipping beside her. It was a picture of Derrin in *All the Queen's Men*, her play, her baby. He played the part of a gay union leader, undecided about coming out of the closet. Sonia played his wife and ardent feminist, not sure if she wanted to leave him. They truly loved one another. The play was about friendship, power, and politics. What people would do to get ahead, and not. The characters were forced to draw a moral line in the sand. Many of them did not want to do this, but they were forced to.

Alice looked around at the newspaper and magazine clippings she was accumulating for her scrapbook. The idea of the union flew in the face of the rising pro-business sentiment climbing in the country. She had read several editorials rejecting the play outright because of its strong pro-union sentiment. She was surprised she had not realized this before, but as the clippings accumulated the evidence was unavoidable.

She frowned, wondering what would become of it. Oh sure, she was used to backlash from her plays; the content was controversial. But now people were criticizing the board of directors, threatening to take their anti-union and pro-business rhetoric to a higher power. Alice wondered who this higher power would be.

Albert lay back on the pillow. "Don't you want to hear my dream? Horrid, just horrid." He covered his face with his hands, then rubbed his eyes. He was beginning to grow a beard. Alice liked it.

"You have been working too hard. You get caught up in all your clients' dreams and you can't detach." Alice smiled and rubbed his scrubby beard. She was used to Albert's ramblings about dreams. He analyze their dreams as if they were a Hieronymous Bosch painting—flitting, glorified images of a divine psyche gone askew. He said that he wanted them to make sense of the imagery, to be able to make a puzzle from the incoherent pieces. All people will do this, he said, given enough time.

"Albert, could you look over here and make sense of my images? What do you think is going on."

He rolled over and rested his head on his hand, surveying the clippings she had lain on the bed. "In what order would you like this response? From a psychological point of view, or merely a transcription of events?"

Alice looked at him. Sometimes she wondered whether he was serious. She was an American, used to the slang and the informality of the Midwest. He was British, a Londoner, and he spoke in clipped, proper phrases. But such eloquent speech. Sometimes Alice was jealous of the fluency of his language, how it trickled like water across stone, flowing from the source.

"You tell me, whatever comes into your head."

"Okay, my dearest." He lay back on the bed with his hands clasped behind his head. "It was night and we were walking across a bridge– "

"Albert, look at my clippings, please."

"My dream."

"Alright. Go on." Exasperated, Alice lay another picture of Sonia next to Derrin. She liked this one, the expression on Sonia's face was tremendous, but that was why she had chosen her for her lead actress in most of the plays she produced. She had great range of intent and expression. "Look at this one of Sonia."

"Darling, please.

"Sorry, sorry, I'm agitated tonight. There is something else I must tell you that goes along with the pictures."

"What?"

"No, you continue."

"That isn't fair. You tell me. I need to know what goes on with your pictures."

"No, really, let's do this one thing at a time." she said.

Albert picked up a picture of Derrin. Gazing at it a moment he lay it back down in a different place. Alice felt like she was watching a detective look for clues at the scene of a crime.

"I don't know. I don't see anything that precipitated this backlash."

Startled, she looked at him.

"Of course I know of the criticism, love. I read the papers. You have been too busy with the play, and I didn't want to bring it up. It would have only added to your stress, and God knows we can't have that." He put his hand on hers trying to draw her to him.

"Wait," Alice pulled away. "Now it's your turn."

"Yes, the dream." He lay back, hands interlocked behind his head. Alice looked at his nipples, the hair on his chest. She gently touched a nipple and he took her hand. A sudden pain crept up her throat and she became tense.

"Wait, is it bad? Will it make me cry?"

"You broke my heart," he said. "We fell off the bridge together, and you flew away, vanishing into thin air."

***

That night Alice had a dream. The moon shone brightly in a sky filled with clouds littered with light. The light, silver, gold, and streaked with blue hit the water. A man swam there, crossing a large lake bordered by granite stones. Trees filled the distance and the moonlight fell upon their leaves. He swam sure and strong, and she saw his arm lift from the water and breech into the next stroke. He swam in the path of the moonlight, his dark hair shining against his face. His face was full of longing, for he was swimming toward his love.

He was tired. As he moved forward the lake seemed to grow;it became larger and larger, and he knew he was caught. He could no longer see the shore. Terrified, he spun around and around in the water, looking for land, looking for relief from a watery grave.

"Alice," he whispered. "Alice…please…" His head bobbed in the water as he struggled to stay afloat, his mouth choked with water and he went under. As he sank into the depths, his hair floated like seaweed, splayed out around him. The moonlight filtered down into the green depths as he sank, darker and darker…

She awoke and sat bolt upright in bed, gasping for air. Albert lay silently beside her. The moon shone brightly, spilling light onto their bed through the open window. The white curtains undulated in the soft breeze.

She lay her hand in the slice of light, illuminating it into a ghostly pale.

Chapter 4

She couldn't concentrate and constantly glanced at the clock on the wall, watching as the seconds ticked painfully by. Her students shifted uncomfortably in their seats, deliberating over their timed essays. She gave these essays once a week to improve their writing skills. They groaned because the timed essays were always on Friday afternoon at one o'clock; right before school let out. Heads popped up and eyes stared out the window.

She drummed her fingers slowly on the table lost in thought. The real reason she gave these essays was to give herself a break. By Friday she was drained and had precious little energy to think of herself, of her plays.

After a production she was always frazzled. It would take her some time to get back into the semblance of normality.

Dion, always the first one done, slapped his essay on her desk.

"Done." He glared at her.

She picked up his essay. "Looks like it comes pretty easy to you."

"Yeah, it does." Dion looked proud in spite of himself.

Alice recognized sharp and pretty sentences next to the pile of chicken scratch Dion routinely put forth. "You want to start editing it?"

"Nope."

Dion walked down the aisle and pulled at Charlane's new hairdo. She instinctively put a protective hand to her head.

"Nah." He slouched in his seat, his pants falling below his underwear.

"Ten more minutes, everyone."

More groans and sighs. She glanced towards the window which looked out on Main Street. A bum staggered next to the old Goodoff's Department store. He stopped when he found the wall would support him, and easing himself against it, sat down. Alice frowned, making a mental note to call social services about this guy—he had been stumbling around out here in front of the school for the past week and obviously needed help.

The bell rang, jarring her from her thoughts. The kids all whooped and jammed into each other in their haste to get out of the door.

"Mother fucker!" Dion slammed Roberto Gomez on the floor.

"Hey!" Alice grabbed Dion by the back of the collar. "What is with you two? It's Friday, doesn't that mean anything?"

"Yeah, time to kick some ass!" Dion lunged for Roberto.

"Roberto, go." said Alice.

Roberto looked uncertain, ready to pounce if given the chance, but his faced changed quickly into a mask of neutrality as he eyed the open door of the classroom. He sulked out the door.

She waited a few moments as she held onto Dion's shirt, feeling the blood pounding in his neck. She was reminded of a raging beast and thought of Othello.

"Let me go." He strained in his shirt.

"Alright." She let go of his collar, and motioned for him to sit at a desk. "What's this about?"

"The man trying to home in on my woman." Dion looked out the window, watching the kids pour out of the building.

So it was like *Othello*.

"Well, you two seem pretty tight. I doubt if Renita is going to switch sides."

Dion, still staring out the window, began to get the beginnings of a smile creeping around the corners of his mouth. "Yeah, but she live in that neighborhood."

Alice understood that he was referring to the Hispanic side of town.

She hooked her hair behind an ear. "We will be studying what it means to be betrayed and stabbed in the back on Monday."

"What?" Dion dragged his eyes from the window and looked at her.

"We will be reading a play called *Othello*, by William Shakespeare."

"That old, bald, English guy? That be *boring*, Ms. Petrovka." Dion frowned.

"Well, I must admit that the language is a little hard to get used to, but once you get used to it, you kind of flow along and fall prey to the spell of the bard."

He snickered, grabbed his books, and headed out of the room.

"Hey!"

Reaching the doorway he looked back at her.

"Girls like poetry, you know."

"Yeah, right, Ms. Petrovka. See ya Monday." He turned to go.

"Wait!"

"What?" Dion turned again, impatience in his eyes.

"You're turning into quite a good writer."

Dion hesitated for a second, and smiling, headed out the door to freedom.

Alice sat on top of the desk and looked out the window and watched as Dion exited the building. He immediately lapsed into his long, lopey stride, catching up with a few of his friends.

The room seemed big and quiet without all their noise. She stared out the window waiting for her interior world to quiet down, waiting for some peace. She smiled and hopped off the desk and went over to the window to inspect her plants.

She had deliberately chosen hardy types—philodendrons, and ivy—plants that could take a beating. But now they were thriving. *Hardy like these kids. Just a little extra care, that's all they need. A little water, some light – someone to care.*

What do I need to thrive?

The thought surprised her, catching her unaware with her fingers in the dirt, checking the moisture level of the philodendron. She thought of Albert. They had been married for two years now. It was going okay; there was nothing to complain about. *Then what is this all about?* A nagging unease settled itself in the back of her mind.

There was a quick rap on the door frame, and Alice turned her head. Joannie stood there, a smirk on her face.

"I see you can't get enough of this place. Time to go, Petrovka. It's time to relax, and we've got the beer—Miller beer." Joannie swung her arms around in an exaggerated display of a waitress holding a tray full of beer.

"All you need now is the little skirt to complete the Pauli Girl ensemble," said Alice. "Give me a few minutes, will you? I want some time to think about Monday's lesson plan."

"Oh, wing it. You always do. All this English literature stuff…c'mon. What do you really need to know anyway? Reading, writing—what else is there once you get the basics down?"

"There is a thing called thinking, Bryant," Alice tapped her head with her index finger. "I suppose you math types have forgotten how to put two and two together?"

"Ha. Four. No more riddles for today, I'm consciously forgetting how to put things together."

Alice surveyed Joannie; her earnest face, framed by blond hair and steel blue eyes. She thought of how they contrasted each other, yet were very similar.

"We sound like we're married." Alice said.

"Married? Never. Not in the cards for me, my sweeting. I'm outta here. Are you to follow, or not?"

"In a few, Math Mind."

"Okay, see ya at O'Leary's." Joannie said, hitting the door jamb twice upon her exit.

It is quiet now, so quiet.

Sweeting. Who was it that had said that? Alice shut her eyes and thought of lips kissing hers. Warm and moist, a slight dip of a tongue lightly touching hers, then, a hand caressing the back of her neck. It felt good, warm, and she thought of the man in the doublet with red slashes. The Renaissance man. Or was it a woman? A woman dressed as a man?

Take pen to paper and write, scarcely blotting a line...

There was a poster of Shakespeare that Alice kept on the wall, and she went and stood before it. It was a copy of the Droeshout portrait; a picture of the supposed Will, vacantly staring. *There is no introspection here, no feeling.* Alice tilted her head and examined the picture. *Who are you? Something is missing...something is lacking...*

"We will start with you Monday, Will. Will you agree?"

Alice watched the eyes. They stared back, empty and silent.

Impatient, she turned and grabbed her keys off the desk, heading out the door.

Chapter 5

Kate was worried about Mary. She had been curled up on the bed for a week now, coughing and spitting up blood. She had kept the house as warm as possible, boiling water and keeping the fire going. Taking the pot off the fire, she poured the water over some herbs. She took the pan over to Mary and let her breathe in the vapors, then she came back and poured a little cup of the brew to steep for a while.

Christopher came to where she was resting and tugged at her dress. Kate picked him up, tickling him under the chin. He had been constantly underfoot since Mary had been ill.

"You miss yer sister. Don't you?" Kate looked at him, examining his face.

He peered up at her with large brown eyes. Eyes that seemed to see everything; took in everything. Kate would catch him sitting on the floor watching her as she did the daily chores. She wondered what he was thinking. Once, she had mentioned it to John.

"John, look at Christopher's eyes, they are so large. He has the eyes of a monk, or a holy one."

"Don't be silly Kate, he's just a boy."

Christopher sat and looked from John to Kate.

"He has your eyes, John."

"Well I a'nt no monk, am I now Kate?" John winked, then turned and went back to his cobbler's work shop in the next room.

Kate took Christopher from her lap, and set him on the ground. She took the cup of steeped brew into Mary. She was getting worse, her face was flushed and her breathing was labored. Kate dipped a rag in water and lay it on her head, then wiped her neck with it.

"Mary, sweet, Mama has something to drink." She cradled Mary's head, putting the cup to her lips.

Mary pushed the cup away. "Water."

"Mama will get some water."

Kate stood, catching Christopher watching her.

"Mama, why is Mary sick?"

"I don't know Christopher. We need to keep her warm."

Christopher looked over at Mary. "She is warm."

"She is. Very warm. Come Christopher, we need to go, let Mary rest now."

***

In the early morning light Christopher crept from his bed, and went to his sister. It was still dark in the room but he could see that her eyes were slightly open.

"Mary."

She did not answer.

He pulled back the bed covers and touched her face. It was cold; her skin was blue. He crawled in next to her, snuggling as close as he could, trying to keep her warm.

"Mary, we can get apples today, then you will feel better."

When Kate came into the room she found them this way. She put her clenched fist to her mouth and sobbed.

Chapter 6

O'Leary's was always crowded on Friday night. Alice surveyed the bar from her table close to the swinging doors of the kitchen. There was a deer mounted on the wall, pictures of well endowed women in tight racing clothes standing next to fast cars, and a lighted O'Doul's sign in the window.

It was a rough crowd composed mainly of Oldsmobile workers getting off their shifts. They poured out of the factory in droves to get a beer and get in a fight. Alice could never figure why Jeannie chose this bar for their Friday night forays and wished they would go somewhere a little more upscale in downtown Lansing. This place smelled like old tires. She wrinkled her nose, taking a sip of chardonnay.

Alice casually looked around for her father. She hoped she wouldn't see him. He usually didn't go to this bar, so she felt pretty safe.

Joannie burst through the door and was greeted by a few men jubilantly yelling her name. She saw Alice and went over, sat down. The waitress quickly approached, and Joannie ordered a Bud, smiling all the while and laying her hand on the waitress's arm. The waitress, her name tag read, "George," laughed at something Joannie said. More men came through the door dressed in clothes lined with soot and oil. George left when she caught their eye.

"A friend of yours?" Alice coughed. The place was full of smoke and she could hardly hear. Someone leaned over the jukebox pushing buttons, and the sound of Bob Seger's "Hollywood Nights," started to play. There was a loud whoop from a table in the corner.

"I like the drums in this song." Joannie drummed her fingers on the table. "Oh yeah." Joannie lay a hand on Alice's arm, "She was, is a friend. We were dating. God, I hate that word. It always sounds like it's leading up to something. Don't you think?"

"It does lead up to something."

"Maybe for some people." Joannie smiled as George brought her beer, a Budweiser. She took a long, hardy gulp from it.

"This place is so loud, can't we go somewhere else?"

Joannie had a perplexed look on her face as she watched George walk around the room. "I can't believe she likes guys now."

Alice looked over at George. She had her arm around a guy who looked to be around thirty, blond, and muscular.

"Maybe she's looking for something more stable." Alice smirked at her.

"Who? That guy! Give me a break. Pretty soon she'll be calling herself Georgiana." Joannie looked dispirited.

"Is that why we came here? To watch George?"

"No."

Alice felt like a little kid looking for attention. She wanted to yell *Well, pay attention to me, damnit!* The hurt from being ignored as a child flooded her full force. But instead of yelling she looked in her wine.

"Come on Alice, this place is alive; I love it here! Where else could you get all this action?" She nodded to a group of guys who had gotten up dancing and singing to Seger: *He was a Midwestern boy all on his own...*

"Well, it's quieter downtown."

"Downtown," Joannie said. "Amongst the lawyers and government cronies? Forget it! Not for me. C'mon Alice, lighten up. Sometimes I wonder what side of the tracks you came from. Didn't you write a play about this stuff?"

Alice smiled weakly. "Well, yes, it's who I am. It's what I know. You know that." She thought of a little girl with brown hair and brown eyes, sitting on a pink banana seat bike. Looking for popsicle sticks in front of the Dairy Queen so she could make a little box for her treasures. *Who was that girl? Where did she go?*

She watched the guys doing their karaoke imitation of Bob Seger. "I don't know Jeannie, I just can't really relate to any of it anymore." She bit her lip and turned to catch Jeannie's reaction. But Jeannie had gone. She was off talking to George.

***

She arrived home to find that Albert had all the mail spilled out on the table, sorting the junk mail from the bills. He tossed a letter towards her and she deftly caught it. It was a letter from her niece Jasmine.

Alice looked at the envelope. It was pink and decorated with little flowers, hearts and mermaids. She brought it to her nose, inhaling deeply. It smelled like patchouli. She flopped on the couch and extracted the letter.

Dear Aunt Alice,

Hi! How are you? I am okay. School will be over in another month! Do you think I could come stay with you and Uncle Albert? Mom says it would be okay with her! Yesterday I went shopping with my friend Kayla and bought the coolest pants. They had mermaids and flowers on them! Can you believe it!

Mom has been traveling a lot. I have been staying with my babysitter (which I don't like as much as you!) That's all for now! Please write back soon!

Love,
Jasmine

Alice's sister, Pam, had divorced her husband when she claimed to have found out he had an affair with someone whose hair was blonder than hers.

"It's because he's Arabic!" Pam had wailed, "All Arabic men want Baywatch blonds."

"Don't be ridiculous, Pam. Any guy could have done that. Don't you think it had something to do with the marriage?"

Pam shook her head and pouted.

Now Pam was the corporate head of a major cosmetics firm. She neglected her daughter and tried to make up for it by buying her expensive presents. Alice figured she was richer than dark chocolate mousse, but that's what she had always wanted.

Alice slowly fanned herself with the letter, wafting the smell of patchouli to her nose. She lay the letter on her chest and looked towards Albert. He was still sorting the mail.

"You know, Jasmine is the only normal one in my family. Thank God I have her."

Albert nodded, preoccupied with his letters. Now, he was sorting the mail from his new clinic from their personal mail.

"Where were you tonight, love?" He glanced over towards her through the opening from the kitchen to the living room. All the townhouses had these little openings.

"Out with Joannie."

Albert nodded. "Doesn't she have a drinking problem?"

She wondered how much she should divulge. It was true, Joannie had claimed she had had a problem, but it was taken care of now. But she knew she could never swing that by Albert, who had the hawk-like perception of an analyst.

"I really don't know Albert. She hasn't said anything about a problem. I stayed awhile and came home, that's all." Alice figured feigning ignorance was the safest thing with Albert.

"Where did you go?"

"O'Leary's."

"Hmm. That's a rough place isn't it?" He watched her carefully.

"Not really. It's where the Oldsmobile workers hang out. You know, five o'clock shift ends on Friday, and they all pour out of that factory. Like oil." She fingered the fringe on the pillow, thought of changing the subject. "What about having Jasmine this summer?"

"Jasmine? That's fine, love, fine." He was momentarily distracted by the mail again.

"She needs someone to pay attention to her, and my sister cares only about herself, her money."

"Yes, an insatiable narcissistic desire. But Joannie now—

"Albert!"

"You see, I haven't forgotten; I keep track of these things. And you thought you could throw me off the track." He shook a letter at her.

"Never. How could I be so bold to actually think that?" She rolled her eyes.

"Really, these friends of yours...you know they will only drag you down. And then there is this Sonia and Derrin—"

"Who are two individuals that are extremely talented...please Albert, can we stop?" She put her hands over her face.

Albert put down the letter and sat by her on the couch. He took her hands off her face. "You know I worry about you. You have been working too hard—teaching and this theatre business—why don't you take a break? It would do you good. Go somewhere fun." He kissed her on the forehead. "I know what you are trying to do with your plays, darling, and I know how this press bothers you— the business press taking a stab at it—calling it communist, anti-American and whatnot. You'll see. It will get better." He rubbed her cheek.

"I don't know Albert. Maybe you're right, maybe I do need a break." She looked out the window; the street lights had come on. "I miss watching *Oprah*. Did you tape it for me?" She looked at him hopefully.

"Yes, of course I did, programmed it for the week. It's in the machine."

"Good." She grabbed the remote from the side table, turned the machine on, and hearing the faithful click and whine of the tape unwinding, settled back on the couch. "I hope it's Dr. Phil."

"That armchair quack? I suppose you love him more than me?" Albert pretended to pout in the kitchen. He opened the cupboard and extracted some onions, placing them on the counter. "I'm making stir-fry. Want some?"

"No, it's too late. I don't want anything. I had a sandwich after school." Alice waited through the commercial. "No Dr. Phil. Darn."

"Good. That guy is silly, a father figure really—barking at people. Is that what they want in America?"

"You're just jealous 'cause the guy's a millionaire and you're not."

"Right."

Alice watched as Oprah announced the day's guests. She said they were distinguished Shakespeare scholars who were investigating the authorship controversy. One guest was a Stratfordian, who believed that William Shakespeare had written the plays; another was a Marlovian who believed that Christopher Marlowe had written the plays.

"Will you look at this. Wow. Something intellectual on *Oprah*. See, you can never tell with her." Alice looked over at Albert. He glanced at the TV.

"What's that, love?"

"Shakespeare and Marlowe."

"Oh? Well, that should be old hat to you."

"What?"

"You've heard of the authorship controversy."

"Yes, but I never thought much of it. Thought it was silly, really."

"You should listen." Albert nodded towards the TV. "The Marlovians are quite strong in England."

"Really?"

"As a matter of fact—well, Bernie, of all people, is a real Shakespeare buff. He's convinced that Marlowe is the author."

"No way. Bernie?"

"Yes, Bernie. It really is fascinating how this Shakespeare thing is kind of like a religion to some people. Just fascinating." Albert shook his head in disbelief.

Chapter 7

The bells had tolled for Mary and they had buried her. As they turned towards home in the hot noonday sun, the dusty streets seemed worse than usual. More and more people were coming to the city, and the streets were packed with the filth of animals and humans. Kate almost tripped over a beggar lying huddled in the street, realizing that he was probably dying.

John took Kate's hand and gave it a squeeze. Tears streamed down her face, and she wiped them away.

When they got home, John went straight to his cobbler's shop to work. Kate sat numbly in a chair in the next room, listening to him pounding leather with a hammer. Christopher sat huddled at her feet sucking his thumb. She picked him up and sat him on her lap.

"Damn it to hell!"

Kate heard John throw the hammer against the wall. Then: silence.

She stroked Christopher's hair, but he wriggled from her lap and climbed into Mary's bed.

"Christopher , no." Kate felt that it was a bad omen for her son to sleep in her dead daughter's bed. He might die too.

Dear Jesu, please—make it stop, make it stop...

Kate picked him up and put him in her bed. He lay there clutching Mary's old poppet. Staring into space.

Chapter 8

Alice, Sonia, and Derrin sat cross-legged on the stage, pouring over old scripts. Sonia had found a script which she showed Derrin, and they both read it. Alice stretched and looked towards the audience. All those empty seats. There was a tangible presence out there. A collective energy that remained hidden until opening night.

Alice dug through the pile and finally found what she was looking for. She placed it next to the manuscript of *Othello*.

"Remember when I had you read from this Derrin?" Alice tapped the script of *Othello*.

"How could I forget? Then I thought, what is this woman going to throw at me next?"

Sonia looked up. "Yeah, Alice. what are you going to throw at us next?"

She pushed the script towards them.

Sonia snatched it up. "*The Jew of Malta?*"

"Is it one of those homoerotic Renaissance plays?" Derrin said. "Then, I say let's do it." He grinned.

"Not exactly. The play is by Christopher Marlowe. And I think you're thinking of *Edward II*, Derrin. If you are thinking of one Marlowe's plays." Alice knew Derrin was all for gay empowerment, having just come out of the closet. "It's very similar to *Othello*. In fact, many scholars believe that Shakespeare's *Othello* is based on *The Jew of Malta*."

Alice didn't really want to talk about how she felt about the Marlowe versus Shakespeare controversy. After watching *Oprah,* she was starting to think that Marlowe could be the author of Shakespeare's plays. In essence, Marlowe was Shakespeare. The idea had captured her imagination, and she recognized it as one of those artistic obsessions.

"What I propose to do," she began, "is to do a run of *The Jew of Malta,* then *The Merchant of Venice.* Back to back."

"What for? If the plays are very similar it will be too much of one thing." Sonia said.

"You watched that *Oprah!*" Derrin laughed.

Alice smiled, relieved to be off the hook. Now she wouldn't have to explain her obsession.

"I don't know," Sonia said, "I really don't see the reason for this."

"Well, for one thing it would be a good thing for us, artistically, to compare the plays of Shakespeare and Marlowe. We could only grow artistically from doing that. And for another thing: the audience would be able to compare the talents of Shakespeare and Marlowe. And, quite frankly, I don't think that Marlowe is given enough air time. Why not give him some? And, for another thing..." She trailed off, unsure how to broach the next topic.

"Good enough for me boss. Did you know Marlowe was gay?" Derrin lay back on the floor, arms crossed behind his head.

"Yeah, I've heard that. Maybe he was, maybe he wasn't. Relationships were different between men back then."

"What *one* other thing were you going to add Alice?" Sonia said.

"The other thing...," Alice looked out towards the audience again. The empty auditorium waiting to be filled. Kind of like a womb. She thought of the masks of tragedy and comedy, of Dionysus. "I think the theatre is a good medium to present controversy. The two plays represent Jews in an unfavorable light, portraying them as greedy, never having enough wealth. But they also represent

Christians unfavorably, portraying them as hypocrites." She stretched her legs in front of her. The wooden floor seemed extremely hard today.

"Sure, I'm all for that education and controversy stuff. Hell, look at my life—out of the closet and into the fire!" Derrin grinned.

"That's out of the frying pan and into the fire, dummy." Sonia said. "I can understand your sentiments Alice, but what about all the negative press from the first play?"

"We can't please everyone Sonia."

"I understand that. But why don't we take a breather? Why get right back in people's faces? You know people don't like that. For the most part, people don't like to be challenged. They would really rather sleep through life. Get the paycheck, get the house, la-dee-da-dee-da. You know what I'm saying." She crossed her legs in front of her and ran a hand through her dark curls.

Alice, too, crossed her legs and felt the blood rush to her face. "Well that's not me. You should know that by now. I play by the rules when I have too, but after that, try to jiggle people a little, wake them up." She picked up the cup next to her, took a sip of coffee.

"Jiggle? A little? C'mon Alice, it's more than a little jiggle. It's like a serious *push*." Let's do something fun. How 'bout *Guys and Dolls*?" Sonia said.

"*Guys and Dolls*? No." Alice rolled her eyes.

Sonia frowned. "Look Alice, I'm trying to help. You know we have a board meeting coming up."

"Girls, please!" Derrin threw up his hands in mock exasperation. "Let's not come to blows over this. We can be friends here, right?"

Alice did not see anything friendly in Sonia's eyes. All she saw was a face full of triumph and malice.

She's challenging me, Alice thought. *Challenging me.*

∗∗∗

Alice sat for a long time by herself after Sonia and Derrin had left. She sipped her coffee and half-heartedly hoped the Renaissance man would make an appearance, but the theatre was quiet. She thought of his red slashed doublet, and the portrait of Marlowe as a young man wearing an identical doublet. *It is uncanny*, she thought, *uncanny*, the way the past is intruding on the present. She knew she would have to tell Albert about her obsession, about all the things that were coalescing to carry her along on this path. She would tell him about her dream. It would be uncomfortable…

She walked behind the curtain, picked up her bag and walked down the long aisle to the door. Locking the doors she stepped back, admiring the large wooden structure. The doors been carefully stripped and varnished. Sanded to perfection, Alice thought. It had all started as a dream a long time ago.

The theatre has been built in 1902, and after closing in 1984, had fallen into a state of disrepair. The final blow had come when a fire in an office building next door caused damage to the old theatre. Abandoned and alone, the theatre played nothing but its ghosts.

Alice remembered going to the theatre as a kid sitting through previews of dancing popcorn and corndogs, then the cartoons. Before the movie started she would gaze up to the dark ceiling painted with a million stars.

It was magical, enchanting, and she had fallen in love with the old theatre. She loved to stare in at the marquee posters when she wandered downtown, sister Pam in tow. They had scrutinized the new movie advertisements: *Benji, Pippie Longstocking, The Bad News Bears.* Equally fascinating was the adult entertainment: *The Exorcist, Carrie, The Great Gatsby.* Alice had admired Robert Redford dressed all in white as Gatsby. Her mother had a crush on Robert Redford. She had carefully examined his face and wondered what it would be like to be a famous movie star. Robert Redford was handsome, clean, and well-mannered. Alice had figured he probably didn't sit in a La-Z-Boy and guzzle beer like her father did when he got home from working first shift at Oldsmobile. He probably even paid attention to his family, Alice had thought. She had started thinking what it would be like to have Robert Redford as a father. She had imagined him holding her hand and smiling down at her, having a conversation with her. She had pressed her nose to the glass. Then Pam would tug at her hand, rudely disrupting her fantasy.

That has always been her way, Alice thought, rudely disrupting my life.

Alice told herself to stop. That it was useless dragging up old memories about her sister, about her family. Her shrink had told her to reprogram her thought processes. Told her to get the record off the old groove and on to another one.

Alice had met her shrink through Albert. "A classical Jungian," he said. "You'll love her."

Her shrink, Selina Goldberg, was married to Bernie Heidleman, a fellow professor at the university and a good friend.

Bernie was fascinated with how the world worked, was always trying to figure it out. Bernie's thing was quantum mechanics, the cutting edge of physics. He was also a consummate storyteller, and after a few glasses of wine after dinner, would entertain them for hours about fantastical stories about reality. Because reality for Bernie was not just something you saw with your eyes, or heard with your ears. There was far more to it than that.

"As a matter of fact," he had said, "We are all probabilities. It just appears that we exist."

"Then would you *probably* like another glass of wine?" Alice had asked. "Or just the *illusion* of one? I can easily fill your glass with water."

Bernie had laughed. "Alright, smart ass. I'll tilt my glass towards the heavy probability of securing some more vino. Please." He had flourished his glass before her.

Alice thought Bernie would be a good actor and often told him so. She remembered he had looked pleased when she mentioned it.

At first she thought that it would be uncomfortable seeing Selina, because Selina and Bernie were married, but so far it had been okay.

Anyway, it's just for a little while, she told herself. Just a little while to stabilize after the *episode*. She shivered, pushing the old anxiety from her mind—that heart numbing, pounding anxiety that had coursed through her veins and threatened to rule her life.

She gave the theatre a parting glance—The Lion, she had named it. It was safe to her, like home. The stage had always been like a womb, she thought. *Where you can be reborn.* The outside world was big and chaotic, nothing could be expected or relied on. Selina had told her she was looking for that stabilizing thread running through her life.

"You want to weave on your loom, yes?" Selina had peered over her glasses at her.

"Loom?" Alice thought a minute. The session had been dragging on. She just wanted to get home and eat a pepperoni pizza with mushrooms. Selina was staring at her. If she didn't say something to break the never ending shrink stare it would go on for eternity. Alice pushed back a cuticle, thought.

"Like the Fates?" Alice smiled brightly, believing this was a clever answer in regards to spinning. Maybe Selina would think so, too.

She continued to stare at her.

Alice never did give the answer Selina had wanted, or *thought* she had wanted, she corrected herself, but now that spinning image continued to haunt her. She thought of things connected by string, by fine gossamer twine. Like a spider's web, space and time were connected in a way that was unfathomable to her. But could it be that perhaps they were poised to catch something spectral and special? The thought comforted her as she drove from the theatre and towards home.

***

When she unlocked the door and went inside, she smelled spaghetti sauce. The windows were fogged, and the pasta was on the stove in a rumbling boil. Albert sat in the living room, feet propped up on the coffee table, reading the paper. She tossed the keys on the table.

"How's it going?" She bent over the paper and gave him a kiss. His lips were warm and moist. The paper crinkled as she attempted to put her arms around him, drawing him into something further.

"Please...dinner will be ready in a minute." He gently disengaged himself from her embrace.

She sat on the chair next to him. "What's wrong?" Alice noticed the bags under his eyes, the five-day stubble. "Are you growing a beard or just forgetting to shave?"

Albert brought his hand to his face and absently rubbed his chin. "I suppose a beard would be in order. I keep shaving the stubble off. It has been awhile, hasn't it?"

"Do you mean the beard, or us having sex?"

He quickly broke her gaze, looked out the window. "I'm sorry. I have been preoccupied."

"Albert, what is wrong? Is it me?"

"No, no..." He got up and went into the kitchen. Alice followed him, suddenly frightened. "You've met someone?"

"Don't be silly." He frowned, then smiled at her. "I could ask you the same thing. You have been pretty preoccupied yourself."

Alice sat down at the edge of a chair. "Yes, I have. It's been strange. *Synchronistic* really, the way things that have been happening."

Albert observed her. "What things?"

Alice told him about the Renaissance man she had seen opening the theatre door. Then about the dream she had had.

"You know, I really didn't think much about the dream. Thought it was probably some sort of nightmare regarding being swamped and all that. You know the kind of dream one has when one is too busy. So I was literally drowning."

Albert nodded.

"But the strange thing was, after I had seen that show about the mystery regarding Shakespeare? Well, I picked up a copy of *Hero and Leander*, written by Marlowe. The poem is about Leander trying to swim over to Hero, his love, and he eventually drowns." Alice wrinkled her brow thinking about it.

Albert took the noodles from the stove, dumped them into the colander. "Could it be that person symbolizes another type of preoccupation that you have been having and haven't been able to articulate yet?"

"Like what?"

"Well, as you said, this man was drowning. Perhaps your animus feels unexpressed. Perhaps it is drowning." Albert openly gazed at her, looking for her feelings regarding his interpretation.

"You sound like my shrink."

"I am your shrink."

Alice pulled him towards her and felt a readiness in him that she was looking for earlier. "No more talk about shrinking—just growing." She stood and deeply kissed him, feeling him melt against her.

"I think the noodles can wait." Albert brushed the hair from her face.

"Yes, the noodles, the noodles, the soft, warm noodles."

Giggling, Alice took his hand. Then they raced to the stairs and into bed.

Chapter 9

Kate stirred the stew over the fireplace. She had prepared it when she arose from bed, and it had been cooking the entire morning. John had managed to snare a few small birds from the pasture beyond the walls of the city, and Kate had added them to the stew. The aroma of marjoram, potato, and quail settled in the air.

Goody Frye sat by the fire on a stool smoking a pipe. She mixed the tobacco she had bought from a merchant in town with an herb she knew would bring good health and cleanliness. She was matter-of-fact and not given to rumination. People thought her eccentric and independent but left her alone until they needed help or advice. She sat smoking in silence.

Christopher stared up at her from his place on the floor. Goody caught his eye. "That one's still lonely, eh?" Goody tapped her pipe on the hearth, extinguishing the spark. She rubbed the inside of the bowl with her thumb.

"Aye, yeah. He is always about, playing with the old poppet and never wants to go outside." Kate wiped her brow with her hand. The steam from the soup made the house warm.

"Been quite awhile?"

"Since Mary died. He has become...fearful. He is getting smaller too. Look at him." Kate sat on a stool next to Goody. She picked him up from the floor and sat him on her lap. Christopher sat sullenly sucking his thumb, clutching the old poppet.

Goody watched him a moment, then deftly grabbed the poppet from him. Christopher screamed, raising his arms towards the doll, "Mary, Mary, Mary!"

"Mary is dead boy!"

Christopher went on screaming.

"Goody, I think—"

"No thinking, Kate. He needs to waken up. He has been asleep, wasting away. He will be next, I tell you."

Goody gave the poppet back to Christopher. He sat on Kate's lap glaring at her. She extracted a bundle from a pocket in her skirt. It was a little cloth bag filled with herbs suspended from a string. Goody put it around Christopher's neck.

"Let him wear that now. Morning and night he should be wearing that charm. I woke him up, now he can smell it fully. Gave thee quite a scare!" Goody wrinkled her nose at him and made a face.

Chistopher, alert now, watched as Goody's eyes twinkled at him. He lay back on Kate's breast, comforted. "Will he be healed from this sickness?" Kate smoothed Christopher's hair. Her brow was creased with worry.

"The boy will make that decision. He will decide to follow his sister or not. I came in here, and felt...he might take leave. He was't not all the way there...in his body." Goody extracted her pipe, and took an ember from the fire to light it.

Kate had gone white. She squeezed Christopher closer to her. He wiggled free and jumped from her lap. Goody laughed.

"Aye, there's a good sign." She puffed on her pipe, a twinkle in her eye.

Kate blanched, as if stuck by an invisible hand.

"You can't keep him to ye, Kate. Let him be. Let him heal."

"I must keep him safe! I must...he is leaving this place!"

35

"It's the boy's decision."

Kate put her hands to her face and sobbed. Goody puffed quietly on her pipe, and Christopher stared at them both. He fingered the herb bag around his neck. Goody winked at him.

"It's part of his nature. He is not always *here* Kate. Look at his eyes. He has the eyes of a seer."

Kate looked up, wiped the tears from her face. "That's just what I was sayin' to John!"

"Aye. I remember when this one was born. He had that caul around his face. I knew this one would be lookin' inward. He will be special Kate. He will be like one of the old ones, of the old times. He is of Merlin's race. Words will come to him in a magic way."

Kate's eyes had gone big. "He will be a poet? A scholar?"

"Aye, a poet. A Merlin. He will be a bard, a conjurer of words." Goody smiled down at Christopher, holding out her arms. Christopher cautiously went to her. Touching her knee, he smiled. Goody picked him up.

"Tell him the old tales, Kate. The old stories. Never stop talking to him. That will be this one's cure."

"The old stories…And the songs?"

"Aye. All of it. All of it is a good balm for the heart. His soul will bind up with it, and it will make him strong."

"And what of the poppet? Should I take it from him?"

"Nay. Let him be with it awhile," Goody whispered in Christopher's ear. He giggled. "He will never forget his sister. Never. Those two had a bond. A strong one. They were like the oak and the mistletoe, bound together, always together. And because of it…he will be a friend to women. Always."

Goody looked towards the window, staring at something at once inside and far away. Christopher followed her gaze, and watched her eyes. He carefully touched the old face; the old wrinkled skin. He touched her old, bulbous nose; then, softly touched his own.

Chapter 10

Alice tugged at the corset that bit into her side. Mercer La Mer at All Occasion Costumes told her it would take awhile to get used to it, but then she could swing into the Renaissance in style. Alice went to Mercer for the costuming of all her plays.

Alice had pulled up the corset, feeling her bosom creep into her neck. Coming out of the dressing room, she saw that Mercer had been waiting for her.

"Ah, madame, exquisite. It fits you, oui?"

"No, it doesn't. It's too damn tight. I don't like it." Alice had stared sullenly at her reflection in the mirror, secretly hoping the corset would pop open, freeing her from this torture.

Mercer had lifted her long brown hair. "Now you can braid the hair Renaissance fashion. It will be very beautiful."

Alice had smiled. At least Mercer knew how to make her feel good. Tousling her hair in her hand, she piled it up on top of her head, sticking out her tongue at her reflection. Mercer laughed.

"My dear Alice, you have a bit of the imp in you. You will be at home in the Renaissance."

Sitting at her desk she wasn't so sure she was at home in the Renaissance. She didn't know how to get these kids interested in it. Maybe dressing up in a costume would do it. Sitting awkwardly at her desk, she stared at the clock on the wall. The bell sounded, and students poured into the halls. Alice got up from her desk and stood in the corner. She put her hands on hips and waited.

Dion, always the first to enter the class, bounded into the room, followed by Alex. The two were playfully pushing each other. Dion looked to the desk, frowned, then noticed her standing in the corner.

"Hey, yo, look at Ms. Petrovka. She gone *Renaissance*." Dion slid into his seat staring at her.

The rest of the kids filed in and sat in their seats. Most of them giggled when they saw her. Alice stood quietly watching them, trying her best to remain motionless like a mannequin. She vaguely felt like something from the wax museum. They talked amongst themselves, quietly at first, then loudly, to see if they could elicit a reaction from her. Finally, when the bell had rung for class to begin, they stared at her expectantly. She stared back. When she couldn't take it any longer she burst out laughing.

"This is the longest I've ever had you stay quiet. Maybe I should dress up more often," Her corset dug into her again, and she tugged at it. "Well, I suppose you all are wondering why I dressed up like this. As Dion guessed, it is to launch ourselves back in time to Elizabethan England, during the time of the Renaissance. Incidentally, Renaissance means rebirth, and we will be birthing ourselves into a new art form: that of Mr. William Shakespeare." She flourished her hand towards the poster of Shakespeare on the wall. The class groaned.

"Now, now. Before you get all pooh pooh on me, we will be having some fun. I want us to get in the spirit of this. Plays are meant to be read out loud, that means performed. So everyone, take out your standard issue text books."

Howard Bennely timidly raised his hand. He wore glasses and a tight Izod short sleeve shirt.

"Ms. Petrovka, what book do you mean?" Howard gazed confusedly into the contents of his backpack.

"Yeah, we got about five hundred books in here." Roberto disinterestedly tossed books onto his desk.

"Roberto, you exaggerate. The book that we have so fervently skipped through to get to the juicy morsels of literature," The class stared at her. "Oh c'mon people, the school issued textbook!"

They promptly took out the book with Lord Alfred Tennyson on the cover. There were a number of loud thumps as they let the book fall onto their desks.

Alice rolled her eyes. "Let's hope you exhibit a little more finesse while reading the bard."

They snickered.

Alice gathered her skirts around her. They rustled as she walked. She sat down at her desk.

"How do you pee in that thing?" Renita said. The class laughed.

"Carefully. Alright, everyone, please turn to page eighty-five. We will be reading *Othello*."

"The play about a black man?" Dion said. "A black man in a turban." He gazed at the picture in the book.

"Well, in Shakespeare's time they would have called him a Moor, thus the title, *Othello, the Moor of Venice*. Shakespeare probably thought that he was from Northern Africa. Skin color is really irrelevant. It's just a human concept, a way of judging each other. Don't you think?"

They looked up from their books, puzzled.

"Nah, it ain't no concept Ms. Petrovka. It everything." Dion said.

"Everything? How is it everything Dion? We're all human. Isn't that everything?"

"Shoot, you know how it is. People judge you by your color. You *know* that."

"I am not so inclined to notice if people judge me by my color because I'm white. I notice that people judge me by my sex though, being a woman."

The girls in the class nodded.

"Some of us have it doubly bad, being black and a woman." It was Kim Reynolds who spoke. She had a wide, shiny, black face, and wore her hair in dreadlocks.

"There are many issues in this play. There is the issue of what it means to be black, in Shakespeare's time. And also, what it means to be married to a black man, and how one woman is treated because of it."

"Who's that?" Renita said.

"Desdemona, who is married to Othello."

Renita shot her hand straight up.

"Yes Renita?"

"I'm playing Desdemona."

The class whistled and catcalled.

"Then you *know* I'm Othello." Dion said. There were louder whistles and cat calls from the class.

"What makes you think that I'm assigning roles for this play?" Alice smiled in spite of herself. She was pleased they were getting into it.

"Ms. Petrovka, don't be playing…naïve on us. You know that you were going to get us to act this thing." Dion leaned forward in his seat.

"Alright. You got me. I was."

"Renita, what are you doin'?" Roberto glared over at her.

"You know what I'm *doin'*." Renita glared back.

Roberto stood up, knocking his desk over. "I ain't playin' this shit." He sulked towards the door, and the class hissed and booed.

Alice felt the tension press against the walls, poised to bounce back and explode.

"Roberto wait!" He turned at the door.

"I want you to play the most important character in the play."

"What are you talking 'bout Ms. Petrovka?"

"Please Roberto, you know if you leave you'll be suspended again. And there's nothing I can do about that." Her eyes pleaded with him.

Roberto glared at her and hit the door jamb with his fist. "Then what? What do you want me to do about that puta taken my woman? The class jeered and Dion rose from his chair, anger straining his face.

"Okay, okay! Sit down, Dion! Roberto, I want you to play Iago, he breaks Othello and Desdemona up and gets them to kill themselves in the end." She spit it out quickly, stumbling over the words as they raced out of her mouth.

Dion and Renita looked over at one another, shook their heads. Roberto glared at them, then at Alice.

"Alright. I'll do it."

***

After class, Alice peeled off her costume and hung it in the closet. *I'll have to be sure to tell Mercer it was a hit*, she thought as a bitter smile crept across her face. But she wasn't sure her introduction to Shakespeare was quite the hit she wanted it to be. It seemed too explosive, letting the threesome involved in a love triangle play the parts of Othello, Desdemona, and Iago. *Maybe they will learn something from it. Maybe they will realize how literature can help you figure things out.* She swung the car keys in her hand, trying to content herself with these thoughts.

She pulled up to the public library well past five. It was relatively quiet, and only a few cars were in the parking lot. Alice often went here to gather her thoughts, sort things out. The place was full of knowledge and wisdom and it had a warm comforting feel to it. When things seemed chaotic in her life, it was here Alice went to look for answers and meditate amongst the quiet volumes. They never told her anything, never lectured. When she needed advice she would delve into a text, or pull one open haphazardly, searching for an answer.

Today she was on a mission.

She pulled the heavy doors open and entered the library. It was dark and quiet inside. Slowly climbing the stairs to the second floor she thought about how the events in her dream had paralleled those in Marlowe's poem. She had had the dream before she had read *Hero and Leander. Shouldn't it have been the other way around?*

She went to the computer terminal and typed in the name Christopher Marlowe, and for the next hour she pulled books from the library shelves, looking for anything that might be able to shed light on what she was feeling inside.

She placed her stack of volumes on the desk in front of the window looking out on a flower garden. The cherry trees were filled with blossoms and a bevy of yellow daffodils were in full bloom. The flower beds were gracefully designed towards a center fountain where a water nymph held a vase from which water poured. Late afternoon light descended on the garden, and the shadows grew long among the trees, catching the light between the leaves as they softly blew in the breeze.

A man and a woman entered the garden and stood by the fountain. The woman had long dark hair, *like mine*, Alice thought, unconsciously bringing her hand to her head, she felt the small braids, continuing along the side of head, joined in the back by a cluster of pearls. *Geez, I forgot to take this stuff out.* The couple embraced then stood apart gazing at each other. The man put his hand on the small of the woman's back and drew her to him. They kissed. *Spring love.* Alice smiled and turned towards her books.

She read Calvin Hoffman's careful account of all the parallelisms he had drawn between Marlowe and Shakespeare — sentences and phrasing that were similar or often identical between both writers. How Hoffman believed that Marlowe's death in Deptford had been faked and that Marlowe was the true author of all the plays and sonnets that had been attributed to the man known as William Shakespeare.

She read about the account of the death, of the coroner's inquest. How silly it all sounded. Four men had strolled in a garden outside of Eleanor Bull's rooming house. They had supper inside, and Marlowe had argued over the bill with the men and attacked one of them with a knife. In turn Marlowe was stabbed in the eye and killed in self defense.

Engrossed in her reading, Alice barely noticed that it began storming outside. There was a crash of thunder and she lifted her eyes from the page. The man had pulled off his jacket and was holding it over his companion's head. The couple ran laughing from the garden.

Alice compared Shakespeare's *Venus and Adonis* to Marlowe's *Hero and Leander* and noticed how similar they were.

She then turned to the sonnets and was struck by the sadness, the fear, and the shame of being an outcast that permeated the poems. And of the longing for love—for one love. She felt as if she had never read them before.

During the course of her reading she felt a strange sense of *deja vu*. Her eyes strayed to a picture of Marlowe on the cover of book she had put aside. It is you, isn't it?

Calm descended upon the library. The storm had stopped. Alice continued reading.

Since brass, nor stone, nor earth, nor boundless sea
But sad mortality o'ersways their power,
How with this rage shall beauty hold a plea,
Whose action is no stronger than a flower?

She was reminded of the Blake poem, about "heaven in a wild flower," of the madness of swirling space, and of this thing called time. She thought of Bernie and the strange physics of quantum mechanics.

Attention library patrons, the library will be closing in fifteen minutes. Please check out all materials at the front desk. Thank you.

Alice stretched in her chair, yawned, and looked out the window.

It was there she saw him. He stood in the mist by the lilac bush, holding a flower. He held it to his nose, then, up to her. Smiling, he cocked his head, as if beckoning her. Then vanished.

Alice's face went slack with astonishment and her mouth dropped open. Later, she would remember her reaction and how silly it seemed.

The chair crashed behind her as she stood. She ran past the research librarian who shot her a puzzled look.

"Ma'am?"

Taking the stairs in leaps and bounds she jumped from the last three. She ran towards the door and threw it open, flying into a sticky, humid air that clung to her skin and wet her hair.

She scanned the garden, saw the lilac, and ran over. Nothing. He had vanished into thin air. She turned around and around then circled the garden. *I'm crazy*, Alice thought. *Plumb crazy. They will all say I have gone off the deep end.*

She walked back to the lilac where she had seen him. Her feet were soaked and she glanced down at her tennis shoes. There, by her feet, was a small, delicate flower, a white and red rose. Her heart thumped, then pounded in her chest. She picked it up and placed it gently in her palm.

***

Driving home Alice glanced at her watch; it was almost six. Sighing, she realized she would never get over to the campus quick enough. She would have to content herself until the morning when she could get in touch with the botanist.

Pulling into the apartment parking lot she noticed that Albert's Jeep was gone. *Odd*, she thought. She unlocked the door and spied a note on the kitchen table. Before she looked at it, she pulled a sandwich bag from the drawer and carefully placed the tiny flower into it. She then placed the rose in the refrigerator on top of the butter dish.

She grabbed the phone book and dialed the number for the botany department at the university. As the phone rang she picked up the note from the kitchen table.

Darling,

Had a conference I forgot to tell you about. Had to fly to Houston for the annual transpersonal psychology blah dee dah. Be home in a few days.

Love,
Albert

Great, just great. Alice chucked the note in trash cannister. It was overflowing. He needed to pull more weight around here. She was getting sick and tired of doing all the chores around the house.

"Botany department."

"Hello, I was wondering if I could get someone to identify a flower that I found."

Silence on the other end. Alice wondered if they had heard her.

"Well…What is it?"

"It looks like some kind of rose."

"Is it wild?"

"Ah…I really don't know."

"Only do wild stuff. Try horticulture." The person hung up. Alice listened to the sound of phone buzz in her ear.

She dialed the number again.

"Hello?"

"You didn't give me the number to horticulture"

"Did you ask?"

Alice waited patiently. Wrote down the number. Hung up the phone. *Crazy plant people.*

"Hello, Hort Department. Can I help you?"

"Do you identify plant specimens? I have a flower I need to identify. I think it's some kind of rose."

"Sure. I can meet with you tomorrow, first thing. Say around ten?"

"That sounds fine."

"Oh wait! Is it wild, or a cultivar?

"Culti...What?"

"A plant you find in a garden."

"Oh. I really don't know."

"If it's wild I'll have to refer you to botany."

"Great," Alice rolled her eyes. "I'll see you tomorrow."

"Do you know how to get here?"

"Yes."

"Okay. See you then."

She opened the refrigerator, picked up the rose. Beads of moisture had formed in the bag so she poked a little hole in the Ziplock to let out some of the condensation. Shutting the refrigerator door, she decided she would make an early night of it. She picked *The Jew of Malta* off the table and went upstairs to bed.

Chapter 11

The days was hot and bright, and Kate took Christopher outside with her whenever she could. Kate swept the floor, trying to keep the dust to a minimum. It was hard to keep the dust flying up from the floor with so little rain.

Christopher stood next to the table watching her. He no longer played underneath the table with Mary's old poppet. He was now content to leave it lying in the bed.

Mostly silent, he had been getting over Mary's death slowly. He was content to listen to her tell stories and quietly play by himself outside or in the corner. Kate had noticed that he would stare into the sky and watch the clouds, a smile on his face. She would watch as he would sit in a patch of sun by the window. He could sit like that for a long time.

But today he looked a little sad, a little forlorn, and Kate became concerned. She placed her broom in the corner and picked up a basket.

"Come Christopher. Let us pick some apples." She smiled and held out her hand. He took her hand and let himself be led out the door. Kate left baby Margaret with the neighbor woman, Anne, who often helped out in return for watching her small ones.

A few doors down they were met by a beggar.

"Hungry, please." The woman held out her hand. A hand that was dirty and skin and bones.

"Go, *tush*." Kate waved her on. She was worried about the increasing amount of beggars who roamed the streets of Canterbury. She heard they were coming because of the plague in London. Creeping along the streets, they slept alongside the houses for warmth. When they opened their doors in the morning there often was a beggar in front of it. Many of them were drunks who waited outside taverns for a keg to burst. Then, they'd fill their mugs.

They walked past the market square where vendors hawked their wares.

"Bread! Fresh bread!" A woman called out to her.

Kate smiled. The woman was Bess Parker, a neighbor.

"Surely Bess, you have saved the plumpest loaf for me." Kate handed her some coins.

"Christopher looks well." Bess placed the loaf in Kate's basket and handed him a piece of bread crust. "You'll be working with your father soon enough." She nodded.

Christopher clung to Kate's skirts. "Yes, soon enough. He has been ill. Ever since Mary's death, you know. Goody said to take him out, get him some air. Tell the old tales to him. That sort of thing."

Bess frowned. "The old tales? I've heard it said that Goody Frye is a witch. Can charm the moths from the shadows with the light of her eyes."

"The old tales are for healing, Bess. Christopher needs to be talked to, not shut up in a room with his father, mending and making soles." She had forgotten how pious Bess Parker was—this was a woman with Puritan leanings.

"Souls mama?" Christopher tugged at her skirt. "Like God making them? Is papa like God?"

The two women laughed. "He is a clever one my Christopher. He'll be a poet, this one. Thank you Mistress Parker, for the bread. We will gather some apples now." Kate bowed her head in deference to the older woman.

They walked away.

"I'll see you in church, Kate?" Bess called after her.

Kate turned, nodded. Christopher looked back, noticed that Bess was frowning, watching them walk away.

"Mama, why does that woman say Goody is a witch?"

"Because she thinks that…Christopher, there are some people who care only for what *they* think God is. They do not care for the old stories or old festivals." Kate didn't understand what it had to do with the old festivals: the maypoles, or the Morrice Dancers, but somehow it did. Now some folk were even raising objection to the mystery plays.

Kate thought of the plays. The traveling guilds usually arrived in spring, bringing with them their troop of actors. They had performed *Mary Magdalene*, during a particular fragrant spring full of flowers. In this play Jesus had sung a beautiful song to his mother, the Moon. He sang of how he rested with his moon mother, the vessel, and then ascended to the Sun. Christopher had been fascinated with the play. She remembered how wide his eyes had grown after Jesus had disappeared in a puff of smoke. He had watched the actors on their portable stage long after everyone had left. An actor had noticed his interest and invited him up on the stage, showing him the hole where smoke was emitted and Jesus had disappeared.

Kate's reminiscence stopped when they had arrived at a small grove of trees. Christopher had fallen silent. Kate examined the apples, which appeared small, probably from lack of rain.

"What is a witch, mama?" He held a small apple in his hand, looking for worm holes.

"A witch? I don't know what a witch is Christopher."

"Is a witch bad?"

Kate thought for a moment. She looked at the clear blue sky, lacy clouds moving towards the center. It was going to be another hot day. "The people who call women weird, or witches, yes, they think they are bad."

"Bad? How are they bad?"

"Ah...Perchance they cast evil spells on people and that sort of thing."

"Goody is not bad." He looked at her, concerned. Satisfied his apple did not contain a worm hole, he took a large bite.

"No, Goody is not bad. Goody is wise. She knows things that women younger than her do not."

"Does she know where our Mary is?"

Kate stopped, looked at him. His eyes, they were so big and brown. She wanted to cry out then. Why had this happened? But it always was happening. It could happen again, would most likely happen again. And yet, she needed to get on, they all needed to go on. Even Christopher. But he was so curious, his mind was always spinning.

"I don't know, Christopher. There are some—such as Mistress Parker—who would say Mary was with God in heaven."

"Is she mama?"

Kate smiled, thought of the mystery play. "Mary is resting with the mother Moon, and after a time, she will come back again."

"Where will we find her then?"

She looked down at his face, those trusting eyes. At his feet was a small delicate flower. She picked the tiny thing and handed it to him.

"In something small and lovely. Something that is beautiful and comes back year after year. Something that is not destroyed."

Chapter 12

Rows of daffodils and tulips lined the streets turning the campus of Michigan State University into a kaleidoscope of color. Alice drove past the old Botany building looking for a place to park. Every available space declared, "University Vehicles Only." Disappointed, she took the winding drive past Forestry and Horticulture, then past Administration and around again.

She finally found a spot next to the music building. A mile from where I need to be, she thought. She slowly walked past the statue of Sparticus, trailing a robe behind him. Nicknamed Sparty, the university mascot stood in the middle of one of the campus's many traffic circles.

She followed the curving drive lined with ancient maples to the old part of campus and found the Horticultural building. Alice opened the heavy wooden doors and checked the office numbers listed on the wall, looking for an Anita Bernadino. She found the office in back, nested tightly in the corner with two offices on either side. She knocked, reading the cartoons on the door, mainly *The Far Side* comics concerning plants.

"It's open."

Alice walked inside. The girl who sat at a desk looked about twenty, had short blond hair, and wore thick glasses. A smear of acne was on her forehead.

"Anita?"

"It's me."

"I'm Alice Petrovka." She stuck out her hand which Anita grabbed and pumped enthusiastically.

"The rose woman. This is great, just great. I haven't had an ID in a while, been bogged down in all of this professorial research. Well, you know how it is, huh? Didn't you say you were a teacher? I hope you treat your grad students better than this, my major professor works me to death." She smiled, rolling her eyes.

"Actually, I'm a high school English teacher."

"Oh." Anita looked dismayed.

"But I understand completely. My husband was in research for a while at the university before he branched off into his own business. He always treated his grad students well."

"Really? What is his field?"

"Psychology."

"Oh." Anita looked disappointed and pushed her glasses up the bridge of her nose.

Alice had a feeling that if they didn't talk about botany there wouldn't be much to talk about. She pulled the sandwich bag out of her purse.

"Ah...The treasure." Anita reached for a pair of tweezers and opened the bag.

"Do you mind?"

"Of course not."

She carefully pulled the flower from the bag. "I'm really glad you called. I have a real fondness for roses. Do you ever walk the MSU gardens?"

Alice nodded. "There must be at least twenty different types of roses there."

"Twenty-two to be exact."

The flower dangled between them.

"Wow. Where did you get this?"

"In the garden in back of the library."

Anita frowned. "On campus?"

"Oh no, sorry, at the public library."

"I could see you getting it, maybe, just maybe, around here. But not over at the public library."

"Why do you say that?"

"I don't think someone would be toting this little beauty around behind that library."

"I'm sorry Anita, but will you tell me what it is?"

Anita had been staring intently at the rose; reached for a book. "I think what you have here hasn't been around for at least three hundred years. Maybe four."

Alice felt her heart begin to pound. "What are you saying?"

"Just that. No one has seen this type of rose for a very long time. Well, maybe in someone's special collection. We have people here who do that sort of thing. Have special collections they've developed from rare plants. But other than us hort nerds, I just can't see anyone running around with this sort of thing."

Alice felt as though all the oxygen was being sucked from the room. Her face flushed and she felt dizzy. She sat in a chair next to Anita.

"What's wrong? You don't look so hot. Or, maybe you do, your face is all red."

"I'm alright, it's just that..." She debated telling Anita any more.

"So, you just found this thing lying on the ground, you said?"

"Yes. Well, a young man dropped it, and I...picked it up. I felt that it was different somehow, so I called you." Alice wondered if the story sounded plausible, or if she sounded like a complete idiot.

"Maybe the young man was four hundred years old." Anita smiled.

Alice swallowed. Anita had no idea how close to the truth she actually was.

"This much I do know: this type of rose was cultivated in England around three to four hundred years ago. Of course, it isn't just any old flower, only the English

53

aristocracy would have such things. But I'd like to keep this little thing and confer with a professor here who, believe it or not, knows more than I do." Anita dropped the flower back in the bag.

"Sure. Keep it and let me know."

"It shouldn't take very long. I'll give you a call later."

"Alright, thanks for your time." Alice opened the door as Anita placed the flower in a small fridge by her desk.

"What we can't ID, we eat." Anita laughed. "Just kidding. I will take good care of your flower."

Alice smiled. "Bye." She closed the door behind her.

She slowly walked down the hall and stopped at a bulletin board and pretended to read it. Someone had just pulled the rug out from under her feet. She felt as though she were floating in space, as if everything she knew or thought she knew was wrong.

***

Don Gibbs got up from the heavy oak table and walked deliberately over to the coffee pot in the corner. He poured black coffee into a Styrofoam cup.

"Have to remember to bring my own cup. These things are disgusting. Anyone else want any?"

Yeah, you do that, get your own damn cup, then. Alice wished he could read her thoughts.

"Look," she said, "I feel like I'm locked in some sort of jury deliberation. This is a board meeting for God's sake." She wished Derrin were here. He would lighten things up. He had that knack.

"Where's your sidekick?" Brad said.

"What?" Alice looked at him quizzically, suddenly realizing who he was talking about. Derrin. She had the oddest feeling he had read her mind.

Brad, the used car salesman. Of all people, he probably *could* read her mind. He had come to the board meetings for a year now, usually lighthearted and jovial, but lately he seemed to have an agenda. Alice couldn't quite figure him out. He sat there in his white shirt, tie loosened. She noticed he had been keeping up the tan that he got in Tahiti, vacationing with his wife. Recently he had sported a little gold hoop in his right ear.

"You know, *Derrin.*" He smirked at her when he enunciated the name.

Alice realized that lately he had been trying to compromise Derrin somehow, was always taking pot shots at him.

"He called and said he had a headache. One of those migraine things."

"I just saw him on campus less than an hour ago. He seemed fine to me." Sonia looked down at the cup in her hands, then her eyes moved towards Brad. She took a sip of coffee when their eyes met. His expression changed somehow, softened.

These two are having an affair.

Alice shook her head, incredulous. *It must have just started,* she thought, *or I would have noticed it before. Or maybe not.* She wondered what she did, and didn't know.

She looked over at Jim Schelling. Of all the people here she at least knew that he was her friend. He was an English professor at MSU who specialized in Shakespeare. At least he's on my side, she thought. He smiled at her when he caught her looking at him.

"Yes, I agree with Alice. We don't need to stalemate over it today. It's all new information. We could have a decision next board meeting." Jim said.

"But I would like to start work on production now," Alice said. "There's a lot to be done if I get the go-ahead to produce the play."

"What is all this *I* Alice?" Sonia said. "What about me? I'm the one who has to learn all the lines. I do not want to do anything Renaissance. I want something light. Something fun." Her eyes moved towards Brad again.

"Something fun?" Alice drummed her fingers on the table. *How long was this going to take? How long were they going to grill her?* "And what would that fun thing be, Sonia?"

"Like I mentioned before, *Guys and Dolls*...something like that." She looked brightly at Alice. The innocent little girl look.

"I'm with that," Brad said. "Why don't we have something that is a little more *now*. We had your serious play. And need we remind you all the negative press given by the business end of it around here?"

"If we let business guide our art we are in a sorry state." Jim said. He was soft spoken. Alice followed his eyes as he looked out the window. A robin clung to a branch and gulped down a worm.

"If you don't worry about politics we'll lose a big portion of our funding." Don stood by the coffee pot. He still held the Styrofoam cup in his hand.

"I agree." Larry said.

Larry and Don reminded Alice of a couple of book ends. They both were in their mid-forties, both were small business owners: Larry's was office supply; Don's was a hardware store. Both had red hair.

No one said anything. They all sat with practiced smiles on their faces and thought about their next move. Alice looked out the window. The robin had flown away.

"I think it is very important to keep the public aware of issues that may be socially uncomfortable. That's one of the purposes of art, to enlighten and instruct." Alice said.

"What about entertain? Isn't that why people go to the theatre? The number one reason is they want to be entertained." Sonia nodded, pleased with herself.

You're always pleased with yourself. Alice was sorry she had gotten to know Sonia so well, to discover that she didn't like her.

"Let me remind everyone," Jim said. "We came up with a list at the beginning of the season. And on that list were two plays from the Renaissance. We're at the end of the list, and we need to put these plays on. Fair is fair, everyone."

"We should be able to get a vote too, Jim," Brad said. "*Fair is fair.*"

Jim held up his hand as a conciliatory gesture. "Okay, let me propose this: We do the Renaissance plays, and in the fall *Guys and Dolls.*"

Larry looked over at Don, who was crumbling the Styrofoam cup over the wastebasket, and Brad looked at Sonia, who had a serene smile on her face.

Alice felt like punching the four of them.

***

When they had all said their niceties, had shaken hands and filtered out of the room, Alice sat by Jim. They stared out the window in front of them. Another robin, or maybe the same one, landed in the tree.

"Robin Goodfellow." Jim said.

"Robin, the patron of housewives." said Alice. "Maybe of our plays, also. So, what do you think of all of this?"

"Hmm. I didn't think the quartet would corner us like this." He shook his head.

Alice looked over at him. His shoulder length hair, steel gray and curly, was clasped in a pony tail. She gave the pony tail a tug. "I like your hair like this."

"Really? Moira says I should cut it. Says I look like a hippie."

"So?"

"So what? Looking like a hippie or the quartet?"

"Don't call them that. It sounds too good for them." Alice looked towards the window again. The robin was gone. She wondered why it kept flying to this particular tree. "They are four corners of a square: inharmonious." She laughed.

"Don't let it get to you."

"How can I not? They are trying to take complete control Jim, and you know it."

"They definitely have their ideas."

"What I would like to know is when this whole thing started. Maybe it was when Brad decided to get out of his neutral zone. Sonia had something to do with it."

Jim looked at her. "You noticed it too, huh?"

"Yeah. The two of them sleeping together is a real mess for my theatre." Alice laughed, but the sound rang hollow in her ears. "Sonia has it in her head that she needs to sing and dance. She views my theatre as her personal springboard to bigger and better things. She wants to start off Broadway and then work her way up."

"Ambition. Politics. What are we to do?"

"I don't know, Jim. I don't want to haggle with this group any more. I'm getting weary. I don't know why we have to bow before the business community. Art and business don't mix. It's ridiculous and humiliating." Alice examined her nails. She felt her face turn red; felt like she was on the verge of losing her temper.

"Unfortunately, art and business have to mix. We get a large portion of our funding due to the business community. But business is largely conservative. It disturbs them to see the status quo upset; maybe it will upset their profits."

"That's silly! It brings hordes of people downtown! My play had the best run of anything else we have put on here. And that has to be good for business, mine and everyone else's."

"Yes, but these people are selling products. They have a vested interest in people not questioning the status quo, not thinking too much."

"I think you give these people way too much credit, Jim."

"I think it operates unconsciously, but it's there."

"I don't see how *All the Queen's Men* has anything to do with buying tools at a hardware store."

Jim got up from the table and walked to the coffee pot. Poured himself a cup of Styrofoam coffee and dumped in a load of Coffee Mate. He picked up a plastic spoon and stirred.

"Think of it—people acknowledge how gay people feel oppressed in the work force; start feeling some empathy for them, and that empathy translates to other things—worker rights in China, for instance. How people are making a pittance there for constructing American doodads." He stood sipping his coffee.

"That's a little far-fetched Jim. I don't see how any of that is related."

"Oh, it is. All attitudes are related. One swings into another. And besides," he cupped his hand by his mouth as if doing an aside in a stage performance, "I used to be one of those radicals in the sixties."

"Right." Alice stretched and yawned, "Let's change the subject," she too cupped her hand by her mouth, "I think Marlowe was Shakespeare."

He stiffened, clasped a hand to his forehead, and shook his head. "Alice. Don't do that. Don't become a *Marlovian.*"

"Now, who's the conservative here?"

"Alright, I acknowledge that it might not have been William Shakespeare from Stratford who wrote the plays. I think any Shakespearean scholar has honestly entertained that at one time or another in his or her academic life, but I would need more evidence either way."

"Really? What kind of evidence?"

"Good, solid evidence. Proving beyond a doubt that Marlowe wrote the plays, the sonnets—the whole shebang."

"But, no one in the Shakespeare industry questions that William Shakespeare was the author of the plays. And there is very *little* evidence to support that."

He frowned. "Just be happy that we're doing *Othello* and *The Jew of Malta.*"

***

Alice returned home to find Mrs. Johnson watering the front lawn. Alice smiled. They lived in an apartment complex and there was no need to water the front lawn. Invisible sprinklers buried in the grass turned on at night during the summer.

"Hello, dear."

"Hi, Mrs. Johnson. How are you?" Alice stopped in front of her door.

"Oh fine, just fine. How are your plays coming along?"

"Well. Really well. We're working on Shakespeare down at the Lion, and at school too."

"And how are those teenagers liking it?"

"I think I tricked them into...appreciating the bard."

"I could never seem to get the high school kids interested in those plays. Oh, and I tried everything. I was sort of different that way back then. Unconventional." Mrs. Johnson adjusted the nozzle on the hose, turning the water into a soft drizzle.

Alice jingled the keys in her pocket. "I guess I'll go in now. I'm awfully tired tonight."

"Oh, I should think. You are such a busy woman. And your husband, too. Why, just yesterday he flew out of here like a bat out of hell."

"He had a conference to go to. He must have been late."

Mrs. Johnson just nodded.

"I'll see you soon." Alice walked in the entry way.

The apartment seemed unbearably still. She went in the living room and opened a window. Inhaling deeply, she savored the spring air. She flopped down in the easy chair, and kicked off her shoes. The answering machine light was blinking. She sighed. *It might be Albert.* She got up and pressed the button.

"Hello. This is Jack McGill, I'm a botany professor here at the university. I understand you had a chat with my graduate assistant, Anita Bernadino, about a rose? I have been examining the specimen, and I would like to discuss it with you. I thought—cough—because I had a lot of information to discuss, it would be a good idea for us to meet. The rose is quite rare. Please call. Thank you."

A lot of information? Quite Rare? Alice glanced at her watch, quickly dialed the number which McGill had listed. It was after hours, but sometimes these professors worked late.

"Botany department."

"Jack McGill please."

"May I ask who is calling?"

"This is Alice Petrovka."

"Oh yes, Ms. Petrovka."

Alice waited not more than a few seconds.

"Hello? Mrs. Petrovka?"

"It's Ms."

"Oh, yes, yes, sorry. This is Jack McGill. I would like to speak to you about the rose? Would you like to meet for lunch tomorrow? Say around noon?

Alice hesitated. She had planned to to lie in her bed and lounge half the day away reading a good book. *Anything* but Marlowe or Shakespeare.

"Okay. Where?"

"Do you know the Lion Theatre?"

"Yes."

"There is a little café over in that part of town, that has the best soup and sandwiches."

"Margrites?"

"You know of it?"

"Yes. Eat there all the time."

"Okay, then. See you at twelve?"

"See you then."

She hung up the phone.

***

She would recall that the moon was hanging in the clouds. It was a full moon, shining white and yellow like a pearl in the clouds. Candles lined the room and they flickered across the walls and across his face as he looked down at her. There was a roaring in her ears as he disrobed, pulling the white shirt over his head. He lay beside her.

A tear ran down the contour of her face, settling in the corner of her mouth.

"Nay," he whispered, kissing her cheek. "Don't cry."

He kissed the salt from her lips; tasted her neck, her nipple. Lower, there was a rush like a river.

The sound of the sea was a gentle rocking rhythm. And as the waves crashed on the shore, theirs was a momentum, then an explosion,–the swollen eastern tide bursting upon itself, flooding, then receding. She gripped him tightly as the water ran between them; circling their legs as tears from the sky. A wave of love soothed her, retreating into her heart and she was gently lulled to sleep.

She awoke feeling like a stranded starfish in a long-dried tidal pool. Her arms and legs were splayed out before her and there was a scent of sea in the air. Sex. There was an inescapable soreness between her legs. Opening her eyes, she blinked, struggled to her elbows. The sun was beating down on her face, heating it like an egg in a pan. She glanced at the clock. She had overslept.

Alice shut the shade and opened the window. She let the soft breeze blow over her as she sat on the edge of the bed. The rustling of the tree tops soothed her as she tried to make sense of things.

After a quick shower she tried to eat some toast. It stuck in her throat. She promptly threw the remains of the bread into the trash.

As she drove towards the restaurant she felt like she was inhabiting two skins. She was living in one world, and at the same time, another world which she could not see or feel, but occasionally visit, albeit, in a strange, disconcerting way.

I'm losing my mind.

She shook her head. No, it was different than before. Before, there had been a depression, then a quick dip into something dark and strange. And then she had met Albert. My wizard, he walked me out of it. He had shown her the path through the dark forest; had given her a light, a lantern back to reality. But could he help her through this?

Her mother had whispered that she had the secret madness of her grandmother on her father's side. She had gone blind, but it only made her sight all the more penetrating, all the more intense. Alice knew little of this Russian grandmother, the one who could feel the weather, the pain of other creatures, and could see into the future. Her father was dismissive, "It's a bunch of old wive's tales." Now, she wondered.

She parked the car in front of the restaurant next to a blue sedan. Alice walked into Margrite's and saw him sitting by the window reading a paper. He smiled, beckoned to her. She walked over to the table.

"Hello, Ms. Petrovka. Sit, sit."

She sat. She could tell he was accustomed to being in charge. Instead of the casual attire most people wore on the weekends, he was dressed in a Kelly green sport coat with a white polo shirt underneath. She thought of Ireland and leprechauns. He looks like a leprechaun, Alice thought, suppressing a laugh. He was short and compact; had reddish blond hair, and slightly pointed ears. His blue eyes twinkled at her.

He pulled a small cooler out from under the table. "You have heard of the War of the Roses?"

"What? You mean the movie?" Alice was taken back. She thought of easing into things with some small talk, not an instant quiz.

"No, no, no. The history. The Tudor-Lancaster war?"

"Oh, yes, vaguely. Shakespeare refers to it in some of his history plays."

"Exactly. And what we have here," He pulled the rose from the cooler, setting the cooler underneath his feet. "is the merging of those two warring factions. It was thought to have been a myth, but then you produced it."

Alice looked down at the rose he had placed on the table. "I'm sorry...Mr. McGill, I don't follow you." She felt like a dumb undergrad, not getting the professor's clues during an important lecture.

"Please, call me Jack."

"Okay, Jack. I'm all ears."

"The war of the roses was symbolized by the White Rose of York, or *Rosa alba Maxima*, and the Red Rose of Lancaster, or *Rosa gallica* "Officinalis." As a sign of reconciliation, the victorious House of Tudor chose a new type of rose with inner white and outer red petals as its heraldic symbol. Do you follow so far?"

Alice dutifully nodded her head.

"No rose breeder has ever succeeded in creating a rose of that heraldic symbol. The closest anyone has ever come was with developing a plant that contains both reddish pink and white flowers. And at times, there are even flowers combining both colors in one, but...never this." He placed the flower in front of her.

"So, what is the significance of this?" Alice said.

The waitress approached them, smiling. "Can I get you something to drink?"

"What would you like my dear, it's on me."

"Oh, that's thoughtful, Jack, but I can pay for my own meal."

"Really," McGill straightened his tie, "I would like to pay for this. I asked you to lunch."

Alice nodded. She felt like she had been doing a lot of nodding, agreeing. "Yes, you did. Okay, you pay."

"Would you like anything to drink?" The waitress looked from her to McGill.

"I'll have a Cutty's. Neat please." McGill said.

"Just water." Alice still felt like a fried egg. Sixteenth century hangover, she thought.

The waitress went to the bar to get their drinks.

"What I'm trying to impress on you is that this rose is quite rare."

She looked up from the menu.

"I don't suppose your gentleman will be dropping any more of these in front of you?" His eyes twinkled at her.

My gentleman dissolved into the mist. Alice felt a creeping antlike anxiety rise up her neck. She scratched her shoulder. "I'm afraid it was one of those strange…coincidences."

What could she tell this guy? She was harboring a secret about roses that she planned to divulge to the world? She didn't even know why she brought the damn thing in herself. *To make sure I wasn't crazy. To verify his presence.* She had verified it alright.

McGill had been studying her. "I don't want to disturb you, Alice. I merely wanted to fill you in on your wonderful find. However you may have come by it."

She stared at the rose and thought of Kit Marlowe. *What do you want from me? What should I do?* She felt inextricably pulled into the mystery, as if she couldn't help herself. It was if she knew him somehow; had been with him before. Lost in thought, Alice didn't notice when the waitress brought the drinks. She ordered in a daze, something with chicken.

The veil had been getting thinner. At times it was as if she was watching a movie of him. She could see him laughing, interacting with actors on the stage, or sitting in a tavern, talking with his fellow playwrights. There was even a time she had been sitting by himself in a room somewhere. Crying.

Alice snapped back to attention. She found herself nodding as McGill elaborated on the history of the rose.

"…so due to centuries of breeding, the original botanical relationships between rose cultivars are far from clear." McGill sipped his whiskey.

The waitress returned with plates of food. She put the chicken dish in front of her. Alice felt as if she could not recall the last fifteen minutes. Time seemed to sometimes speed incredibly fast, and then at other times slow to a standstill. She glanced at her watch.

"Ah, steak." McGill dug into the bloody piece of meat. "Am I keeping you from something? I feel as though you have been distracted."

"I'm sorry. It's just that, well, I wonder what all of this has to do with me. Of course, it's very interesting, but really, I just found the rose. No more, no less. I'm not in any way interested in getting into the rose business."

"I realize that, Alice. But just let me add this—," he waved his fork at her, "if you did know of the plant that produced this rose, a person would probably be willing to pay thousands of dollars. Perhaps *more*."

Did you here that, Kit? Maybe next time you'll leave me an entire plant.

Alice held McGill's gaze. "If you're suggesting this is some sort of bribery, Jack… it's not. I don't have any tricks up my sleeve. I was just curious as to what type of rose this was."

He shrugged. "I can understand your curiosity. But yes, it is hard to believe you don't know something more."

"No more, no less. You can keep the rose if you like. I was just wondering about the significance as to why breeders would take the time to develop such a thing."

He looked up from his steak. "To merge the competing factions I suppose."

"A synthesis?"

"Sure. A combining of the impossible."

She smiled. "What's in a name? That which we call a rose, By any other word would smell as sweet."

"Shakespeare?"

"Yes, *Romeo and Juliet*. A combining of the impossible."

The owner of the restaurant, Margrite La Mer, approached them. She was smiling, holding a tray full of deserts.

"Alice, try one of my éclairs. I made them fresh this morning."

"I'm stuffed. Your food is so good I never leave room for desert."

Margrite set the tray down and waved a finger at her. "Tut, tut, you must always save room for desert. You Americans with your Atkins, counting all those calories. How are you to live? Maybe your gentleman friend would like a treat? Eh, sir?" She held the desert in front of him. "On the house. You tell me if you like, then I will keep the recipe the way it is."

She set an éclair before McGill and he promptly took a bite. "Magnificent, madam, magnificent." He nodded his head enthusiastically.

Margrite turned to Alice. "Mercer tells me you are ordering Renaissance costumes for your Shakespeare and Marlowe plays. How wonderful! I am so anxious to see *The Jew of Malta* at your theatre."

"Yes, I will be picking them up tomorrow."

"Good, good. I will see you soon, Alice."

Alice nodded.

"You own the Lion?" McGill said.

"Yes."

"No wonder you were so quick quoting Shakespeare."

***

She had shrugged off any further mention of payment; telling McGill she was happy she could be of service in the light of such an important find. McGill had seemed unbelieving. *Thinks I'm some sort of rose extortionist.*

Alice drove slowly home, taking the old neighborhoods with their old-fashioned street lamps. She passed some girls playing jump rope.

Her thoughts kept coming back to the strange symbolism of it all. When McGill had told her that there had never been a successful cultivation of this mythical Tudor rose she had felt a sense of apprehension followed by euphoria. She wanted to tell McGill that he would never again find his special rose, that it was developed especially for her.

Yes, at that exact moment when McGill told me that…it had never been developed…then I knew. Something so exquisitely rare, never to be seen again. That's what Kit gave me.

Alice thought of everything she could think of concerning roses. Of course they symbolized love, white for purity, red for passion. And what was it in Spencer's *Fairie Queen*, that poem he had written for Queen Elizabeth? Oh, yes, the fairy queen had a bower of bliss symbolizing her sexual nature, and the central holiest of holies was the Rose of Love. And in Britain there was a traditional Mummer's dance known as The Rose. Five dancers formed a five-pointed star of swords over a victim, called the Fool, who was symbolically slain and then resurrected with a mysterious elixir, which signified the semen of the God reincarnating himself in the Goddess. The Dewdrop in the Rose.

She parked the car, noticing Albert's Jeep. When she entered the apartment he was talking on the phone.

"Yes, yes. I do know that. Um, hmm. Interesting stuff." He nodded and smiled as she walked in. She sat on the edge of the chair watching him.

"Alright. Good-bye."

"Who was that?"

"Francesca Mann. Thinks she knows everything there is to know about Transpersonal Psychology. She is so tiresome. Followed me around the whole conference. Really, she is very insecure." He ran his hand through his hair.

"Maybe she likes you."

"Likes me?"

"Don't be a dummy."

"*Please.* I think she likes to attach herself to a male for some reason. Probably issues she had with her father, or something like that. Stunted animus. Anyway, darling, it was great," his eyes shone, "Stan was there," Alice took this to mean Stanislov Grof, the founder of Transpersonal Psychology. "He had all sorts of people from all walks of life talking about their mystical experiences and how it has affected their lives and their patients' lives. It really was groundbreaking. I was glad the mainstream press was there." He scribbled something in a notebook.

"Albert?"

"Yes?"

"Well, I...found this rose...and I wondered...didn't you say that often people had synchronistic circumstances which lead them to a breakthrough in their lives?"

"Yes." He looked at her cautiously. "What are you getting at darling?"

"You know I have been working on Shakespeare and Marlowe plays. It's Marlowe who is haunting me. I have dreams about him, and then I found this rose in the garden..." She stopped, realizing how Albert was taking this. He had a strange look on his face. Fearful. "Albert, it's not that. I'm fine." She looked out the window, feeling defeated.

"Have you been having your anxiety attacks?"

"No."

"I don't understand."

"There is nothing to *understand*. I need you to hear what I have been going through!" She twisted a curl around her finger.

Alice told him everything, beginning with the man in the slashed doublet opening the door to the theatre, and ending with the sighting in the garden. But she didn't tell him about the sexual dream, it felt too personal, too embarrassing. Albert listened intently. She knew many years of listening to patients had effectively turned his face to stone, and she could not tell what he was thinking. Though it was part and parcel of the trade of psychology—do not betray the patient with your feelings—it bothered her.

When she finished she was looking down at her hands. She looked up at him. He avoided her eyes.

"I know you told me some of this before…but I thought you were over your obsession. Are you are going to tell all this to Selina?"

"Selina and I finished our work together."

"Alice….I think you should talk to someone." He let out a long breath, brushed the hair off his forehead.

"You think I'm crazy." She felt the blood rise to her face.

"No, I think you're under pressure. You remember…the same thing happened before when you were under pressure."

"That was different! I had people threatening to fire me…The baby."

"Yes, but you know how your mind works. You started concocting things, putting things together that didn't exist –"

"Goddamn it, Albert! I will not live the rest of my life in the shadow of that breakdown! It's not fair." Her lungs gave out and she heaved a huge sob. She ran towards the bedroom, slammed the door, and quickly locked it.

Albert twisted the knob. "Alice, Alice…please…it doesn't have to be this way."

"Leave me alone!" She buried her head in the pillow and cried.

Quite some time later Albert finally left the door.

Chapter 13

Christopher sat in front of the window. He listened to the sounds of his mother and sisters talking quietly among themselves in the next room. The light was getting dim and he was having a hard time reading his book, Ovid's *Amores*. He took a candle from the mantle and lit it from the fire. Placing it on the table, he began to read again.

The Latin was difficult but it kept him occupied. He was absorbed in Ovid wooing the fair Corinna and finally making love with her.

Little Anne stumbled into the room. She ran over and tried to pry the book from his hands. Christopher held his arm out in front of her.

"Get ye gone, ye saucy imp!" He smiled. Anne was his favorite sister. She was the most playful and the most daring.

"No. Play with me, Christopher." She sat on a stool next to him and took off her shoes.

"Mother won't like it when your feet become black."

She stuck out her tongue at him. "Play." She tugged on his arm.

"No. Do ye have eyes? I'm readin'." He had lost his place. He couldn't pick up the thread of the translation again. "Play with Margaret."

"Meg's mendin' with Mother. Play with me, Christopher."

He sighed then got up and lit another candle from the mantle. He set it down on the table. No use in reading now anyway, the light was too poor. He listened to the sound of the rain on the roof. John's hammer echoed along with the lonely sound of the rhythm of the rain drops. It was fall— harvest time—and the rain was a constant companion now.

"Thou art stubborn, bootless giglet." He ruffled her hair. "I will tell ye a story."

Anne sat and looked at him expectantly. He listened to the tapping on the roof, thinking.

"There was a knight lookin' for his faire lady in the rain. Clink, clink, clink, on his armor the rain did patter as he rode. His horse razed up at the fork he did come to. There stood one of the wee folk. Somethin' of a fairy or a dwarf."

Anne's eyes grew big. "What say the dwarf?"

" 'I give you three wishes faire knight,' sayeth he, 'and if ye can guess my name, you can marry yer faire lady, and be kingdom of this land, and all the gold in the wide world will be yours. The knight peereth down at the wee one. 'How do I tell ye are one of the fair folk, and not of a base sort? The dwarf doth plucked a hair from his head. 'Take this hair, brave knight, and drop it down on the table at dawn. Thou will't see—"

John appeared in the doorway.

"I need ye in the shop."

Christopher nodded. Anne jumped off the stool. "Father, Christopher's tellin' me a tale. He can't go yet." She stood in front of him, eyes pleading.

"Go to. Find yer mother and sisters."

Frowning, Anne went into the other room.

Christopher followed his father to his cobbler's shop. The shop and the house were built together and separated by a thin door. The family could sometimes hear John beating the leather for shoes far into the night.

"The Tinkler's have ta'en their harvest in, now they all be in want of shoes. I have made the patterns, and ye can sew

72

the leather; fix it to the sole." John handed him a needle and thread, setting the leather and soles before him.

"The Tinkler's have ten?" Christopher said.

"Aye. And one on the way."

Christopher began sewing.

They were silent as the rain kept its constant beat upon the roof. John glanced over at Christopher once in a while.

"What were ye readin'?" John said.

"Ovid...*Amores*."

"I see you can read the Latin as good as gold. *Amores*...the boy's thoughts turn to fancy now, eh?"

Christopher blushed, stole a quick glance at his father.

"Oh, I know a wee bit a Latin."

John went back to working the leather. It came stiff, from the tanner. It needed to be worked long and hard to become pliable for shoes. Most often it was cowhide, but at times he could get deer. He used this for finer shoes, when the ladies wanted something special.

Christopher felt as if the room grew warmer as the tension between his father and him started to build. He knew that he had to say something. He had been waiting, procrastinating really, all summer.

"Father, I—"

"I need you here for harvest, and then beyond—"

"Father, Jonathon Parker got me a scholarship."

"A scholarship?" John looked up, twisted some leather in his hand, set it down. "Bess Parker's son?"

"The same."

"Did Parker give ye the book also?"

"Yea."

"Hmmph. And he himself thinkin' on such piety. I suppose you will be a priest?"

"Nay...aye," Christopher jabbed himself with the needle, shook his hand hard, trying to release the pain. "I don't know." He stuck his finger in his mouth.

"You'll break yer mother's heart."

"Father…I want to be a scholar. I know it has been oft' said that I would become a shoemaker. And 'tis a most honorable profession, but father…I cannot do it. I want…to study."

John threw the hammer down. "And you won't be eatin'! That's for certain – there's no money in it. How will ye marry?" He stared at him, accusing, questioning.

Christopher avoided his eyes. "I didn't do it for spite father. I think…'tis a gift." He looked at him, pleading.

John picked up the hammer. "Yer my only son, Christopher." He pounded the leather, then pulled it and stretched. Taking a sole cutout from the wall he stared at it.

"I cannot make ye what I want. Can I now?"

"Father, I—"

"There's naught to say son. You do what you want. Whatever 'tis, you'll make me proud. That I'm sure of."

Christopher stopped stitching and watched his father work. His father never looked over at him but he sensed it had passed between them; it was done. He had his father's blessing, and he could study at Cambridge.

Chapter 14

Alice awoke with the curtain drawn and the shades down. The bedroom was pitch black. She lay a minute thinking: *yes, we had a fight, and Albert thinks I'm losing my mind.* She drew the covers over her face. Then threw them back down and looked at the clock. Eight thirty. She was late for school.

She ran down the stairs. Albert had a pot of coffee going and plates on the table. The smell of bacon was in the air. He stood at the counter beating some eggs.

"Hello, love." He came over and kissed her.

"This is horrible! I'm late."

"No, I called in for you. Don't worry."

"Don't worry? You think I'm crazy." She plopped down in a chair at the table. Albert went back to the eggs.

"I never said that. You know we don't use that terminology in psychology."

"I am so reassured. Crazy is crazy."

Albert turned from the counter. "I think you are under stress, and were under stress before. It causes you to...invent things."

"I do not invent things Albert."

"You need a break. School will be done soon. You can rest. We can go somewhere. How's that?"

He popped bread in the toaster and stirred the eggs in the pan, then took the orange juice from the refrigerator and poured two glasses. All of it seemed so mechanical in this sterile apartment.

"We need to get out of here, Albert. I hate it here."

"But you wanted to move here after the baby."

"That was then…I couldn't stand to be there with her gone. It was frightening. The house seemed haunted with her ghost."

Albert nodded. "Our lease is up in the summer. Maybe we could start looking for houses."

Alice ran her hand through her hair. "I don't know. I was thinking…"

"We could even start today if you want." He smiled at her, and for a second she saw the old Albert. The old Albert she had fallen in love with. *Was it so long ago?*

What had happened?

"I was thinking…that maybe we should try again. For a baby." She watched his face, and felt the tears well in her eyes as he blanched.

"Alice, I can't just yet…I need more time."

"How much more time, Albert?" She thought she sounded level enough, but he looked at her like she had pained him.

He placed the plates before them and sat in a chair opposite her. The light from the window over the sink shone on the table. It reflected in Albert's glass as he picked it up and drank.

"I don't know. I want to heal…not start all over again."

"We can't heal, Albert, if we don't start living." She took a mouthful of egg.

"Healing is living. I need time. Please don't pressure me."

"But, it's my life too. I think we need this to get on with things."

"Maybe you need this…pregnancy to get on with things. I don't."

Alice looked at the wall in front of her. She felt trapped. She thought of how big and bland the expanse of wall looked. It needed a painting hanging on it. "This argument, if I can be so bold to call it that, is sounding circular."

Albert shrugged. "There's nothing to say."

"I think there is and you're just trying to avoid it."

"What am I trying to avoid, Alice? I told you how I felt. What more is there?"

"There's the fact that we are living in limbo here. It's like we regressed by moving into this apartment. We have no roots, no connections…"

"Your family is here."

"My family." Alice snorted. *I will not think about them now.* But her Russian grandmother popped in her head regardless. Alice had only seen pictures. She was a very pretty woman: high cheek bones, long dark hair, dark eyes. She resembled Alice. That's what her father had always told her. Maybe that's why he is an asshole, she thought.

"Anyway," she drank the last of her juice, "It's better to do something than nothing at all."

"Sometimes nothing at all can be something." Albert took a sip of coffee, put the cup down and placed his hand over hers. "I promise. Just not now."

***

Later that afternoon Alice drove down the side street that ran north of the park. She parked the car and got out, walking down the hill. A fountain sat in the middle of the park, cascading water into a shallow stone enclosure. Alice peered into the water, saw her reflection. She smiled at the reflection as the water undulated around it, breaking it up into a wavy pattern. She wondered if all things were like this wavy pattern and people just couldn't discern it. Pennies lined the bottom of the fountain. Among the pennies were a few sparkles of silver. People who needed the extra assurance of a wish coming true, she thought. She put her hand in her pocket, groping for change. All she brought up was a quarter. She fingered the small piece of silver, as if seeing money for the first time.

What do I want? She looked up to the sky. The trees were filled with leaves which alternated in light and shadow. The green against the blue sky reminded her of an earlier time. She saw Marie in her stroller, looking up at her. Her baby's view, which was whole and complete trust. Marie looked at her and then beyond her, towards the sky.

"What are you looking at, little munchkin?" Alice smiled at her, then followed her gaze.

The doctors told her it had been a heart condition that had suddenly gotten worse.

A heart condition? What did they know. What she wanted to know was why her tiny baby's heart had broken. She blinked back the tears. A crow flew overhead.

She took the coin and flipped it into the water, creating a pattern of circles. The circles continued from their entrance point, slowly becoming weaker until they dissolved into the whole of the water.

Alice watched as the watery circles subsided into a glassy surface and he became visible. He stood behind her. Her heart pounded and her eyes grew large. He placed his hand on her shoulder. She felt the warmth, the pressure from his hand. She placed her hand over his. It didn't disappear, but stayed warm and solid as a hand should.

"Don't leave me, Kit."

He smiled. She closed her eyes and savored the warmth, the closeness of him. There was a tug on her arm and she turned.

"Will you push me on the swing?" A little girl stared up at her.

Alice blinked, trying to focus. "Of course I will."

The girl grabbed her hand, pulling her towards the swings.

***

Alice sat on Jeannie's porch with her fingers linked behind her head. Jeannie emerged from the house with two glasses of lemonade. She handed one to Alice.

"What's wrong? You're as white as a ghost."

"Oh, I'm okay. I suppose I'm just tired." She tried to smile, but it felt cheap, so she quit.

"Cut it out, Petrovka. You know I'm perceptive. For a Math-Mind that is." Jeannie winked at her.

"Just give me a minute," She tasted the lemonade. "So what's up with George?"

"Well...," Jeannie stretched luxuriously, indicating she was pleased. "She spent the night last night."

"Is that good?"

"What do you think? I haven't been laid now for what...two months. Yes, of course it's good."

"What about the blond muscle man?

"She decided that she liked it one way. My way." Jeannie split a grin.

"You look like a goddamn pumpkin with that grin on your face, Bryant."

"You mean a jack o' lantern. Yes, well, I do feel a bit hallowed out after last night. If you know what I mean."

Alice rolled her eyes.

"Hey, maybe you wouldn't be so depressed like if you got a little more sex in your life, Petrovka. What's with your man?"

"Everything is fine in that department." She glanced over at Jeannie. Her eyebrows were raised, questioning. "Sort of." Alice sighed, took a sip of lemonade and launched into the mystical man thing with Jeannie. She watched her face for signs of disbelief. When she got to the part about the rose Jeannie's eyes grew big. She stopped the porch swing and stood up.

"You think I'm crazy."

"No, no. Just a minute. I'll be right back." Jeannie went into the house.

Alice sat against the wall, then stood up and sat on the porch swing. The taste of the story in her mouth felt strange. Did it make sense? Did Jeannie believe her?

The screen door slammed behind Jeannie. She had a bottle of vodka in her hand, and promptly poured some in Alice's glass of lemonade.

"What are you doing? It's the middle of the day?" Alice stared into her glass.

"Sometimes a tonic is called for. Time of day doesn't matter. So, go on." Jeannie nodded at her.

Alice continued her story, ending with the park incident a few minutes before.

"So after that, I came right over. I didn't know what to do." She shook her head.

"Wow." Jeannie took a gulp of lemonade. "So, Albert thinks you're crazy?"

Alice nodded. "It's so bizarre, of course he thinks I'm crazy. My mother says it runs in the family. Not being crazy, but psychic ability. My Russian grandmother had some gift…" Trailing off, she wondered. *Would her father tell her anything?*

"Didn't they burn people at the stake for that sort of thing? Seeing into the future and all that?"

"I'm not really worried about being burned at the stake, Bryant. Just crucified at home."

"What does it feel like?" Jeannie said.

"What do you mean?"

"Seeing this…guy. What's his name?"

"Marlowe. Christopher, or Kit, Marlowe. Kit is his nickname." She took a sip of lemonade. "You put *way* to much vodka in this."

"Yeah, I know."

"It's like time is split, and I can see into the past. Like I'm living on two levels at once: back in the sixteenth century and here." She couldn't think of any other way to explain it. She knew that Zen masters said if you could explain Nirvana then you had missed it. Maybe that was how it was with this.

"Hmm." Jeannie watched the tree tops rustle in the breeze. They sat silent in the swing together, a gentle rocking motion on the porch. Alice felt transported back to her childhood home. Things were simpler then. She thought of the night and shadows. Of playing with the neighborhood kids.

"It's like hide-and-seek." Alice said.

"What?"

"He wants me to find him for some reason."

"For some reason?"

"Yes. And I don't know what it is. But, I get the feeling he has something to tell me."

"You need to see someone."

"Thanks, Jeannie. You sound like Albert now." She stood up, ready to leave.

"No, no. Don't get all huffy on me now, Petrovka. I mean someone who knows about these things. Like a psychic."

Alice hesitated at the door, felt the lightness of the vodka in her head, and sat back down. "What are you talking about?"

"I know a woman. Reputable. I have seen her several times as a matter of fact…"

Alice started to laugh, "Math Mind sees a psychic? Does not compute."

"What you see here before you is just the tip of the iceberg, Petrovka. I am a woman with depth and substance. Did I ever tell you I used to paint?

"No."

"Well, I did. For a long time, too. Anyway –"

"What a minute. Why didn't you tell me you painted?"

"It just never came up."

"Why did you stop?"

81

Jeannie snorted. "Numbers are safer than naked models, that's why. But really, I asked this psychic about it and she said I wasn't ready."

"Oh, that's profound."

"But she said something else…"

"And?"

"She said that there was a problem with my femaleness. Of course at first I thought she was alluding to my being gay, but she said there was a dark energy centered around my uterus. She said I should get it checked out."

"The ovarian tumor."

"Yeah. I would have died, Alice. Imagine if I didn't see her when I did."

They sat rocking together, lost in thought.

"I don't know, Jeannie, it sounds so strange…all of it."

"Just do it. What do you have to lose?"

"Maybe that's what I'm afraid of."

Chapter 15

Sonia and Derrin sat in the audience. Sonia made her disinterest clear as she read the paper, but Derrin leaned forward, arms wrapped around the chair in front of him.

"This place smells great."

Alice looked to where they sat, shielding her face with her hand, warding off the harsh glare of the spotlight. "Yeah, it does. Could you dim those lights, Derrin? We're being blinded down here."

She had had the carpet shampooed yesterday, much to the disapproval of the board. It was filthy dirty, and hadn't been cleaned since the theatre opened. The place pulled in more money every year. She didn't know what they were concerned about.

Dion, Roberto, and Renita stood on stage. They quietly read their lines for Act IV, Scene III. Dion glanced up from time to time, taking in the lights, the stage, the audience, in awe of it all. Alice was pleased. She thought this would be a good experience for all of them. The whole class had proved so enthusiastic about performing Othello that Alice had decided to finish the year with the play. It was a rare thing to have an entire class interested in a subject, so she knew she had to go with it.

Roberto positively relished the role of Iago. And Dion was noble and tragic as Othello. But Renita had a problem with Desdemona. She made Desdemona out to be too cocky, too headstrong. Alice tried to explain that while

Desdemona was a strong female figure for the time period, she wouldn't sound, or act, like she was from the West side of Lansing. Renita said that's who she was, and she couldn't change.

"Renita, that's the point of acting. You are no longer you. You are the character. Let me show you the difference...Sonia, could you come down and read the part of Emilia?"

Sonia looked up from the paper, gave it a shake, then carefully set it down. She maintained her bored expression and stood beside them on the stage.

"Now Emilia," Alice said, "Is, as you know, Desdomona's servant. She is usually portrayed as slightly older and wiser than Desdemona. Why? Because I think it is inherent in the script; in the language. You will understand Desdemona's character better, Renita, if you understand the difference between these two women. In a way, she is like Othello. They are rather naïve, while Emilia tends to be more headstrong."

Renita stood, hands on hips, smacking her gum at Sonia.

"Please Renita, get rid of your gum. They did not chew gum in Elizabethan England. Desdemona, take it from line fifty nine—*these men, these men!*

She walked down the aisle and sat next to Derrin, listening. Made them go through it again. Then again. They went through it until she saw a change in Renita; saw that she was defining Desdemona out of Desdemona, not Renita.

"Good! Good! Bravo you two! Bravo!" Alice and Derrin applauded. Sonia bowed, then ran off the stage. Renita stood fixed in the center of the stage, her eyes shining. She was a butterfly emerging from a chrysalis.

"I remember when Sonia used to look like that." Derrin said.

"Me too."

Alice wasn't altogether surprised when, after everyone had left, Derrin followed her into her office. Red curtains with gold lions draped the window, tied back with gold cord. There was a slight breeze outside ruffling the papers on her desk. She put the paperweight down on them. The temperature was rising, and they were expecting a storm later in the day.

"We should get out of here before it rains." Alice said.

Derrin nodded. "That's kind of why I wanted to talk to you."

"Okay." Alice sat back.

"It's just not the same anymore," he ran his hands through his hair, "Christ, this is hard Alice."

"Just tell me what's on your mind, Derrin."

"Well, you see how Sonia has been acting, so buddy, buddy with Brad, and she just doesn't care about the acting anymore. You know, she had those big dreams about going to Broadway. Now she can't wait to hightail it out of here after we practice."

"Yes, I'm aware of that."

"I'm not saying she doesn't put her time in, because she does. But she knows exactly how much time she needs to put in, no more, no less, and that's what she does. The magic is gone for her. It's like a job."

Alice nodded.

Derrin swallowed so hard his Adam's apple moved up and down. He took a deep breath. She put his hand over his. "It's okay Derrin, really."

"The thing is….they are so…mean…I mean, they are unforgiving of my sexuality. They make little jibes here and there. Sonia never used to be like that. Not before *Brad*." He broke down, sobbing. Alice, realizing there were no tissues around, went into the bathroom, grabbed a handful of toilet paper and handed it to him.

"Anyway, I want to quit. I want out of here!" He dabbed at his eyes and blew his nose.

She sat in her chair again. "Don't let them run you out of here, Derrin."

"I can't stand it! They've turned everyone against me. I thought the theatre was a safe haven for gay people. Yeah, right. Ha. Ha." He blew his nose again.

"They haven't turned everyone against you. Am I against you?"

"You're the only one."

"No, that's not true. What about Jim Schelling? He thinks you're a superb actor, and an admirable person."

"Oh, cut it out with all the grandiose adjectives Alice."

"It's true."

"I know they want to get rid of me."

"I'm the only one who can get rid of you. And that's not going to happen. No anti-gay conspiracy here. But you know Derrin, you will have to be dealing with this kind of thing for the rest of your life. It's not easy. Once you come out of the closet…well, you're not hidden any more. Kind of a sitting duck for people's sexual insecurities and general lack of understanding and open mindedness."

He sighed. "Yeah, I know. All they care about is the money."

Alice frowned, cocked her head. "The money? Who? I don't get your drift, Derrin."

"Well, once this place started pulling in the bucks…that's all they were concerned about."

"By they…do you mean the board?"

He nodded.

She looked out the window. A robin flew into a tree with a worm in its beak – gulped it down.

"Looking for easy pickings, I suppose."

She thought it strange there were so many robins around. She did enjoy their song.

"I'm sorry, what did you say Alice? Easy pickings?"

"Oh…I guess I was thinking out loud."

There was the sound of thunder in the distance. The sky turned a murky grey, threaded with a venomous yellow.

"Looks like a doozy." Alice said.

"Yeah. I'm out of here. Thanks for the pep talk boss." Derrin stood.

"Just let me know what you're thinking. Okay?"

"Sure. See ya."

A boom of thunder echoed throughout the sky. Alice closed the window as the wind whipped rain drops over the desk. She noticed the faux-silk curtains were fading, turning a shade of dark pink where the sun had been baking them. Alice fingered them between her fingers, thought of what Derrin had said. She wondered how much he really did know but didn't want to tell her.

She watched the rain, and thought she would wait for it to pass before she ventured outside to her car. Lately she had been thinking of Kit when it had rained.

She thumbed through a pile of bills on her desk. The phone rang. She picked it up and explained to the caller that this was the Lion Theatre, not the Lion Strip Club. The person on the other end seemed to think that they were one and the same, *a theatre is a theatre.* Disgusted, Alice hung up the phone. Out of the corner of her eye she saw a number written on a piece of paper tucked under the phone. She picked it up and examined it. Not recognizing the handwriting, she frowned. Turning the scrap of paper over she noticed the initials D.J. *Derrin James? How would he have gotten into my office?* Alice made a mental note to ask him when she saw him again.

No, no, I want to know now. She dialed the number.

"American Bank and Trust."

American Bank and Trust?

"Sorry, wrong number." She hung up the phone. Looking out the window she noticed the rain had stopped. She carefully closed the blinds and the curtains. She crumpled the paper, and her hand hovered over the waste basket. Instead, she shoved the scrap in her pocket.

***

The address that Jeannie had written down for her lay in the console of her car. She picked it up. It looked like it was by the school. Backing out of the parking lot she turned down Lake Lansing, towards the west end of town.

The road was the link between two different worlds. If you lived on the west end you were most likely Mexican, and if you lived on the east end you were most likely white. Somewhere in the middle the houses became smaller. Yards started to contain plastic Virgin Marys. These were placed in grottos with masses of fake roses or geraniums in bright blue pots. Children littered the unkempt yards. Some toddled in diapers with bare feet. Young girls sat on the porches watching them. Alice became lost looking for the address. She stopped by a yard full of small children chasing a kitten. A young girl sat on the porch steps with an older girl sitting behind her.

"Do you know where Maria Serna lives?"

They looked at each other, then at her. The young girl giggled. She had on blue eye shadow and had a red ribbon tied at the end of her long braid.

"*No lo se.*" The young girl said.

"Oh," The older girl appeared lost in thought. "You mean Mimi?"

Alice didn't know. She nodded her head yes.

"She lives on Baker. Go up three streets, go left. You'll see it."

The girls looked away, dismissing her.

Alice turned the way the girls had told her and went down the street. There was a corner grocer advertising Budweiser and chorizo, but no Mimi. She pulled into the store parking lot and parked the car. Running her hands through her hair she tried to decide what to do. Roberto Gomez came out of the store.

"Yo, it's Ms. Petrovka." Smiling, he walked over to her car. "What you doin' here?" He placed his arms in the window, leaning in.

"Oh, I…am getting chorizo. Only place I know that carries it."

"Yeah. You white people eat that boring food."

Alice nodded. "What are you doing here, Roberto?"

For some reason Roberto didn't think this was a dumb question. "Getting some tortillas for my mom." He held the bag up as evidence. "We ran out when Jimmy and Shay came over for dinner."

"Oh. Well, I better get going." Alice started the car.

"Okay Ms. P. See ya at school."

Alice pulled out, defeated. She twisted and turned back to Lake Lansing and drove east.

Chapter 16

Christopher sat at a long wooden table. He knew he should be getting back to his room, but he was engrossed in the translation of the *The Amores*. He finally had the parchment and quills to do what he wanted. In the excitement and intensity of translating works from the Latin he often stayed up much later than his fellow students. The candle sputtered and he brought it closer to the book to see the printed words. It was slow and tedious work.

The hall was drafty and the books were chained to the tables. Students would often try to take the books back to their rooms so they could read in more comfortable quarters. Christopher noticed that the chain on the *The Amores* had gauge marks in it. His fellow students had tried unsuccessfully to remove the book from the table. It was no surprise, the book was full of erotic poetry, easily the most popular volume at the table.

Although the poetry engrossed him, lately his thoughts had been turning towards the plays of Seneca and Plautus, the Roman playwrights of antiquity. When he read their plays, he could vividly envision the actors, the movement, the rising and falling of their voices.

Earlier in the year the headmaster had caught him in the midst of his imagining and he had become stone silent. When Christopher broke from his fantasy he found that everyone was staring at him. They then began to laugh. The headmaster had banished him to his room with no dinner and extra morning prayer.

The other day the students were expected to take part in a performance of one of the English mystery plays, *Everyman*. Christopher found himself engrossed in the direction and the performance. He was praised for his efforts, and called upon to direct the next school performance of *The Second Shepherds' Play*.

After *Everyman* Christopher had shut himself in his room during free time. He was gripped by a vision of something he wanted to write. He had an idea of a play of a hero who was bold and full of himself. But how? He vaguely had an idea of something like Seneca or Plautus, where the actors would speak normally, in blank verse, prose style. Of course, there would be poetry, too. Poetry was beautiful, and would add romance and allure to the stage. But the blank verse, it was like bold brush strokes on the stage. Yes, yes, that's it, he thought. Too many plays were all in the rhyme of verse. It became tedious and boring and too hard to follow. The audience often lost interest halfway into the play. Mine, he thought, will be different; it will be exciting.

He thought of his play and the main character. This hero would rise to great heights of glory and fame. Christopher fanned himself with the quill, thinking, then he brought it to his face, caressing his cheek. He would be a great lover also, and his wife would love him intensely, passionately…

"How now, Kit?"

Christopher jumped in his seat and quickly turned his head. "Ah! Nick, what say you, snekin' up on me like that?"

Nick sat down next to him. He picked up the book Christopher was translating.

"Ovid. *The Amores.*"

Christopher held a finger to his lips.

"All your time spent on this?" Nick laughed, slapped Christopher on the back. "There's much to be learned about becoming a priest in it? Ha!" He picked up the book and read, scratching the back of his head. "Where will you find a woman like this?"

Christopher shrugged, smiled.

"What about a wench, flesh and blood? Naught in yer head, but real."

"Aye Nick. I suppose ye have one hidden in yer room?"

"Perchance...yea, I do." Nick raised his eyebrows.

Christopher looked up from whittling his quill.

"Ha! There's the rub!"

"As you will, Nick. Prithee leave me be." He waved his hand in dismissal.

"Ah, get ye to town, lad. What say you? Wenching, drinking... enough time spent on this." Nick grabbed the book from him.

Christopher grabbed for it back. The headmaster walked by and they began conversing in Latin. If caught speaking English they would be severely reprimanded. Christopher and Nick nodded, waited until the headmaster passed.

"Surely yer not studying for the priesthood?" Nick whispered.

Christopher smiled again. "Aye, and what of it?"

"There's naught to be gained by becoming a skinny priest. Always hungry, bowing and praying. For what?" Nick snorted.

"Surely there's heaven? A just reward."

"Heaven? What, that fairytale?"

Christopher looked at him, astonished. "Nick, ye better be careful. What ye say is blasphemy. Ye know that."

"Aye." Nick leaned back, a cocky expression on his face. "I know ye feel the same, Kit."

Christopher avoided his eyes. "A just reward, Nick. A just reward." He turned toward the parchment and dipped his quill in the ink pot.

Nick covered his writing hand with his. "Are ye hungry, Kit? Tell me that. Are ye?" Christopher glanced at him and Nick looked at him fiercely, fire in his eyes.

"Aye," He admitted, nodding slightly. "And cold."

"Then I pray you meet me on the morrow in my room...after we sup."

"Nicholas Faunt!"

Christopher and Nick jerked their heads up. The headmaster stood over them, crooking his finger towards Nick.

"Ades dum abo." Come with me.

Nick nodded at Christopher and stood. *"Valere iubere."* Goodbye.

The head master cuffed him, then pushed him forwards. Christopher watched as they walked down the long hall together.

Chapter 17

They had barely spoken a word together as they drove through town. Alice had gotten the call unexpectedly— *would you like to come to dinner? Pam is in town.*

Pam. Who was she anyway? Alice wondered. Her mother's favorite, a smashing success. *What about me? What about my theatre? My work with all these kids?*

She knew, logically, that it didn't matter. That her parents held different values than hers. Besides, her work with Selina had taught that families were often illogical, and had hidden agendas of their own. Agendas that were seldom acknowledged, and sometimes handed down throughout the ages as a kind of familial birthright.

"Who knows when the dysfunction gets started?" Selina had said. "It could have been anything that caused the family stress – maybe a psychotic family member?" Selina had looked at her, questioning. That shrink look said: *fill in the blank, please.* Albert played this with her, also. She glanced over at him. He stared straight ahead, hands gripping the wheel.

"Talk to me. You know how I hate this."

"Why are we going? Why didn't you beg off? You know they cause you great discomfort." Albert turned the wheel down the street where her parents lived.

Alice panicked. "I don't know."

"Well, I can always turn around." He patted her hand and parked the car in her parent's driveway.

"Sure, Albert. Wouldn't that look strange? Now that we're parked here."

He shrugged. "You could say you were sick and had to leave."

That wouldn't be too far from the truth. *No, I will go through with this.* Alice opened the door and got out, vaguely feeling like she was going to her execution. Albert followed close behind her.

Jasmine met them at the door. "Aunt Alice!" She flung the door open, and jumped out onto the porch.

"Hey!" Alice gave her a hug. Jasmine jumped from her to Albert.

Albert gently pried her off, and the three of them went inside. Alice noticed a rash on the side of Jasmine's neck. "What's this honey?"

"Nothing." Jasmine nervously put her hand to her neck and started scratching.

"Something under your skin, kiddo?" Albert patted her head as Jasmine ducked under his arm.

Alice and Albert walked towards the back of the house where the living room was. There sat Pam, as on a throne, in the middle of the room, surrounded by remnants of wall paper and fabric. Her mother sat on the ground at Pam's feet. How perfectly worshipful in its design, Alice thought.

Ever since Pam had become head of My Face, Your Face, their mother had absolutely doted on her. Pam could do no wrong. Everything she said had relevance, every word was precious. There was a grand design to what Pam said, and Myra basked in its eloquence. Alice on the other hand, as always, felt disregarded. She had felt this way since childhood. But the eminence of Pam had taken on royal proportions since her elevation to corporate executive.

"Hi." Alice stood in the doorway with Albert. Albert took a seat by the window.

"Oh hi, Alice." Myra barely glanced up.

Well forget the fact that you called me, wanted me to come over, Alice thought.

Pam's eyes scanned her face. She had a smug expression on her face, secure in her queenly role.

"I only stopped by to say hi," Alice said, sensing how the trap had been laid. She was merely bait to make her mother and sister feel elevated, feel good about themselves, while she was made to feel small and worthless.

But in the back of her mind she felt that maybe just once...just maybe...it could be different. Of course it never was.

"We're redecorating the living room. Want to help? Here, see if you can come up with a color combination for this piece of wall paper." Pam threw the wall paper remnant at her feet and went back to sorting through what she had arranged in front of her.

"No...I don't want to be a part of this...task. I need to talk to dad." Alice backed out of the room. Behind her she heard Albert make polite conversation. The forced sound of Pam's laugh rang in her ears.

The door to the family room was open a crack. Family room, what a quaint phrase. The only family here is my father who sits in front of the TV with a beer in his hand. Thin light filtered through the window as she entered the room. She couldn't tell if her father was dozing or actually asleep. Two cans of Budweiser lay perched on the table beside him. A game of baseball flickered on the TV.

"Dad?"

Her father lay there in his recliner, snoring. The smell of beer hovered around him like a thick smog, heavy and filled with years of perspiration. Alice fought back the urge to cry and picked up the beer cans. She walked to the kitchen and placed them on the counter hearing the sound of her mother, sister, and Albert conversing in the next room. Alice marveled at the fact that Albert could so easily talk to them.

She walked back into the room.

"Dad?" Alice touched Sam's shoulder, shook it a little.

"Huh? Whadya want?" He opened up a bleary eye towards his daughter.

Alice sat next to him on the couch. Sam rubbed his eyes.

"Is your sister here?" He spoke gruffly, eyed the table for his beer. "I had a good swallow left in that one, Alice."

Alice said nothing, stared at the baseball game.

"She wants to redo the living room. Like that will change anything." He stared to laugh.

"What's so funny?"

"Nothing."

Sam settled his face into an impenetrable mask. It reminded her of clay, and nothing could make her more angry.

"Nothing?"

Alice couldn't figure him out. Sometimes he would have little outbursts like this, as if he was on the verge of saying something real and authentic about their family. Then he would shut down again. Alice kept waiting. Always the waiting. She sighed. But today she had bigger fish to fry.

"Dad, what can you tell me about grandma Petrovka?"

He looked over at her. "Why do you bring that up?"

"I heard she was psychic."

He snorted. "She was a nut. Who'd ya hear that from?"

"Mom."

"Another nut."

Alice waited a few minutes, realizing she had to pick the right moment of balance. If she waited too long her dad would wave her off, and if she didn't wait long enough he would probably explode. She hated walking on eggshells.

Alice knew that her grandmother, Ireni Petrovka, had survived the Russian Revolution of 1917. She had managed to come to America soon after. Apparently she had suffered a nervous breakdown after the birth of Alice's father. When he was barely two she had had to put him in an orphanage until she was able to recover. Her grandmother had died before she was born. That was all she knew.

Alice went to the kitchen and opened the fridge. She grabbed a Budweiser from a twelve pack, opened it and set it in front of her father. He accepted this gesture as a token of affection and patted her hand.

"Bobby tells me you were down at O'Leary's the other night with some blond."

"Her name is Joannie. Yes, I was there." And left as soon as I could, she thought.

Alice felt very small, like she was ten years old, alone in her bed with the window open and the moon shining down, watching the pattern of light reflect on her bedcovers, moving from one end to the other, waiting for the sounds of her dad coming home from the bar.

"So what about grandma, dad?"

Sam chugged down half the beer. Set the can down and wiped his mouth with the back of his hand. He shrugged and glanced over at her. "I really can't remember much. It was so long ago."

Bullshit. You remember everything, that's why you drink so much.

Alice felt the heat rise to her face. She snatched the can of beer from the table.

"Why don't you quit drinking, Dad? What are you so afraid of?" She glared at him.

Sam's mouth dropped open. "Well, I guess you have her temper." They stared at each other for what seemed like eons ticking away over the centuries. *Something has got to give.*

"She picked your name, you know."

Alice sat down, grateful the spell had been broken. She didn't realize it would be so hard. She was shaking.

"She knew things. That's all." Sam took an active interest in the game on the television, craning his neck towards it.

"What things?

"She knew things about people, what would happen to them. Or, if they were sick, she could tell them what was wrong."

"And?" Alice encouraged her father.

"They locked her up for it."

She knew she was treading on dangerous ground. "But why?"

Sam shifted in his seat. "It wasn't like the old country here. There was a long tradition of healers over there. People were suspicious, my mother could barely speak English. Some religious…person…claimed she was psychotic. I think the person thought she was a witch. I don't know…it was so long ago." He waved her off.

She realized this was the most Sam had ever told her.

"Thanks dad."

He took a swig of beer. "Don't mention it."

***

During the ride home Albert listened to Alice excitedly speak of her grandmother. She told him what she could piece together. She stopped short when he adopted his shrink face.

"What's wrong?"

"Nothing, love. I suppose I'm just tired." He managed a weak smile.

"Great. I get to play the guessing game with everyone tonight? What? Tell me what you're thinking."

"There's a fine line between the psychic and the psychotic, you know."

Alice felt a crushing vice wrap around her chest. It became hard to breath. She looked out the window, watching the street lights flash by and the headlights approach in the distance.

"I just don't understand. Your profession tells you to regard the psychic as a healing process. Yet, you sit here and denigrate me."

"But you have a history of *psychotic*, not psychic, disturbance. Of course I'm alarmed. And now this Marlowe thing."

Alice looked over at him. "You're jealous."

"Jealous? What are you talking about?"

"You know damn well what I'm talking about. If it was anything else besides Marlowe, you would listen to me. In fact, if it was one of your precious clients you would be all ears, I'm sure." She slumped in her seat.

"I'm sorry I ever brought up this Marlowe thing." Albert pulled in the parking lot.

"It has nothing to do with you bringing it up. Did you ever think that it might be something that I have tapped into? Some sort of psychic link? Can't you understand that finding this information out about my grandmother has made me feel good about myself? Why can't you understand that?" She peered at him in the dark.

"Of course it has to do with me bringing it up, or you never would have latched on to it." He picked up her hand. "Don't you realize the obsessive nature you have? This happened before with that Pirondello play, and then with Mr. Gronsky."

"Pirondello didn't come back to haunt me, and Mr. Gronsky was a tyrannical ass. You *know* that, Albert."

"Yes, but the point is, you were obsessed with the play, and Gronsky, and then you had the psychotic break."

"Well, it was a nice place to be at the time, Albert." She withdrew her hand from his, thinking of the blissful feelings she had felt after she had broken through the paranoia.

"What are you saying Alice? That your breakdown was some sort of defense mechanism?"

"Maybe."

"I don't buy that." He took the keys from the ignition.

"Mr. Big Shot Transactional Analysis is now telling me what I should feel. I thought that was the point of transactional analysis Albert, that the patient is guided by her own intuition, and not led on by the shrink!"

"You have a past – "

"Look, Albert, my life is fine. I am not under the same stress I was before. You cannot imprint one circumstance upon another. I am a changed person."

He shook his head. "I wish you would talk to Selina."

"Our work together is done Albert, I told you that! Damnit! Don't you listen to me?" She hit the side of the door with her fist. "And what about you? Are you a changed person? When's the last time you saw Marie? You never put flowers on her grave." Alice felt tears stream down her cheeks.

"Marie is dead Alice. She doesn't care if I see her."

"Well, I care! And it seems to me you are the one not dealing with things, not changing. Look! We're still in this damn apartment!"

"May I remind you that – "

"No, you may not remind me. I'm sick and tired of being the patient, Albert, while you are the great and sane analyst." Alice opened the door, got out, and then slammed it as hard as she could. She walked to the apartment door and realized she didn't have the key.

Chapter 18

One evening after dinner they went back to Christopher's room. Nick talked of the theatre in London and of a certain clown, Richard Tarlton, who brought down the house with his antics.

Nick laughed, remembering, "And this Tarlton, moving about, suddenly flipped back after he had recited his lines. Now, hear me, all the way back, in the air! Why, his cap was still upon on his head! The man is most fluid." He shook his head in amazement.

Christopher frowned. "Do ye mean limber?"

"Aye, that too." Nick lay back on the bed with his hands behind his head.

Christopher cleared his throat and went to his desk, inserted a key and opened a drawer. "Ye asked what I ha' been workin' on Nick? Here 'tis." He handed his manuscript to Nick.

Nick flipped through the pages. "Marry, Kit...'tis long. What say you....ah," He turned to the first page, to the title of the play. *"Tamburlaine?"* He looked at Christopher, a quizzical expression on his face.

"Timur the Lame. I ha' been readin' the Turks. He was a great lord, except lame. Now, mind you, my Tamburlaine, is not. As a warrior he is strong and undefeated."

"And what say you now, Kit? Will ye be ta'en the play to London?" Nick smirked at him.

"Aye. *Deo favente*." Christopher retrieved his manuscript, placed it in the desk drawer and locked it.

"Certes, with God's favor. But I see ye plan to be no man of God, nay Kit, you aim to be a playmaker?"

Christopher smiled, pulled the tie on his robe tighter. "Tis true. A poet is what I'll be Nick. But, I aim to make money at my labor, and a poet needs a patron. Marry, not being gentle is my plight. And being noble fares better than naught." He frowned, scratching his leg. "Ah, this cloak scratches so. The roughest wool, 'tis all my mother could afford."

Nick sat the edge of the bed. A smile crept across his face. "Verily Kit, I cannot change base stock into gold. I'm no alchemist. 'Tis rough you are, not gentle." He laughed. Christopher threw a pillow at his head.

"Fie Nick, you lightminded giglet. I ha' the same brain as any noble, perchance e'en better. In the main, thou wilt see my plays in London. Thou wilt *see*." Christopher's eyes gleamed.

"Ha! But, I know a way to make this wealth thou art craving. On the morrow Kit, *on the morrow*."

Christopher looked at him, doubtful. "What say you Nick? Prithee tell me the length of it."

Nick stood and went to the door, listened for a minute, then came back to the bed. He sat next to Christopher.

"Ye know of Walsingham?"

Christopher frowned. "The man of state, Sir Francis?"

"Aye, the very one."

Nick leaned closer to Christopher and explained.

Chapter 19

Alice didn't plan on driving to Mimi Serna's, but after finally locating her house the pending visit became an obsession. She drove around the block a few times, working up her courage. She wondered what she would say to this woman. *Will she tell me I'm crazy?*

Getting out of the car she walked across the street to the house. In the window there was a small sign of a palm with an eye in the middle of it. *Hand of seeing?* She knocked on the door.

"*Un momento!*" Someone yelled from inside.

A small boy of about eight answered the door. He had a crew cut and was dressed in a Batman shirt and a pair of jeans. He stared at her.

"*Es su madre...,*"

He nodded. "Ma!"

Mimi quickly appeared at the door, a load of wash in her arms. Alice was slightly taken back. She wasn't sure what a psychic would look like, but Mimi Serna did not seem to resemble one at all. Dressed in black slacks and a white shirt, she resembled a waitress or a receptionist. She had dark hair that was held back with a barrette and she wore glasses. *Where's the turban, the bright colors...*

Alice shook her head, embarrassed at the thought. Mimi smiled.

"Can I help you?"

"A friend of mine mentioned you, said I should pay you a visit…"

Mimi nodded, and ushered her in the door. "Come in, let's go to the office."

Office?

"I'll be out in time for supper." Mimi said.

"Okay, Ma."

She nodded at the young boy, and he ran up the stairs.

"Down here." Mimi started to descend the basement stairs.

The basement was comfortable and refinished. A carpet was on the floor, and a litter box and dishes of cat food and water lay against the wall. Mimi led her to a door and opened it.

"My name is Mimi, by the way."

"I'm Alice."

"Hi, Alice."

The room was small. There was a table with two chairs up against the wall and a bookshelf full of books. She picked up a thin volume of poetry by Dylan Thomas, set it back in its spot, scanned the titles of other books – a novel, *House of the Spirits,* by Isabel Allende. How fitting. There were novels by Alice Walker and Barbara Kingsolver, Raymond Carver, and Stephen King. A whole row of books on Tarot and astrology. A book on car mechanics stopped her.

"Car mechanics?"

Mimi laughed, sitting down at the table. "Sure, why not?"

"It just seems strange sitting here amongst the literature. So practical somehow."

"Yes, well I'm a single mother and, believe it or not, we have no mechanics in my family, so here I am. A psychic car mechanic." She laughed again. "But my main job is nursing, over at Lansing General. I work the cardiac unit. What about you, you like to read?"

"Oh, yes. I'm an English teacher over at the high school."

"Ah, *that* English teacher."

"What?" Alice's face fell.

"They talk about you. In a good way."

Alice smiled. "Teaching is something that comes naturally to me, you know, like a life process – like living….," Alice looked towards the small window to the outside, "and like dying…what is that poem? Oh yeah, "Time held me green and dying / Though I sang in my chains like the sea."

"Dylan Thomas. 'Fern Hill.' " Mimi said.

Alice nodded.

"My favorite," Mimi said, "Is: The force that through the green fuse drives the flower / Drives my green age; that blasts the roots of trees / Is my destroyer."

"Yes, Dylan was great. Wasn't he?" Alice sat down opposite Mimi.

Mimi was looking at her strangely, focusing, then, unfocusing. She took her glasses off, put them on again, peered at her.

"*Quod me nutriet, me destruiet.* Yes, that's it." Mimi took her glasses off, rubbed them on her shirt.

Astonished, Alice could only stare at her.

"It's quite a bit like Dylan, wouldn't you say?"

"Well, yes…how did you know?"

Mimi shrugged. "What nourishes me, also destroys me. The message is for you not me. I'm only the antennae. I pick the stuff up and broadcast it."

Alice slowly nodded. "It's Kit Marlowe's saying. He had it painted in a corner of his portrait. You can find it all over Shakespeare's works too—it's in the sonnets, in the plays—everywhere."

Mimi frowned. "Well, whatever it means, it's all over you, Alice. You literally vibrate with it." Mimi placed a small bundle wrapped in velvet in front of her. "Now, let me tell you what I usually do. I read the cards and see what type of impressions I get."

Mimi took the Tarot cards out and shuffled them. She placed them in front of Alice. "Please cut the deck in two."

She dutifully separated the pile into two halves.

Mimi placed the cards together. "The reason I use cards in guiding my intuition is because the cards tell a story. They use ancient symbolism that is contained in our unconscious, but we have access to it when we see and use the symbols. It is like a memory bank that we can tap into."

Alice nodded. She was well versed in symbolism. Her work as a writer and in the theatre had taught her there were no coincidences. There was a purpose behind everything. Albert felt the same way in his psychology work. They used to talk about the symbols they found to be inherent in their work. But all that was over now, Alice thought.

Mimi lay the first card down. It was an image of two people united together. Cupid rose above them with his bow, aiming an arrow towards them.

"The lovers," Mimi said. "The sign of Gemini. It is the journey of the twins. Someone you feel very close to is reaching out to you."

Mimi looked at the card, a quizzical expression on her face. "That reminds me of something." She stood up and went to the bookshelf, withdrew a volume and sat down again. "There is something in the Book of Changes, the I Ching, which relates to this...," she quickly thumbed through the pages, "Here it is: *'when two people are at one in their inmost hearts, they shatter even the strength of iron or bronze.'*" She looked up from the book at Alice. Sometimes I just feel inspired to look into something further for a client. Does it mean anything to you?"

"No... well, maybe."

Mimi drew more cards, all relating to the archetype of the lovers. "This is strange, usually I get a series of different cards, not the same type of card, over and over. The symbolism is very strong here, the odds of pulling these cards would be quite low. Then again, I don't believe in chance."

Mimi drew a few more cards and then stopped to study them. She looked up at Alice.

"I feel as if you're holding something back, something that you don't want to talk about. But that's okay. What I do is give you the information relating to your psychic state and you process it. You don't have to divulge anything you don't want to."

Alice looked down at her hands, felt void of anything to say. Mimi was silent for a moment. "Maybe I should answer your first question."

"My first question?"

"Yes. The first question you had when you pulled in here, 'will she tell me I'm crazy?' The answer is no. You're not crazy, Alice."

Alice felt her heart start thumping, then pounding, in her chest. She suddenly wanted to be anywhere but here.

Mimi stared at the cards a moment longer. "Something else."

"Something else." Alice responded faintly. Perspiration broke out on her forehead.

"Yes. Look into some sort of Russian nesting dolls. I think it might be important."

Chapter 20

Christopher and Nick walked through the streets of London, towards the house of Walsingham. The sights and sounds of the city were like a tonic to Christopher, who hadn't been out of the cloistered environment of the university for months.

Happy to shed his scratchy robe, he donned breeches and shirt, then pulled on the boots his father had made him, admiring himself in the glass.

"Fit for a king, Nick."

"Ay, fit enough for Sir Francis. But he hath no eye for ye." Nick laughed.

They passed by the brothels where prostitutes stood in the doors, hoping for a customer.

"There be yer fair Corinna." Nick elbowed him and nodded towards a whore. "Ye have small change? That is all they require."

The woman surveyed Christopher. She was short and buxom, with blond hair and blue eyes. She smiled and walked boldly towards them.

"What say you," she whispered in Christopher's ear, then placed his hand on her breast.

"Ah, by your leave m'lady, there is naught to say." Christopher removed his hand.

She glared at him, then strode back to her perch in the doorway.

Nick stood a few feet away, doubled over in laughter. "How now, Kit? Ye won't let the whore filch ye? Go to!"

"Go to? Nay, perchance you will risk that ill humor, but not I."

"Ah, these whores are not ill."

"They filch yer will, and there it will rot. And in the nose of thee...burning, burning, red lamp fire to light our way." Christopher smiled and shook his head as they passed the whores.

"Marry, I see perchance ye wilt like a thing...ah, more costly."

"Costly?"

"Ay Kit, costly. Costly like a courtesan, now that ye be close to a man of means."

Christopher laughed. "Ah Nick, ye be a man of tall tales. Mayhap one that I cannot afford, and hidden ones, perchance under yer bed?"

"Ha! Well, la; I know of one courtesan. Receives me well, she does."

They continued walking up the street and turned a corner, passing a group of minstrels. A dark man in a brightly colored turban and red velvet gerkin played a lute, while another dark-skinned man strummed a guitar.

Nick noticed him watching the musicians. "They be Berbers of some sort. Ethiopes. Perchance Jews." Nick shrugged and continued walking.

Christopher walked up to the men and threw a small coin into their pot. The turbaned man smiled, nodded towards Christopher, and continued playing.

"I see ye like music more than ha'en yer will filched." Nick rolled his eyes.

"What say you, Nick? Is that a not a lovely hue for a gerkin?" Christopher stood admiring the musician's clothing.

"Ay. Come, come. Sir Francis will be wait'n on us." He pulled on Christopher's sleeve.

"I shall get a gerkin of that hue, red, and perchance ha' a portrait made, when I come to London wi' my plays." His eyes glazed over, thinking of the future when he would bring Tamburlaine to the stage.

"Ah, go to. Yer head is stuffed with plays."

Christopher felt himself enter a dream where the present and the future seemed to merge. The people around him became fuzzy, and he saw others that seemed to be more part of the future than the present. The language became strange as he struggled to understand it. Some, too, were people of the past. A robed figure that appeared to have lived many years ago glided by. The robed figure was a monk, with the shorn hair of an ancient order. He followed the monk with his eyes, and the monk nodded at him as he passed.

He noticed a woman standing still in the throng of past-present-and-future. She had brown hair and eyes, and she was watching him from a distance. Although she was dressed in the present, he sensed that she was part of the future. Christopher felt drawn to her, and his heart pounded. She disappeared in the haze of people, and Christopher turned looking for her. As he turned, the present street sounds coalesced around him. There was a loud buzzing in his ears. His vision tunneled and all the colors of the past-present-and-future kaleidoscoped together. As the present time layered itself on the moment, he felt himself looking at another woman who had been watching him.

She was an older woman with deeply set eyes. Her dark hair was visible in the red kerchief she had wrapped around her head. She sat at a table with cards in front of her and nodded at Christopher as she held up a card. The woman was a great distance from him, but the card shone with a florescent intensity. It was of two people embracing.

Christopher moved toward her. He felt a vague tug on his arm and realized it was Nick.

"Tut, it is a gypsy, Kit. If ye want to be hanged and quartered for consort'n wi' the likes of them…then go to." Nick frowned and pulled his arm, forcefully this time.

Christopher looked at the woman, and she calmly held his gaze. It seemed an eternity as they gazed at each other.

"Sir Francis, Kit, Sir Francis."

Christopher felt himself be led away, the gaze of the woman lost. A visceral pull wrenched his gut as his eyes were ripped from the gypsy's.

***

They stood before a heavy door. The wood was ancient; it had stood the test of time. He stared at the door, his heart racing. Nick grabbed the door knocker, and Christopher placed his hand over his.

"Nick, perchance this is not right. We can go."

"Come Kit, you are just scared. This fear of yours will leave ye."

"Aye?" Christopher felt beads of sweat form on his forehead. "Sir Francis is a master of spies. We could be killed—"

"The work pays, Kit. You want to be a scholar? How bad do ye be want'n that?"

The knocker banged loudly against the door. It was opened quickly by a manservant. Dark in appearance and questioning, the servant stood at the door.

"Nicholas Faunt and Master Christopher Marlowe to see Sir Francis." Nick nodded.

The servant ushered them in.

They stood in a spacious entrance hall. Brocade tapestries lay against the wall in a room just beyond. The house smelled of spices and something Christopher couldn't quite identify. A large vase of roses was on the table.

"This way." The servant led them to a room with a fire. Like the rest of the house the room was wide and spacious. Books lined an entire wall. The room reeked of knowledge and Christopher was instantly enamored. At first glance it appeared that the room was unoccupied, then Christopher noticed someone sitting by the fire. The figure stood up and turned towards them.

The servant bowed. "Masters Nicholas Faunt and Christopher Marlowe Sir."

Sir Francis nodded, and the servant left.

He stood looking at them a moment, and Christopher had the distinct impression that Sir Francis Walsingham could find out anything about him he needed to know. The eyes of the hawk penetrated him, looking for a weakness, but the words that came out of his mouth were warm.

"Christopher Marlowe, the best at Cambridge they tell me. I am pleased to make your acquaintance."

"Sir, the privilege is mine." Christopher bowed slightly.

"Would you like something to drink, eat, perchance?"

"No, sir." Christopher shook his head. Nick also shook his head.

"He likes to keep his head clear?" Sir Francis addressed Nick.

"Aye sir," said Nick, "and has a good head for puzzle making. And solving. Kit has been translating Ovid."

"Ovid?" Sir Francis raised an eyebrow. "He's a bit of a lover. Wouldn't you say Master Marlowe?"

"Aye sir. But love and war are equal. We cannot have one without the other."

Sir Francis looked at him with interest. He ushered them to sit, and then he sat and crossed his legs. "Please, tell me more."

"To truly love, sir, one is passionate. And passion is also the mark of the warrior. It is passion that makes the lover or the soldier." Christopher felt his heart hammering in his chest, wondering if he was saying the correct thing.

"Aye. Perchance. But, is it not better to subdue the passions in order to have a clear head?"

"A clear head is the mark of a gentleman sir." Christopher felt his leg shaking.

113

"In matters of state, yes…A game of chess Master Marlowe?"

Startled, Christopher met Sir Francis's gaze. He wanted to question Nick if he should enter into this game with him, but he dared not look towards his friend. He sensed that it was between him and Sir Francis now, and matters of logic must be pushed by the wayside. He would have to rely on his intuition.

Sir Francis sat behind a chessboard with pieces carved out of a white material that Christopher had never seen before. He picked up a piece and examined it.

" 'Tis ivory Master Marlowe. Is it not a lovely substance?"

Christopher nodded and put the piece down.

"You may have the white colour. White is the colour of good, no?"

"White is a colour you cannot see."

Sir Francis laughed. "True enough. But the enemy may hide in the shadows. And the shadows are the colour of ill, black. You must mix with the black to root out the evil."

He felt a sudden tug at his gut, realizing where Sir Francis was leading him. It would be a matter of black and white to Sir Francis, a question of all or nothing. He was questioning his loyalty and where he would draw the line.

Slowly and deliberately Christopher played his moves.

"When entering the shadow, I will never lose myself." He checkmated Sir Francis.

"Ah," Sir Francis looked up from the board. *"Ars est celare artum."* It is art to conceal art.

Nick looked over from the bookshelf and raised his eyebrows.

"Aye, sir. But pray tell, if it is art to conceal art, how may'nt I not turn gray? How can the black and white mix?"

Sir Francis glared at him. "Are you not a cobbler's son?"

"Ay. That I am sir."

"Ne supra crepidam sutor iudicaret!"

Christopher looked down at his feet, his cheeks stinging.

114

***

They walked through the town square. It was almost to be deserted. Only a few stragglers ventured forth on the cobblestone. But Nick seemed optimistic, even happy. Christopher didn't share in his feelings. He felt as though something precious might be taken from him.

"What say you Kit? Marry! To France you'll go! I ha' not seen the likes of it. Ever. Verily, Sir Francis trusts ye."

Christopher shook his head. "What of my studies? It will be a hard place to be, Nick."

"Think on the money, Kit. Ye won't go for wont of hunger now."

"Aye. But for wont of something else. Ye heard Sir Francis, 'the cobbler should not judge above the sandal.' I shalt always be a pawn to Sir Francis, Nick, ne'er a man."

They walked in silence. As they made their way through the narrow streets, Christopher felt a building sense of apprehension. He felt a presence, a fear, as the city was filled with the approaching twilight, and the shadows lengthened.

Chapter 21

Alice sat nestled in the corner of the couch watching them. She did not particularly feel like conversing with anyone, although Albert seemed to be in good spirits. He had invited Selina and Bernie over for dinner, and now he and Selina sat at the kitchen table talking shop. She heard the words "manifest complex," and "narcissistic disorder," then faded out again. At one time, she thought it interesting to understand how Albert thought about these things, but that seemed so long ago. It eventually became just a vocabulary. A way of discussing complex ideas. And then the abstraction seemed to disassociate itself from reality. It seemed to her that Albert had become more interested in talking about the theories then about actual people.

What happened to their common imagery? Their common language they once shared together? Alice didn't know. She sat on the couch fingering her wine glass, then swallowed the last of the chardonnay.

"Anyone care for pate? I made it yesterday. It's onion." She looked over at Selina and Albert.

"Oh yes, that sounds divine." Selina smiled, white teeth gleaming.

Alice got up and went to the kitchen. Bernie was staring out the window above the sink.

"What's up?" Alice said.

"Oh. Nothing much. Lost in thought."

Alice poured herself some wine. "Join me in a drink?"

"Sure."

Alice opened the cupboard and got another wine glass. "Chardonnay or merlot?"

He frowned. "What are we eating?"

"Just pick. Who cares."

He gave her a weak smile. "I suppose...chardonnay."

Alice sat in a kitchen chair. "You're more of a party pooper than I am."

"Really? Do I appear to be? " He sat next to her.

"Well, we might as well pair up seeing those two out there are interested in nothing but shop."

"Yes." He sighed.

"What's wrong?"

"Oh, nothing."

"C'mon tell me. It would be nice to talk to someone other than a shrink for a change."

"Yes, we could talk about alternative realities."

She thought she caught a gleam in his eye. "It's a start."

"Then move on to sex." He laughed.

"Actually, *I* could mix the two." She took a sip of wine.

"I know," He said, eyes twinkling, "I heard about Marlowe."

"Really? It doesn't surprise me. " she said. "Let's talk about you."

"Funding for my project has been cut. Can't go all the way without funding."

"I'm sorry to hear that, Bernie. I know you were really into this project. No wonder you're depressed."

"Yeah." He sighed, sipped his wine. "It's more important for them to have bombs than to investigate the nature of reality."

"What do you mean?"

"The defense industry bid us out."

"Shit."

"Yeah, that's what I say. Shit. Who cares about reality? We can blow it all up, anyway." He held the stem of his wine glass between his fingers, rolled it between his thumb and index finger. "You know, the nature of reality is imperative to our understanding."

"You don't need to tell me that."

"I know. But what a loss you know? There are only a few other of my colleagues who are working on Bohm's theories. And, my baby...how the past, present, and future intermix—are one, essentially—in the implicate order. Now it's shelved."

Alice's ears picked up. "What is the implicate order?"

"The underlying nature of all reality. What we see is the explicate order. All of the explicate order is folded within the implicate order. And the mean thing about this funding cut; I was getting so close to it in my equations."

"But what does it have to do with time?"

"Time and space are constructs of our mind. They are illusions, just as the sages of the past have been telling us for countless generations. I know it's hard to understand being stuck in a body, living in this so-called three dimensional reality." He shrugged.

"I have been living in two realities. What do you think about that?" Alice challenged him.

He got up from the table poured himself some more wine, sat down again. "Tell me."

She took a deep and began talking. She left nothing out, and as she recounted everything that had happened over the past months she felt relieved, then drained, as if storing up all the information had been a kind of sickness and needed to be purged.

"And Albert is worried you're losing your marbles?"

"Yes."

"So Selina says."

"And that's another thing, look at those two, so cozy together, doesn't it get to you?"

"No. They care about you, that's all. Believe me, I would be the first to know if there was anything between the two analysts, analyzing everything." He laughed.

"Hmm."

He patted her hand. "I'm sure these past months have been hard on you."

"Yes, very much so. But what do you think? Is it possible?"

"Anything is possible. If you want to be a good scientist you have to have an open mind. As they say in Zen, have a beginners's mind. A mind that is not full of what you think reality is like."

"But, is what I experienced explored in your theories?"

"Well, I don't study parapsychological phenomena, but yes, I believe that it is possible to tap into some sort of other reality. Rip the fabric of the space-time continuum, so to speak. Maybe you have found a point that's not so continuous."

Albert walked into the kitchen. He was smiling and jingling something in his pocket. Alice had the distinct feeling that he was going to say something important.

"Albert," Bernie said. "Just commenting on the lack of judiciousness in our scientific system. But I'm sure Selina has filled you in?"

"That she has. Sorry to hear it. Do you think you'll be able to do anything about it next year?"

"I don't know. It's a sorry thing when the economy dictates what we need scientifically. Can you believe they want me to work on that missile project? I told them to forget about it, that it would be a sorry day in hell when I was involved in developing weapons of mass destruction. That's what they call these things these days. Say, when is the revolution anyway?"

Albert scratched his head. "Haven't you Yanks had enough of that? After World War II I think the entire world has had enough of that sort of thing."

"The world has had enough, but what about the people in power? Where are our compassionate leaders? We need another person like Gandhi here in the states."

Alice laughed. "To stand up to our oppressors, the capitalists?"

"Substitute the capitalists for the British. Cheers, mate." Albert slapped him on the back, sitting down across from him.

"Laugh if you like, but we need to do something. The people are getting apathetic. Set in their ways, and content with their white bread and cheap gas." said Alice.

"It is quite cheap here." Albert said.

"You two are missing the point." Bernie said.

"The point," said Alice, "is always being missed. It's fluid." She swirled the wine in her glass, watching the liquid catch the light.

"Well," Bernie knocked on the table. "I'll see what Selina is up to. Maybe she has fallen asleep."

Albert took Bernie's seat. He swallowed hard, and appeared to be trying to keep his composure, as if he might start crying.

"What is it?' said Alice.

"I have been a complete ass." Albert said. "I know I haven't been listening to you and your feelings. I know this Marlowe thing has become important to you."

"Did Selina tell you to say that? Why don't you have an original thought of your own, Albert? Just once."

Albert stared at her. A tear slid down his cheek and traveled down the length of his face and fell on the table.

"Fluid." She whispered.

"I brought you these." He said.

He reached into his pocket and pulled out two keys, tied with a red ribbon. She picked them up fingering the ribbon. It was smooth and satiny.

"Two keys? What are these?"

"The keys to my heart. One unlocks mine, and the other, yours." He put his face in his hands and sobbed.

Uncomfortable, Alice shifted in her seat. "I'm sorry." she said. "I don't know what to say to you."

"Why do you say you're sorry? *Are* you sorry?"

Alice did not want to get into the particulars of what sorry meant. Of course, it was just simply something to say when you felt uncomfortable. Everyone knew that. And yet, she felt that she owed him something more than sorry, but she didn't know what it was. She had already given many years of her life to this relationship. She was thirty-one years old. They had had a child together. But what did any of that mean?

Was she sorry that times were bad for them now? She looked towards the door. Escape was easy.

"What are the keys for, Albert?"

"The keys." He looked up at her with red eyes. Putting his hand in his pocket he rooted around, withdrawing a slip of paper. He placed it on the table.

Alice picked it up. "An address?"

He tried to smile. "You'll recognize it when you see it."

Chapter 22

She got off the highway in an area that she hadn't seen in a while. It was in Livingston County, farm country. She recognized it as an area where they had gone picnicking. She bit her fingernail remembering. The trees were filled with misty sunshine and the smell of coolness and country gathered around the hedgerows.

A ring-necked pheasant darted across the road and Alice slowed the car. It ran into the field and stood alert, craning its neck, aware that she was watching.

She pulled over to the side and sat in the car watching the sun cross the horizon and glow against the field. She got out of the car and stood next to the field. It had recently been plowed.

She took a deep breath, and the smell of the earth made her stagger. The scent was so rich and removed from the city that it was like a tonic to her mind. She felt her spine straighten and her senses heighten. The hedgerows seemed to speak to her. She went towards them, listening. *It's only the hum of insects.*

A monarch butterfly fluttered around her head then gently wafted towards a cone flower. As Alice watched, she crept towards it, observing how it probed with its dainty proboscis, looking for the sweet nectar.

She looked up from the flowers and away from the field. The house stood on the hill. It was an old farm house. Albert said it had been built in the late eighteen hundreds.

The shutters had been painted a bright pink, contrasting with the white of the house. Alice thought of the Tudor rose. I will walk inside the rose, she thought.

She jangled the keys in her hand and pushed the key into the lock. The door swung open and she walked inside. Alice smiled, noting where she would hang the pictures and place the furniture.

The staircase was directly to her left with a curving banister. She placed her hand on it, looking up the stairs. She mounted the first step and felt her body tingle with an electricity settling itself at the base of her spine. The warmth radiated through her legs as she ascended the steps.

At the top of the stairs she turned towards a bedroom. Light spilled around the door, and she entered the room and sat on the bed covered with a lace crochet spread. She lay down on the bed, drowsy with longing and desire.

As she pushed the hair off her face something in the closet caught her attention—something shiny. Intrigued, she got up and opened the closet door. A billowy dress spilled out—a Renaissance dress, sewn for a lady—all silk and lace. She stared at the dress, then shut the door and lay on the bed, drifting off into a deep sleep.

***

Joannie extracted the tea bag from the cup. She gave it a final squeeze, milking the last remnants of herbs from the bag. She sat down with her tea and promptly jumped up to shut the window.

"The wind has shifted. Now it's coming from the north. Damn it, I thought spring had sprung." Joannie sipped her tea. "You need some sort of tea for nerves, Petrovka."

"Maybe I should just take a pill."

"You might want to after I tell you what's going down at the high school."

Alice looked up from her nails. "Pray tell, Bryant."

Joannie shook her head. "I'm surprised you haven't heard the rumors.

"I've been busy."

"It's understandable you don't want to hang with us in the teacher's lounge with all the off color jokes that damn jock jerk tells."

"I don't have much in common with those people. Sad, I know. They are my colleagues."

They fell silent for a moment. Joannie got up and shut the rest of the windows on the first floor.

"I think I can guess. Layoffs right?" Alice called after her, looking at the wall. Her eyes fastened on a movement. A spider was crawling lethargically along a window ledge.

Joannie sat down. "Yes. That's the rumor."

Alice watched the spider. Joannie turned toward it with interest, then registered disgust. Alice put her hand on her arm. "Please. Leave it."

"Albert is trying to buy me off with a new house."

"Buy you off?"

"Yes. He thinks all our troubles will be solved by this house. He even put a Renaissance style dress in the bedroom closet."

Joannie frowned. "Wait. I don't get it. He is upset because of these so called fantasies you're having...and then he sticks a period dress in the closet?

Alice nodded. "Exactly. It's almost as if he wants me to go crazy, somehow throw me over the edge, and then...rescue me? I don't know."

Alice looked towards the spider. She was possessed with an urge to free it. Getting up, she placed the spider on her palm, walked outside, and carefully set it in a patch of sunlight. The spider moved away, settling itself next to the wall.

Chapter 23

He gazed into the mirror. The image in the before him spoke of wealth and confidence. Christopher breathed a sigh of relief. He had returned from France trusted and well-regarded in elite society. Walsingham had christened him: "Master Marlowe, a most wonderous spy." Smiling, he had promised him patronage for his poetry; he would introduce him to his young cousin, Thomas Walsingham. "A most noteworthy gentleman," Walsingham had said. He had said all of this with conviction, but Christopher could never tell by his eyes. Walsingham was one man he could not read.

He ran his hands over his arms. The doublet was made of the finest velvet – black, with slash marks showing the red velvet underneath.

"Come, come. If thou coiffest further, ye wilt wear out the fabric." Gascoigne, the painter, ushered him down from the stool.

"Ah, ye hast no idea how fine 'tis this cloth for me." Christopher looked about the room. "Whereon shall I stand for this portrait, sir?"

"Methinks…here." Gascoigne positioned Christopher in front of the wall. "'Tis enough light in front of the window." Gascoigne unwrapped his brushes from a leather cloth. He mixed the paints on the table before him. "I ha' most of what I need, except some saffron." He stood mixing paints, glancing up at Christopher. "'Twill be black, the background."

"Can I move?"

"Nay, none for an hour."

Christopher stood still, settling his eyes on the movement outside the window. His thoughts once again turned toward France and what he had accomplished. Walsingham promised that the mission would take no longer then a month, but as he sent reports back to England, Walsingham pressed him to stay further.

"This Baines," Walsingham had said. "'Tis sneaky. He may be dealing in doubles. You must watch, till thou knowest."

Walsingham had concerns that Richard Baines, who had been sent to the sanctuary in Rheims to gather information on Catholics, was a double agent, spying at once for England and France. Baines worked for the Privy Council, but Walsingham was sure that he had been singled out by the Archbishop, John Whitgift, also on the Privy Council, for his own political and religious purposes. Because Whitgift's ambitions conflicted with Walsingham's, Walsingham had sent Christopher to France because he was a new agent and unknown to Baines.

Once in France, Christopher had carefully monitored Baines's movements. He had disguised himself, with help from a monsignor also working for Walsingham, as a novice priest. He sat in the back of the cathedral at Rheims and carefully watched the imposing figure of Richard Baines kneeling in the front pew. Christopher took out his rosary and fingered the beads, alternating an Our Father with a Hail Mary, one prayer per bead. Peering out from behind his woolen hood, he watched as the figure of Baines rose from the pew and then genuflected in front of the cross. A young priest entered the sanctuary, and Baines rose up to greet him. He kissed the priest on both cheeks and then softly on the lips. The priest placed something on the altar and then left. Baines watched him go and then turned his eyes to Christopher.

Holy Mary, mother of God
Pray for us sinners, now
And at the hour of our death Amen.

Christopher switched beads, and felt Baine's eyes on him. He looked up.

"Dost thou believe...priest?" Baines's eyes sought his.

Christopher made the sign of the cross and then rose from the pew.

"You wish to speak with me Father?"

"Aye. Speak to all initiates I must. I pray thee, we meet in my quarters after sup. Converse we will...and pray together."

"We shall, then, Father."

"Give you good morrow." Baines clasped his shoulder, rubbing his fingers along his back, down, then lightly across his buttocks. He patted him, and turned to leave.

Christopher watched him walk the aisle. Baines did not turn around.

"Will ye be clasping thine arms the entire day?"

Christopher blinked, and the face of Gascoigne came into focus. He had unconsciously folded his arms in front of himself when he was thinking about Baines.

"Sir, shall I put mine arms down?"

Gascoigne looked at him, then at the canvas. "Nay, keep thine arms the way they are. Methinks it suits you. And the look upon thy face, barely a smile. Keep that look upon ye face." Gascoigne started to paint.

Chistopher let the face of Gascoigne fade again from focus—thinking of his play, *Tamburlaine*. He decided then he would take it to Phillip Henslowe—to the Rose Theatre.

Chapter 24

Alice took her hanging plants from the window and carefully set them in the box by the door. She was pleased that the philodendron had gotten so long. She examined one of its long stems, remembering when it had been nothing but a cutting that Joannie had given her. Looking around the room she realized she was almost done cleaning up. School was out for the summer.

The afternoon sun was high in the sky when she heard the knock at the door. She had been planning to spend some time reading, with her feet propped up on her desk, and wasn't entirely surprised when she opened the door to Mr. Bonham, the principal.

"Hello, Alice." He cleared his throat.

"Hi. Pink slip time?"

Mr. Bonham blushed. "Well, yes, to be so blunt. We won't be renewing your contract. I'm sorry, Alice, but you know the school had been under pressure—budget cuts and all. We have had to let some other teachers go also. Fine teachers. Excellent teachers." He fingered his tie. Alice noticed it was decorated with lettuce heads. She thought of gardening.

Mr. Bonham leaned against her desk. Alice crossed her arms in front of herself.

She didn't care about this anymore, and because of Mr. Bonham's lettuce tie she had begun to think of gardening and of roses. She wondered what had become of the rose expert, Mr. McGill, and her rose. She wished she had pressed it between two sheets of paper, setting a book on it, preserving it forever. But nothing lasts forever, she thought. *Or does it?*

Mr. Bonham elaborated on budget cuts and Alice though of lettuce heads. She tuned into the conversation when he looked at her intently and expectantly.

"I know why I'm getting fired Mr. Bonham, and it isn't because of budget cuts. I see what is happening to this school. The character has changed; the agenda has changed. It's not designed for free thinking anymore. No, you don't want us to promote independent thinking. You want us to teach for tests." Alice took a breath, not quite sure she would go on.

Mr. Bonham blushed again. "Alice, that's not correct. We value you, and we think you're an excellent teacher."

"We value me, Mr. Bonham.? Just who is we? Do you mean the school board values me?"

"Why…yes, of course."

"Well if they value me so much, then why didn't they give me tenure two years ago?"

"The board, like any school board, felt you had to prove yourself. Any school district is like that." Mr. Bonham nodded, pleased with his performance. He reminded Alice of a peacock, ready to preen. What a smug bastard.

"These school board members, two of them are on my theatre board also. I know what they're looking for…I know." Alice swallowed a lump in her throat.

Mr. Bonham looked uncomfortable. He adjusted the tie around his neck. He assumed a mournful face and stuck out his hand. "I'm sorry, Alice. Truly sorry."

"Truly. The pleasure was mine Mr. Bonham." Alice turned her back on him, unwilling to shake his hand.

She heard the door open, then close behind her.

Alice walked over to the wall where she had hung a picture of the class after their performance of *Othello*. The pain in her chest brought tears to her eyes. They all looked so happy and proud. Her trio—Alberto, Dion, and Renita,—had rejuvenated her as a teacher. And she had rejuvenated them. She would never see them again.

The sudden loneliness gripped her like a vice. Picking up the phone she quickly called Bernie.

***

The late afternoon sunshine spilled onto the tables in the front of the window, but did not touch the table in the corner where Alice sat. Alice lay her package, purchased at Ballard's Antiques, on the chair next to her. She looked around for Margrite, but did not see her. A waiter pulled the blinds down to shield the restaurant from the sun. The restaurant was shrouded in semi-darkness. He approached her table and lit the candle in the center of the table.

"Will anyone be joining you tonight, mademoiselle?"

"Yes, a gentleman. Thank you."

"Would you care for something to drink?"

"A glass of chardonnay would be fine."

Alice watched the waiter walk over to the bar and give her drink order to the bartender. The bartender was someone Alice recognized, an older man, probably in his late forties, dark hair and eyes, with a moustache. A good looking man, Alice thought. He and the waiter laughed at some joke he had told. He caught Alice looking at him and winked at her. She looked away.

The waiter came back with her chardonnay. He placed it in front of her along with a little note. Alice unfolded the note.

Beautiful mademoiselle,
My name is Antoine. I shall forever be enraptured by your loveliness, and continually at your service. The wine is on me. Please, do not bid me adieu.

Alice felt his eyes burning through her as she read the note. She quickly looked up, meeting his gaze. He winked and blew a kiss. She laughed. Bernie walked into the restaurant, spotted Alice, and sat down.

"What's so funny?"

Alice, still laughing, looked towards Antoine, who smiled knowingly. "Oh nothing."

The waiter appeared.

"A Corona please." Bernie picked up the menu. "Are you hungry? I'm starved."

Alice sipped her wine. She did not pick up the menu. "A little."

Uneasy, she felt at once intimidated and unsure of herself. *And with Bernie of all people.*

Bernie looked up from the menu. "Spit it out. Do you want to talk about getting fired?"

"No. I wanted to know more about...time. How is time treated in physics?"

"The chicken *cordon bleu* sounds good. Maybe I'll get that."

"Bernie."

"Yes, time. The proverbial which came first, the chicken or the egg thing."

"What do you mean?"

"Well, without matter you don't have time, and without time, you don't have matter. So which comes first, time, or matter?"

"That's beyond me."

"Me, too. That's why I'm a physicist. It drives me crazy. And you know how I love being crazy."

"Not me, Bernie."

The waiter returned with the Corona. Bernie filled his glass and took a long swallow. "Very good. Just what I needed. So why all the interest in time? Are you writing a play about time travel?"

"In a way, yes."

"Hmm." He gave her a searching look. "Back to the Marlowe man, are you?"

Alice didn't say anything, looked down at the table. "You're one of the only people I can talk to about this Bernie. I just want a connection."

He nodded. "What about Albert?"

"What does Albert have to do with this?"

"Maybe you are trying to run away from the here and now."

"I'm content to be where I am."

"Okay. Fair enough."

The waiter appeared and they ordered. Alice noticed Antoine watching them.

"Well, it's ironic, but Bohm's theory states just that: the past, present, and future all exist simultaneously."

Alice shook her head. "But how can that be? It doesn't make sense."

Bernie took a swig of his beer. "Okay, it's like this." Taking a pen from his shirt pocket he wrote on a cocktail napkin. He drew three circles with smiles inside them. Each circle was slightly bigger than the other.

"Very cute, Bernie."

He smiled. "Alright. Perhaps time is like this: let us say, the biggest circle is the future." He pointed to the figure. "The next biggest circle is the present, and the smallest circle is the past. Are you with me?"

"I think so."

"Now," Bernie picked up his pen and drew circles nested inside of each other. "Each level, or layer of time, is separate from one another, but each level is constantly influencing the other two levels. So, in this way, they are inseparable. Bohm's theory suggests that time is not only something that happens in the present and now, but also something that happens in the past and future, shown by the way the circles represent the interconnection of past, present, and future."

Alice stared at the napkin and Bernie became more animated.

"We are really beings who live in parallel, concurrent nows. And maybe, just maybe, sometime in the future, we might even be able to reach into this super holographic level of reality and pluck out scenes from the past. Fascinating!" Bernie flung his pen down, looked up at Alice. "Does this help or did I totally blow you away?

Alice reached over and pulled the bag she had brought from the antique store onto the table. She pulled from the bag what she had purchased from the store: a trio of Russian nested dolls.

Bernie laughed. "I believe our spouses would call this a synchronistic moment."

Alice nodded. She took the three dolls apart and placed them side by side. "Time is not real then?"

Bernie scratched his head. "Well, I think it would be more accurate to say that our ideas of time…are not reflective of reality."

"But what I wonder is, how do we access these different levels or layers of time?"

He smiled. "That's the key. Who knows?"

"What about the idea of ritual and connecting with the past?"

"Yes? And what about it?"

"I've heard that, at least metaphorically…it might be possible."

The waiter brought their dinners, setting the plates before them. Alice looked at the shrimp in front of her. It smelled of the sea. Thoughts of Britain came drifting before, after, and into her.

Chapter 25

The street was moving, full of people. It had stopped raining, and the sun shone brightly, warming the cobbled streets; steaming the puddles. Christopher kept his head up, proud to be a man of means, able to afford his velvet doublet and fine wool hose. Strutting proudly, he felt his foot sink into something. Horse manure. Disgusted, he lifted his boot and scraped it on the ground, trying to knock off as much as he could. A beggar boy walked by, laughing at him. Christopher smiled and motioned him over.

"Cleanest mine boot, boy, and I shall give ye this two pence." He reached in his pocket, holding up the coin.

The boy nodded and Christopher pulled off his boot, handing it to him. The boy ran off with the boot, and Christopher watched him as he ran over to the blacksmith's shop trying to secure a rag.

It wouldn't do to smell like the street when he saw Sir Francis.

Christopher had asked Nick to come, but Nick had begged off, complaining that he wasn't feeling well. The water in France had given him the runs. He, too, had just come from France, mopping up after the Baines fiasco. Nick had said that Baines had been powerfully angry when he had been thrown in jail. He had known he had been routed out by a spy and was bent on vengeance.

He thought about this as he carefully balanced on his right foot, waiting for the boy to return his boot. Hearing footsteps, he looked up to notice a gathering of women watching him. They had come from their perches to cluster in front of him.

"How now, bootless bawcock?" A woman yelled.

The group erupted with laughter.

Clearly the leader of the group, a small blond woman stood with hands on hips, ready to shout another epithet at him. He recognized her as the prostitute who had placed his hand upon her breast. Christopher frowned, anxious for his boot to be returned. He looked around for the boy.

"M'lady, a boot and a bawcock shall be matched." He smiled thinly.

"Comest thou then, dare ye put a bauble in the bawdy house. Bliss bestowed on such small change." She winked, and the group laughed again.

Christopher swallowed, a larger group of town folk was gathering around the women. "M'lady, I cannot make beef of such a kindly poet. And that thou art." The boy returned with his boot. Christopher gratefully dropped the coin in the boy's hand and pulled his boot on. "I shall go."

The woman glared at him. "Yea, go to. Thou art none for women, thou art attired for a man. Pricked for him, thou art." She stared at him, a sly smile spreading on her lips, while the crowd jeered. Christopher was reminded of a cat and he was once again a mouse, cornered; he gulped, thinking of Sir Francis. He would be late.

He folded his arms across his chest, and glared at the woman, who gladly took on the challenging gaze. A little girl picked up a stone, and aiming it at Christopher's head, let it fly. He placed his hand on his head; warm blood met his hand.

The crowd was becoming vicious, leering, laughing, and threatening him by pushing closer.

Christopher strode forward and pulled the woman by the elbow into her house. He shut the door on the laughing crowd and pulled the woman close, peering into her face.

"Thou hast coveted me before. I know ye; I remember."

The sound of a crying infant met his ears. He turned toward the sound and noticed a small cradle by the door. The woman pushed away from him and went to the baby, unlaced the front of her gown, and placed the babe at her breast. She sat on the bottom of the step leading to the upstairs room and looked up at Christopher, standing in front of the door.

"I know ye too, thou art Christopher Marley, playmaker. Playmaker of *Tamburlaine*. How dost thou feel Christopher? Now that thou hast no more trouble with money? Now that ye stomach is full?" She looked down at her babe.

He sat next to her on the step, noticing a sore on top of the baby's head. *Goody would have a certain cure.* "What is your name? And your babe's?" The room felt damp and smelled of rot and human waste.

He reached in his pocket and pulled out a coin. Picking up her hand he pressed the coin into it. Her fingers clasped around the coin, holding it tightly. A tear squeezed out beneath her clenched eyelids. Christopher gently wiped the tear from her cheek with the edge of his sleeve. She hugged the baby closer to her.

"My name is Mare MacPhaine. And this is Mary. I named her after myself."

Christopher smiled. "From Scotland are ye? The Clan Gunn?"

Her eyes widened. "How do ye know?"

He rose from the step. "There are things I know from travels I have taken. Perchance we meet again, Mare. I must take my leave. I am expected."

Mare rose quickly and placed Mary over her shoulder, rubbing her back. "Expected? In that attire thou is won't to see none but Sir Francis; he lives at the end of the street. That I know." She smirked at him.

Christopher froze, his hand on the door knob. "'Tis true Mare. I have business with Sir Francis." He felt his mouth go dry. "I still am hungry, Mare. There is naught to be had...being a scholar."

"I can help ye Kit. I know of people that travel with secrets." She implored him with her eyes, searching him.

Christopher opened the door, letting himself out. "I aim to be back. Whether thoust know of Sir Francis, or not. Take care of Mary." He nodded, shutting the door behind him. Wondering what had just taken place.

The light outside hit him like a wave, making his eyes water. He strode quickly into the street, past the houses of the poor and of those in ill-repute. A dog ran out, snarling at him, and a woman pulled the dog back, apologizing. As he walked the scenery quickly changed; the streets became cleaner and there was less human discord. Housewives carried baskets with bread, nodding to him, taking in his velvet doublet. He looked to be a gentleman, or a man of means. He scratched the back of his neck, feeling otherwise, as if the dust and grime had settled on his skin. Canterbury had not left him. He was the son of a shoe-maker.

A gypsy hovel lay at the end of the street proper. He stopped and stared at it. Should he go? Should he risk talking to the proprietor? Sir Francis was close. He was surrounded by those who knew and those who would know. The radiating influence of his intelligence web was the thickest where he lived; he was nestled as a spider in the middle of it. Christopher glanced around. No one seemed to notice him.

He walked over to the hut. A woman opened the door before he could knock and pulled him inside. The room was dark, lit only by a candle. He noticed through the flickering flame that something lay on the table. A plate full of some sort of leaves.

He turned to the woman and recognized her. It had seemed so long ago as he had walked the street with Nick and had come across this woman. This woman who had pulled his gut, his very will, with her eyes. Now her deeply set eyes warmly regarded him..

She pulled a card from her dress, the card of The Lovers, handing it to him.

"Dost thou not speak?"

She shook her head no.

A small man waddled into the room from the back of the house. *A dwarf.* Christopher looked at him curiously. The dwarf was lighter skinned than the gypsy, and fair-haired. He was dressed in a green gerkin with a metal-linked belt, and he wore a small, slouched cap of a darker shade of green. Christopher glanced down at his feet, expecting to see small slippered feet, but the dwarf had on well-made leather boots. Christopher could make out fine stitches on the exquisitely crafted boots.

"What say you, cobbler's son? Fine boots, eh?" The dwarf winked at him.

"Ah, that they are, sir. That they are. And so small."

The dwarf frowned.

"I mean the fine stitching." Christopher quickly added.

The dwarf climbed upon a chair, and standing, beginning rubbing the leaves on the plate into a fine powder. He pulled from his pouch a small bag, and poured the herbs into the bag.

Christopher looked around for the gypsy. She had disappeared.

"Christopher Marlowe, the playmaker," he handed Christopher the bag. "I know of Mare, and the babe Mary. Give this to her, and let her be well." He bowed slightly, and jumped off the chair, heading towards the back of the room.

"Sir?"

The dwarf turned.

"Do ye know of her? The woman of my dream?" Christopher extracted the precious card from a pocket bag.

The dwarf nodded. "She shall be forged to ye – in another time. The breath she speaks shall be of yours, in remembrance." He turned again to go.

"Sir...?"

"Be gone now. Sir Francis awaits."

"Pray tell sir, what 'tis your name?"

He waved his hand in dismissal, and Christopher opened the door, positioning his hood over his head. He bowed slightly to the dwarf, and left quickly, neither looking to the right, nor left, but straight ahead to the street. Before he turned the corner he looked back, to memorize where the hovel was.

It had disappeared.

Christopher stopped, rubbed his eyes, and opened them again.

It was still gone.

***

The door was slightly ajar and he let himself in. Christopher felt flushed, as if the dirt and grime from the street still stuck to his face. He brushed his face with his sleeve; saw the outline of dirt. Trying to rub the dirt with his fingers, he became aware of the stillness of the house. Standing there waiting for the manservant, he rocked slightly on his feet; feeling the boards creak, felt a twinge of fear.

"Guliet?"

The voice rang clear and sharp, feeling for any uncertainties. Christopher stopped brushing his shirt sleeve, and felt his muscles tense.

"No, sir, 'tis Christopher Marlowe. At your service." He listened, poised and alert.

The air felt thick, pungent with intelligence. It seemed as if Walsingham cut through the air with his thoughts, tendrils of cunning uncurled, feelers put forth to grip their host. With heightened awareness, Christopher walked into the room to meet Walsingham. He did not turn his head to greet him, but sat immobile, staring into the fire.

"Sir?"

"The matter of Baines is ta'en care...I see you are waiting to matriculate?"

"Aye. That I am, sir."

"We have given the order to let you proceed. The manner in which you skillfully made Baines...bound Baines, was most pleasing to her majesty. There 'tis nothing more irksome to her than the seminary situation at Rheims. Though I have spoken to her continually of matters that are of more import...," Walsingham turned his gaze towards Christopher.

There is of naught that he cannot see...

Christopher tore his eyes from Walsingham's piercing gaze. The fire continually danced, bringing a soft glow to the surroundings. On the table in front of Walsingham lay an object of wood and glass.

"What will you do now, Master Marlowe? Now that you are finished at university?"

"I shall continue in London, sir, as a scholar and a poet."

Walsingham nodded, and bringing the tips of his fingers together, he placed them near his chin. The effect was something like praying. He waited for Walsingham to speak again, and, growing uneasy at the silence, studied the wood and glass object that lay on the table.

Walsingham watched him with amusement. "They make such things in Barbary lands, the southwest portion of Spain. So Raleigh doth say. He brought back this artifice."

Christopher nodded, waiting. There was no use wasting time in idle conversation.

"And what say you, Master Marlowe? Are you not ta'en with things fantastical? Did you not conjure Baines?"

Christopher shifted from one foot to the other. "The conjurer is easily conjured, sir. But 'tis no matter, I brought forth that which came from his own accord."

Walsingham laughed. "How will thou decide, who fore art the conjured, or the conjurer? Are you not the same? Thou art a spy Marlowe, lest thou forget."

"These entanglements are easily unknotted, if the side thou art fashioning is true and fair. I know my own true cord, 'tis heart felt of queen and country. "Tis the tapestry of my heart."

Walsingham nodded. "But what of true and fair on many levels? As such is this?" He gestured towards the object of wood and glass. It was an elaborate chess set, built upon three tiers. The players had to maneuver amongst all three levels.

"The levels are one, sir. Thou must remember tha—"

"That is the thing, these levels. How cans't thou remain true and fair amongst all three: players, council, and queen? Cans't thou do it?"

Christopher felt a presence. He felt as if the dwarf were in the room with them, watching him.

"A game, Master Marlowe?"

"Sir...I must beg off. I have been too much in the world."

Walsingham nodded. "Rightfully so."

"I beg your leave, sir. I have affairs I must attend." He felt the tension begin to drain, and the knots release themselves. His muscles relaxed. He would soon be safe.

"There will come a time, where we must enter into the game. Betwixt the two of us. I will be in touch with you for further service. Go to."

Christopher nodded, taking his leave. Guliet had entered the hall. He placed a hand lightly on Christopher's shoulder. Slipping a note in his hand, he whispered in his ear.

"Alvis said ye forgot this."

"Alvis?"

"Aye," Guliet looked at him strangely. "Ye met him earlier." He led Christopher out the door. "And Lakshmi?"

"Lakshmi...the woman?"

"Aye, the one."

There was a faint smell of spices and incense on Guliet. His eyes were a deep sea green, set in a swarthy face. Christopher tried to read his eyes, but Guliet shut the door, leaving him standing outside.

141

Christopher turned the note over in his hand. It was the card that he had shown the dwarf. On the back were written four words. He brought the card to his eyes, for the writing was faint and old and spidery. Twinned hearts in time. Turning the card over again, he noticed a sun and moon above the lovers clasped in their embrace. And above the picture of the sun and moon was a small eye in the middle of a doorway. As he looked at it, it seemed to blink, and then change into the figure of a tiny woman.

Chapter 26

Alice sat on the stoop of the doorway of their new house. The day was clear and bright with a thin strata of clouds in the upper most layer of the sky. A feeling of peace settled around her, even though she had come to the house with a profound feeling of disturbance and agitation. The agitation started when Sonia and Brad ran off to Acapulco a week before the opening of *The Jew of Malta*. There had been no word from either of them. The understudy for Sonia, Lucy Branard, was sick with the flu. And to top it all off, Derrin had been embezzling money from the theatre company. He had a cocaine addiction. Alice had tried to get in touch with Jim Schelling, but he was in London.

The garden trowel fell from her hand, clacking on the stone step. White roses surrounded her. Roses she did not know if she would plant or not. *White of marriage, white of the sun*....it didn't matter anymore. The thoughts trailed off while she sat thinking of white.

Earlier, she had placed the daffodils that Albert had given her as a housewarming present on the counter by the sink. *Of course,* she thought, *the only reason he gave them to me was because of guilt—guilt that he couldn't be here on the formal day of house closure.* It was the first house they had owned together, and now he wasn't here.

She had admired the petals of the daffodils and how translucent they were. The luminescence shining through the petals cast many shades of light and white—*pale green in the innermost sanctum of the flower...* She thought how sensual flowers were, and why men gave them to women.

The late afternoon light had shifted, and a breeze began to blow. She stuck her legs out in front of her to capture the last warming rays of light. Warm sunlight felt so good after a long Michigan winter.

In lieu of everything that had happened it had been a phone call that had unnerved her. The call didn't surprise her, but she felt that this could be the untied rope that set the boat out to flow in the open ocean. *I must be careful to shield myself from this anxiety...*

Bernie and Selina had left for some remote region in Brazil. It was Bernie who had called her with barely constrained joy and enthusiasm. He tried to cloak his jubilance because he felt by leaving he was letting her down. Selina had recently received a grant to study with tribal shamans. She would document their mythologies and relate this to her developing thesis of the commonalities of all world mythologies. She would do most of her research when the shamans had taken ayahuascera, a powerful psychotropic drug known to bring about fantastical visions and insights. Bernie had said he was amazed at what knowledge and insight he had received after partaking in an ayahuescara ceremony. He was especially jubilant because he said the plants seemed to be communicating on a molecular level with the people who had taken the mixture. In fact, the shamans claimed that it was the plants themselves that told them how to mix two very specific substances together to get the psychotropic effect. He claimed that participants had gained knowledge of DNA through their visions of snakes and other serpentine creatures.

She was skeptical. It all sounded like *Alice's Adventures in Wonderland* to her.

"Well, now that you mention it, I believe Lewis Carrol was on opiates when he wrote that book."

"Maybe. But Bernie, what does this have to do with quantum mechanics?"

There was a sigh on the other end of the line. "Alice, I had to let go of that job for a while. This work with Selina inspires me. We were fortunate to be able to work together."

There was a crackling noise on the line.

"What's that?" she said.

"We've been having trouble with the phones. I've got to get going. Take care Alice."

As she hung up the phone she realized that Bernie's journeys with ayahuascera were not so far removed from her own.

A loud thunderclap sounded, and she looked to her left down the road, amazed at what was transpiring. Cutting across the blue sky, a series of black thunderclouds were making their way towards her. They were nestled on the horizon, punctuated with unearthly streaks of green and yellow. Bright bursts of lightening flashed through the black clouds.

The roses could wait until tomorrow. Now she would take a long soak in her claw-footed tub. She carefully snipped three roses from the potted plants to place in a vase next to the tub.

"Ouch! Damnit!"

A thorn from a rose had punctured her thumb, bringing blood to the surface of her skin. Scrutinizing the small bead forming she stuck the thumb in her mouth and sat on the steps looking down the road towards the horizon, where the light was becoming fuzzy and unclear.

Near the end of the road, a small figure approached. Alice thought it odd that someone would be out walking with an impending thunderstorm threatening to burst forth. It was an isolated road, with the next house at least a quarter of a mile away. As the figure neared her house it stopped near the old oak at the crossroads. Unbelievably, the figure seemed to blink on and then off . One moment it was here, and the next, gone.

She rubbed her eyes - surely she was tired and imagining things. How could a person blink on and off? How could a person be here one moment and gone the next? She decided the person was ill and wandering around, possibly out of their mind. She stood and made her way to the end of the walk, hands on hips, waiting. The figure turned towards her. Alice squinted, trying to make out who the person was. He, or she, was wearing a little red, pointed hat. Alice started laughing—*a dwarf, that's what it is! Someone from the theatre thinks they're pretty funny, trying to bring me out of my funk…Maybe Jim…*

Smiling broadly, she started walking briskly towards the dwarf. The dwarf continued to stare at her. Alice noticed something strange about the dwarf's eyes. Fascinated, she slowed her pace. The dwarf stood motionless, one eye seemed to grow exceedingly large. As Alice watched the eye enlarge, she saw people moving inside it. The pupil had disappeared, along with the dwarf. There was nothing but what seemed like a round, growing movie projection, full of people in motion. Mesmerized, Alice could do nothing but stare. She wondered vaguely if she was losing her mind, but she felt so much at ease she dismissed the idea.

The ball had grown so large that the people appeared life-size, and Alice felt her every day surroundings fall away. The very edges of her world were pulling down at the edges, and for one brief moment she felt a sense of panic. Either she would enter this world completely, or wake from what seemed to be a dream. She ran towards a rapidly dissolving corner meaning to grab the last bit of present day reality and pull herself through it, but bumping into a motley jester who playfully pushed her away, she ran headlong into a wooden plank and everything became black.

Chapter 27

The dream was about something hard and flat. A surface with no ridges and contours. She became aware of odors, the smell of urine and brine. Alice wrinkled her nose, and pulled her arms up her chest, fetal position, trying to escape the smells and the hardness of the dream. There was a tugging on her legs and she braced herself. The tugging on her legs became more intense and she opened her eyes. This was no dream. She quickly sat up and banged her head.

"Ow!"

She was met with a pair of eyes staring into hers. They blinked, and Alice peered beyond the eyes into the space behind them. It appeared to be a market square. People milled about in the dusty street dressed in clothing styles from the sixteenth century. Alice laughed.

"What part of London is this, Jim? This is a great set-up. I almost believed it." She brushed off her arms. They were covered in dust and grime. "Geez, my legs, too. You went to a great deal of trouble, Jim. The thing is, how did you get me here?"

She gazed at the face cloaked in shadow. The bright eyes met hers again.

"Have you need of anything? A girl of small size found ye under here." The eyes inquired unto hers.

"Need of anything..." Alice looked at her, and then at the marketplace. She crawled out from under the structure she found herself under, when the voice stopped her.

"Aye, I wouldn't do that. You haven't the proper dress."

Alice stood up anyway and surveyed her surroundings. It looked too real. As far as she could see, it was all...authentic.

"Where's Jim?" She asked faintly, putting a hand to her forehead. She was starting to feel dizzy.

"Jem? I know no Jem. It ha' a Turkish sound to it. Is he a Turk, this Jem?"

The eyes had materialized into a pleasant face. Alice felt a sense of foreboding creep over her. The dizziness became acute and she dropped to her knees. The images of the people in the marketplace swam around her but did not dematerialize.

"Make it stop." she whispered.

"Lady? Are you ill?" The woman crouched next to Alice, laying a hand on her arm.

"Where is Jim? Who are you? I haven't seen you working at any theatre company..." She trailed off watching as people walked by.

The woman laughed. "Theatre Company? You speak strangely. Are you from the low countries?"

Alice nodded slowly, realizing where she was.

"This is England."

"Aye. My name is Mare MacPhail. Would you be in need of any help?" She rose to her feet, and Alice slowly stood beside her.

"I don't know. I just need to talk to Jim."

"I know of no Jem, Lady."

"It's true isn't it? How did this happen?" She wondered if she should give in to the despair or the hilarity of the situation. The feelings rose like bubbles inside her, either one threatening to pop and overwhelm her.

"Surely I must be mad. I fell off the porch, or something."

"Lady? What is it you are saying? Why do you speak so to yourself?"

"I saw a dwarf before it happened."

"Shh." Mare whispered in her ear, "Be careful what ye says't. They will say witch, or conjurer."

"His eye became huge, and I just kind of...fell into it. Is the best way to explain it."

Mare nodded, as if this was entirely probable.

Alice laughed. "It sounds ridiculous."

Mare continued nodding. "Aye, there are some things which cannot be rightly spoken of. Such as Alvis."

"The dwarf?"

"Aye."

"Maybe it could be described correctly in a painting."

Mare frowned. "A large eyeball?"

Alice laughed. "Aye!"

"It resembles a play. This fantastical eyeball. I should speak of it to Kit. He will enjoy the thought."

Stunned, Alice asked: "Kit? Christopher Marlowe?"

"Aye, befriended me he did. Myself and Mary. Ye know of him?"

"Are you real Mare?" She touched her arm, felt the solidness of it.

Mare patted her arm. "Come now, Lady. We will go to my house. Let you sup. Methinks you ha' not eaten in days the way you carry on."

Alice let herself be led by Mare as they walked through the market square. She felt like a child being led by the hand. People stared as they walked by. She had no idea that madness could be so enticing, so entertaining. She thought back to the earlier demons in her manic state. No demons that plagued her past occurred now, just a state of being entirely enfolded in the present.

"Mare, what happened to me?"

"What happened? I don't rightly know. Two lasses found you under the fish monger's stall. Dressed in your underwear," She glanced at Alice. "We must dress ye lady. There are laws of bawd and lewdness."

"Laws of bawd."

"Aye."

"I assure you, I'm not a whore." Alice laughed.

Mare slapped her face. Shocked, Alice stopped and placed a hand to her stinging cheek. Mare continued walking, adjusting her shawl around her shoulders, above her breasts. Tying a knot in the shaw, she shrugged.

"Tis no consequence of thou'st thinking better of thou self. Thou art a bawd. I was trying to give thou'st succour. Sustenance."

"But Mare, I assure you, I'm not a—"

"Fie! That thing betwixt your legs will feed thou, will it not?

This woman is a whore, and I have just offended her by thinking better of myself.

"Mare, I—"

"Pish! Leave me."

Mare walked ahead, walked proud and erect. Alice realized that the friendliness of the world was swallowed by that receding back. People stared at her, ugly and mean – there was no disguising the contempt in their looks. Panic overwhelmed her.

"Mare! Please!"

The receding figure turned. And waited. Alice ran to catch up. "I'm sorry."

"Thou name and thou are full of strangeness." Mare frowned and continued walking.

So this it it. This was the movie. She didn't quite know how to digest it, but it was. There was no mistaking. She took her hand, held it to her face, and realized that it was just a hand.

She glanced at her shorts; her bare legs. "People think I'm in my underwear."

"Aye. And the words thous't speak art strange."

"What can I do?"

"Thou will know of men whens't they come, but be not too bold." Mare gripped her arm, pulling her close. Alice realized she was speaking of prostitution.

She thought she would change the subject – a subject beyond whoring. A profession, she wondered, if she would be able to pull off.

"How did you meet Kit Marlowe?"

Mare did not answer right away, but instead gazed at the horizon. The dust from the heat of the day rose above their feet. People let them pass, but the men still jeered at her. She wondered how women survived this type of misogynistic climate. The very air vibrated with it. Mare had given Alice her shawl, and Alice now fashioned a skirt with it, tying it snugly around her waste. It amused her that the sight of a bosom pushing from a gown did not draw looks, while a pair of bare legs did.

"Fie! Get thou'st eyes in thy head, giggling piglet!" Mare made a motion with her thumbnail, scraping it across her teeth in an exaggerated manner, towards a jeering man. It was a motion Alice recognized from the theatre – a sign of Elizabethan swearing. The equivalent of giving the finger.

"Kit bestowed a kindness on me. He gave me herbs for Mary, a medicine. You shall see." Mare smiled to herself. "He ha' a room with Thomas Kyd, the playmaker. Ye know of him, too?"

Alice nodded. It was so odd to hear these names. Names that she had seen set in type on a page regarding the beginnings of theatre four hundred years before her time.

It isn't real! An ancient piece of her identity hung on for dear life, trying to keep her in her place and in her time. Some thread like consistency that had evolved through the eons, keeping the two separate.

The air became heavy, and the twilight set in. As they walked, the street became narrower, with half-timbered Tudor row houses crowded on either side. A juggler stood by the side of the road. He was dressed in motley green, topped with a hat of a jester. He dropped a ball when he saw Alice, but quickly picked it up and began juggling again.

"How dost thou, sweet lady, pretty lady? A visage for mine blind eyes!" The fool, pretending to be blind, let the balls drop by his feet, which he promptly stumbled and fell over. Looking up, he smiled broadly at Alice, two dimples speckling his cheeks.

"Ah! Get thee gone, Hadeus. Cans't thou see there is no light for yer jests?"

"All the light I need is here." He winked at Alice, and bowed deeply. A tuft of dark curls protruded from his jester's cap. "Tell me your name, pretty lady."

Mare stood in front of a door, ready to turn the latch and enter the dwelling.

"This one comes from afar; she has no need for a motley such as yourself."

"I beg of ye women of the world, worldly women, what say you to a poor soul such as myself?"

"Tarletorizing he is, Alice. Thinks he is the image of that famous clown, Richard Tarleton," Mare smirked at him, "What say you, clown, caught in the shadow of that tumbler Tarleton? Ye think that ye are famous now? Now that you have played a jest in *Tamburlaine*? And *The Spanish Trajedy*?"

"Aye. Kyd and Marlowe use me wisely."

"Wisely, I'll say fool, is something naught for thou." Mare opened the door, ushering in Alice.

"Good even, clown." Alice returned his smile.

"Ah! She speaks! She speaks!" Hadeus swooned, falling to his knee, bowing deeply.

Mare firmly shut the door. "Enough of that clown. Puts on airs, he does. Ever since he played a jest in those plays. And his name is Aaron." Mare spoke confidentially, in a whisper.

"Oh?"

"Aye. Aaron. A Jew he is." Mare nodded, as she walked to another room in the back of the dwelling. A young girl sat next to a cupboard, tending to a baby in a cradle.

The baby began to cry and Mare picked it up. "Calls himself Hadeus, but he's naught but a Jew."

"I see." Alice knew that it was common for Jews to hide their identity in Elizabethan England if they didn't want to be ostracized within the walls of the Jewish ghetto, where the gates were locked at night.

"There's many here in the theatre." Mare said. "Jews, I mean."

She crooned to the baby. "This is Mary, my little one. Take a peek." She held the baby out for Alice to see.

Alice was presented with the spitting image of her Marie. Confused, she stroked the baby's cheek, looking into her eyes.

"Have thou any children?" Mare asked softly.

"Yes ...No. I did. May I hold her?"

"Surely." Mare placed the baby in her arms. Alice felt transported back to a warm, secure, place. She felt like the mother she once was. The baby looked at her, cooing.

"Marie?"

"No, Mary, her name is." Mare looked concerned, and took the baby from her arms. "Perchance ye should lie down Alice. You look tired. I ha' to go soon. The night is coming, and I'll be makin' my way to the Mermaid."

Alice looked at the silent girl who sat next to her on the bed. The girl had lanky brown hair, and was wearing an old, dirty gown of a greenish hue. The candle on the table next to her made her glow with a sickly cast.

"Hello." Alice smiled, but the girl merely looked towards the floor, saying nothing.

Mare looked despondently at the girl. "I don't know this one's name. I found her wandering the street, almost starved. I brought her back here. A good nurse she is. She took an instant like to Mary. Never leaves her side." She looked at the girl.

"How long have ye been here, sweet?" Mare said.

The girl looked at her feet and mumbled something. She looked traumatized, as if she had seen things that she shouldn't. Her eyes were big and haunted.

"We must take care of one another. Who else will?" Mare looked at Alice, tying her shawl around her shoulders.

"And may I stay with you Mare? I have no one else."

Mare checked her appearance in the mirror against the wall. She smoothed her blond hair from her face and spread something from a little pot she pulled from her dress pocket on her eyes. Stepping back, she admired the effect. She watched Alice from the mirror.

"Aye. You mays't. I knew when I first saw ye that would be the case – thou was alone." She motioned towards a trunk in the corner. "I ha' a spare gown in that trunk. You mays't wear it and accompany me to the Mermaid." Alice hesitated, and Mare stopped applying her makeup and turned to face her. "Go to. It shall fit ye."

Alice swallowed a lump in her throat, thinking of the difficulty that this scenario presented. She walked to the trunk and opened it, pulling a gown of mulberry from its depths. She felt the cloth, rubbing it between her fingers, and held it to her body. Standing behind Mare, Alice looked at the effect. Gingerly holding the gown to her, she pressed the extra fabric around her waist.

"I think the gown is too big."

Mare looked up exasperated. She set the makeup pot down and stood behind Alice. "Pish. The gown is fine. Look, I can pull it in. See?" She showed Alice the drawstrings in the back. Alice looked at these doubtfully. "What say you now." Mare threw the gown on the bed. "Ye ha' next to nothing to wear. Put it on." Mare stood looking at her.

Alice tentatively picked up the dress from the bed and removed her shorts.

Mare laughed. "Why dos't thou take off these underthings?"

The girl looked up surprised.

"My underwear is underneath." Alice removed her shorts and stood in the middle of the room in her underwear.

Mare walked over and pulled her underwear back, peering in. "Ah, ye are a woman." She snapped the underwear back in place. "The thing stretches!" She laughed, looked at the girl. The girl smiled.

Alice stepped away from her, quickly pulled off her shirt, and pulled on the gown. She stood in front of the mirror, admiring the affect. "I don't see what is so funny. Can someone help me with these?" She pulled the drawstrings behind her, but they were too loose to pull tightly.

Mare stepped over Alice's clothes on the floor. Grabbing the drawstrings, she pulled tightly, and deftly tied the strings in a knot. She stepped back from Alice. "'Tis truly a gown made for you, Lady."

The cloth was light, a finely woven mulberry, with intricate beadwork sewn in the bodice. The top of her bosom was exposed. She knew gowns were designed for breast feeding, or, when whores were trying to sell their wares, the breasts could be released from the gown. Alice fingered the silk fabric sewn into strips in the skirt of the gown. She pulled the pin from her bun, and her dark hair cascaded around her shoulders.

Mare winked at her admiringly. "Ye shall have all the pence ye may need with the likes of those on display."

"Please, Mare. I won't be doing that."

Mare frowned. "What? With the airs again, I see. Come Lady, let us take leave. The time is late."

Alice cringed. The thought of drunk and drooling seventeenth century men made her stomach clench. She thought of lice and venereal disease. She thought of their hands pawing her flesh.

"I think I will...wait a few moments. Go without me, Mare. I know where the Mermaid is." She offered a weak smile, hoping to deter Mare for as long as she could. Mare smirked, opened her mouth to say something, thought better of it, and walked out the door. A whoosh of dust blew behind her as she left. The thin light that filtered through the window illuminated the floating specks. Alice stood looking at them for a few moments, and then turned to the girl on the bed.

"I don't think I can do this." Alice said quietly.

The girl quickly looked away.

Alice walked to the window. The light was fading, covering the street in mellow gold and soft shadow. An old blind beggar walked slowly down the street, tapping a cane in front of him. When he was almost out of view he stopped, and carefully set himself down a few feet from a street vendor. Most of the market people had left, but there were a few late proprietors. A woman selling bread reached into a basket and gave a small roll to the blind man who sat next to her stall. The beggar gratefully took the bread and lifted his hat to her.

"Will you tell me your name?" Alice said, still looking out the window. She didn't expect the girl to answer, but it was worth a try. Silence covered the room. Alice turned and looked at the girl. Her hair was dirty, and she didn't look up. Alice sat next to her.

"My name is Anne."

She said it so quietly that it seemed to come from a ghost. Alice wondered if she imagined it. "What?"

"Anne. My name is Anne."

"I thought that's what you said." She patted her hand. "Will the baby wake soon?" Alice looked at the sleeping baby in the cradle. The baby looked peaceful enough sucking on her finger.

Anne continued to stare at the floor. Alice realized that the girl was probably deeply disturbed. She wondered how much time Mare had for her.

"Are you hungry?"

Anne nodded. She then sighed. It was a deep sigh that seemed to reach to the bottom of her feet. "I want for sleep too, Lady." Anne lay back on the bed and pulled her hands up to her chin. She pulled her body into a fetal position, and her eyes became glassy. Alice became alarmed.

"Anne?"

Anne lifted her head.

"Don't fall asleep yet. I'm going to get you something to eat." Alice looked around the house. She walked from the back bedroom to the large room in the front. Large wooden beams lined the ceiling. Amongst the sparse furnishings there was a jug on top of a wooden side board. Alice poured the contents into a small earthen cup. She lifted the cup to her nose. It smelled like sweet wine. Taking a sip she recognized the potion was sack—a cheap wine found abundantly during the Renaissance.

This won't do...I need water.

A trunk stood against another wall, and Alice pulled the lid open. She pulled out a few gowns and tiny baby dresses. In the corner of the trunk was a small wooden box, carved with the initials MM. She opened the lid. It was empty. Alice put the contents back in the trunk. Sitting back on her haunches, she put her arms around her legs, trying to think. She felt something small and hard press into her leg. Feeling on the outside of the gown she discovered a small pocket. Alice excitedly groped inside the pocket, pulling forth some coins. She examined the coins – two pence. Jingling the change in her hand, she quickly walked out the door.

Across the street the bread vendor was putting her wares away.

"Wait!"

The woman looked at her quizzically.

"Yea?"

"Do you have any more bread?"

"Surely I do."

"How much for a pence?" Alice held the coin in her hand.

"Even dozen."

"Here." She handed the woman her coin, and realized she had no way of carrying the bread. The woman looked at her doubtfully.

"Do ye live near?" The woman asked.

"You wouldn't happen to have any water?" Alice gathered the bread in her skirt. "I have another pence."

The women looked around. "The water I brought today." She picked up an earthen jug. "'Tis half full." She handed it to Alice and collected her pence. "Good even, Lady. I hope you fare well." She nodded, and continued to place her bread in baskets.

Alice walked across the street, managing to twist her skirt around the bread, forming a sort of bag, carrying the water jug in the same hand. She extracted a roll and bit into it, realizing how hungry she was. The bread had a hard crust and a soft interior. It melted in her mouth.

As she approached the house a shadowy figure appeared outside the door. Her heart beat faster.

She held the jug tight between her finger and thumb, ready to use it as a weapon.

"How now, pretty Lady?"

She recognized the voice but couldn't place the face. "Who is it?"

"It? It is a thing, and I am no thing, Lady. Perchance a thing of jest will riddle you."

He stepped in front of her.

"Aaron?"

"Aye, the one."

Feeling instant relief, she stopped in front of him. "What are you doing out here? It's pitch black."

"I protect the fair ones of this house. Mare might not say so, but 'tis true. I watch them well."

Alice bit into her roll. "Want one?" She offered the bread from her skirt.

"Gramercy Lady, I am starved." He took the bread, and, after taking a bite, did a backwards flip. Surprised, Alice laughed. It seemed as though he had vanished into a blur of green and white.

"Where do you live, Aaron?"

"Hadeus." He looked embarrassed.

"Hadeus, then, where do you live?"

"Where I can, Lady. Where I can." He deposited his roll into a side pouch. "I know not when I eat again." He bowed before her. "If thous't grant me the chance to be so bold…The question Lady—what parts dost thou hail from?" He watched her carefully, and Alice felt he was memorizing her face.

"I..ah…from the low countries."

He nodded. "I ha' been across the sea to the place. Perchance you hail further then that? I know not of your accent." He looked at her slyly. "Perchance, a place we have not heard of?"

Alice said nothing.

"We both have something to hide Lady. I am a Jew, and thou dost know it. You are conjured, from a far place. I dost know it. I will say naught to a soul, Lady. Thou can keep a secret with me." He smiled in the dark—white teeth gleaming. She wondered how he had managed to keep his teeth this long.

"What do you mean by that, Hadeus? That I am conjured?"

He shook his head. "Some things cannot be spoken of, Lady. Some things are known, but not. It is a magical art."

Alice felt confused. "You sound like Mare."

"Aye. We are all in the theatre, one way, or another."

"That sounds suspiciously familiar."

"Familiar?"

"The world is but a stage…You know, from the play?" Alice stopped, realizing he wouldn't know. The play hadn't been written yet.

"Ye know of playmaking? Are ye a poet, Lady?"

"My name is Alice. And yes, I do write plays." She smiled broadly, wondering if her teeth gleamed as his did.

"I ha' naught heard of a woman…playmaker."

A dog barked. Alice turned towards the sound and then turned back towards Aaron. "I must make my living somehow. I'm afraid Mare thinks I must be a whore to make money."

He nodded. " 'Tis hard for a woman. If ye must make your keep, ye can try your luck at the Mermaid. Many of the whores make change there."

"I don't think you understand Hadeus. I don't want to become a whore."

He scratched his head. "There is a playmaker that stays late until the night working. Perchance you could speak with him. He knows of much theater work. I do jests in all of his plays." He puffed his chest out proudly, and Alice expected him to do another backward flip, but instead he bowed. "I must take my leave Lady, 'tis late and revelers will be about. They expect to make merry on my head, and I need to take care."

Without so much as a glance back he disappeared into the shadows, and Alice was left standing alone in the night. The dog had stopped barking, and the night was growing still and quiet. A cricket chirped close by her feet, startling her. She pushed the door open, and walked to the back room where Anne was holding the baby. A candle flickered on a nearby table. Mary had begun to get fussy, and Anne was bouncing her in her arms. With her wails growing increasingly frantic, Anne looked increasingly harried.

"I know naught what is wrong with her. She usually sleeps 'til Mare returns."

Alice placed the bread and water on the table. "You go ahead and eat. Give the baby to me." She held out her arms, and Anne gratefully handed over the baby. She fell on the bread like a hungry animal, quickly gulping and stuffing as fast as she could.

"Go slow; you're going to get sick."

Anne nodded, stopped, then took a drink from the jug. Panting, she let the water dribble down her chin. Her eyes shone her thanks. "Grammercy Lady. I ha' not eaten…it seems like days."

"Doesn't Mare feed you?"

"Aye. She does. As well as she can. She has made little change as of late. More and more whores come to town, she says."

The baby continued to wail, and Alice knew by the sound of her cries that she was hungry. She stuck her finger in Mary's mouth and she sucked hungrily, screaming when she discovered there was no milk.

"I better get Mare. I don't think there is much choice in the matter." She gave Mary back to the reluctant Anne.

"I'll hurry as fast as I can."

Chapter 28

She looked up and down the road hoping to see Aaron. He was long gone. Few people wandered the street at this hour, and the ones who did—madmen, whores, and drunks—kept to themselves in little groupings.

The street widened at the crossroads, and she looked to the left. She knew she must make her way towards the London Bridge, but she was confused about which way to go. She knew the bridge lay somewhere to the south, but it was dark and hard to get her bearings.

A man dressed in rags approached from her left, and she thought to ask him directions.

"Booged lone tame 'ha da row!" He laughed and stumbled past her.

Alice realized he was drunk or mad, or both. She wondered how far Bedlam, the insane asylum, was from here, trying to will the old map of Elizabethan England into her head. She realized there was no one in authority to turn to if she needed help—no policemen, no ambulance…no nothing. There were only these people, the common people, wandering the streets who might help her.

She continued down the road and soon heard the sound of laughter. A stone building with a sign which read The Boar's Head stood before her. Shutters had been thrown back and light spilled from the windows. A man approached carrying a mandolin. He had a red kerchief on his head and was wearing a white shirt. The man entered the tavern.

"Play, Michel! Play!" The sound of fresh laughter erupted and then the sound of string instruments playing a popular ballad. Voices started to sing along.

Alice tentatively pushed the heavy door open to the pungent smell of ale and tobacco. There was a small crowd gathered around two musicians. A few people looked over when she entered, then went back to conversing with their companions. In the corner, a bald man was smoking a pipe, merrily eyeing the musicians and tapping his foot to the music. Alice approached him.

"Sir, how do I get to the Mermaid?"

"Sir?" He looked up, surprised. "I ha' naught been called 'Sir' not once in my short life!" He pulled her close. "Stay. Stay awhile. I'll bring ye a pint o'ale." He looked at her beseechingly.

"I must get there…to the Mermaid." She gently pried his arm off her waist. "If you would be so kind…"

"You. Mark that! She calls me 'you' too. Like a gentleman!" He stood up and swayed, joining the crowd clustered around the musicians, singing a little ditty: "You too, and you. Shall be a good gentleman new." He collapsed in a chair, and then rolled off, hitting the ground with a thump. Alice was reminded of a large sack of flour.

She wondered if anyone was sober. A woman who had been watching the scene unfold approached.

"I heard ye would be lookin' for the Mermaid."

"Yes. Do you know where it is?"

"Aye. Go from here, straight. There shall be another Tavern. Listen for the Thames, and look for the torches." She nodded, and walked away.

Alice looked after her, wondering if anyone could possibly be more obtuse. She pushed the wooden door open and walked out onto the street.

The street gave way to another and she turned, hoping she was heading south. Continuing along she smelled a putrid odor. It was rank and old, like a disused urinal. An outhouse smell. *Maybe it's a ditch leading to the river…* The

London Bridge came into view. And sure enough, she saw the torches.

Relieved, she knew she was on the right track. As she approached, she heard the sound of moaning. There on spikes in front of the bridge was the horror she had only read about.

A head was stuck on a spike. Drawn by repulsion and terror, she could not help but look. The lifeless eyes bulged, glassy, and its tongue, stiff, protruded from the mouth. A woman stood in front of the head, sobbing. Horrified, Alice wanted to comfort her but could not. Her stiff legs carried her past the scene.

She made her mind blank and thought of nothing, and the moaning and sobbing finally receded. She crossed the bridge with a sigh of relief, only to realize she had to walk it again to get back to Mare's dwelling. Stopping, she looked back, watching the flicker of the torches that signified death and the crossing. The dark water gurgled under the bridge and she thought of the river Styx and its quiet, boatman, who merely asked that travelers paid their way before he ferried them to the other side.

Alice continued on, realizing the Mermaid was not much further. Her feet ached. *I need a good pair of tennis shoes if I'm going to be walking round this place...And a horse.* Her toes were numb as she approached the tavern. Larger than the Boar's Head, the tavern greeted her arrival with a wooden sign painted with a portrait of a blue mermaid. Raucous laughter erupted from inside. She pushed the door open to be met by a cloud of tobacco smoke, and something sweeter that she faintly recognized from another time. *Marijuana!* Incredulous, Alice looked around. It could be any one, there were many people smoking pipes. She remembered that it was Sir Walter Raleigh who had first brought tobacco to England from the Indians. Could the Native Americans also have given him marijuana?

Her eyes scanned the crowd and quickly fell on Mare. She had her arm entwined within a man's beefier one. He was a smallish man dressed in the rough wear of a sailor—cutoff pants below the knee and an old worn shirt. Alice moved towards them.

"Sailed with the navy, I did. Until something finer came along in the West Indies." He winked at Mare. "Come, sweet, I'll pay you a pretty pence or two."

Mare smiled, and looking up caught Alice's eye.

"Alice! Come, come! I ha' been waiting for ye." She looked to the sailor. "See? Just as I told ye. She's a lovely girl, is't she not?"

The sailor critically appraised her. His eyes narrowed, and he motioned to a man sitting at a nearby table. A candle flickered on the table throwing light on the male occupant. Alice identified him as the man smoking the marijuana. He sat with a pipe and stared at her with dead eyes. He took a puff off his pipe and then a swig of ale.

"What say ye, man?" The smallish man inquired.

The pipe smoker nodded. "Come to, wench." He held out his hand.

When she did not reciprocate, he grabbed her and pulled her onto him. He smelled of stale urine and ale and laughed deeply as he held her close. Alice recognized the bump of an erection underneath her; horrified, she tried to get off the man's lap.

He twisted her arm beneath her back. "Ye will be goin' nowhere but the bed wench." Laughing, and still holding her arm behind her back, he pulled her to her feet.

Terrified, she looked at Mare. Sympathy flickered in Mare's eyes.

"John, she'll go willingly. Let her be." Mare forced a laugh, and tried to pull the sailor from Alice, who only shoved her away. "Get ye gone, whore. I ha' mine here."

He shoved her forward towards some stairs in the back of the tavern. She screamed, but few people even looked up from their ale. Out of the corner of her eye she caught a glimpse of Mare. Her eyes were wide and her face pale.

A man emerged from a back room. Her eyes met his. Brown eyes and shoulder length hair.

"Kit!"

A flicker of recognition flit over his face.

"Let her be." Christopher said.

Mare laughed uproariously, "Ah, there you are!" She stood beside Alice and took the sailor's hand from her arm. "Prithee be, sirs, this wench ha' been promised to the…ah, how shall I speak it? The bawdy bawcock that he be!"

"What?" Alice looked at her incredulously, knowing that the words roughly translated to dirty pimp.

"Aye. The best…as bawcockery goes. How now, Kit? What say you?" Mare slipped her arm through Christopher's. The sailor narrowed his eyes and tried to grab Alice.

Christopher forced his arm down. "Pray tell, what have ye with my wench? Care ye for a tangle?" He pulled his dagger from his side. Surprised, the sailor stepped back.

"Get ye gone. All of ye."

The sailor hesitated, then walked back to his companion, mumbling something under his breath.

The companion looked incredulously at Mare, "What of mine?"

"What of it?" said Mare. "Besides, ye paid me naught…And anyway, for the likes of ye and yer fellow, I'll have naught!" She stuck her thumb in her mouth and pulled it out, scraping the nail against her teeth.

The insulted man looked down at his ale, face red and ashamed, while his companion stared dumbfounded.

Christopher ran a hand through his hair, and nervously chuckled. "Baseless bate-breeders. What say you, Mare? I shall have a wig and staff for you yet for that performance. Come to the stage? It pays better than whoring. "

"Tut, tut. Stop yer jests Kit, ye know as well as I that women cannot play upon the stage."

"'Tis a pity. And what of the wench I paid for? How now, wench?" He looked at Alice. "Dost thou have a name?" He smiled warmly and picking up her hand, lightly brushed his lips against it.

Electricity ran up her arm and down her spine, but Alice tried to remain calm. "Mare, the baby is awake and screaming; she needs to be fed."

Mare's eyes grew wide. "Ah, I wish I had a wet-nurse! How long has Mary been awake Alice?"

She shrugged. "Over an hour. Anne will be fit to be tied when you get there, I guess."

Christopher looked at her quizzically. "Your speech…'tis strange. Of where art thou from?"

"I am gone," Mare gathered her shawl from the back of a chair. "Alice, bring home some change, will ye now?" She shot her and Christopher a parting glance and left the tavern.

***

A few stragglers sat next to drunken men, hoping to lift a coin or two when they passed out. Christopher sat next to Alice for protection, but Alice suspected it was more of a matter of curiosity. He became animated when they discussed the theatre, and his eyes grew large when she told him she could read and write.

"Hallo! A whore who cans't read! This I must see."

Taking her hand, he led her to the room where he had emerged earlier. A candle flickered on a table, next to an inkpot with a quill. Paper lay in front of the inkpot. He picked up the paper on the table.

"My play," He held it out to her. "Dost thou care to read?"

She held it, looking at the title. "*The Jew of Malta.*"

"And this?"

She took hold of another paper he held out to her, "*Hamlet – The Prince of Denmark*?" Incredulous, she read the title again. "How could this be?"

"Is not that a good title?"

"It is said that Shakespeare wrote it."

His face darkened. "I cans't assure ye Lady, that I, and my fellow, Thomas Kyd, wrote this play." He grabbed the paper from her hand. "Shaksper is a cobbled country base...," He spluttered, ...coming to London to make his fortune, leaving a wife..."

"An actor?"

"Aye, and barely. He does naught work for Strange's Men. The theatre company. Ye know of it?"

"Well, I—"

"Who are ye lady?" He stared at her.

Alice knew then there was nothing to say to appease him. And that he would probably try to test her in some way. He probably thought she was a spy. Perhaps from the low countries. A man snored in the corner. He garbled once and turned over.

Taking a deep breath she held it for a few seconds then let it escape. "I come from a country you have barely heard of. And no, I am not a spy. But I am a playwright."

He frowned. "A playmaker?"

"Yes. A playmaker."

"Pray tell, what brings you here then, Alice?"

She shrugged. "I woke up under a market stall. Mare pulled me out."

He looked at her doubtfully.

"It's the truth."

The candle flickered in front of them, casting uncertain shadows on the wall. It had burned down to a small nub. Alice thought that it must be near three o'clock in the morning. She felt profoundly tired, like she had jet lag, but this was going back-in-time-four-centuries lag.

Her mind was wired differently from everyone else's here. She could feel it. She knew about things like space travel, mobile phones, and Captain Crunch. These people, if they were educated, knew about Ptolemy. There was no running water, and no toilets—none that flushed anyway.

As she thought of all of this the candle gave one last sputter and went out.

"Do you know who I am?"

"Hmm. Perchance, Lady. Perchance."

She listened to the sound of their breathing. It was quiet in the room, and the only sounds were the eruptions of loud talking and frequent bursts of laughter from the other room. She wondered how long they would sit in the dark.

"Who am I then?"

He took a taper to the fire embers to light the candle. It flickered and sputtered, going out again.

"I suppose is naught to be...this candle."

He sat next to her again. "Thou art from a place...I cannot explain."

"From the future?" She wondered if he would buy that. People were beheaded for a lot less than proclaiming to come from the future.

"There was a conjurer—" he said.

"A conjurer?"

"Aye. She dealt in cards. And a dwarf."

"A dwarf? " It was like a rip in time and she had fallen in. She remembered that Mare too, had said something about the dwarf. Maybe if she could find him he could get her back—back to where she belonged. Alice was beginning to feel that if she didn't hurry, there wouldn't be a future to come back to.

She stood up and felt for the door. "I've got to go, Kit. I need to find that dwarf...I need to get back."

He laughed. "Back? Back where?"

It was disorientating in the dark. She felt smothered, claustrophobic.

"Is there another candle Kit? We need light."

"Nay. 'Tis no more. Perchance if I ha' a pence..."

"I have one." She rooted around in her dress pocket, feeling for the last pence. "Here," She felt for his hand and curled his fingers around the coin. "Please...get us a candle."

Kit stood up and walked towards the larger tavern. Alice watched his shadow exit the door frame, wondering how much she should say, what would she tell him?

Chapter 29

Christopher returned with the candle. He set in on the table and lit it with a taper he carefully pulled from the fire embers. The room came into view again. He looked over at her.

"Thou art lovely, as Helen, and now'st thou will tell me thou art a phantom as Helen." He smiled. "Where there should be a whole, here is half a candle the hostess sold for a pence. 'Hostess, quoth I, thou art stingy with the candle. Quoth she, 'Tis all I have troublesome playmaker.' What say you, Alice, will you tell me your whole story with half a candle?"

She watched the flame flicker, thinking about that day in the garden with the rose. The silence grew between them as her mind worked for answers.

"And what of Shaksper? Thou seems to know something... of that actor."

She realized then why she was there. Call it madness, call it a scientific blunder—a rip in the fabric of time and space. None of that mattered. She knew what she must do.

Alice lay her hand on his arm. "Kit, please, whatever happens...don't let them take your name. Don't hide behind another. You're not Shakespeare."

Christopher snorted. "Aye, that I am *naught*. Shaksper is a simple man."

"Just leave some evidence. Or no one will know that you wrote...all of it."

"Alice, you speak in riddles. Ye must ha' hit your head hard." He took a drink of ale.

She frowned. "I do know a thing or two."

"'Tis true. And like a conjurer, thou knowest the circle I am in."

"Like Walsingham."

Christopher choked on his ale. "Ah! The truth ha' come —thou art a spy! Tell me, lovely Lady, dost thou think thou will bed me...and bleed me? I'll ha' naught of this." He stood up.

"Wait!" Alice grabbed his arm. "Please! Sit a minute, will you? I can help."

He looked at her doubtfully, but took his seat again. Alice noted the corner of his eye twitch. It gave him the appearance of an epileptic or a man who had sworn off the drink.

"Have'st ale, Alice, or wine?

Alice nodded, realizing how thirsty she was. She knew that ale or wine wouldn't satisfy like water, but in sixteenth century England she had little choice, it was either ale or sack. Both had been purified in the fermenting process.

"I'll have ale."

As he left to fetch her ale from the main tavern, Alice quickly ran over historical events in her mind. He was part of Sir Francis Walsingham's spy network. The network had been formed to keep Queen Elizabeth, and England, safe. Sir Francis was notoriously clever as a spymaster, but Elizabeth never gave him quite enough money to maintain his clandestine operations. He used his own money to maintain his vast network and died broke. But all of this would be in the future of where Alice was now. *The Jew of Malta* was Christopher Marlowe's last play before he was brought before the Queen's Privy Council on charges of sedition and treason. He would have started the epic poem, *Hero and Leander*. Alice wondered how long they had before the end.

Christopher returned with the beverage and set it before her. She took a sip of ale. It was surprisingly bitter, and strong.

"Are you finished with the play, *The Jew of Malta?*

"Aye. It 'ha been at the Rose, um…," He scratched his head, "perchance a month? I am not certain," He looked at her. "You remind me of Bellamira, dark hair, eyes. The very one. 'Tis a pity boys must play her part. They, being not women, know naught their ways, and…," pausing, he looked at her, "their desires."

Alice swigged down half the ale. It was in an earthen mug, warm, but quenched her thirst. The drink went right to her head.

"I suppose not." she said.

"What say you, Alice? Disguise is your nature. Would you care to be a player?"

"A player?" She laughed and ale came out her nose. She wiped her face on her sleeve. "You have no idea."

"I ha' an idea—perchance, one or two."

Alice took the quill from the inkpot and ran it along the bridge of his nose. "Pray tell, Kit?" Giddy from the ale and exhausted, her eyes drooped.

He took the quill from her hand and put it back in the inkpot.

Chapter 30

She heard the creak of the hinges as the shutter swung open. Sunlight flooded the room, and she pulled the covers over her head. She buried her head in the pillow and heard the sound of muffled conversation. Something hard and pointy bit into the side of her cheek and she sat up. Her head was pounding.

"Ah! The Lady wakes. Dost thou care for any breakfast?" Christopher nodded towards a table set with a loaf of bread, a mug, and a pitcher.

Alice pulled a piece of straw from her mouth. "Not if it's that God-forsaken ale we have been drinking. I never want it again."

He laughed. "The Mermaid hath strong ale. 'Tis a good thing that Tom believeth the same." He turned towards a man who seemed to emerge from a dark corner of the room. The man was taller and thinner than Kit.

He nodded in her direction, and picked up an inkpot and quill off the table. "Good morrow, Lady. Your name be Alice?"

She nodded.

"I am Tom. Thomas Kyd." He whittled a writing edge on the quill.

"Of *The Spanish Tragedy*." Alice said.

Tom turned towards Christopher. "Thou art correct. This lady knows the theatre, and playmaking. Thou writes too, Lady?"

"Yes."

"I want for Alice to play Bellamira. Does not she fit the part?"

"Aye," Tom said. "A courtesan who beds scholars."

"Wait a minute. I am *not* a courtesan, and I do not bed scholars."

"I crave your pardon, Alice. What is thy profession?" Tom looked at her expectantly, and Alice knew that Christopher had had a hard time explaining who, or what, she was.

"Methinks the lady's a spy," Kit said. "And she wishes to conjure me with her tall tales."

Tom nodded. "She dost speaketh strangely. I ha' never heard this speech before. But ye say she is a woman?"

"Aye. Carry her home, I did, with her head falling about my neck, and grabbing me about the waist. Whispering—"

"Just a sec..." Alice chewed the bread in her mouth and swallowed. "You gave me the ale to see if I'd talk!" She thought back to the tavern. She couldn't remember leaving. "What did I say?" she ventured meekly.

"Thou thinks on me very highly," The beginnings of a smile played around the corners of Christopher's mouth. "And thou...," He frowned, then waved his hand in dismissal. "'Twas naught but bed talk any courtesan would say."

Alice felt her face go red. She poured the liquid from the pitcher, noting it was water. Gratefully, she took a sip. It did nothing to quench her embarrassment.

"I'm sorry. I don't usually act like that."

Tom burst into laughter. "A modest whore! No Bellamira. But, she plays the part."

Christopher nodded. "Aye. 'Tis true."

Alice sat glowering over her mug. "I am not a whore. Did you hear that? But you...," She pointed an accusing finger at Christopher, "Most people think you're gay!"

He nodded, smiling. "Aye. I dress well."

Alice rolled her eyes. "Not fancy, gay, but ...people say you fancy men."

Tom snorted. Christopher raised his eyebrows. "I desire patronage, Lady, if that is what thou...meanest. Gentlemen prefer kind words of a poetical nature. It moves them."

"Oh, I'm sure it does." Alice raised her eyebrows.

"Tut, tut, Alice. Thou speaketh like a glover's wife. And thou art gentle. How else could ye learn to write?"

Alice sat in a chair next to the table. There was a small blue vase full of quills. She pulled one out. It had a blunt edge. She put it back and picked up the vase, holding it to the light. The light shone through it, turning it a brilliant sky blue.

"Beautiful." she said.

"'Tis glass Kit brought from Italy."

"Ah, Italy. A romantic place, full of papists and spies."

Christopher and Thomas exchanged a look. Thomas gathered paper, quills, and an inkpot, placing them in a bag. He sat on the edge of the bed and pulled his boots on.

"I shalt take my leave. To the Rose."

"Ye ha' a new player?" Christopher said.

"Aye, a simple one is he, but remembers well. Shaksper is his name."

Christopher laughed. "Alice says he wrote my plays."

"I said, some people say that..."

"Nay. This man cannot write. 'Tis true though, Kit's plays could be improved. I ha' been saying since *The Spanish Tragedy*."

"Get ye gone, Tom." Christopher tossed a quill in his direction, and it lazily floated through the air. Tom deftly grabbed it.

Thomas turned towards Alice and gave a slight bow. "Adieu, my Lady. I am sure we will meet again," Then towards Christopher, "Wilt thou be coming soon? There 'tis much to do. I ha' heard Henslowe is a thither about dragon noises and devil's costumes."

Christopher nodded. "Aye. I shall be there."

Thomas left and Christopher sat next to Alice, taking the blue vase from her hand. "It would be better if thou dids't not speak of papists and spies."

Alice glared at him. "I don't know what kind of game you're playing, but I'm tired of it. I don't want to pretend I don't know who Walsingham is, or that you work for him, and that the papists are plotting against the queen."

Astonished, Christopher raised his eyebrows and smiled.

"Did anyone ever tell you your eyebrows look like cupids bows?"

He broke into a grin. "Aye. And did anyone tell ye that ye smell of cow offal?"

"Well." Alice felt spent.

Christopher pointed to a basin sitting on a table. "There. You may refresh yourself. Get the cow off ye."

She walked over and dipped the cloth in the water, rubbing it over her face and between her breasts. "I suppose privacy is a thing unheard of here?"

Christopher averted his eyes, and took a coin from his pocket. "I suggest also, lady, you visit a seamstress, and have another gown sewn. I will pay ye this wage...now, for services ye ha' yet to render."

"If I told you once, I have said it a million times! I'm not—"

"Nay. Ye shall play Bellamira in the *Jew*. And there is another matter of disguise...A little matter of a man named Baines. Dost thou know of this man?"

Alice nodded. "The man deals in doubles. He is an agent provocateur. I would rather not speak of him. And, as such, you mentioned you would rather not speak of papists and spies."

"'Tis good to stray from such things. Let us come from the shadows then. Dear heart, what say you? The light of day beckons and we have much work to do."

***

Alice stood in front of the thrust stage. The groundling area in front of the stage had been swept clean, but the stench of old dirt and sweat was overwhelming. She was trying her best not to gag.

Kit and Thomas were arguing about a scene in the *Jew*, and Alice concentrated on what they were saying. Aaron appeared from backstage, and did a somersault, then a flip, noticing her when he had completed the maneuver.

"Ah! My fair one, my lovely mistress! What say thou? Come to, come to!" He held his hand out towards her.

Alice smiled, moving towards the stage.

"Mistress? What say thous't clown? This woman, Alice. Dost thou know her?" Kit said.

"Oh, aye. She is my fair Alice, living with Mare she is." He turned to the absent audience, and with an aside added, "I aim to make her my wife."

Kit frowned. "I'll not ha' a clown and my playmaker make the bare-backed beast together. Nay…" He walked over to the foot of the stage. "Come to, Alice, time for Bellamira." He held out his hand and smiled.

Alice grabbed Kit's hand and he pulled her upright onto the stage. She looked down onto the empty groundling area. Kit pulled her close and spread his arm across the stage area. "Look. 'Tis not a view? You shall be my lovely Bellamira."

She saw the eye of Alvis blink, enveloping them into a thousand and one things. She shook her head, dislodging the vision.

"I want this to last." she said.

Aaron grabbed her arm, pulling her from Kit. "Bellamira!"

She laughed and grabbed his hand. "And who shall be Pilia-Borgia? Who?"

Thomas smiled. "I am to play Pilia, infamous pickpocket."

They faced each other and Alice began Bellamira's lament over losing her scholars. She recited the lines perfectly and when she was finished Kit nodded approvingly. "Well said, Alice." He squeezed her hand. "And thou art my lovely Bellamira. Dost thou know?"

Thomas looked from her to Kit. "We shalt pull it off. Can'st thou play a man too, Alice?"

"Of course."

Although the camaraderie of the play bound them together, Alice felt an impending sadness flowing in with the muted sunset. Time here was not immortal. It was as efflorescent as the blink of a dwarf's eye.

Chapter 31

The bed was warm, but the sheets felt rough. Like a cat's tongue. He had his quill, and she playfully grabbed it from him, running it up his thigh. He held his breath, and she touched his cheek, his hair, teasing the feather across his nose. Kit gently took it from her hand.

"Over, my Alice."

She turned on her back. Feeling the quill move over her skin, she laughed. "What are you writing?

The movements against her flesh were at once short, long, and sensuous. When it was finished she promised that she would let it dry, and after what seemed like hours she finally turned over.

"Mmm." She kissed Kit, feeling the warmth of their bonding washing over her.

He pulled back and propped his head underneath his hands.

"What did you write?"

"Ye shall see my Alice. Ye shall see."

She took his hand and held it between hers. "Again?"

Kit laughed. "Ah, give me time woman! Thou art insatiable." He snuggled next to her. "And now we will speak of the spy Baines."

Alice felt stung, literally slapped. She sat up in bed and looked long and hard at him. "Now who is bed…and bled." She grabbed the quill and made a slicing motion across her throat. "You might as well cut my throat then use me so."

"Ah, now the drama comes…"

"How could you do this to me? How could you! Right after—this." She stood up and grabbed her gown, pulling it roughly over her head.

"How could I?" Kit grabbed her wrist and pulled her to him. "What of you lady? What of these bed vows you speak? Who is pulling who? Art thou a spy? What do you want?" He took her hand, placing the quill in it. "This, my mistress, is what binds us."

"And Baines will soon bind you."

Kit stood and went to the window. The street was dark, and there was no movement. The dawn was just beginning to show on the rooftops. He placed his hands on the edge of the window and leaned out. She watched him stretch, then turn towards her.

"He haunts me still. He is waiting in late for me."

"Aye."

"Alice…do not taunt me with an accent that not suits you. Why do ye speak such?"

"I know of Baines and what he is capable of. But I would rather not speak of him directly after…" She got up from the bed and stood beside him. He looked down at the people walking the dusty street.

Alice touched his tattooed arm. "And what of this?" She touched the leaves circling his arm. "What does it mean?"

"How do ye know of Baines?" He looked suspicious.

"I have learned of him through my studies."

"Studies," He scoffed. "Dost thou trivel with my affections Alice?"

"No. The circle of all we do unites us together again."

He glanced down at her fingers circling the chain of leaves around his bicep. "In Espana I received it. It means I believe in all things. The magic of alchemy. It cans't be broken, this chain. Working for Walsingham I was," He sighed. "As of now. And at a time when I believed in what

181

could be done for England. As an intelligencer. He cupped her chin in his hand. "Cans't it be, sweet Alice?" "I know not. Tell me, love. Tell me of Baines."

She shook her head free from his hand, sensing that the things that bound them were beyond the both of them. "I don't know what he is planning next."

His eyes met hers. "Find him. Tell me what of him I can take...and unmake,"

"But what of his whereabouts? He is undercover, and I know not where he is." she said.

"He may be a priest. He is in a village not far...ever angry at me since I knew him at Rheims. He is hell bent to kill me, he is."

Chapter 32

She awoke to the toll of church bells. Someone had died. Alice placed a hand behind her feeling for Kit, but he had gone. Thomas was sitting at a table dipping his quill in an ink pot. He placed the quill on the parchment and wrote. He looked up, and she realized she was naked. She quickly grabbed a sheet, wrapping it around her body.

Thomas smiled. "I shall avert mine eyes, lady. Though 'twill be hard. Thou art lovely." He started writing again. Alice watched him for a moment.

"Thomas, do you know the date?"

He looked up from his writing. "Aye. 'Tis the 25th of May."

"The year?"

He looked at her quizzically. "'Tis the year of our Lord 1593."

"Oh, God."

"Aye. Exactly." He continued writing.

"I don't have much time."

"Time lady? You mays't pass the time with me if thous't care. I shall go to the theatre soon enough. But thous't art welcome to stay." He stopped writing. "Kit speaks well of ye. It seems he knew of your coming."

"Yes?"

"Aye. He spoke of a woman through a dream he had. 'Alice, her name is Alice,' quoth he. He told me his very thought then. The dream is like that of that man, Leander, swimming to his love, Hero. Dost thou know the story?"

"Yes. I do." She clasped the sheet around her and sat up. "Thomas, you have to leave. You're in great danger."

Thomas frowned. "Art thou unwell Alice? Thou speaketh strangely of danger. Thou hast come too far, and now are ill. Rest awhile."

"You're in grave danger. They will find you and torture you. Kit too. I must find Baines."

"Lady, you are too much in yourself. 'Tis safe here. Ye have no need for such worries, for whatever has plagued ye is in the past. Kit will take good care of ye. Of that I am sure."

"No Thomas, you misunderstand."

"Ah, no. Ye speak in tales I don't understand. Ye shall be safe here, lady. I guarantee it. Sir Cecil holds us in great regard, as does Sir Walsingham. There is nothing to fear."

"I must dress."

He turned and averted his eyes from her as she pulled on her gown. She quickly fastened the buttons, and pulled on her shoes, hopping on one foot as she pulled on the other. "I have to find Kit."

"He 'tis at the theatre lady. The Rose." Thomas watched as she quickly left the dwelling, then turned again to his writing.

***

Growing increasingly faint with hunger Alice hurried down the street. There were no bread vendors in sight. She was worried Kit would go to the stationers at Saint Paul's Church Yard, and she would be too late. He would be an easy target for the authorities at Saint Paul's. They knew where to find their scholar, their playmaker who loved to read.

Time was running out. There were only five days to the end. The end of history for Kit Marlowe, and the beginning of history for one William Shakespeare.

She turned the corner and was engulfed in a throng of people coming to the market selling their wares. Fishmongers took their catch off the carts, bearing the fish in huge baskets. They set up their stalls, and basket weavers, and bread minders took their place beside them. Alice stood in line in front of a baker. The smell of the bread caused her stomach to grumble. She licked her lips and rooted in her side pocket for a pence. Her hand came up empty. Frantically she searched harder in her pocket. It was her turn in line.

"I ah…" Her hand came out empty, and the baker turned to the next customer.

The little girl behind her pressed a pence in her hand. "Lady."

It was Anne. She smiled broadly at her then shyly looked away. Alice hugged her and collected her bread from the baker woman, who shooed them away from the front of the stall.

"Will ye be coming home lady?"

Alice broke off a piece of bread and handed a piece to Anne. She felt tears well in her eyes, touched that Anne thought of her this way.

"I don't know. I must find Kit. I fear he is in grave danger."

Anne nodded distractedly and looked at her feet. "I would like ye to look after me lady." She tried to smile, but her eyes were full of sadness.

Alice felt her heart would burst. She held Anne's hand. "I'll do the best I can. I'll try to come back as soon as possible." She gave her hand a squeeze, then brushed the crumbs from her hands. "Tell Mare I'll be back in a fortnight."

Anne looked at her longingly. "Grammercy Lady. For the bread." She walked down the street. Alice watched her pick her way among beggars and vagabonds. She did not look back, and Alice knew why. Her back stood tall and strait. She was like a strong willow, bending with the wind, but snapping back.

I won't fail her...

***

The Rose was full. The play was ready, and Kit stood standing in the groundling area. On his head was perched a velvet hat that matched his black doublet and hose. He held his hand out and directed the players on the stage. His face was lit with anticipation and joy. Alice stood at the entrance of the theatre and watched him.

Kit finally turned and saw her standing. "Alice!" He walked over to her, still smiling. Alice wanted to forever remember this image: the beginnings of a beard; tousled hair under his hat; and smooth velvet of a self-made man. He took his hand gently in hers and bent to kiss it.

"My mistress." He then took her in his arms and swung her around to the stage. "You shall be back soon to play Bellamira?" He whispered in her ear. "Look at the player in her gown. Is it not an apparition?"

She laughed. "Bearded he is. And not of my stature."

"No. There is no one of your stature, dear heart." He rocked her in his arms.

"I need money, Kit."

He nodded and pulled shillings from his pocket. He placed them in her hand.

"Take care, sweeting. I shall wait for you." He pulled her close and brushed his lips with hers, then kissed her deeply. She felt herself melt against him and the line between the two of them dissolve. The distant sound of clapping and shouting arose. Alice pulled away, and saw the players watching them, applauding.

"Where is the stage, my love? There, or here?" He smiled. "Go. Come quickly back to me."

She wanted to tell him of her fear, how it might not possible for her to do this. Yet, on the other hand, all she wanted to do was make sure he was safe. And save Thomas. They had no idea how close to death they were. The fear was a palpable taste in her mouth. It was visceral and tasted of metal. She wiped her brow and turned to go.

"Alice."

"Yes?" She half hoped that he would tell her to forget it, it didn't matter. To stay, that was all that mattered…

"Fare ye well."

***

The seamstress assured her that this was the fashion of all vicar's wives. The gown was a mixture of dour matron with a slight hint of cleavage. Alice smoothed her hair, then wrapped it behind her head, secured it with a pin, then brought a few soft curls forward to frame her face.

Kit had said that Baines could most probably be found in the village of Staffordshire, according to news from Walsingham's intelligencers. They claimed to have seen him there. Now it was up to her to validate the sighting.

Alice mounted a horse she had paid for in a town she could not remember, except for the fact that it was outside of London, and the men were rude. Even to a vicar's wife. She didn't want to remember, only to get through it.

Kit had only five days before he became a footnote in history. Whitgift even now was planning his revenge against the Puritans, and since Kit worked for Walsingham, Whitgift's rival for the Queen's attention, he would be made the scapegoat for this long standing rivalry between the two men. It was a complex scenario. According to Whitgift, who was a defender of the Anglican faith, the flowering of the English Enlightenment was a cause for mass hysteria, and all unruliness and anarchy must be brought down. There was no room for independent thinking, and Kit Marlowe was the exemplar of all of this.

She rode hard and fast. As the cold wind whipped her face she turned once at the sound of bells. The church bells were forever tolling. *Grave diggers will soon be afoot...*

The town of Staffordshire drew near, and she dismounted at the nearest inn. The thick door held up against her fist, and she rubbed her hand when she was done. A woman who answered the door had a tired and worn face. She was wearing a red cloth wrapped around her head and was thick around the waist. Alice asked for a bed, and it was granted. When she lay down she thought of Mare, and Anne. She wished they were with her.

Chapter 33

A long morning of riding led her to landmarks that Kit had described. She took an old side road heading through a field and came to an ancient oak by a bridge that stretched across a river. The church where Baines was deacon would not be far. The horse trotted amongst stones she did not see, quickly stepping over them, and she was glad he was surefooted.

When the church was in sight she dismounted. She led the horse to a tree and roped the animal. He brushed his nose across her hand, and the warm breath from his nostrils warmed her hand. She patted his nose.

"Wish me luck."

The horse snorted and stamped his foot.

Alice walked to the door and rapped smartly, trying hard to muster the courage she didn't have. A woman answered the door.

***

Christopher leaned out the window while Thomas lit a candle in the corner. A wine jug sat on the table. The bed was still unmade. Soon, the laundress would come and collect the dirty clothes and linens.

"This, Thomas is what *The Spanish Tragedy* needs..." Kit dipped his pen in the inkpot, looked at the parchment in front of him, then set it down. "All in all, a woman like Bellamira." He rose and went to the window.

"Ah, Kit. Thou art spell bound by Alice."

"Ha! Thou art thinking of *Doctor Faustus*. He dost conjure the fair Helen to do his bidding…with a kiss." Kit leaned far out the window. "Hey ya! Man! Dost thou believe in love?" He yelled down to a young couple. They looked up, smiling.

"My friend!" Thomas grabbed his doublet, pulling him from the window. "Thou art love struck. Come, come."

"Listen, Tom." Kit went back to the table and took up his quill. "There have been women, but Alice is a jewel."

"What of Emilia?"

Kit ran his hand through his hair. "'Tis true they say I deal in doubles. But in love, Tom? Nay. Emilia is betrothed to her cousin by orders of the queen."

"Betrothed? What say you?"

"She is with child."

"Ah, Kit." Thomas shook his head.

Kit shrugged. "She has said naught to me but has said so to Lord Hunsdon." He scoffed. "'Tis no matter. She hopes to gain from our Lord. He is…was, her paramour."

"And of court?" said Thomas.

"She is wont to be at court, but may no longer be. I will learn of it soon. The queen will soon be merrymaking."

"You are there?"

"Aye. Tom, thinkon't! I am a most beloved poet of her majesty, our queen."

Tom whittled a quill, a sly smile on his face. "'Tis true, Kit. I wish you well in juggling your many women. Take care not to drop one."

Kit laughed. "Tom, ye jest. Ye play me well, my friend, but I am true and straight as an arrow."

***

Alice was led into the house of a man who had made well for himself. Italian tapestries lined the wall, as well as portraits by Van Mander. She undid her cloak and laid it aside.

"Dost thou care for refreshment lady?"

"No. Gramercy. Is Master Baines here? I've come from far." She adjusted her skirt, proud of her accent and the way she carried herself.

The house woman studied her with an eye of the jaded and long apprenticed unto the ways of people trying to take advantage.

"He may be back soon, Lady. Perchance not. Do you care to come later?"

Alice studied the house. This was a house of a man who took chances. The beams were crooked, and the glass was askew. She thought of getting up and looking at herself but sat still. Her eyes traveled to the woman.

"No. I shall sit." She smiled.

The woman shifted from foot to foot. With a sigh she left.

Alice laughed inwardly as the door moved. *I knew it.*

She stood as he entered the room.

***

Kit stood and stretched. The last of the wine was gone. Thomas had left after the laundress collected the dirty linen.

The day was coming alive, and he must make haste. But Alice had not left him and would not. Thoughts of her drifted before his eyes.

He went to the window, watching the people below. A man walked by with an eye that could not see. He dragged his foot behind him.

"Aye!"

The man stopped and took his hat from his head, holding it towards the window. Kit threw a coin, aiming for the hat. The coin fell near the beggar's worn out shoe.

"Dost thou feel it man?

The man nodded and carefully felt by his foot, picking up the shilling.

Kit retreated from the window, pulling his frame inside the room. An angel, dost thou think I'm an angel...

O, if she only knew.

***

Baines smiled when he saw her. "Lady?"

She stood and courtsied. "I need advice. Sir." Alice looked at him wide eyed, playing the awestruck housewife. Would he suspect her? She felt the blood rise to her neck and creep up her face.

He sat next to her. The clock that was all the rage amongst the rich kept ticking. The velvet of his doublet rubbed against her arm. He took her hand in his.

"Ye are new to the place?"

She turned as red as his doublet and turned in her seat. She didn't know if she should laugh, or faint. To be so near to someone that determined life or death overwhelmed her. She waved her hand in front of her face.

"Tis most difficult, sir."

"Your accent, 'tis hard to place. Are ye from the low countries?"

Alice watched the clock. The clock meant that time could be measured and discovered. But she knew that time was something that could be quite malleable. She remembered Bernie and it seemed far, yet close, and suddenly her head felt very light. The silks and warmth were getting to her. She must remember her place.

"Aye. I need advice on one that hath cost me much..." She left it there and continued to fan her face.

He rubbed her back. She wondered if it would play out as Kit had said, that he would try to look for any weakness and stop at nothing to get at it. Alice coughed lightly in her hanky, and Baines leaned forward expectantly. "Mistress?"

"The wonder of it 'tis...the Queen...she is worried about papists, and ye...ye are worried about...what sir?"

His face grew hard, lines appeared around his eyes and his mouth turned into a straight line.

"What do ye want, wench."

"Sir, I am very worried and scared of what is happening in town." Alice adjusted the skirts of her gown. "I know this is not something ye would care to think of...but will the playmakers have a gain? I say this only because my husband is worried of it. He reported that Sir Whitgift said the crowd is like a downed woman—may I speak such vulgarity? Do ye think, sir?"

"Oh, aye. The crowd knows not a thing. Not a thing. Say your name Mistress, I did not catch it?"

"Benchly, sir. Ann Benchly. My husband—"

"I know not of any Benchly." He looked at her warily. "What is it he does?"

"A musician sir."

"Aye? A musician? I know of quite a few musicians. Who does he play for?"

"He plays for the court sir, but recently he has been sent to play for a playmaker, name of Marlowe. The one who wrote that play...*Tamburlaine*."

"I know of him." Baines snapped, all thoughts of her husband put aside. "Blasphemy it 'tis. You know this man?"

"Sir?"

"This Marlowe, wench!"

"No, sir," she stammered, happy that he entered the trap. Would he suspect her as a silly woman, worried about playmakers and their blasphemous plays? Or would he begin to suspect her. Her breath quickened, and she felt a strong flush creep up her neck.

"Mistress Benchly, are ye ill? Or 'tis something... else?" He lay a hand in her lap and rubbed her thigh.

Alice watched his hand in horror. "Sir, I assure you! I am a most pious woman! I am worried for my husband's safety. He will be branded as a heretic, making merriments with this Marlowe, and his other assorted bawdies."

"Oh, aye. That I can assure ye, mistress. But we...but I can protect you." He leaned forward and kissed her neck. Alice pretended to swoon, but she must not appear to eager. She thought of Mare's words, and how it was a woman's way to be a whore.

"Sir, I must not. I must..." He placed a finger to her lips.

"We will speak of this, and the matter of Marlowe later. We can find a way to put him away. Forever. And ye shall help."

"Help, sir? How can I be of service to ye? Pray tell. I will do as ye bid." She hung her head, the picture of piety.

He laughed, a high-pitched sound that Alice had only heard in the mentally disturbed.

"I know what side I'm on. I know how to get him. That bastard of a cobbler's son. He hast not a thing on me. Trying to coin money? Well...that is not what happened..." He babbled, and Alice listened. "Yea, he is a spy, like myself. Dost thou think likewise? That I was put here by Whitgift, to give the sacrament to those like yourself?" He laughed in that high-pitched sound that scared and fascinated her. "And when it ends I shall have a pretty penny, while our Kit will be strung and quartered." He stood and motioned towards the door. As if summoned by magic, the housewoman appeared.

"Mistress Benchly will be by on the morrow. Good day mistress. We will meet on the morrow." He bowed deeply, and kissed her hand. "And if thou are not back on the morrow...it shall be set in place without ye." He nodded.

The housewoman shut the door behind her.

***

Christopher stood in Saint Paul's churchyard. He thumbed through a book of Ovid's poems. It was a good translation.

He smiled once again at the exploits of his favorite lover and the fair Corinna. He looked up, and noticed two whores watching him. He smiled and smoothed his shoulder length hair. They approached, and he waved them away. He would wait for Alice. She was the one he wanted. If Ovid was the one who began the spark, she was the muse who ignited the fire. Kit placed the book on the table. He swung his cape around him, adjusted his velvet hat, and walked down the dirty street.

A notice pinned to a big oak caught his eye. As he approached the tree he saw Alvis out of the corner of his eye.

"Nay...not yet. Please..." The whisper trailed from his lips, and he found himself standing where druids had gathered and mistletoe had once hung.

Written in the language of *Tamburlaine*, the note spoke against the immigrants who were moving to England. Astonished, he stood opened-mouthed and turned to see at least a dozen identical notices pinned everywhere he looked.

***

Figuring she must be ten miles from the city, Alice dismounted. A winding cobblestone road had brought her to this little hamlet. She knocked at an inn door. Waited. When there was no answer, he walked to the back of the inn where a little girl wearing a gray, woolen dress approached her.

"Hello. Where is everyone?" Alice smiled waiting.

Frightened of her strange speech, the girl looked at her wide-eyed. She turned and ran. "Please! Wait!" Alice looked after her. "I can't...go any further..." Her voice trailed off and she sank to her knees.

If she didn't get to London to warn Kit, she would have to return and speak again with Baines without speaking to him. And she had no idea what kind of game Baines was playing. Alice stood, grabbed the reins and led the horse to the small lake behind the inn. The horse snorted, pawed the ground, and gratefully drank the water. She patted his nose.

"You've been good to me friend." She looked across the lake. She saw a fire lit on the other side, and heard the sound of laughter, then song. Shielding her eyes against the water's glare, Alice watched. She smelled the acrid smoke. The horse stamped his foot, and she again patted his nose. She nervously wound her hair around her hand, pinning it back. If she did not leave soon towards London all would be lost.

Alice mounted the horse and whispered in his ear.

"Once more, friend. Then we'll be home."

The horse snorted and bore his mistress in the direction she led him.

***

"Thomas!"

Kit stormed into the room, sweat on his brow. The room was empty. The laundress had not been there. Kit ran to the window. Fear seeped from every corner. Paper, libels, everywhere, pinned to doors, and posts. He stepped back from the window. Wary.

"They 'ha come for us."

The room was closing in, and Christopher dashed from it.

***

Few people walked the streets as she entered town. The wind had turned the River Thames a grey chalk where no glance of sunlight reflected. She pulled her cloak around her against the gusts. The horse slowed to a mere crawl. Alice dug her heal into his side, but he only tossed his head then swished it from side to side. Alice dismounted and walked.

She turned towards the Anchor Inn hoping to find Kit there. A cluster of papers blew into her skirts and tangled in her feet. She bent with reins in hand to retrieve one.

Ye strangers y^t doe inhabite in this lande
Note this same writing doe it vnderstand
Conceit it well for savegard of your lyves
Your goods, your children, & your dearest wives
Your Machiavellian Marchant spoyles the state,
Your vsery doth leave vs all for deade
Your Artifex, & craftesman works our fate,
 And like the Jewes, you eate us vp as bread…

Her heart pounded and she shook the note from her hand. Picking up another, it was the same, and another, and another…Alice realized in horror that Baines had been here before her. Way before. She only wondered why he would want her back. It certainly wasn't to frame Christopher, because the note made certain of that. Signed Tamburlaine, it did all but say that Kit had written it. That, or someone close to him.

There was only one place to find answers: to the spymaster himself.

***

Walsingham turned from the great fireplace. Kit sat in the chair nearest the fire, knowing it was only a matter of time before Whitgift and his allies closed in on him.

"He 'ha the queen's ear. And methinks sometimes her very soul." Walsingham said slowly.

"But what of France? What of the Armada? We have secured England for her grace."

Walsingham narrowed his eyes and stroked his beard. "The queen's favor is not with her spymaster. The lady tolerates me because she has to, but she has no stomach for the affairs of state." He walked to the table and picked out a rose. It was a deep red color, reminding Christopher of blood.

"This rose, it 'ha no idea of the thorns that live upon it." Walsingham twirled the flower lightly in his hands, avoiding the sharp thorns. "But I...I ha' becometh quite aware." He tossed the flower to Christopher who caught it, but let it drop when a thorn punctured his thumb. He looked at Sir Walsingham suddenly aware that he had been nothing but a pawn, and like a pawn, he could be sacrificed. He put his thumb in his mouth, tasting his blood.

"I thought Sir, that my good affairs for the state would procure me—"

"Think not of that, Marlowe. Ye may ha' been saved once from falling from favor, in the university, but that was much easier. Ye wert but a small player then. Now, ye have risen higher, flying amongst the nobles and heads of state. And know ye, that like Icarus, flying close the sun is exhiliraring. And deadly." Walsingham stared at him.

Guliet rushed into the room. He brought his hand to his head, as if to keep the yellow turban from tumbling off.

"Sir, there is a woman at the door who says she must see you." Guliet bowed deeply.

"Sirrah!" Walsingham waved his hand, dismissing him. "Thou'st knows I said no visitors!"

Guliet bowed even deeper, and firmly pulled the turban tighter on his head. Christopher stared at his feet. Guliet straightened and caught him staring.

"Most noble sir, the woman will not be persuaded. I feareth a ruckus from the state this woman is in, I—"

"Silence! I will see to it!" Walsingham stormed from the room.

Kit looked into Guliet's eyes. "Aaron?"

"Aye. sir." Aaron said, a gleam in his eye. "Methinks thou noticed mine shoes." Aaron stuck out a foot for him to examine.

"What?"

"Only a cobbler's son would notice the lack of toe."

"Aye. They art not pointed."

"'Tis true." Aaron hopped on one foot.

"Why art thou here?" Christopher quickly scanned the door for Walsingham.

"My dear Alice sent me, sir. And Guliet is a friend. He did laugh –"

Walsingham stormed into the room with Alice in tow. He pushed her in front of him.

"Sirrah! Explain this woman!"

Christopher gaped at Walsingham, who glared. He did not blink.

"She is an intelligencer, Sir." Christopher offered.

"An intelligencer? And for who dost thou *intelligence*, wench?"

Alice winced at the word *wench*.

"Master Marlowe, sir. But it was only for your sake, sir, that I did spy. I looked into Baines's affairs."

"Ah." Walsingham nodded. "And how much does she know?"

Kit glanced from Alice to Walsingham. "Everything."

"'Tis to be expected with bed mates. Go to, I will speak with the woman alone."

Christopher and Guliet left the room. Alice sat by him in front of the great fire. The firelight softened Walsingham's features, yet there was a steeliness behind the facade. He sat observing her for several moments.

"I think thou should understand, Lady, that the queen's ear is mine. 'Tis not a simple game of courtiers playing for favor. I am privy to the most sensitive of matters regarding state. Dost thou think that thou would miss my gaze? Come, come." He patted her knee.

She cringed. There was something deadly behind his eyes. She pushed away visions of torture, but England's deadliest truth-telling devices quickly came to mind: being pulled apart like a chicken wing on the *strappado*, or stretched on the rack until the victim's very screams thinned and grew faint. Terror welled in her heart and the sickeningly dull thudding of her blood grew in her ears.

"Why does Master Marlowe trust ye?" He sat back and cupped his chin in his hand.

"Sir, I stay in a trusted house on the Bankside."

"And to whom does this house belong?"

"To one Mare MacPhaine."

"Ah, yes. It is said she has connections amongst the nobility in Scotland. She has Master Marlowe's babe, does she not?"

Alice felt her stomach drop somewhere below her knees. She frowned. "No, I know naught."

"You are faire, and well provided for. I see how ye could easily travel among the folk along there. And capture their secrets. For who would thinkest twice that a common whore would do them wrong. Care you for our court, lady?"

"I have never been."

Walsingham laughed. "Surely a lady with your breeding and education would care for the manners and intrigue of court. "Tis much better than the Bankside and the hovel you reside in. Elizabeth would delight in your presence. She much enjoys the company of beautiful and educated ladies as yourself. They are much hard to come by, you know."

Alice managed a faint smile. She counted the roses on the table. There were eleven.

Walsingham lit a pipe, pulling on the embers and exhaling towards Alice.

"I know who you are, lady. I have watched your movements for several weeks now. But whereof dost thou come from?"

He watched her, puffing silently on his pipe.

"If I know naught of your origins, lady, you are not to be trusted. It is my duty to protect the realm from any threat. And although the queen holds me at arm's length, she begrudgingly gives me this suit. And more..." He nodded, leaving the and more hanging in the air, tempting her with thoughts of torture.

"*Insanus omnis furere credit ceteros.*" she whispered.

Shocked, Walsingham leaned forward. "Did I hear correctly? Every madman thinks everyone else is mad?"

He stood, and Alice felt the players on the board sliding forward, as if a life-size chess match were in progress, and now was the checkmate; off with her head.

"Sir, it was the Navarre I left from France." She carefully reached in her pocket and pulled out a worn letter, handing it to Walsingham. He snatched the letter and stood by the fire reading.

After a moment he looked towards her. "The note is signed by the Duke of Valois asking a Lady Blanchett to release you to England to gather intelligence. Because of your impeccable breeding and knowledge of English."

"Sir, the duke's habits are strange. I could no longer stand to be in court. I have released myself of my bonds of mine own accord." She hid her face behind a lace hanky.

"Guliet!"

He instantly appeared at the door. Alice looked at Guliet carefully. There was something strange about him that she could not quite place.

"Bring me a copy of the letter with the Duke of Valois' signature. I have it in the study in the wooden box."

"Sir, I beseech you," Alice began, "The Catholics are becoming cruel and cunning. They no longer seek to know the message of Christ. They are immersed in adornment and power. It is my only hope to have peace."

"And what of your religion, my Lady?"

"I lean towards the pure."

"You are a Puritan then?"

"It seems to be a comforting middle ground."

Walsingham nodded, engrossed in her answer. "I also seek the pure in matters."

He no longer gripped the arm of his chair and his eyes had softened.

"This country has been divided perchance by religious struggles, which has given us an opportunity to become strong. Our queen plays it well. She is the Virgin Spectacle, remnant of the old religion, yet, holding to the new Anglican faith. She walks a fine line, our queen. And although she is tolerant of other faiths, it is the Catholic plotters who grieve her most."

"And Baines sir?"

"We believe that Baines is working for Archbishop Whitgift. As you know a member of our Privy Council. The same faith as our queen, and she pits us against each other." He frowned. "Whitgift has no use for the theatre either. He believe it is the devil's staging ground."

Guliet returned with the letter. Walsingham carefully compared the note to Alice's, scrupulously inspecting the two signatures. After what seemed an eternity to Alice, he looked up, face impassive. "It is the duke's signature." He handed the two letters to Guliet. Guliet winked at Alice. She suppressed a smile and smoothed the wrinkles in her gown.

"I commend you for discovering Baines, lady. I am sure it was at Master Marlowe's bequest. Are you in love with him?"

Her face flushed at such a bold inquiry. "I have grown fond of him. Sir."

"He has a certain skill, I suppose. Playmaker that he is. Very fanciful. A delight to the ladies."

"It is my suit to help the realm, sir. I think naught of my own...entanglements."

"I would advise ye to think first of this one, my lady. Master Marlowe is a most cunning spy, one of my best. He walks freely in all manner of circles. You have been advised."

Walsingham stood and nodded towards her. "My lady." He then turned to the fire.

Alice watched him for several moments, realizing she had been dismissed. A cold fear like a fall frost crept over her.

"Sir? What am I to do about Baines, then?"

Walsingham turned his face from the fire.

"Go to him as promised. Explain to him the nature of this libel note pinned to almost every door in London. Watch his reaction. He has already confided in you, and he will again." With that said, he again turned towards the fire.

Alice felt like sinking to the floor in despair. She was in no mood to rush across England again. And she hardly knew who to trust anymore, after Walsingham's disclosure about Kit.

She walked through the larger room, and secrets seemed to spin themselves out in corners. Guliet opened the door and followed her out, urgently whispering: "The Anchor, my lady. Tonight. We shall meet at the tavern."

He stepped inside, and Alice was left alone.

The sky had turned to grey mist and the air felt pregnant with rain. Blackbirds pecked in the grass of the spacious lawn.

She walked to the post where her horse was reined, and noticed Walsingham watching from the window. He disappeared from the window, only to walk out the front door towards her. Her horse stamped impatiently as the spymaster watched her take the reins from the post.

"I have further thoughts. We shall go to court, my lady. Elizabeth will be wont to meet with you."

Alice held the reins in her hand. The horse snuffled for a bit of sugar, and she patted his nose. Walsingham stepped forward and his long, lean fingers deftly grabbed the reins and tied them again to the post.

"There is a banquet at St. James Palace. In a fortnight we alight for court."

"And if I say…Nay?"

He leaned back observing her, inviting a vague terror as he silently stood there with the misty air between them.

"There is Topcliffe to deal with, lady. I dare say he is not as welcoming as I."

He turned and strode into his manor, and all that Alice could think of was chicken bones and burning offal.

Chapter 34

Light filled the windows of the Mermaid Tavern, casting brightness into shadows outside. Pulling open the heavy pine doors, Alice entered the tavern. Kit, Aaron, and Guliet sat at a far table in a corner.

Alice sat next to Kit. "I feel as though I've truly entered the theatre with a performance such as that," she said.

Aaron stood and bowed deeply. "My lovely, you have. Is not she a sweet chuck, Guliet?"

"Aye. She 'tis. But betrothed to Marlowe she is. Pity."

"But how did Walsingham not notice you, Aaron?" Alice said.

"He knows only my outline, not the face. He does not trouble himself with things that he need not look closely at. And look, are not Guliet and I doubles? He is my twin." He grasped Guliet around the shoulders.

Alice carefully studied the pair. Indeed, they did resemble each other with an uncanny likeness – the same curly hair, the same dimple.

"As you and Master Marlowe, Alice."

Kit smiled.

"Speaketh your mind now Alice," Kit said. "did Walsingham not lure and bait you?"

"Yes. He did. I was afraid for my life."

"Did he not stand at the fire during his famous dismissal of ye? The beard of that man must be tarnished in soot with all the dismissalings he doth do." Kit said.

"Aye," Aaron said. "And speaketh of his smoldering beard – his hair naught catch flame yet is a wonder."

"'His hair hath caught a flame," replied Guliet. That is why he wears it shorn under a Puritan cap."

The men laughed, and Alice allowed her eyes to graze over Kit. She felt his searching stare.

"Truth be told now, Alice. What say Walsingham?" He asked softly.

"He said enough."

"Sweet chuck, tellest me." He rubbed her palm with his thumb.

"He threatened me. Threatened me with Topcliffe." She put her hands to her throat, as if to ease a binding.

He gently took her hands from her throat. "'Tis all talk. Fear not."

She looked down at his hands. They were rough and brown. "He said we are to go to court.

Kit's eyes grew wide. "Court? When?"

"A fortnight."

"A fortnight." A shadow passed over his face and his eyes grew dim.

"What say you now?"

"'Tis naught to say. I shalt be there at court, Alice. Try not to read me."

Chapter 35

Alice had tossed and turned all night, knowing full well what Walsingham was up too. He wanted her to perform; he wanted her to be in Queen Elizabeth's graces. He was testing her to see if she had ever been in the English court, or any court.

Today would be a day of presentation. And acting.

He also had seen her with Kit. There could be no other explanation. Walsingham was planning his counter move against his own intelligencer. He was parlaying for position. Perhaps he would use this knowledge to get Kit to do what he wanted, or perhaps he was just collecting information.

They had left in a steel gray dawn. But finally the sun had spilled across the horizon and the day had broken open into rays of golden sunshine. Alice opened the carriage shade to catch the dew on the grass and dream of better things than where she was now.

Walsingham sat on the opposite seat watching her, as usual. She was plagued with an uneasy wit that wished to do nothing but counter-balance him and put him in his place. But she simply smiled at him and contented herself to look at the window.

The palace reared its head as they rounded a turn in the road, and the carriage drew nearer as if in a dream. They hit a rough spot and bumped along for a little stretch that was mostly rocks and potholes.

She lifted a handkerchief to her face, breathing in deeply its scent of lavender. As they approached the palace Alice saw the twin towers flanking either side of the great doors. Small figures appeared from the side of the palace and moved in a hurried pace towards the great doors.

She lay back on the cushions. Walsingham had his face turned from the palace, and was looking in the opposite direction. *What do you see?*

"What am I to do in this place?" she said.

"*Do,* lady?" He let the words waft weightless in the air, to evaporate like the morning dew.

"You threatened me with Topcliffe."

The smile that spread across his pockmarked face did not touch his eyes. Alice wondered if *anything* touched his eyes. His soul, if he had a soul. Shrewdness and aversion were his game, and now she had been caught up in it.

The wheel hit an unusually large bump and the carriage jolted and rocked from side to side. Alice bumped her head against the side and tried to regain composure by smoothing her silk gown. She clenched the cloth of the gown as her thoughts swam and the dizziness subsided, leaving her with the sick residue of oncoming headache.

"We are wont to dismount here." Walsingham smiled as he held the door open for her.

She stepped down from the carriage and a hand instantly appeared holding hers, helping her descend. The hand taker was dressed in green velvet trimmed with brocade. He smelled faintly of rose and musk. His forehead was damp with moisture and a slash appeared alongside one of his cheeks and disappeared into his dark hair. He bowed before Walsingham.

"Our queen awaits ye sir."

Walsingham nodded and placed Alice's arm in between his, patting it as smiling attendants opened the doors, and they were admitted into the Great Hall. The doors closed behind them and they were subjected to a sumptuous banquet of the senses: the flickering light from hundreds of candles illuminating the silks and brocades of attendants, courtiers and ladies in waiting; the thick smell of musk and lavender on throbbing pulse points; the scent of roast duck and pork, sage and chervil; the rustling of silks and the languid movement of bodies dressed to display prestige and charm. Musicians coaxed melodious notes from their instruments; simple little quartets set to catch the court in a joyous mood. In the middle of the gathering sat the queen.

It was a magical stage and Alice held her breath.

All eyes turned towards them as the music stopped and a hush fell over the crowd.

"Ahhhh." Queen Elizabeth stood.

Her face was an impenetrable mask of white, and her eyes were richly brown and devouring. The gown matched her red hair which was gathered on top of her head and tressed with diamonds and rubies. Alice heard the woosh of her gown as she walked towards them.

Alice deeply courtsied. The queen regarded her quizzically.

"Ye know of the Duke of Valois, Lady?" She said this without a hint of malice, but as you would ask an old friend of some common matter.

"Yes, my queen."

The queen looked to the court. All eyes were still upon them. With a dismissive gesture of her hand, she waved them into animation again. "Get with your merriments."

This time the instruments sounded with more gusto. The bassoons leapt into a jig, the queen's favorite.

The queen smiled and turned towards Alice.

"I think," Alice said. "That the duke is much regarded amongst his people. The people of France love him, and are quite loyal. He is very concerned with the papacy, but order and harmony among the people are his main concern."

The queen sighed and looked towards the court. Her eyes roamed the faces that stood at various stations in the Great Hall. They pretended to dance and make quiet conversation, but they were trained to understand the undercurrents of their queen, and sense whatever that might mean to them. The ladies in waiting whispered behind their hands, and looked to the color of Alice's dress, and the way her hair shown in the light.

"This is information any intelligencer can give me." The queen put her finger under her chin and gazed at Alice. "I am wont to know how the man conducts himself."

Alice caught the eye of Walsingham. He had made his way to the corner with other members of the queen's Privy Council. She understood suddenly that this move had been choreographed long before the short meeting she had had with him. She thought again of Topcliffe, the queen's psychopathic executioner.

"Let me make myself clear, lady," The queen lay her finger on Alice's wrist, as if to feel her pulse point. Her heart beat faster, and the smell of musk burst through the air.

"Perchance ye understand...Now." The queen's eyes were always kind, but there was the solid rock of England behind them. "I would like to know of his appetites."

Alice's breath caught in her mouth and she laughed. Her eyes bounced over the musicians who now were merrily playing a minuet. To the right of the musicians stood a group of men – the poets. Poets in the queen's favor. She made out Kit in the small gathering. He had his arm around a beauty with glistening black hair. He did not look at her.

Alice watched him a moment. "He enjoys verse which speaks of satyrs, nymphs, and young folk. He delights when he and his entourage chase one another through the forest glen. There is much tanglement after the chase which results in rolling in the dew, and sighing...that is all my queen. Oh, and I almost forgot," Kit had his arm dangled carelessly over the woman's shoulder. His finger grazed slowly over the top of her bosom. "There is a device he uses, perchance a sheep's bladder?" She frowned, as if in remembrance. "That was all I knew of before I was dismissed from the chamber. There were many young boys."

The queen dropped her wrist. "As I suspected." She clapped her hands, and all eyes were riveted on her. "A dance." There was a roar of approval from the court. She took a few steps from Alice, and her ladies in waiting floated towards her. She suddenly turned.

"He does not like women?"

"No, my queen. Not at all."

The music spun around her and she was caught up in the throng of the smell of civet and rustling cloth. A young courtier took her hand lightly and bowed. She smiled and declined. The figures started dancing, and Kit stood at the tail end of the line of people with his dark haired beauty.

Chapter 36

She entered the tavern and found the men huddled in the corner drinking ale. Alice sat at the table.

Kit fiddled with a torn piece of parchment in front of him.

"It hath been decided that you should go with Aaron to converse with Baines." Kit said.

"Thanks for deciding for me."

"Please, I knowest the way to safety, lady. That is why I came with Kit to the residence of Walsingham." Aaron clearly wanted to diffuse the tension. He glanced from Alice to Kit. "And we don't trust Baines with ye."

"I've managed so far." Alice got up from her seat and ordered a pint of ale from the barmaid who drew the amber colored liquid from the keg. The barmaid had a large mole on her left cheek and was wearing a yellow scarf wrapped around her head. Alice thanked the woman and took the ale back to the table.

"You sent me to see Baines. By myself, as I recall." She sipped her ale.

Kit raised his eyebrows. "He grows most savage, dear heart. When he is trapped he will seek to tear at whatever binds him. He is not to be trusted. Especially with my most blessed." He held her hand under the table.

"Another game of yours Kit?" Alice's eyes were blazing.

Guliet and Aaron looked at one another.

"Game, Lady?," Kit said. "Perchance you can speak your mind on this matter? It is troubling you."

"Come, come Aaron. I see a gentleman we know. There, by the window. Sirrah! Sir Toby!" Guliet and Aaron stumbled over benches to reach a drunk who was mumbling to himself in a corner.

Kit's eyes did not leave her face as he smoothed her palm with his thumb.

"Naught is packed for you and Aaron. Perchance we should pack them now? It shall help your troubled mind."

"I doubt if packing the horses shall help my troubled mind. What do you want with me Kit? Why do you lead me on like this?"

"Lead you? Why art thou so untrusting of me?"

"You are a spy. You play doubles."

"I know right from wrong in matters of love, my dear heart. What has Sir Francis said to make thou so bereft?"

"He says you have a child with Mare. Mary."

He laughed so hard that everyone in the tavern turned to look. He bent over the table and whispered feverishly, "You believe the *spymaster*?"

"Who *should* I believe?" The ale was getting warm, and Alice drank down the last of it. She felt the warm glow spread through her innards.

"Aye." Kit turned to look around the room. Everyone had gone back to talking quietly amongst themselves. "The spymaster pits spy against spy. That is how it is played, Alice. You must keep above it. Sir Francis has possibly more to lose than I. He seeks the queen's favor."

"And you? What do you seek?"

"My love. My art. The two are one, Alice."

"Why should I believe you?"

He gazed at her, musing and still, and a silence fell between them like softly falling snow.

"'Tis not a matter of belief. 'Tis a matter of knowing. You know, Alice. I can feel that. The day in the garden. Remember, my love? I saw you standing in the window?"

212

"It wasn't a dream then."

"I held a flower for you. A flower through time. It 'twas not a shadow, 'twas the gift of knowing. What more can I say?"

"And of the dark haired woman at court?"

Kit looked away from her. "Thou may believe, or thou may not. 'Tis no matter. We must play this thing out, my love. There is naught else to do." He banged his fist on the table. "Hadeus!"

"Aye!," Aaron and Guliet helped the drunk to his feet. "We seek the service of all good things Sirrah, and this one in his cups!" The drunk belched and sat heavily upon the bench in front of him. With a great sigh he lay his head on the table and began to snore.

"Aaron, go with Alice to Baines. Guliet, I thank you for your service." Kit held out a handful of coins. Guliet shook his head.

"'Tis no need of that, Master Marlowe." He bowed deeply, then scratched his head. "On second thought, I shall take them in good stead."

Kit chuckled. "In the matter of money thou art not fickle clown. Go to! Walsingham will be waiting for ye. He will think ye 'ha fallen into a bush."

Guliet took the coins, and hugged Alice. "Lady, Godspeed you, and keep you from harm." He left. Alice looked after him.

"I would have never thought..."

"Nay. There is much you don't know Alice. 'Tis better that way. But ye know enough."

She turned on him. "How dare you say that! When I have done nothing but help you!"

"In matters of state—"

"State! I could care less about *state*."

Kit stood and fastened his cloak. "There is the matter of the play, lady, that I must attend to. I am obliged to keep my eyes and ears open. I am but a thread upon that gown."

She understood that he was referring to the dress that Queen Elizabeth wore in her portrait. Woven into the gown of *The Rainbow Portrait* were a multitude of ears and eyes, the very symbols of surveillance. Elizabeth could count on her innumerable intelligencers to protect her and her realm.

"You're more than a thread, more than a pawn," Alice whispered. "You are, will be, the greatest playwright that ever lived."

As if listening to a muted jest, Kit cocked his head and laughed. "Who shall grant me that favor. You, lady?" He smoothed his black hair. "If I, the playmaker am to write, I must be in the right. Aye, my Alice?"

She slapped him across the face. "Stop making puns! Shed this cloak of intelligencing, it will only get you killed!"

Aaron lightly touched her elbow. "Lady, we must go. The hour grows late."

Alice shook him off.

Kit touched his face where she had slapped him. "I am afraid that I have been woven too tight, my Lady. The thread that binds me through and through will unravel if 'tis pulled. I must protect England from her enemies."

"I'm tired of your riddles. Come, let's go, Aaron. I grow weary of this."

Kit's face grew dark and venomous, but after a few moments he softened. "Always the wretch upon the wheel I shall be with you, woman. Shalt you return to me?"

"I will think on it." She pulled her cloak around her.

He smiled weakly. "I need my Bellamira."

"If that's all you need, you're in trouble."

Aaron looked at Kit and shrugged his shoulders, then he and Alice walked from the tavern.

Kit ran a hand through his hair, and sat down at the table. He fiddled with the piece of parchment in front of him, taking a quill and a knife from a pocket on his side. He whittled the tip of the quill.

"Always the ending, Alice. You seek the end," he whispered to himself. "What of forever?" The room grew quiet, and he looked around him.

"Traitor." Someone hissed.

He left before the crowd turned on him.

Chapter 37

Outside the city center of London the wild countryside spilled before them. The cover of heavy darkness cloaked the land. Aaron chose a secret route through the thickest trees where there was a small lane, well-traveled, but hidden from view. He rode in front, and soon the reassuring clomp of hooves was the only sound they heard.

She pulled up beside him.

"How long before we reach Baines?"

"Half a night. Perchance more. We must make as much haste as we are able. Then we will rest for the remainder. Is that agreeable, Lady?"

She nodded her head, too tired for talk. The feeling of dread was overwhelming. She felt like a pawn herself, acting out some plot she no longer had any control over. As the gnawing pain of doubt seeped into her like venom, she distrusted herself and her feelings. She said nothing to Aaron and the silence between them lingered.

Aaron moved in his seat.

"Lady?"

"Please, call me Alice, Aaron. We are equals."

He laughed. "Ah! Two fools together, traveling. We are equal in foolery."

She looked at him. It was dark, but a bright moon illuminated him, turning him and his horse into an apparition of ghostly blue.

"I 'ha been searching for some time Alice. I am alone now. My family, friends…all gone."

"Gone?"

"I am a Jew, as you well know. The Inquisitors in Spain…laid waste to my people."

"I'm sorry." She glanced at him and saw him cringe. The painful thoughts of the past impeding on the present.

"Nay. Nay. 'Tis no time for sorrow, la—Alice. 'Tis no time. I will rot if I let the sorrow take me. Henceforth, I am a fool!" He chuckled loudly.

Alice said nothing.

The horses' plodding turned into muted thuds upon the deeply layered leaves. The trees were thicker and the night wind blew through the leaves.

"Mine own wife…and daughter. My daughter was all of three. Were killed."

He had pulled the hood of his cloak over his head.

"There is nothing for me to say," she said.

"Aye. There is naught to say, except we 'ha our own inquisitor here. In England. Whitgift has been using Baines as a pawn to set his trap."

"Aaron?"

"Aye?"

"What do you know about Kit? What is the truth?"

The path forked in the forest and they stopped at its juncture. The middle path was wide, but the two branching paths were narrow. Aaron lowered the hood of his cloak. Sharp moonlight landed on his face. Alice could see he had been crying.

The horses stood silently, waiting to be prodded on towards their destination. They nuzzled each other's noses, then bent down to sniff the leaves.

"If there is no merriment, if there is naught…misrule within the cruelty of the realm…Alice, we shall all perish. Kit understands the secret musings of people. He gives a certain hope. He knew I suffered and offered me a place as a player. He has been kind to our people."

She nodded, and wiped her nose with the back of her hand. The forest damp clung to her hair.

"Baines expects me by daylight."

"Yea. So he does. He expects you to lay the trap for Kit. We hath been watching his moves, and then he escaped us. And you found him." He motioned to his horse to head left, and they slipped quietly onto the narrow path.

They heard the jingling of bells and stopped their horses to listen. Three horsemen and two women passed them. Even in the moonlight Alice could see that their cloaks were made off a fine weave. They merely nodded in passing.

Alice wondered who they were and why they would travel by night.

"Surely they are escaping something. They are on the path towards London. No matter, travelers shall be scarce now."

After they passed, Aaron seemed to relax. He started humming, and then sung in a low voice:

Jean de Nivelle a trios enfants
Don't il y en a deux marchands,
L'autre escure la vaisselle

Alice rubbed her nose, then gathered the reins in front of her. "That song sounds familiar."

"Ah. Remember court, Alice? It is one of the queen's favorites."

She could not remember the queen's face when she had heard that song, she only remembered Kit watching his dark haired beauty. The melancholy song brought it all back to her. The court was perfumed in civet, that musky concoction that seemed to inspire the passions. The queen commanded dances: pavans and guillards, and clapped her hands when she was dissatisfied, which, seemed to be often. Her Italian musicians, those which she inherited from her father, looked up expectantly, seemingly never perturbed.

"The queen seemed unhappy with the courtesans and their dance." said Alice.

"The queen herself is a most excellent dancer. She is our Virgin Queen, a perfectionist in all things. She is rarely pleased...with anything, for that matter. You see," Aaron brought up his hand in a small flourish, as if to indicate the scene of the court that he was describing, "the queen seeks to keep everything in a state of perpetual unrest. In this she thinks she will find rest. But, we are still waiting." He shrugged. "Perchance, forever."

Chapter 38

The door to the house was open. Alice entered slowly, cautiously She walked into the spacious room. Baines lay with his head on the table. She walked to him. A cup of mead had spilled by his hand, and his fingers lay against the base of the cup. The mead had turned to honey, and a trail of ants crept from the floor to the table. They circled again and again in the sticky trail. Out of the corner of his mouth dribbled a line of spittle.

The smell was vile. Alice waved the flies away as she picked up a note which lay on the table. It was a copy of the Dutch Libel implicating Kit as the writer. Someone had written across the top. She squinted and read the line: *The dye has been cast.*

She let the note flutter to the ground and walked out the door.

***

They had said little on the way back to London. Aaron asked how far Baines had progressed in implicating Kit within the ensuing religious scandal and how she might stop him. Alice answered his questions with curt replies, and he soon gave up. He seemed hurt, but she didn't care. She didn't want to play the game anymore.

And there was always the matter of the play. Always the play. She thought of Bellamira, and how she had been cast in that role in more ways than one. She thought of Faustian bargains, and how the themes in Kit's writing had come back to visit his life in material form. They both had to choose between what was ethical and sane, and what was degraded and insane.

She let herself slip into a place that felt removed from her physical reality. Her mind went back to the stage where she had been lying. Like the opening of a womb to a new world previously unknown to an infant, only one floodlight had illuminated her prone body. *There are faces peering above me in masks...*

"Lady? Are you well?"

She felt the dream dissolve. "What? What is it?" She shifted in her seat and pulled her cloak tighter around her body.

"Baines, lady. Of what import to us is this matter?"

She shrugged, realizing Aaron had been speaking for some time. "He was dark and dangerous and lived in a poisonous place that got the better of him. He would have only entangled me further."

"But how do you know, lady?"

"Why are you calling me lady again?" She snapped.

"Pray pardon, Alice. But you seem...distant. It is a matter of distance and inequality I imagine."

"Please stop." She drew up the reins, and the horse snorted and threw his head back. She met his eyes, hoping the stationary placement of their bodies along the path would stop the endless motion of the movie of their own making – of the fluidity of their thoughts and actions.

"Listen to me, Aaron. There is nothing we can do. There are shades of entanglement, and the further you delve into intelligencing, into the device, the tighter the knot becomes."

"Is there nothing to report back then?"

"Of what can we report? Baines is dead."

"But who—"

"It does not matter. There is plot and counterplot. *Ad infinitum.*"

"I'm sure we can help untangle it, lady."

"I think not. No pun intended." She turned her horse towards the path again, decided against it, and again turned towards Aaron.

"Her majesty asked me about the Duke of Valois' appetites. Now the circulation of this information will circle around court. And who do you think will write about it?"

Aaron took off his cap and scratched his head. "Pamphlets will be made mocking the king, and people, scholars, if you will, will stop at Saint Paul's church yard looking for some merriment, picking up these pamphlets."

The horse stepped from side to side, and she pulled back on the reins. "Kit will write about it. He will use the information for his plays."

"Aye, perchance like Gaveston...in Edward the Second? Master Marlowe cares not for rules, he cares for misrule. He is master of that."

"Maybe. He finds rule within misrule. He exploits it, as the queen."

"The queen seeks the truth, lady."

"The truth," she said, "is as fleeting as the sun's ray. The truth cannot be captured in stone. It is as changing as women's fashion."

"Nay, lady, the truth *is* set in stone. It is there for the wise, and willing, to perceive."

"The truth is in the telling, Aaron. It is lost in the tale that is told. People will fashion it the way they choose, to their own benefit."

He was silent a moment. "You did not *lie* about the duke, Lady?"

"It is all in the perceiving of the tale, Aaron," She waved her hand in dismissal, turning her horse to face the trail. "At least I've given him something to write about."

As they rounded the hill towards the city they did not at first see London, but smelled it. There was a cloud hanging over the city. As they approached they realized that the cloud was concentrated around the tower, and they strained to make out where the fire originated.

They dug their heels into the sides of their horses and rode at a full gallop, following the plume of mushroom smoke drifting into the sky. They rode until the smoke stung their eyes and they heard the screams of the people.

People struggled with buckets of water as they made a human chain dipping the water from the Thames onto the licking flames. Many buckets were being utilized through the chain, but many people ran down to the river and dipped their single buckets in the water, bringing them back to dump them on the roaring flames. They did not realize that their frantic efforts were like a drop of water on the sun.

The horse reared back, and Alice watched the chaotic scene. Aaron pulled up alongside her.

"What say you, Alice. Is it what methinks?"

She could only stare dumbfounded. Heavy wooden timbers crashed to the ground, engulfed in flames. She thought of the tower card in the tarot. It was all exploding around them. The Rose Theatre was burning.

A group of skull-capped men stood apart from the commotion watching as the theatre burned. They had the look of the self-righteous—smug satisfaction lit their faces. They stood entranced, as if sitting in front of a sitting room fire.

Aaron rubbed his face and coughed. "Ah, Kit. What will ye do now?"

A street urchin ran by covered in grime carrying a bucket. He was an arm's length from the horses.

"Aye! Boy!" Aaron yelled, "What burns?"

The boy paused, "The Anchor. The tavern there." He stood with his wild hair sticking up all over his head.

"Not the Rose Theatre?" Alice said.

"Nay. The Puritans say 'tis the will of god to demolish this unholy of holy places. The play place of the filthy playmakers. But I know better." He grinned and took off running, water splashing his legs.

Aaron raised his fist to the sky and looked upwards. "Ah! Thank holy heaven, Alice! The play continues." He turned his horse to walk along the river. Alice followed.

The streets were full of people moving towards the fire. Alice had a feeling of trepidation as they moved against the crowd, as if they were making their way towards the next fiasco. *Surely Kit would have heard of the fire?*

They continued down the cobbles of Bishops Gate until the land narrowed into Norton Fulgate, the place of the theatre people. Black and white timber-framed houses crowded each other on either side of the narrow street, making the passage dark and dismal. A casement window opened from above, and Alice quickly side-stepped the horse to avoid being doused in excrement. The woman pulled the chamber pot back inside the window.

"Thou art quick." Aaron nodded.

Con-men and pick-pockets surveyed them with narrowed eyes as they walked past. Their dirty faces matched their soiled clothes.

On the east side of London where the poor lived, clothing regulations were strictly enforced for class distinction. The poor shuffled by in woolens and leather, while the slightly richer free men and women wore garments that imitated those of the rich.

A woman in a yellow silk dress stood inside a door-frame watching as they passed. Her black hair was piled high on her head, and she had a painted white face with red lips.

"You would be looking for Kit?" She called out.

"Yea," Aaron turned towards her. "What of it?"

"He's not here."

"Where is he?"

She shrugged and turned her head, waiting for a customer.

They stopped in front of the black and white timber frame that Kit and Thomas shared. Aaron roped the horses in front of a trough of water. The door was not bolted; she pushed it open.

The place was cold and damp. There had been no fire for some time. She walked to the table. A pewter plate with encrusted gravy lay there.

"Kit?" The shuffling, muted conversations and clip-clop of horses hooves outside the house was the only sound she could discern. Aaron suddenly grabbed her arm, "Listen!" he whispered urgently.

He took the stairs by twos, and Alice followed, wondering what had provoked him. They entered the bedroom. Tom lay on the bed facing the wall, with his limbs splayed at unnatural angles.

"Tom!" She ran to him, turning his head towards her. His face was red and puffy, but he blinked his eyes. Flies buzzed around his body. The place smelled of urine, excrement, and death.

"Flinging coppses." Aaron swore under his breath, and flung the casement window open. A breeze blew in, whisking away the tang of the pungency.

"He's been tortured. *Strappado*." Aaron sat on the edge of the bed.

Her face turned white as she cradled his head. "Get him some water, Aaron. He's dying of dehydration."

"Lady?"

She realized he would not know the word dehydration; it hadn't been invented yet.

"Get him some water!" She shrieked.

He ran down the stairs and returned with a basin of water and a goblet. She took a section of the sheet, dipped it in the water, and wiped his hot grimy face. He blinked up at her.

"Shh...shh." She lifted the goblet to his lips, and trickled the water into his mouth. His throat constricted, and then he drank greedily.

He gasped and sputtered, trying to grab her arm but his elbow was dislocated. He began to cry, and Alice rocked him.

"Mare," Alice whispered through his hair. "Can you find Mare, Aaron? Tell her—no matter, she will know what has happened."

Aaron silently slipped from the room. Alice rocked Thomas for a long while. The shadows shifted in the room, and the sky became a steel gray. The carefree sounds of children playing in the street drifted through the air.

Thomas struggled to speak and Alice gave him sips of water.

"Kit is gone." He rasped. "Sir Thomas Walsingham's. Privy Council is on him. Found papers," He winced. "In mine."

"Papers." Alice said. She looked up towards the window. Swallows flew by catching the evening bugs. Predator and prey.

Twilight had come.

Chapter 39

Under the cover of night, Aaron and Alice set off towards Scadbury, home of Thomas Walsingham, Sir Francis's cousin. Alice was still robed in the travel dress she had worn for the queen's visit, now torn and soiled. Her hair was matted, and she had not bathed in a week. The stench of her body repulsed her.

Aaron did not seem to mind as they set off. He rode high on his horse and took command of the way along brooks and the little lanes that had been in use since the time of the Celts. Tiny fireflies pricked the darkness, dancing along beside them and up ahead of the lane. Twice she saw movement in the bushes.

"'Tis the old ones. Or vagabonds. Cony catchers." He said. "Perchance they will stop a rider and ask for money," he looked at her. "and sometimes more."

Alice shuddered to think of being pulled off the horse, raped, and pick-pocketed.

"They know me, Alice." He puffed out his chest. "You are safe with me, lady."

"How so?"

"I 'ha paid the way to travel this trail."

"I would rather believe in fairies, Aaron."

"Nay, they art large, that folk. They may beguile ye, and lead you astray."

***

The lane branched off and then became narrow as they made their way towards Scadbury. Aaron said that they were close, but trees crowded on either side, shielding the manor from their eyes. Alice finally caught a glimpse of it. Rising from the trees, three towers proclaimed their dominance to the sky. The horses stood, pawing at the earth while they looked at the large manor. Alice wiped a grimey hand across her brow.

"Is that a moat, Aaron?"

"'Tis. Truly we are amongst nobles." He urged his horse forward.

Lights twinkled in the glass as they approached, and a shadow moved in front of a window. Alice quickly moved forward and motioned for Aaron to stop.

"Are we in danger? "

"Nay, Alice. Ye shall see."

They dismounted, secured their horses, and stood in front of the moat waiting for the bridge to be lowered. Gardens surrounded the estate, and the air smelled of sweet rose.

The bridge was slowly lowered. They walked across and were met at the imposing wooden doors by a man dressed in a plain jerkin and trousers. He nodded and led them into the interior. The front opened into a vast hall ensconced with tapestries and paintings. Candles and torches lined the walls and the floor was an alabaster marble with a center pattern of a rose, a lion and a boar.

The heard echoing footsteps. Alice watched as Kit walked towards them down a long hall with another man. The early morning sun backlit them from a hall window, lining the figures in light. The man was taller than Kit, and they walked easily together.

Sir Thomas Walsingham bowed before them. Kit took her hand and brushed his lips lightly against it. The featheriness of his kiss reminded her of the quill and the night spent in bed professing secrets and love. She took a sharp intake of breath as the electricity again ran down her spine.

"My mistress who art master of my passions, Thomas. Alice."

It was not clear to her if he was speaking of her or of Thomas. Kit's eyes burned into hers as riddles and spider's webs weaved together in her chest, creating a tight knot.

"Lady, I have heard wondrous tales of your intelligence and beauty. I must say I can certainly vouch for the beauty that Kit spoke of." He bowed slightly before her.

"And here 'tis our clown, one Hadeus." Kit said.

"Clown, care you to sup? There are ample provisions in our kitchen. The servants have taken leave to dine. I dare say you look in need of refreshment." Thomas said.

"Aye, sir. I shall water and bed our horses. And, if I be so bold, to bathe, sir? I am afraid the scent of offal is upon us from the long journey." Hadeus held his nose.

Thomas laughed. "Merriment is refreshing, clown, and the smell of one so bold should be clean. Take care and find old Harry. He shall be in the stable now, and will lead you to clean and care for horse, stave your hunger, and perchance find some nightly merriment."

Aaron bowed deeply and doffed his cap. Leaving, he walked the long hall where Kit and Sir Thomas had come.

"And you, fair Alice? You look weary. Perchance you would care to bathe before we sup?" Thomas said.

"Sir, if I may be so bold. I must speak with Kit alone, I—"

"Come, come, Alice. You are weary. It is written on your face. Bathe and then we shall sup. Perchance we shall walk in the garden. It has been said that my gardens are the finest in Kent." He placed his hand on the small of her back, leading her towards the stairs. "One of the women shall help with your bath."

Alice moved from his hand. "But sir, it is of the gravest importance that I speak with Kit. He is in grave dan—"

"Soft, lady, soft." He held a finger to his lips. "If there is something to say, you may say it to both Kit and I. We are one in the same mind. Is not that true, sweet heart." He ran his hand along Kit's arm.

Kit blushed. Rubbed the back of his neck. "'Tis true, Tom. But Alice has come riding hard a long way. 'Tis nothing to listen to a few words."

Thomas looked towards the hall window, lost in thought. The sun had gone behind a cloud, and the hall had turned a somber gray. "A few words. Lady, I know of the danger you speak of. All of London is being bitten by the plague. Kit is here for his protection. He seeks solace to write and replenish his wit."

The flush of anger rose to Alice's voice, molding the words strong and clear: "Sir Thomas, the plague is not the disease that I speak of. The disease I speak of, this plague, is being propagated by the very church masters of which Elizabeth keeps council, she—"

"Peace!" Thomas gripped her arm. Alice cried out and Kit pushed Thomas away from her.

"What say you! She seeks to protect me, Tom, and you treat her this way?"

Thomas held up his hand as a gesture of appeasement, then ran it through his hair. "I pray your forgiveness, fair Alice. I am not of right mind...as of late. I desire fair action and fair speech within my house. We must take our discussion at dinner, where we will all be refreshed and of like mind. Come, Kit."

Kit briefly met her eyes. He and Thomas walked past the stairs to the great room of the house while she began her long climb up the stairs to the upper reaches of Sir Thomas's dwelling.

***

The bath left her feeling refreshed. She was surprised at how at ease she felt being scrubbed and dried by Celeste, a

230

Frenchwoman who spoke little English. Alice used hand gestures to make herself understood. Despite the language barrier, Celeste seemed to understand the tension and pressure that Alice was feeling.

She helped Alice into a fresh chemise of cool smelling cotton, then a farthingale that fit like a hoop along her waist. A corset which lifted her breasts was secured around her waist. Celeste then tied a petticoat dotted with stars and moons—a delicately patterned luminescent needlework around the ensemble. Then came an overskirt which was a deep purple velvet and cut low at the bosom. Celeste handed her a bottle of lavender cologne and attempted to place a feathered hat on her head. Alice brushed it aside.

"No! I feel like a stuffed cabbage as it is, Celeste."

"Eh? *Cabbage*? What is?" Celeste rhymed the word with mirage.

Alice shook her head, tugging on the dress. "Too hard to explain, this dish."

"Ah. *Oui*. Go?" Celeste pointed towards the door.

"I suppose we are finished with all of this nonsense." Alice held a mirror and examined her face. Nothing had changed. The image presented her with no solution to the problems at hand. The dirt form the road had been washed off, leaving her with a fresh facade to tackle the dirty problems on the floor below. She wondered about the growing animosity between her and Sir Thomas Walsingham. Would she soon be wanted at dinner? She looked towards the window. The sun was still high in the sky. Too early for dinner.

They began their long descent down the stairs, Alice with skirts gathered in one hand, the other hand on the stairrail. When she reached the bottom of the stairs, Alice wondered where Kit must be. Laughter erupted from the kitchen, and she walked towards the jubilant noise. Aaron and a man she had not previously met sat at the servant's table drinking ale.

Aaron held his cup towards her in a toast. "My fair Alice. Refreshed and feeling fond of the poet that Sir

Thomas does fancy?" He chuckled and held his drink high, toasting her. "You're a sight better than Sir Tom, I might say. This is Hal, the cook and bright woodsman. Bringing us warmth of the wood. And ale. Aye, Hal."

"Oh, aye. A jack of all trades be I."

Aaron looked at Celeste standing behind Alice. He let out a low whistle. "Marry, here's a well made bed," He stood and bowed deeply, doffing his cap. "Who is this beauty of the manor?

"This is Celeste, Hadeus."

Celeste curtsied.

"Ah, celestial heavenly Celeste. I am enraptured." Wide eyed, he took a sip of ale.

" Shall I tell her your *real* name? asked Alice.

"She shalt find out soon enough. Trimmed as a wick am I. A pocketful of poking Sabbath." He winked at Celeste, and she smiled broadly with a blank look upon her face. He frowned, searching her face for an understanding of his jest. "She is deaf or knows not a lick of English."

Hal chuckled.

"Nay, Hadeus. She is French born and bred. She knows little of our language." said Alice.

Celeste smiled. "Born and bred a Frenchwoman, 'tis true. But of your language? Of this I know of the Jews and their Sabbath, one Aaron. The Sabbath is as long and wide as the course of the river Thames through the fertile valley. Sustain many a Jew it does." Her eyes sparked as she looked at him slyly.

"Aye, Celeste, touché to you. You have rapt me soundly. Come sit, join our merriment. A bit of good wine? We have uncorked the best the master has in store."

"You have earned it," began Hal. "Celeste and I have heard of your coming from Sir Tom. We have played the jest and the fool for you, fool," He nodded towards Alice. "Pray pardon, my Lady, but it couldn't be helped. We had no idea what your suit and countenance would bring."

"I see. But what of our host? Truly, what does he think of us?" Alice said.

Hal rose from the table and went to the latticed window facing the garden. He held his hands behind his back. "Truly? Sir Tom is a good man." He looked out upon the garden, his face turned away from the others. Alice could not read him.

"Tut, Alice," Aaron chided. "Let us not fret about the man that Sir Thomas is, may be, or may become. Let us relax in our merriment."

"I have come to warn Kit, Aaron. You know that."

"Master Marlowe knows of the gravity of the situation, lady. He has little choice in the matter but to plan his escape." Hal said.

"Escape. For what length of time?"

Hal and Celeste looked at one another.

"Lady," Hal said softly. "Sir Tom is fond of Master Marlowe. He seeks to preserve him from tanglements of the court. It is thought that he should disappear from England. Forever."

"Who will decide this?" Alice said.

"It is being decided now." said Hal. "In the garden."

A hush fell over the conversation and Alice walked to the window where Hal stood looking over the garden. Late afternoon bees buzzed by. Kit and Sir Thomas stood at the far end of the garden by the outer wall. Kit listened while Sir Thomas spoke earnestly, gesticulating. He looks resigned, thought Alice.

"I will not see him again." said Alice. "We have come for naught, Aaron. Except as interesting supper conversation, our purpose here has ended."

"Sir Tom will give you a few moments with Master Marlowe. He won't begrudge ye that." said Hal.

"Oh, aye," said Celeste. "And how will you manage to pry him from his poet? The man is clung to him as to a barnacle on a ship," Celeste rose from the table. "Not to fear Alice. I shall bait him with distracting deserts and things he does fancy."

Hal frowned. "Unwholesome delicacies."

"Nay. Enchanted." said Celeste.

"Pray tell!" said Aaron.

Celeste playfully cuffed him and held her hand towards Hal. "Come, there are much preparations to be made."

"Aye. Let us ready to sup." Hal took her hand.

Alice turned from the window. "I to the garden to see Kit."

Chapter 40

Alice was jealous of the trio that made their way to the kitchen to plan the large going away dinner for Kit. She had no desire to once again haggle for Kit's ear with Sir Thomas. According to Celeste, Sir Thomas had spared no expense for his friend's last supper before his exile. There was even special wine from France, from one Sir Bandicoot. He made regular trips to the Alsace region in search of fine wine for his noble friends and himself.

She made her way around the tall stone wall enclosing tthe garden. In the center of the garden there stood a large, very masculine statue of Jupiter. Ganymede, his spritely servant, sat upon his knee. She ran her hand along the wall, eyeing the statue and what lay behind it. Coming across an over-grown boxwood she heard the murmur of voices. Convinced that they had not heard or seen her approach, Alice crept closer. The insistent plea of Sir Thomas could be heard beyond the boxwood.

"—stay in France first, dear heart; then, to Italy, one Padua; then, Venice. You shall be among our friends there. I have told them of your coming."

"Tom, I cannot stomach it. Being a ghost, traveling among the shadows. When will I return?"

"To be as Ovid, exiled and free. Think on it, Kit!"

"'Tis not a thought that comforts, Tom."

There was a silence. The soft breath of the wind rustled the tree leaves above.

"We must wait for the silence of Whitgift, dear heart."

Alice muffled a sneeze as Sir Thomas held himself erect, listening. It was at that moment she caught a glimpse of two men entering the far end of the garden. Sir Thomas turned towards the men, and Alice stepped again behind the boxwood.

"Holla! Here comes the pair. One Poley and one Skeres.

Alice recognized the names. Robert Poley and Nicholas Skeres: regular members in the London underground, they peddled their services as mercenaries and spies.

Peering through her dense coverage, she watched them stop in front of Kit and Sir Thomas. Their appearances didn't seem to match their reputations. Skeres had a soft face, appearing almost feminine, and Poley had a lopsided grin that stretched across his face in an almost comical way. They were both dressed as members of the upper class. Poley and his grin in green velvet, and Skeres and his gentle face surrounded by lace.

Both men glanced around the garden, wary.

Poley moved out of view and spoke in a low voice. The voice was carved and calculating, it clearly had made secret plans before, and it knew the correct polish and veneer to apply.

Kit's eyes widened and then he looked at the ground, as if searching for a way out of the situation. She had seen him look this way before. When he was working on his plays, his eyes traveled inward, watching a scene in his mind she could not see, but which was simply played out for him. His job was to get it all down. The quill scurried across paper, scratching its way along like a mad chicken. The inkpot would be empty in an hour's time. She had sat on the bed, and watched, and dreamed the dream of knowing what had already happened.

The group moved slightly towards her and she pressed her back against the wall. A branch dragged across her dress, tearing it. She reached to unhook the branch at the precise moment the group moved past her. She stood stock still, gripping thorns.

The group drifted towards the great house, and Alice turned her hand over. In the center was a puncture mark dripping with blood.

***

She gazed at the horizon where sea met sky and clutched something dark and roughly woolen in her hands. Putting the garment to her face she breathed deep. The smell of memory collided with the deep force of regret.

At the edge of her vision a small figure stood waiting.

Twisting her head away from the figure, she walked in the opposite direction on the wharf. The sun appeared from under a cloud and the heat of it beat down on her head and the backs of her arms. She could feel the eyes of the figure burn into her skin as the mists begin to gather...

She awoke thrashing with the bedclothes twisted around her and her face turned towards the sun. The window had not yet been opened, and the room was hot and stuffy.

Alice pulled the wet hair from her mouth and sat up in bed. The sound of voices drifted up the stairs. A harsh burst of laughter erupted and she heard hurried footsteps on the stairs. Celeste knocked and entered.

She frowned. "Mistress, you look like apple rot. Let us get you dressed."

Alice laughed. "Celeste, let the men go about their business. I'm not welcome there." She reclined on the bed.

"Ah, *contraire*, Alice. They have been asking of you. And supper is almost served, and the wine is being poured."

"Wine? Being poured? I hope there is a keg of it to get them all drunk so Kit and I can escape." She sat on the edge of the bed.

"Tut, Alice. It shall all soon be played." Celeste tugged on the back strings of the bodice.

"I wish it were but a dream."

Alice pulled her dress over her chemise, and Celeste helped with the buttons in the back. She then arranged her hair into a neat chignon.

They descended the stairs and a cloud of trepidation fell over her. She lay her hand on Celeste's arm.

"Soft," she whispered. "Do you hear them speak?"

"Nay. 'Tis a matter of serious import. They speak in hushed tones."

"I cannot go through with this, Celeste. My heart is begun to stop." Alice sat on the middle stair.

"Mistress," Celeste hissed. "Come! This shall be the best performance for the player in you. If you can play this, you shall become rich in London. Hail queen boy!" Celeste tugged on her arm, and Alice reluctantly stood up.

The rest of the house was still as they made their way to the dining hall. As they entered no kind eyes looked upon her. A hush fell in the conversation. Sir Thomas stood, and the rest of the guests followed suit.

"Alice. Welcome to our table. We have been waiting in great anticipation of your beauty and wit." He nodded and pulled out a chair for her.

"Sir Thomas, you are kind. I thank you and will reappear momentarily with the wine. Celeste has asked for my help."

He frowned as Celeste waited by the door. She curtsied and smiled.

"A lady such as yourself should not be asked to serve with the kitchen help. You are my guest and should appear as such."

"Appearances, Sir Thomas are…," her words dragged off as the men waited to hear what she would say. Kit looked at her questioningly. A smile played at the corners of his mouth. She wanted to say that appearances are not what they seem, but then he might begin to suspect her of something deviant. Suspicion was the last thing she wanted.

"Beg your pardon," she said. "The appearance of wine at dinner shall mark the renewal of our bonds with Master Marlowe. He is wont to leave, but—"

"Kit is not leaving. Pray tell, Alice, what is on your mind?
" As he abruptly cut her off, she abruptly sat. The other guests followed.

Celeste quietly left the room.

Feeling defeated, Alice stared at a pitcher of water on the table. There was nothing left to do but play her part. Her eyes met Kit's. *Is this our final act?* She looked for an answer in his eyes but there was none.

It was Poley who finally spoke.

"The player wench. How now? We hear thou shalt play the part of Bellamira." His lopsided grin stretched across his face.

"Sir, 'tis true. I shall." She felt a chill creep over her at his offhand words, realizing he was trying to demean her by using the common terms of wench and thou.

"Alice will tend to the monies of the play. She has been instructed to receive them from our Lord Admiral." Kit said.

Skeres soft eyes fell upon her. "Monies? To the wench? This has not been done before, Marlowe."

"I have spoken to the man and he wishes it to be so." Kit said.

Thomas leaned back in his chair. "Dear heart…we need the monies for your stay abroad."

Kit swallowed, lay his hands on the table. Blue ink stains colored the tips of his fingers. The smell of quail drifted through the air and Alice felt her stomach rumble.

Celeste entered silently through the doorway with a jug of wine and glasses.

"Pray tell, Tom, how long shall this be?"

"And how long shall we bear Whitgift? 'Tis too soon to tell the tale." said Thomas.

"Whitgift has the queen at his knee, he does." Poley said.

Skeres chuckled. "Aye. But there it stops." He took a sip of the wine that Celeste had set before him.

Alice looked quickly at Celeste and she caught her eye, giving a quick wink.

Sir Thomas sighed and looked long at Kit. "'Tis true. She plays her spymaster and her church warden well. It is her suit."

The vision of the queen holding the two cards of emperor and devil danced in Alice's head. She could clearly see the red hair and brown eyes shining, as before a fire. The tarot cards had been cast.

Alice shook her head, dislodging the thought. "But what of me, Kit? How shall I find you?"

He smiled. "My chuck, you shall —"

"He shall not be found!" Sir Thomas snapped.

Alice jumped, startled by the venom in his voice.

"Tom, I—"

Thomas lay a finger to his lips and bent over the table. "Whitgift has had her followed. He knows who she is. None of the players know of these doings. Of our plan. They believe Kit shall get the monies. What to do? Give me the monies, love."

Kit looked at Alice. "What say you?"

"They will not know me as queen boy."

Kit smiled. "Aye. The truth is in the telling, Tom. She shall be a woman, but thought to be a boy."

Thomas frowned and sipped his wine. "You shan't stay queen boy for long with such a bosom."

Skeres and Poley chuckled.

"Sir, I shall be bound."

Kit laughed. "And bound to me ye shall come."

"Wine, sir?" Celeste held the bottle aloft, hovering above Thomas's cup.

"There shall be no drama of comings or goings here. Love, as your patron, I tell you—"

"Tell me naught, Tom. The play is to be finished. I must see to it. And Alice is the best one to procure the monies. She is a skilled conjurer."

Sir Tom rubbed his eyes. "Grammercy, Celeste, yes, more wine."

"The puzzle of your disappearance, my dearest playmaker, has been put together wisely. 'Tis no room for error. Every piece is there. And accounted for. Come!" He clapped his hands, and Aaron stuck his head through the door. His jester's hat sliding sideways upon his head. "To eat!"

***

Steam rose from the rosemary-scented quail when Celeste cut into the bird and began to serve. The mist briefly obscured Alice's view of Kit across the table and when it cleared he was looking at her. She touched his leg with her foot and he smiled. He picked up his bird and took a bite.

"Celeste, the bird is succulent. My praise to the cook so faire." Kit said.

"Gramercy, Master Marlowe. I aim to have you savor this last meal with us." Celeste frowned. "Beg pardon, Sir Thomas. 'Tis not my place."

"The truth is well spoken, Celeste. Fear not." Thomas took a bite. "My regards also to the faire Celeste."

Celeste refilled his wine glass, and Skeres and Poley held up theirs. She filled their glasses to the brim.

"Tom, how shall it be played?" said Kit.

"Have I not writ the final act of your disappearance? I have learned well."

"The Lord Admiral will be expecting the monies from myself," said Kit. "I have instructed our player, faire Alice as Bellamira, to take them in my stead. He will be on the lookout for queen boy."

"He will be on the lookout for Poley. As *I have* instructed, dear heart."

"Nay, the Lord Admiral will be seeking Bellamira, for I—"

"Nay!" Thomas glared at Kit, his eyes like knives glittering steel. "Poley is in my service. He does what I am wont for him to do. Let me make it clear to you, my most dear, that the queen has given you a pardon. If not for that, you would be pulled apart by Topcliffe. In pieces." Sir Thomas ripped the leg from the thigh of a quail. As the bones snapped, Kit shuddered.

"It is a grave mistake to be an atheist, love." said Sir Thomas, biting into the quail leg.

"I am a free thinker. A scholar. No one owns me, Tom. No one." Kit ran his hands through his hair and met Thomas's eyes with a level stare.

"Sir Tom," said Alice, "Can we not divide the sum between us? Kit is wont for monies abroad. When he arrives in France he shall be penniless."

"I see you need not worry of Topcliffe. You are pulled apart by this woman." Thomas threw his fork on his plate and stood. "I retire to the great room." He bowed slightly and walked from the room.

All eyes followed his receding back.

"There is the problem of the death." Skeres said softly. He served the cod Hal had lain on the table. His movements were slow and thorough, and as he worked it seemed as if he had become entranced. Skeres stopped, and rested his hands on the table. He slumped forward.

Poley looked at him quizzically, then pulled a knife from the quail and turned towards Alice. She screamed and jumped from her seat as he looked at her, blinking hard. His eyes moved to the knife in his hand as he tried to raise his arm. The knife fell from his fingers and he slumped to the floor.

"My heart is stopped."

Alice lay a hand on her chest as Kit stood behind her, his hands on her shoulders.

Celeste and Aaron entered the room. Celeste calmly nodded as she surveyed the scene and placed the jug of wine on the table.

"See here, Hadeus. As I've said. To the mark they fall. As soon as the cod was placed before them."

"Mark? Codpiece on that. Thou knows very well that you were worried of them not falling. And here is the wine!" He grabbed the wine and danced a jig, pretending to spill the wine, and then not.

"Soft, thou loud limbeck of mirth." said Kit. "What of Sir Tom?"

"Dead asleep. And snoring like thunder." said Aaron.

They stared at one another and laughed, intensely feeling their freedom.

"For the merriment," cried Aaron. He grabbed Celeste and kissed her on the cheek.

"Tut." She blushed and tried to push him away as he held tighter.

"Come quick, gather." said Kit. They huddled around the table as he leaned forward. "The time is now to make our mark. I must leave for a ship bound for France."

"Aye," said Aaron, serious now. "Of when, sir?"

"Soon. In the dead of night I must leave for fear of one knowing my face."

Alice well knew the scenario that was about to ensue. Kit would leave for a ship anchored in Deptford where he would sail to a distant location. Most scholars thought that France was his first destination.

"And of the sleeping?" said Alice. "When shall the tired trio awake?"

"They shan't awake 'till late morn. If that." Celeste said. "And have no memory of the night's events. But we shall move them to their beds. *To keep with the mystery.*"

The room was becoming dark, encased in shadows. Alice got up to fetch a candle from the side board. She lit the candle with a match from the board and placed it on the table. Their faces were illuminated by its flickering light.

"Tis dark now," Kit said. "We must use it wisely to move into the night concealed. The ship will anchor in Deptford soon, and I must make way to Eleanor Bull's."

"Will not the trio turn on you now that you have deceived them?" said Celeste.

"Nay. The love of Sir Tom is strong, and the queen...she uses me well. I dare say Poley and Skeres would turn a quick knife if asked. As they will with the body of Penry."

"Penry." said Aaron.

"Aye, the one preacher. He is dead now as we speak," Kit looked around him when he heard a loud creak. "They will take the body and say 'tis me. A stab wound to the dead man's eye, and they shall say it is me. Whitgift shall have his proof. His sacrifice." Kit grimaced.

"But what of the plays." said Celeste. "You will not be stopped? Nay, say 'tis not so, Kit. You make the world laugh."

"I shall become as one with someone else."

"You will be a motley then?" Aaron frowned.

Kit looked at Aaron, a startled amazement flushing his face. He burst into laughter. "Fool, thank the heavens for such frivolity at this time in my life. Aye. A fool, a simple man I will be hidden in. *Shakspere*."

***

They looked at one another uneasily.

There was nothing left to do but to say their goodbyes.

It had begun to rain lightly, and Alice was not looking forward to riding back to London.

"I'm sorry for this, Alice. But if Sir Tom would have got the money, he would have say and sway where I kept myself."

She waved her hand in dismissal. "Peace. I'm gone. Don't forget what I've done for you." She turned to go and he grabbed her arm, his eyes becoming dark—burning into hers. "I shan't." He said, then softening, "In Deptford we meet?"

Alice nodded and escaped into the rain.

***

She rode hard through the night. The rain pelted her relentlessly but it cooled the horse as he galloped along the paths and roads leading in and out of the forest.

The day gleamed as the sun peeked over a ridge. Framed in dripping wet trees the fog rose from the meadow, heating the damp air. She pulled on the rains and stood silent in the clearing. A magpie flew in the tree next to her and she tried to recall the rhyme that foretold your fate according to the number of magpies seen together. She anxiously looked for another magpie, and when one did not appear, she wondered if this was a bad omen. The bird remained solitary. dropping at first down to the grass, pecking, then flying into a distant tree.

She had only stopped this once to give the horse a break from the fast pace of threading their way through the forest. He was a good steed, a consistent steed, one that had served her well, and she was utterly grateful when the city once again came into view.

She wound her way through the backside of London, smelling the refuse and sidestepping the sleeping beggars. Puddles filled the streets from the night's deluge.

As they picked their way through the streets, they heard the horns. It was barely discernible through the din of the streets but it became louder, more insistent as she approached the Rose. Then, the beat of the drums began, and it feltl ike an echo in the chamber of her heart as they drew closer to the theatre.

The back side of the Rose was crowded with people. The crowd had begun to form a loose line waiting to get into the theatre. A little boy with a pointed cap ran in front of the horse and she pulled back hard on the reins to avoid trampling him.

"Watch where you tread!" The woman jerked on the boy's arm, roughly pulling him behind her. She spit in Alice's direction.

The drumbeat was louder now, and she heard the crowd roaring up in laughter. It amazed her the way the audience became like a living thing, operating as a single organism. There were not individual faces in the crowd; the crowd was the individual face.

These people knew of the myths, legends—the romance that had shaped Britain. And they knew of the simple things that could make a laugh erupt from the gut. A deep belly laugh that would heal the most aching and steadfast of sorrows.

She pictured Richard Tarlton with his drum and tabor, blowing a tune to enchant the audience. Once the spell was cast, he would begin a jig. Not just any jig, but a jig that would tell a story. And in the middle of the story he would flip—completely backwards. The audience could never tell when, although they waited with anticipation for him to perform this stunt.

Making her way through the crowds, she dismounted the horse near the theatre. A girl stood nearby watching her and ran to her asking for a handout to tether her horse. Alice handed her the horse and a pence, quickly gathering her skirts about her as she walked to the Rose.

She hurried, realizing that the tabor was beginning to sound thin and the pounding of the drums less frequent. Like a hungry animal, the crowd howled and clapped, covering the music with their cheers.

The time was now.

She made her way through the opening of the Rose as the crowds in the galleys stood along with the groundlings and proclaimed their enthusiasm for the first actor who appeared onstage. The audience stamped and clapped, drowning out the actor on stage who laughed and held his hand to his head in mock disbelief, waiting for the crowd to become quiet. Alice used this moment to make her way to tiring house.

No one noticed as she slipped around back and up the stairs, making her way to a small room illuminated by a single candle. A trunk full of costumes and attire was situated in the corner and she walked towards it. Hearing sounds of intimacy she looked sharply to her left. Two younger men stood locked in a naked embrace.

Alice grabbed a gown from the hook and threw it at them. Blushing, she coughed into her hand and looked away.

"Bellamira?" One of the young men nervously twisted a red cap around his head while holding the gown about him. His companion had pulled on his pants and was pulling his shirt over his head.

"The very one." said Alice. "And unless you are playing Katherine, I'd advise to put on your pants."

"I am Katherine." he said.

"Oh. Then what of the red cap?"

"Naught." He threw it down. "Will you say anything to the Lord Admiral, lady?"

Alice pulled the gown from the trunk and undressed behind a screen. "Nay. What is there to tell? Affection between two is the business of the two embraced."

She emerged and combed her hair. The makeup pot lay next to a mirror on the wall. She applied the heavy white paint to her face, cringing to know it was full of lead.

"Now, to the courtesan." She outlined her eyes with black kohl and pulled her hair on top of her head, then twisted a necklace of pearls into her hair. Stepping back from the mirror she surveyed her work.

"What say you?" she said.

"Monstrous beauty, lady. You are a charmed mirror." The lad who played Katherine bowed before her.

As the words spilled from his mouth she began to have a vision. A hall of mirrors stood before her and she was reflected in each one as far as her eye could see. Dizzy, she placed her hand to her head.

"Lady? Art though ill?"

She shook her head as the heat crept up the back of her neck and to her face. "Nay. Tired is all. I've been riding hard."

Richard Tarlton appeared at the top of the stair. He did a complete somersault before them and landed at their feet. Jumping up, he surveyed their faces.

"Hast thou seen Master Marlowe?" he asked.

"Master Marlowe is naught to be found." She gave him a hard look, knowing he was one of the privileged few who knew the situation.

Tarlton placed his hands on his hips and like a snake about to strike made himself larger. "Lads! Go to. There is naught here for nary of you."

"Nay, perchance not. But all of London is abuzz with the gossip of our missing playmaker." The lad who played Katherine nodded vigorously while his companion surveyed his nails.

Tarlton frowned. "Alice, I cannot perform the last scene and have asked Hadeus to perform in my stead."

"A lack of a playmaker and a clown does not bode us well," she said.

Aaron rushed up the stairs, a mask of fear covering his face. "Lady, " he said, out of breath, "It is not fortuitous for you to play today."

"Hadeus, why dost thou talk in puzzles?" She turned from the mirror.

"Tis my part!" The boy who was Katherine walked out on stage. The crowd whistled and cat-called.

"All will fall apart, lady."

She looked at him quizzically. "I am to play this part, as you know Hadeus. Then give our Lord Admiral some monies. The rest goes to Kit. I will meet him at Deptford before his ship is to sail to France. And then I go to Italy. We will be together then." She fingered the beads around her neck. "Shh. Listen. I am to go on stage in a moment." She held her finger to her lips.

Hadeus moved towards her. "Lady, if ye are too stay in this time—"

Alice shrugged him off with her hand. "I'm here on stage."

The crowd roared as she appeared. Standing in the middle of the stage she looked down at the groundlings jeering at her, some faces smiling in awe. The dirt and filth of the floor rushed to her nose and she stifled an urge to gag. Staring straight ahead and eyeing the plumed hat of a rake in the galley she became Bellamira:

Since this town was besieged, my gain grows cold
The time has been, that but for one bare night

Pausing, she looked again at the groundlings. *What is my line?* The crowd became hazy, swimming in her vision. The stage rocked, and she moved drunkenly as if on a ship. Holding out her arms, the seasickness came over her in waves. She looked towards the horizon. At the back of the playhouse, on the groundlings' floor, she saw the dwarf. He stood in the midst of a clearing that grew wider as she watched.

She screamed as the clearing became nothing but his eyeball with all else in the theatre reflected and swimming in it. Drowning in the vision, she felt herself fall into a large pool. She thrashed in the water, watching as Kit dropped through the darkness of its depths.

Alvis blinked and all was black.

Chapter 41

Kit watched the shadows on the wharf as he huddled in his cloak waiting for the ship to Calais, France. He tried to calm himself as people hurried by in all manner of dress and occupation. Because it was early morning mainly merchants hurried by. A few drunken stranglers emerged from the dark, staggering towards the brothels—what they called home.

He knew that assassins could come in any form, merchant or drunken sailor, it didn't matter. He had seen them all in his tenure as an intelligencer and there wasn't a soul who could fool him anymore. Intelligence and betrayals had given him a sixth sense into the heart of humanity.

He closed his eyes and thought of her. Trying to conjure her on the dock. It wasn't so much for the money but the fact that he knew he wouldn't see her for a long time.

Waiting there at the edge of the shadows he flinched at the sound of a shrill whistle. It was only a sailor, beckoning passengers to get on board.

Kit touched his shoulder as the sailor approached. "How long 'till we embark?"

"Now, my friend. We leave." Grinning, the red-haired sailor approached the boarding plank and ran lightly up it.

Kit looked behind him. The shadows were growing thin and slowly disappeared as a tired sun rose in the English sky.

He closed his eyes again. "Alice. Come." He fervently whispered her name again and again as a dying man would incite God to protect him.

"All aboard!"

The sound jarred him and the heavy clanking of the men pulling up the boarding plank proved that the ship was about to leave.

Frantic, he put his safety aside and screamed her name.

Jumping aboard the plank as it was rising, he ran onto the ship. The ship unfurled its sails. The docks grew distant as they set out across the channel. Alice did not appear.

Chapter 42

The sound of murmuring voices penetrated the veil of water as she swam to the top and broke through. The words "reaction formation," and "psychosis" clearly percolated above the others.

Her eyelids fluttered as she blinked away the last remnants of Alvis, as he fluttered away, seemingly into a corner of the theatre.

"Ah, she awakes!"

Opening her eyes she saw nothing but fuzzy shapes as she tried to focus. Sunlight poured through a window to her right. She tried to sit but found that her feet were bound to the foot of a bed. Raising herself on her elbows, she opened her mouth but no words came out. Shadows materialized and a woman in white bent over her. The woman held her wrist. Alice lay down again on the bed.

"Alice."

When she heard the voice she turned. "Kit." She whispered, at once feeling safe and secure. She would not be tortured now. But then vision materialized into Albert, someone from the future past who was a distant memory. She recoiled as he touched her hand.

The nurse was scribbling something on a clipboard. Moaning sounded from the hallway, and then an ear splitting scream.

"I'll be back in a minute, hon." The nurse's southern drawl and honeyed voice trailed after her. "Mr. Dempsey, your meds aren't due for another two hours. No, you get back to bed and I'll sit with you soon. Your wife is dead, hon."

The words 'dead, hon' had such a finality that Alice couldn't quite understand.

"Where am I?" she said.

Albert looked pained. "The psych ward."

"The psych ward?" Confused at first, she laughed, a small hysterical laugh that reminded her of Baines. She stopped laughing. "Why?"

He took a deep breath, let it out and looked out the window, then back at her. "You don't remember anything?"

Alice wondered how much she should tell him. They now thought she was a raving lunatic. "Nothing."

"We found you unconscious by the side of the house. It appeared you had hit your head, but you just stared into space when you awoke. We put you through a battery of tests, but apparently there was no neurological damage."

"So you assumed that it was something else?"

"Alice, when we came near, you screamed and tried to run. It was if you were seeing something that we weren't...I —"

"Who is *we*, Albert?"

"Selina and I of course."

She stared straight ahead. "Of course."

"You don't understand, Alice."

"Oh, I do understand, Albert. I am so completely manageable right now. You get to play the role you are so fond off."

"Alice, if you were rational, we could have a conversation but—"

A small man appeared around the corner. He was dressed in green and carrying a tray. She screamed. She felt as if every nerve and synapse in her body was on fire and ready to die. She felt a sharp pinch in her arm as they held her down. Everything turned black.

***

When she awoke, it was dark save for the light streaming from the window onto her bed. She placed her hand in the pool of moonlight and was reminded of an earlier time when things were ready to happen, when she was on the brink of something. Tears spilled down her cheeks.

"How did this go so wrong?" She whispered her question. "Kit, where are you now?" She wiped her face with her hand, trying to make sense of it all.

Perhaps she was crazy. She tried to piece together what had happened. She had bumped her head, yes, but she wound up in another place, in another time. Or experienced one, anyway. She realized she remembered everything. There was not a single detail she couldn't recall—from the silk of her dress at Scadbury manor, to the feel of Kit's hand on her cheek. She smiled, remembering the ink stained hand, how gentle it was.

But try as she might, she could not remember what had directly happened before they knocked her out with Thorazine. The Thorazine had created an instant stupor and then she had felt profoundly tired. Yet, now she felt refreshed and her mind felt sharp. She had an acute sense that she was missing a block of time.

A shadow appeared at her door. There was a glint of light on metal and she made out two wheels as they turned in the light. Then the wheels stopped.

"Hello? Who's there?" Alice held the covers around her.

A woman with long, grey, disheveled hair wheeled herself into the room. She wore a red hospital gown.

"I've never seen a red hospital gown." said Alice.

"That's because you haven't been here long enough." the woman snapped.

"I don't see why you're so irritated with my response."

"We're in a mental hospital and you would expect some sort of....behavior. Now wouldn't you?"

"Yes."

"Good." The woman did a complete, neat three hundred and sixty degree circle in her chair. "You gave everyone quite a scare. Screaming like that."

"I saw a dwarf."

"A dwarf?"

"Yes. He came into my room."

The woman smiled, clearly not put off by this response. She twirled her long hair around her finger.

"Hmm. But why would you scream? Was he evil?"

"I don't know."

"Well, you should find out."

The woman abruptly turned on her wheels and went out of the room, leaving Alice to wonder if she was dreaming. She searched the room for a clock and saw that it was ticking. Time was still present.

Chapter 43

The room felt warm when she awoke and she wondered if it was summer. Thoughts and memories became more clear as time anchored itself in the present of the twenty-first century. With her eyes closed, she could clearly see Alvis walking up the road to her house. She remembered that it was about to storm. A horrible storm. Green and yellow had slashed the sky.

She did not open her eyes right away when she heard the voices. They were muffled at first but the volume rose and the voices became clear.

"When shall she be able to come home?" Albert said.

"I don't know. She may be in a psychotic state for a few days, weeks...months. I just don't know." said Selina.

"But have you seen this before? A case like this?"

"No. I haven't. I've looked through the literature regarding psychosis, and there is nothing comparable. Usually, people think they are someone else; there is this grandiose fantasy, you know? Like, thinking you're Christ. Usually Christ."

"Yes, it's a wonder more people don't think they're Ghenghis Khan. Or Hitler."

She could sense Albert smiling. She could *feel* it. There was a smugness about them that she abhorred. They felt so confident in their diagnosis, so sure that they had mapped the contours of her mind, and that was all there was to it.

Alice didn't want to talk to them. What could she say? After all, Christ was sacrificed. She rolled over on the bed to smother a laugh.

"I think I'll be going, Albert. Is there anything I can get you, tell you, before I leave?"

Albert sighed. "No, I'm afraid there is nothing I need right now. Or need to know for that matter. What I do need to know you can't provide, and I will have to wait. But thank you so much. You have no idea how much your presence here means to me."

"Well, I can't really say I'm surprised that this happened. Now that I look back on it it seems she, Alice, was being driven up against the wall and had no place to turn but fantasy. Unfortunately, it consumed the totality of her psyche, all of her energy."

"Yes. Quite right. And uncompensated for it all. I will speak with you soon."

"Call if you need anything, Albert. Please."

"Yes. Thanks again. Take care."

The door closed and Selina briefly spoke with the nurse on duty, but Alice could not make out who it was.

Albert got up from the chair. He bent over the bed and smoothed her hair. "I'm sorry, love, but I must be going. I have that class to teach. Beginning Psych. And there's no way out of it. I'll be back tomorrow. "

She lay there after Albert left and listened to the sounds of footsteps and voices in the ward. There was a shout, and a brief scuffle somewhere down the hall. The soothing sound of a doctor eased the hysterical cries of a patient, and the floor went back to its pleasantly normal facade.

She could not be certain where she was. This seemed to be a large hospital, and she tried to remember if Albert had ever mentioned it.

Alice got out of bed and went to the window. There was a spacious manicured lawn with a line of trees by the road. Older patients in wheelchairs were arranged on the grass with staff members dressed in white.

"Hello. Up and around today?"

Alice turned from the window. "Where am I?"

The nurse smiled. "Pinehurst. A resting home for the elderly."

"I'm not old."

"And those whose nerves are shattered."

"So you take in people with neurological disorders? And crazy people?"

A look of surprise crossed the nurse's face. "Well...I wouldn't call the people, clients, here, crazy."

"I'm crazy."

The nurse smiled. "Can I take your blood pressure, please?"

"But I'm not ill. Just crazy."

"I still have to take your blood pressure. It's procedure."

Alice held out her arm and the nurse pushed up her sleeve. The movement of cloth against skin reminded Alice of Kit and his quill. She felt the slow, sensuous movement brushing along her back. She shivered.

"Are you cold? I can get you a blanket."

"I'm hungry. When's lunch? When do I get out of here?" Alice thought she might drive to Taco Bell and get a cheesy bean and rice burrito. Now that she was back in the twenty-first century.

The nurse rolled down the sleeve over her arm. "I don't know. You'll have to ask the doctor."

Alice realized that would be either Albert or Selina.

She got up from the bed and went to the window again. "Will I also have to ask the doctor when lunch is scheduled?"

The nurse laughed. "Of course not. Lunch is at noon," she glanced at the wall clock. "In fifteen minutes."

"And you'll bring it to me?"

"No, one of the lunch aides will." She patted Alice's arm. "Don't worry, you'll be out of here soon. You seem quite normal."

Alice stared out the window. "You have no idea."

Lunch the next day consisted of tasteless ham sandwich on white bread with canned pears in a small, white, ceramic dish. Alice played with her pears and opened the cellophane-wrapped chocolate chip cookie. Dipping it in milk, she watched the people out the window. The woman in the red hospital gown and wild gray hair sat in her wheelchair conversing with another older woman on a bench. Today she had on a grey coat the color of steel wool. The wind picked up and blew her hair around her face. She took a clip from her pocket and arranged her hair on top of her head, clipping it into place.

The door opened and Alice turned from the window. Albert entered with a bouquet of flowers. Red roses.

He hugged her. "You're looking fresh today. Fresh as a flower." He held a rose to her face, caressing her cheek.

She turned her face away from him. "Albert, what am I doing here? And when am I getting out?"

"I told you why you were here. You should be here just another week for—"

"That is complete crap, Albert." She stood and the blood flushed to her face. "I need to get out of here and you try to pacify me with roses. Bullshit."

He sighed. "You need to speak to Selina for an evaluation."

"Says who?"

"It's the standard procedure for dismissal from Pinehurst."

"Well, I don't want Selina for my shrink. I told you that earlier."

"I committed you, Alice. And as a competent spouse, what is in the paperwork goes."

He stood there, so self-satisfied and so firm in his conviction of her madness that she picked up the flower vase and threw it against the wall. It shattered, splashing water and roses everywhere.

His face showed disbelief. "That is an indication. It proves to me that you *need* to be evaluated to leave."

"What it proves is that I'm angry, Albert. Even sane people get angry. Did it ever occur to you that being here, and not being heard, might make me angry?"

"Darling, that's what the evaluation is for, to make certain you can stand on your own two feet, come back into the world."

"I don't need a piece of paper telling me I'm sane. I know I'm sane."

"Let's get through it, then, so we can leave."

"No. *You* leave Albert."

"What?"

"Just leave!"

"What do you mean? The room?"

"Yes."

An orderly appeared at the door. He was a beefy man dressed in white with a blue and green tattoo on his bicep.

"Need any help here? I heard a crash." He said.

"No, thanks. I was just leaving."

"Wait," the orderly looked confused. "you're not the patient are you?"

"No. Ms. Petrovka is the patient. I was just on my way out. It seems she doesn't care for my flowers."

The orderly snickered. "Tough break, buddy. What can ya do?"

He shut the door leaving Alice alone and staring at a wall drenched in water with shattered glass and roses strewn about the floor.

Chapter 44

Albert did not return for an evaluation or to sign any papers. Selina was in to see her every few days, so Alice smiled and acted noncommittal about her state of affairs, or when she wanted to leave. She said Albert would return.

Most days she peered out the window and watched the woman with the long gray hair hold court with a group of women. She animatedly discussed some topic as the wind blew her hair around her face, at which point she always extracted a clip. She expertly flipped her hair into a sort of chignon at the back of her head.

Alice got the feeling she was expert at a lot of things.

She sat in the gray chair by the window and opened a book. There were a great deal of books accumulating near the chair by the window, for she had been requesting books from the university. The staff at Pinehurst did not think this strange. They knew she was a playwright who owned a theatre.

Alice sat back in her chair. No one had visited. Everyone had seemed downright squeamish in fact, Albert had said. Everyone except Joannie. Joannie had gotten in touch with Albert, to check on Alice. She said she would stop in soon to see her. Alice smiled at the thought. Joannie the only one brave enough to check on the crazy woman.

She turned back to her books, picked one up, *Symbols and Mystery in the Renaissance*. Flipping through it, she came to a picture of an alchemist holding a sun in one hand and a moon in the other. The symbol of Venus was stationed above his head.

She had requested everything she could get her hands on regarding Elizabethan history, Shakespeare, symbolism, and the Renaissance. Carefully checking bibliographies, footnotes, and references to a possible trail she might take regarding the research, she made extensive lists of the books she needed. When the night nurse came in to check her vitals she handed her a list.

The nurse always smiled and took the list from her hand.

"I see you've been busy today."

"What else is a crazy playwright to do with her time? Do you give this information to my doctor?"

"What information?"

"The lists of books I've requested."

"Of course I do. I have to share everything I observe about you with the authorities managing your case."

"Of course."

Alice felt like she was under the looking glass. A bug being observed. She wondered if this is how Kit Marlowe felt when he had slipped away to Calais. Did he wonder why she had never shown in Deptford? *What did he think?* All this history had passed since then.

History. She wondered if there was a way to go back and tell him. How had she fallen through this rip in time? *Had it always been there?*

Reading the sonnets over and over she found herself within the words. And the woman who came after her. The dark lady. Was she the woman at court?

She couldn't blame him. How utterly lonely he must have felt sailing away from everyone and everything he knew and loved. It must have been like she felt now, everything had been blown apart and must be put back together again.

Alice wondered if he had made it to Italy. She was determined to find out.

She peered out the window. The woman with the long gray hair was staring at two ducks swimming lazily in the pond. Alice shut her book and let the sun warm her face as it streamed in through the window.

***

She awoke to a brisk knock on the door. Startled, she sat upright in her chair. The night nurse appeared with Joannie trailing behind, peering over her shoulder.

"I have a surprise for you." the nurse said.

"Look what the cat dragged in," said Alice.

"Hey you, Petrovka. What's up?" Joannie smiled, then looked away, embarrassed.

"I'll leave you two to chat." The nurse left the room.

Alice looked at the floor. "Well?"

"Maybe I should have said, you're *definitely* not up."

Laughing, Alice looked at Joannie. "I am so happy, Bryant, you are not going to tiptoe around me."

"I would be doing a great disservice to you, Petrovka. And to myself." Joannie sat next to her in a chair facing the window. "Interesting woman out there with the gray hair."

"Yes. I think I will approach her at the craft session today."

"Crafts? That definitely sounds like something crazy people do." Joannie said.

"We have to do *something* around here."

"Hmm. So, what's up with this crazy business, anyway."

"Had an experience. Went back in time, talked to Christopher Marlowe, found out for certain he was Shakespeare. Was acting in a play and I was suddenly transported forward in time. Boom! Here I am."

Joannie laughed. "Well, well. Quite an adventure. Really doesn't surprise me though."

"You're the only person who'd say that."

"Of course. Playing along with your big adventure of Alice falling into the looking glass, down the rabbit hole—"

"Oh, how weird Bryant! That's exactly the way it was. There was this dwarf, Alvis was his name, eyeball, and—"

263

"*Puhleeze!* I don't think I can deal with it all right now. Remember, I have to pretend to be sane. Unlike yourself."

"Alright. I can see how it could be a bit overwhelming."

"So, what's next on your big adventure?"

Alice looked out the window at the woman with the gray hair rolling away in her wheelchair. "I need to show the world that Christopher Marlowe was, no is, Shakespeare."

"Sounds a bit over the top."

"It isn't."

"What for?" Joannie asked. "All you're going to get is a lot of flak from people entrenched in keeping the status quo the way it is, and—"

"Who cares? I was there, Bryant. *I was there.* It's something I have to do."

Joannie looked at her doubtfully. "You really want me to believe this, don't you?"

"I do."

"If you think you have it hard here, wait until people get a load of your ideas."

Alice took a deep breath. "I know. I'll just have to dig my heels in, I guess."

***

The corridor was gray and quiet as she made her way down the hall. Most people were tucked away in their beds, watching television.

She slipped into the room. An aide was working with a few other patients at a table with some watercolors. One lone patient sat in front of an easel set with a canvas, clearly flaunting convention by painting with oils.

Alice made her way to a small bookshelf in the corner of the room. She pulled out a small volume of the sonnets and sat in the chair next to the bookshelf. Sinking into the plush comfort of a chair she turned to Sonnet 36.

Let me confess we two must be twain
Although our undivided loves one;

So shall these blots that do with me remain,

Absorbed she read on. Clearly the sonnet was about the loss of a friend and the friend's role in getting the plays to the theatre. The ink blots remained with Kit because the manuscripts were copied by a scrivener, and he had blots on his character from the Privy Council Inquisition.

The woman with the gray hair rolled up to her. Alice looked up.

"The rumor is that you have had some kind of *experience*." The woman said.

Alice put down the book. "That sounds vague. Everyone here has had some kind of experience."

"Yes, but yours was, is…quite extraordinary."

"I don't know if I want to talk to you about this. I don't even know you."

"I understand your apprehension. I approached you because I think we have a lot in common."

Intrigued, Alice cocked her head. "Really? How so."

"My husband also had me put away."

"In the old days, I hear it was quite common for men to commit their wives, if they were to feisty, independent, or whatnot. Or, if they wanted something."

"And there you have it. If they wanted something. Like money. And, let me add, the old days weren't so long ago. Treated like cattle, we were. And still are!" Clearly miffed, the woman frowned and took the clip from her pocket, securing her long gray hair.

Alice leaned forward. "He committed you for your money?"

"Bingo."

"I'm sorry."

"I'm Celeste, by the way. Celeste Cecil Chambers. The three C's." The woman held her head high as if she was royalty. "I am a direct descendant of Robert Cecil."

"Of England? Of the court of Queen Elizabeth?" said Alice.

"Yes. That one."

"What a coincidence." Alice sat back in her chair.

"I'm sure." The woman gave her a long, searching look, then turned on her wheels and headed towards the door. "We really should have tea sometime. Alice, is it?"

"Yes…I mean to the tea, too. I would like that. Very much."

"Good. Ta." The woman wheeled herself out of the room as Alice watched her go.

Alice placed the small volume of sonnets back in the bookshelf.

***

Albert did come again. But this time he brought no flowers. He sat on the edge of the bed while she stared out the window at the garden. This garden wasn't as nice as the one by the library. This garden was too formal; too tidy. Not a leaf, not a twig out of place. Everything was trimmed and shaped according to a plan. There was no room for wild abandon. She thought of this as he went on in an even, careful tone. She thought his voice matched the boxwood hedges.

Albert and Selina finally pronounced her sane, and they each signed the release papers.

Alice never once gave into Albert, never agreed that she was delusional. She held fast to her version of events. Albert conceded that it was a magical experience, and he promised not be so quick to dismiss. After all, Bernie had obviously encountered such things in the rainforest talking to shamans. Alice was irritated that, to Albert, Bernie's experiences somehow had more authority than hers. She told Albert that she herself could be compared to a shaman, and he nodded, saying the whole experience was probably brought on by losing the baby.

She was to leave the next morning. But now, she was scheduled for tea.

She had managed to procure a small pot with two tea cups. She showed the kitchen staff her papers stating she was sane enough to exit Pinehurst and they reluctantly gave her an electric kettle to use in her room.

There was a light rap on the door.

"Come on in."

The woman with the long gray hair, Celeste from the present time, wheeled herself into the room.

Alice lay scones on a plate and placed them on the table by the window. Through the window she saw the large willow in the yard blowing in the breeze.

Celeste picked up a scone and took a bite. "Almond." She wiped her mouth with the back of her hand. "Tired of manners." She munched heavily and squinted at Alice. "You like this English tea thing."

"My husband's British."

"Right. And who are you really married to?"

Alice's hand shook and the cup crashed to the floor, breaking into three large pieces. Celeste calmly eyed the catastrophe and took another bite. "No need to panic. That's why we're here."

"I really don't understand your riddles." Alice said.

"Look, I came here for an intelligent conversation and I'll leave if you want to play games." Celeste wiped the crumbs from her lap. "I can get banality anywhere."

Alice picked up the large pieces of porcelain. "Can't believe that this didn't shatter into more pieces. Just three."

"Yes. Like the fates."

"The fates." Alice looked up with the pieces in her hand. "Celeste, do you believe we were supposed to meet?"

She shook her finger at Alice. "I've been keeping an eye on you. I saw what was going on."

"Did you?" Alice decided to play along and humor the old woman. *No harm in that.*

"Don't condescend to me! If you don't believe in yourself and what you're doing, who will? Why do you want to play games?"

Alice walked to the wastebasket in the corner and tossed the three shards inside. They clattered against each other. "I almost wish we had a cauldron here. I could throw these pieces in, and poof! The answer would appear."

Celeste bit into another piece of scone. "Look what happened to Lady Macbeth. And Duncan."

"Are you trying to tell me with your witchery that somehow I am going to self-destruct with guilt?"

"Is that what you think Shakespeare was implying? The man who was Shakespeare?"

Celeste's eyes grew bigger, and for an instant Alice thought that she might become like Alvis and dissolve the past present and future all together into the singularity that it was. The norns knew about this singularity and had woven it on their loom.

"As you came in, there was a rip in the fabric of all that went together and I saw it spelled out all over you. I saw that you had gone back in time, to Elizabethan England, and had spoken with the murderous spymaster. And the man who was Shakespeare."

"I was with him. The man who was Shakespeare." Alice said.

"The masters of intelligence were very well versed in cloaking intelligence in the symbolism of the time. Of all time, in fact, but of course it has been lost to us. But the artists, the writers... they all knew. And had to keep quiet about the old ways." Celeste said.

Alice could only nod. She felt drained, tired, as if everything that had been woven into the fabric of her being had been ripped from her.

"Because you know this, you can never go back to the old ways. Although they will try to make you reassemble as your old self."

"But how do you know? How can you perceive these things?" Alice said.

"I studied the classics. Mythology. I started seeing the patterns in literature and in all of the stories people had been telling each other from the beginning of time."

"There is a reason for all of this Celeste. I feel it. I am not insane, any more than you are."

"No, of course not. We've just managed to find ourselves in this…unwholesome predicament. My husband had me locked up when he found he could. Then got his hands on my money."

"Is there a way out for you?" asked Alice.

"Yes, I'm working on it—many years in the making, but I'll get there. Players…what is that line from *As You Like It*?"

"All the world's a stage, and all the men and women merely players."

Standing, Alice went to the window. Clusters of patients sat in wheelchairs or on blankets in the fresh air. "I've got to prove Kit was Shakespeare. I've got to put all the pieces of the puzzle together."

"You need hard evidence, love. And it's been hidden."

"I know."

Chapter 45

Alice stood there in her smart pink suit feeling very English. Her dark hair cascaded over her shoulders. The rainbow portrait of Elizabeth hung on a wall in front of her. She seemed to be watching Alice with a faint smile on her face. Her dress was dotted with eyes and ears. *Symbols that they loved. Symbols that alluded to something else.*

"Holding onto her secrets."

"Excuse me?" Alice said.

"Sorry. I must have been speaking to myself."

The man who addressed her also wore a suit. He had tousled black hair and reminded Alice of someone from an old rock band. She wondered where she got this idea, and stole a glance at him.

"Do you always approach strange women staring at portraits and start a conversation?"

He laughed. "Yes, as a matter of fact. I work here. A curator of sorts."

Alice looked at his name tag. "Neville Cruise. And what sort would that be?"

"I'm a connoisseur of beauty." He smiled brightly.

"Are you hitting on me, Neville?"

"Only if you want."

"Well, I'm married. In more ways than one."

"What? Like twice? A harem is it? Count me in." He laughed.

She smiled despite horrendous jet lag. Alice wanted nothing more than a hot bath and a bed.

Neville blushed and then turned towards the portrait. Clearing his throat he said, "She learned she was queen in this very house."

"Yes?"

"Actually, it was in the yard. Under a tree. An oak tree."

"Neville, I'd love to stay and chat but, actually I'm here to meet someone." Alice glanced at her watch.

"Of course. Can I take you to your someone?"

"Cedric Cecil."

He raised his eyebrows. "You rise to the top…Sorry, your name?"

"Alice Petrovka."

"And the top we shall go. Mr. Cecil has an office on the third floor. May I ask—"

"You may."

He moved towards a set of stairs on the right and Alice followed. Their heels clapped on the marble.

"To further the plot, Alice, why are you here?"

"To discuss some letters with Mr. Cecil. A Shakespearean matter."

"Uh oh." He stopped on the second floor landing and placed his hand on her arm. "Alice, others have come here to discuss Shakespearean matters with Mr. Cecil. They haven't gotten very far."

She shook off his hand. "I will get as far as I need, Mr. Cruise. Thank you very much."

"I only tell you this so you won't be disappointed."

"What would you know about this anyway?"

"Hatfield House is rife with rumor, despite its size, everyone knows everyone else's business."

Neville continued up the stairs, Alice followed.

"Well, that's the thing, it's rumors you're speaking of." she said.

"Shakespeare is a big deal to the Cecils. All roads seem to lead here, then the trail runs out."

"The trail, Mr. Cruise?"

"The authorship controversy."

Neville rapped soundly on the large maple door in front of them. When a "Yes?" issued from inside he opened the door for her. "Alice Petrovka to see you, sir."

"Oh, yes. Do come in, Ms. Petrovka. Thank you, Neville."

Neville turned to Alice. "Good luck." he whispered.

Cedric Cecil sat at a large mahogany desk facing the door. He did not look up as she sat down.

"Alice Petrovka. Please, sit."

Alice sat in a chair facing him. He still did not look up and continued writing. Minutes ticked by and she looked at the gardens out the window. She wondered why he didn't place his desk in view of the gardens.

He tapped his pen on the desk and looked at her. "Who sent you?"

"Celeste Chambers."

"Hmm. Yes. And how is that you came to know my sister?"

Alice shifted in her seat, uncomfortable. "I met her at Pinehurst."

Cecil placed the pen near his lips and gently bit it. Alice wondered if he chewed his pencils as a child. He stared at her, clearly waiting for her to say more.

"She told me I should approach you about the court records concerning Christopher Marlowe and your ancestors, William and Robert Cecil."

"Did she?"

"Yes, she did. She said you would have knowledge of documents relating to what happened to Christopher Marlowe."

"What happened to Christopher Marlowe." Cecil placed his hands together with his fingertips touching, forming a church steeple. "I think we all know what happened to Christopher Marlowe, Ms. Petrovka. He died in Deptford, with a stab wound to the eye."

"I do not believe he died in Deptford."

"So you fancy yourself a Marlovian, do you?"

"If you care to call me that."

"Quite right. Ms. Petrovka, I assure you, the Cecil estate has no such records proving Christopher Marlowe did not die in Deptford."

"There are other ways to procure these records than to simply ask for them, Mr. Cecil."

"You are not the first one to try to obtain…these phantom records. There have been others. Many others. I have told them all the same thing, the trail stops here. There is nothing to find."

"I believe you are hiding something, Mr. Cecil. It is currently relevant information, and a matter of public trust to the people of England, and indeed, the world."

Cecil smiled politely. "You are assuming Marlowe is Shakespeare, Ms. Petrovka, and that is quite a jump from merely proving him alive."

"I'm not assuming anything. I *know* Marlowe is Shakespeare."

Cecil impatiently tapped his pencil on the table. "You are beginning to sound like a fanatic, Ms. Petrovka, and I've already told you there is nothing to give you regarding information about my ancestors and Marlowe. There is simply nothing."

"You can stonewall all you want. But, I'll get what I need from you. There are ways."

His eyes turned cold. "This isn't America. Things are done differently here and it is a matter of privacy."

"We'll see about that."

"Good day, Ms. Petrovka. Enjoy England." He turned to his document again.

***

Alice shut the maple door behind her. Portraits of Cecils from the last four hundred years lined the hall. She descended the stairs as Neville was ascending.

"Hello! Angry, are you? I can tell by your face."

"Don't tell me you were just coming around the corner, Mr. Cruise."

"Checking on you, so to speak."

"No need to check on me. You already told me I wouldn't get what I needed. And I didn't."

She reached the bottom of the stairs and turned towards the mahogany doors. Various tour groups were clustered together listening in rapt attention to their guides.

"Alice, wait." He touched her arm, turning her toward him.

"Shouldn't you be giving a tour or something." She nodded towards a group of people.

"No. Listen to me...this Shakespeare thing. I don't think you understand."

"What is there to understand, Neville?" She impatiently shook his hand off. "You know, for an Englishman you are very touchy-feely."

"You think we're all a bunch of cold fish, do you?"

"No, not everyone. At least someone who lived four hundred years ago wasn't."

He looked at her strangely. "I don't know what you're going on about, but Shakespeare is serious stuff here in Britain. It could be dangerous."

She laughed. "Serious and dangerous. This is how you describe your fellow countrymen and women."

"There is a vested interest in keeping things the way they are. Always has been." Neville said. "Seekers have come trying to prove Marlowe is Shakespeare, mainly those after the Hoffman prize. But they've always been quietly rebuffed."

"I'm not after Calvin Hoffman's prize and I'm not so easily rebuffed."

"Not after the Hoffman prize? It's a million American dollars."

"I'm after something else."

"What is that, may I ask?"

"Debunking the Shakespeare Industry and exposing them for what they are—a bunch of cons and liars," Alice blurted.

"The English are stubborn, Alice."

"My husband is English. I can find myself around this country, alright."

"One of the harem?"

"We're recently separated."

"I see."

"I really think you don't, Mr. Cruise."

"You're in love with Marlowe. Just like the grand Marlovian dame, Dolly Walker Wraight, was."

"So, what if I am?"

"I'm sure it's easy to love someone in the past who wrote great seductive poetry and some of the best plays in the world. But he's dead, Alice."

"That's what you think."

He frowned. "Maybe there is more to this than meets the eye."

Alice yawned. "I'm exhausted. I need a bath and to go to bed."

"I know the best thing for jet lag."

"I'm not sleeping with you, Mr. Cruise."

He laughed. "Not yet to be added to the harem?"

"Well? Tempt me."

"Tea by the Thames."

"Doesn't sound terribly exciting, but it does sound terribly English."

"You'll see. You need to be by the water right now. And liquidated, yes." He glanced at his watch. "I'm off at five. Ten minutes. Meet me around back?"

Alice hesitated, then pushed open the heavy doors. "Alright, Mr. Cruise. I'll be waiting by my car."

"Good." He smiled. "You won't be disappointed."

***

As soon as she left he locked the door and phoned his contact in the United States. Waiting for the pickup, he stood by the window.

"Jim? Hello, yes, Cedric here. Afraid of a problem. Hmm. Another one. Yes, this one you know. Going to give the chaps a ring and will let you know. Yes, alright...good-bye."

He hung up. Alice and Neville stood at their cars talking. Taking his pipe from the desk he lit it and inhaled deeply. As the smoke filled the room, he watched as the two cars pulled from the parking lot.

Chapter 46

Alice sat on a bench overlooking the Thames. The sun was warm and low in the sky. She waited for Neville to return with their tea. The spot Neville had chosen was not to far from the Rose, Kit's theatre. The new Globe stood behind them. Closed now, patrons stood reading the notices of upcoming productions.

Breathing deeply, she leaned back and tried to feel Kit's presence. Nothing. She felt nothing. Opening her eyes she watched the water. Large barges chugged by, and the smaller boats maneuvered among them. Tourist boats drifted by at a leisurely pace. The sound of a guide's voice speaking urgently about the landmarks and scenery floated across the water.

Neville handed her a cup of tea and placed a plate of scones between them.

"Sorry, I should have asked if you like milk with your tea."

She took a sip. "I like it. And the sugar and lemon. Thanks."

He sat next to her. "Busy place."

"Yes. It's nothing like it used to be."

"There was quite a bit of development in the seventies, yes." he said.

"I mean...earlier."

He gave her a questioning look, and she found herself starting from the beginning. She told him about the theatre visitor who wore a slashed doublet. How she had seen him holding a rose at the library. How she found the rose and had it identified. Then the ending and beginning of her journey, where she had crashed through time.

"It wasn't far from here actually...by the South Bank, on Blackfriar's Road."

"By the Old Vic Theatre?" he said.

"Yes, down that way." said Alice.

"I used to act there."

Alice laughed. "It just figures. I should have known—an actor."

"What makes you say that?"

"You say your lines perfectly." she said. "What was your specialty?"

"I was keen on Shakespeare."

"Do you think I'm crazy, then?"

Voices echoed across the water. A guide was describing the Anchor Inn, its age and earlier Renaissance guests who frequented the tavern. The voices floated across the water and then disappeared, followed by a wake of laughter.

"I do believe you had an experience, and I cannot claim to know what it is. Scientifically, or anything else. The government would love to get its hands on you, I'm sure."

She finished the last of her scone and threw away the paper plate. "I had to do this, you see. Just had to."

"Well...it is your play, so to speak."

"Celeste said I probably would encounter trouble with Cedric. But on the chance that he might have softened regarding the Cecils and Kit, she sent me to him."

"If anything, Cedric Cecil has hardened against the intelligence regarding Kit Marlowe."

"I suppose you've learned a lot working at the manor?" Alice said.

"The eyes and ears of Hatfield House."

"Just like Elizabeth's gown. Acting not paying you enough?"

"No. But rich nobles do. And it's been said that young American tourists of the feminine persuasion fancy me."

She laughed. "Everyone's on the lookout for their proper English gentleman? I, on the other hand, have had enough of that."

"Too many Englishmen in your harem, I suppose. I trust I've been of service?"

"You have. And I thank you for your kindness." Alice said.

"What is next for you on your grand quest, if I may ask?"

"To Venice. I am to speak with Luisa Vernetti. She is in charge of the State Archives and apparently knows a thing or two."

"I hope you find what you're searching for. It seems like you've run into a dead end here."

"Yes, apparently."

"Good luck to you, Alice. I suppose it is appropriate to bid you adieu at this point."

He stood, took her hand lightly in his and brushed his lips upon it, "Goodbye," he said, then walked towards the London Bridge.

Surprisingly, Alice felt more than a little regret as she watched him walk away.

Chapter 47

After she had returned her rental car she took the tube to Paddington station. It was rush hour and throngs of people waited in line to buy tickets or to grab the next tube. She made her way past the maze of people and stood waiting for the familiar red bullet to hurry its way towards the platform.

Because it was so busy, she held onto a metal support and braced herself. The tube pulled from the station and hurtled through the long, narrow passage underground. People packed tight around her, like so many sausages in a can.

She was never completely comfortable moving underground, and had terrible thoughts of being caught in the tube like an earthworm, stuck in the muck of a bomb blow-up and being smothered by smoke.

Paddington station came into view as her calamitous fantasy came to an end. She concentrated on the tube map and the voice telling her where she was in space and time. She fixated on the dots before her stop, there were two, and saw a man reading *The Guardian*. He looked up at her. His face registered something more than casual acquaintance, and slightly alarmed, she turned her head.

She bounded off the steps, happy to be away from the mass of people pressing in on her. She had forgotten how crowded London was, so different from four hundred years ago.

Walking the street towards her hotel, Alice felt as if nothing was left from long ago. The great fire of London had burned most of the old houses and structures, and what had survived existed in little pockets, like a species on the brink of extinction.

A light mist filmed the air and she pulled up the collar of her raincoat as people jostled past her. No, she felt none of Kit in this place. His presence had vanished like the rain. As the clouds parted and the blue sky appeared again, she spotted the white facade of her hotel, the Paddington Arms. Dipping into a shop for a bottle of wine, Alice did not notice that the man who had been reading *The Guardian* on the tube had slipped in behind her.

Chapter 48

Chester Lightley held the phone away from his ear as Cedric Cecil jabbered about his nation's precious secrets. Lightley ran his hand over his bald head as the old drone babbled on. It wasn't the first time that he thought Cecil wanted his job. No, indeed, needed his job.

Tiresome nobles. *They still think they run the country.*

Well, he knew where he stood. A hard working bloke from Liverpool, growing up on the rough side of town, he had worked his way through the ranks to get this job. It wasn't handed to him as an inheritance like Cecil's had been. And that, he thought, was precisely what was so tiresome about the man.

Lightley's hand skimmed his left earring, a small hoop his wife had wanted . In fact, she had wanted the whole package—shaved head and earring. A package common to many balding Englishmen. Lightley didn't mind. The sex got better. Nona wanted him twice a week now.

He walked to the window, looking down from the top floor of MI6. The view was lovely along the South Bank of the Thames from here, he could see Vauxhall Bridge. Cecil's voice receded in the distance as Lightley took in the panoramic view along the river. He unbuttoned the middle button of his jacket, smoothed a hand over his belly: a bit bulging, he thought. *Now if I could only get rid of this...*Thoughts of Nona and him twisting on the bed came to mind.

"Do you know we have someone following her?"

"You wha?" Lightley snapped back to attention, his Northern accent betraying his working class roots.

"Precisely."

Lightley detected the gloating, gilded lilt of Cecil's received pronunciation, made more pronounced by the fact that he thought he had him by the balls.

"You're out of your range here, Cecil. This is our jurisdiction. We have a man on the case."

"You don't seem to understand, Lightley. This is probably one of the most, no, the most important matter regarding the crown, nobility, and secrets for our nation."

"Right. Absolutely." Lightley drummed his fingers on the table, letting Cecil think he got the better of him. "The Italians are in on this, too, you know."

"Of course I know that." Cecil snapped. "The reason for my call is to let you know where we stand in this matter. We don't need to be stepping on each other's toes. I bid you good day."

Lightley held his chin in his hand as he heard the unmistakable click of dismissal from Cecil.

"Bloody hell." He sighed, shut off his mobile and pocketed it. Cecil had just added considerable meat to his already well-heaped plate.

He stood once again and stared out the window thinking of the Cecils and Walsingham. Sir Francis Walsingham had set up England's spy network back in the reign of Elizabeth I, at much personal cost to himself. He spent much of his own money in order to protect the realm. The Cecils too, participated in the spy network, and often hired their own spies for special projects. Many times spies competed against each other within the budding intelligence network.

And this is what I've inherited. Lightley rubbed his bald head, realizing things weren't so different today. The agency had many competing interests and competing projects that turned agents against each other, and against their bosses. The situation was compounded by the fact that the Cecils still maintained their own intelligence service, and employed this service whenever they thought that ancient foibles were to be uncovered. And this ancient foible hit a very personal sore spot of Cecil's. The family had been divided about how to deal with Christopher Marlowe working as a spy for the Cecils and Walsingham throughout the years.

The latest fiasco had involved Celeste Cecil. The family had basically turned against her when she exhibited a mystical streak, giving her husband ample opportunity to act on this vulnerability. And act on it he did. Celeste now sat in a psychiatric ward while her husband rambled in their large estate on the East Coast.

Lightley pulled the dossier from his desk drawer. *Enter Alice Petrovka.* He took the picture from the file. Interesting woman, he thought. He gave a wry smile, knowing the agent in charge of the woman would have no trouble whatsoever in trailing her. Yes, at least *his* agent wouldn't have any trouble trailing this woman. He was unsure of Cecil's agent. Cecil had a tendency to find agents who were rather unsavory underworld figures. Thugs from America. Lightley couldn't be sure what motivated them, although the forensic psychologists on board said like many Americans they operated from a hero complex and were motivated by fame and glory.

He grimaced. This was a dangerous game, and one he did not relish. But Lightley was known for his finesse in sticky situations. That's why he rose to the top of his field.

He stared at the picture as he took his mobile from his pocket.

"Ah, Miss Alice. You have no idea of the danger you're in." The eyes in the picture levelly met his, seemingly unconcerned.

He quickly phoned the agent in charge of the woman.

Chapter 49

She turned the corner and breathed a sigh of relief as The Paddington Arms appeared in front of her. The brief sunshine had been replaced by a heavy rain. She ducked under the awning and shook her umbrella. As she walked through the entrance way and made her way to reception, she could not shake the feeling that someone was following her. She turned around and saw no one but a gentleman in a dark hat.

Alice sat in a chair next to a window, pretending to be interested in a magazine. He hesitated, but did not look in her direction, simply went to the desk, obtained a key, and went towards the stairs. Alice watched him from her magazine. When he was out of sight she went to the reception desk.

"Excuse me, could you please tell me who that gentlemen was?"

"I'm sorry ma'am. We cannot give out guest information. Are you an authority?"

Alice realized she would be expected to produce some identification. "No...I just...he looked like an old friend of mine. I did not want to bother him if he wasn't."

The girl nodded. "Here are your keys. Enjoy your stay at the Paddington Arms."

Alice traversed the stairs to her room located in the back of the building. It was an old building, with many additions tacked on through the years. Thus the stairs rose, then fell again, not going completely up, but continuing their journey in a sort of maze. It wasn't the first time Alice felt like she was in Wonderland. She stopped, hearing foot-steps behind her, and thinking to let a fellow lodger pass, she waited. But the sound stopped as she did.

"Hello?" She stood at a stairwell and waited. Nothing.

Climbing the last flight, she found her room at the top of the stairs. It was a simple but large room, well-made with a pink and yellow bedspread on a white four poster. The dresser contained the usual things found in a fair to middling hotel in London: a tea set with digestives, an electric kettle, and of course, tea.

Alice fished her cell phone from her bag and rang Celeste. She sat on the edge of the bed and waited for her to pick up the phone. Recently Celeste had managed to scrounge up enough money to rent a small apartment in the city. Celeste loved the location, close to the city center and near a park, and she loved her freedom from Pinehurst.

No one home. She set the phone down.

She filled the kettle and plugged it in. As she ate a biscuit, she ran a bath, throwing in some lavender-scented crystals she had bought at the shop along with the wine. The sweet scent of lavender filled the air and she relaxed.

She watched the water. Tomorrow she would be in the water-filled city of Venice. She knew she would find Kit there. She just had to. Sticking her foot gingerly in the tub to check the temperature, Alice wondered again what he had thought when she didn't arrive at the ship with the money. It would have been their last embrace. She slipped out of her clothes and into the water.

As it stood they had simply parted. The water quivered around her breasts as she thought of him and the dream of him drowning. He was seeking asylum, something to give him safety where he had had none. And still didn't.

But what of time? According to Bernie, time didn't really exist, and they all were contained in a dynamic hologram. After a while, Alice reluctantly emerged from the water.

Surely Bernie must be back from South America. Selina had mentioned he had planned an extended stay there doing further research to help support Bohm's theories.

Donning a hotel robe, she wrapped her hair in a matching towel and made her way into the spacious living room area. She was glad now that she had decided to splurge on a large suite. London always made her so tired.

Alice picked up the phone and found Bernie's number. As the phone rang, she hoped it Bernie picked up rather than Selina.

"Hello?"

"Bernie?"

"One and only. At least at this number."

"Good. No split personality for you."

"Are you kidding? With an ex-wife as a shrink?"

"What? Did I hear correctly? You and Selina are divorced?"

"Not quite yet, but soon," He sighed. "You probably haven't heard, have you?"

"What."

"She ran off with *your* ex-husband."

Alice tapped a pencil on the table. "Figures. No matter, they deserve each other."

"You were right about them, Alice. They were always so cozy together. No wonder they locked you up. To continue their sneaky work, and—"

"That's kind of why I called you Bernie."

"To discuss their sneaky work?"

"No. To discuss what happened to me. Why I was locked up."

"Oooh. Okay."

"What I really need to know is what happened to me."

Bernie paused. "Honestly, I don't know, Alice."

"I'm beginning to doubt myself. Maybe I *was* crazy."

"What I can tell you is this…People from all over the world have experiences similar to this…shamans, healers. That's what I learned in the rain forest."

"But what if I wanted to go back? Back in time. Or, you say, time doesn't exist. Then how can I tap into that time period again, when to us…it's all been said and done for four hundred years."

"Well, I don't rightly know. Maybe conditions were just right and you fell into it."

"Do you think it's possible to make conditions right again."

"You could try. Shamans take ayahuascara. These are plants prepared for hallucinatory experiences that lead them to certain revelations regarding sick or unbalanced individuals. I don't advocate that, but there are music and trance states. Rituals if you will. Rituals done throughout time seem to break down the barriers of time, and connect people to times past."

"Rituals."

"Yes, rituals, " Bernie said. "They are a powerful way to connect you to the past. To the logos and knowledge that are in the collective unconscious."

Alice turned on the television. She clicked through the channels, looking for a station broadcasting the weather. She was taking a small charter plane to Venice and was hoping for clear weather over the Austrian Alps.

As she watched TV, absently flipping through channels, she found herself telling Bernie the detailed course of events that had transpired since their dinner date so long ago, and why she was so intensely interested in the nature of time.

"And that," she finalized, "is why I need to prove that Christopher Marlowe is Shakespeare. If I can I can prove that—oh my God!"

A small crumpled body appeared on screen. Alice couldn't believe how small she seemed.

"What is it Alice." Bernie's voice was level.

"They killed her." she whispered.

"Killed who? What is going on, Alice."

"Celeste Cecil. I've got to go Bernie."

"Please Alice, I'm afraid you may be in grave danger. Come back to the States."

"I'm afraid it's too late for that, Bernie."

She hung up the phone and stared at the door. The door knob was turning.

Chapter 50

Jim Schelling wasn't surprised that Cecil had contacted him. As a member of the Shakespeare Society, he knew he could be contacted any time by its governing members, especially since they funded for his work. He already knew most of what Cecil had told him. He knew members had become suspicious when Alice Petrovka had become convinced that Christopher Marlowe had written Shakespeare's plays and sonnets. They knew she was onto something when she had the rose. Jack McGill had notified the society that she had found a rare cultivar, something that only a small cadre of dedicated rose growers in England would know about. The society was concerned about the symbolism of the rose. The symbolism of the rose would perhaps get them to the heart of the matter, they had said.

He wasn't buying her back-through-time story either. Of course everyone had heard about it by now; some found it fascinating, others found it completely ridiculous. Schelling suspected that Alice was easily manipulated by fantasy, dreams, and symbolic images, so her current delirium worked to his advantage.

He sat on the edge of the stage at The Lion and gazed into the empty audience. These things ate at him because he now owned the theatre, and the society wanted a much bigger part in its affairs. Jim Schelling had his own ideas of what should go on in this theatre.

It was a fairly easy matter keeping Sonia and Brad in line with his goals. Once they learned they could have money and power they fell in line. Derrin was a far different matter. He wasn't motivated by traditional tokens of ego gratification, but Schelling had managed to turn his foray into drugs into a big fiasco. Schelling's current worry was how to keep Derrin quiet. It was proving harder than he thought.

Sitting on the edge of the stage, he fingered his pony-tail, wrapping it round and round his finger, thinking. He needed to be more creative in his solutions. The problems now seemed insurmountable, but would soon diminish with the application of his creative abilities. After all, he didn't rise to the top of his profession in the world of university theatre without something of a hassle. But, as he thought of acting and Shakespeare, he was suddenly inspired. There was a simple answer to his problem.

Chapter 51

Alice had boarded the charter jet at Heathrow early in the morning still clutching the note the maid had given her.

As Alice had advanced on the door with the lamp as her weapon, the maid from the hotel had protectively covered her head with her arm. The woman looked harmless enough as she hid behind her cart of towels and cleaning supplies, explaining in broken English that she was merely "dropping towels." As she was about to slip away the maid had handed Alice a note that a gentleman in the hallway had given her. When Alice asked who he was, she said she didn't know. She did say that he was wearing glasses and a fedora.

"Cold, cold eyes." she had said. "Frozen."

Apparently, the eyes matched the words in the note. Alice unfolded it again and read it.

The canals of Venice are long and winding
It's nothing for a body to disappear there under the pilings. Forever.

She had kept it as a sort of talisman to keep her strong, and now the words were losing their power. Of course they had kept her from sleeping last night, and she had tossed and turned on her comfortable bed and soft pillow—a comfort she could not truly indulge, thanks to the note. As the darkness ebbed and light flowed into dawn, she had reluctantly turned on the television and watched a comedy, which only made her sad.

The jet veered towards the Alps, and the white peaks glimmered through the clouds. As she approached Venice, the fear that had so solidly gripped her dissipated. It was laughable really, she had thought. All it did was to serve to build momentum in her. Perhaps she was on the right path. Why else would these people be trying to thwart her investigation? What were their motives?

I must be getting close to the truth. There could be no other explanation. Apparently, there was a lot more at stake in proving Kit Marlowe was Shakespeare than she had at first thought. The Shakespeare industry was a powerful force; many people had staked their careers on it. *But murder?*

These thoughts plagued her as the plane touched down in Treviso. And as she boarded the bus that would take her to Venice, she wondered about all the players involved and all the pieces in the puzzle.

And then there was her life back in the States. *What little was left of it,* she thought. She had called Albert after she had spoken to Bernie. He had been tight-lipped with her, unwilling to discuss anything. He had hinted that perhaps she should talk to Jim Schelling about the Lion, that there were ownership rumors in town.

Albert made it sound like the rumors were a result of their divorce, and questions about who owned what after they split. Alice had been relieved that everything had gone so well with their breakup.. But his sudden insistence that she should check into a possible problem with the Lion while emotionally downplaying the incident caused her to rethink his motives. At first, she had been unwilling to believe the rumor. *Of course he wants to hurt me, he is angry that I set divorce proceedings in place.* He knew how important the theatre was to her. After a time she chalked it up to his passive aggressive tendencies, and applauded her efforts at figuring out Albert's psychological state instead of vice versa.

The emotional fallout was building in intensity, rather than abating, as she had expected. She was not prepared for Albert's anger, or the vindictiveness he seemed to embrace.

That has to be it...

The man next to her looked at her strangely, and she realized she had spoken out loud.

"Sorry." Alice said. She looked out the window.

The bus rolled into the station and people pulled luggage and parcels from overhead compartments. Alice remained seated, waiting for everyone else to finish so she had room to move. People milled around the bus, some hailing taxis, others boarding still more buses headed into the heart of Venice. The faint smell of the lagoons was in the air, musty and damp, like washcloths that had been sitting on a basement floor for too long.

A dwarf appeared around the corner of a brick building in the parking lot. He wore an orange sequined jump suit and a matching sequined mask. A pointed white hat sat on his head. He looked directly at the bus. Alice's heart thumped in her chest, and she waited for the telltale signs of a rip in time. She gripped the seat in front of her. The man looked behind him, and a group of dwarves walked from behind the building. They were all dressed in the same spandex jumpsuit in various bright colors. Alice realized it was for some type of show or celebration, one of the comedie de arte theatre spectacles commonly staged in Venice. She breathed a sigh of relief, familiar pain that it was.

But perhaps it was a sign. A sign that she would see Kit again.

The dwarves clasped arms and circled around, doing a ring-around-the-rosy. People laughed and pointed, and camera clicks filled the air. Alice was reminded of Caravaggio, the Renaissance artist skilled in the arts of light and dark, of the shadows, and of rendering his subjects mysteriously life-like.

She walked towards her hotel out of the busy parking lot. Slowing down outside the concrete confines of the lot, she remembered last time she had been in Venice. It had been many years ago when she and Albert came for the film festival at the Lido. Tickets had been hard to get, although the hotel had been easy enough to procure at the expensive and renovated gothic cathedral. The cathedral had sparkled on the water of the Grand Canal, near the Rialto. The open waterway had flooded the rooms with light, which shimmered on the ceiling.

They had adopted a routine of eating, film watching, and lovemaking, with most of the day centered on love making. Everything was foreplay: the films, the food, the strolls along the waterways into secluded, narrow passageways. The two had left the tourists far behind, eating their spaghetti and gnocchi along the route to San Marco Square.

Even the pigeons flying in the square had added to the amorous effect of their Venetian visitation. A little girl had run into a flock of pigeons, and a shower of feathers had burst on them. A lone feather drifted down, landing on Alice's head. Albert had laughed and, picking it off her head, he had tickled her nose.

She wondered if it had all been a fantasy. She wondered if she was on a wild goose chase that had no substance. She wondered if Albert was completely right about her wild imaginings. Her psychosis. After all, she had ended her marriage for this, this idea that she had clung to. And could she say for sure that Christopher Marlowe was, in fact, Shakespeare?

She was overwhelmed by doubt as she made her way along the narrow street. Perhaps she had been too quick to end her marriage. She passed the fresh fruit and seafood market, and a clerk nodded in her direction. She nodded back, and stopped to admire the firm, ripe fruit in his stall. She picked up an orange and was once again flooded with memories of a four hundred-year-old-romance that was contained like this round fruit in her palm, a small crystal ball she could use to see into the past.

"*Bella.*" The clerk spoke, and she was jarred from the memory, knowing that Kit was all around her.

She put the orange back. "*Grazzi.*" She blushed, imagining the man could read her thoughts.

Happier then, Alice slowed her pace. She felt him here. He was all around, waiting to be found. She was sure this was a good omen of things to come with Luisa Vernetti. Surely things will come to fruition.

Alice laughed then, realizing that the inspiration of fruit had at once led to thoughts of lovemaking, productivity, and puns. The stuff that Kit was made of, and she sensed it here, in this place. The place where he surely had sunk some roots.

Her feet felt light and she barely felt the pull of the suitcase behind her. Turning the corner, she came across the open air markets that stood along the street. Brightly colored carnival masks delighted her eyes. She stopped and gazed at a particularly colorful mask of pink, red, and orange. She picked it up, knowing that this was one a sign. Handing it to the shopkeeper, she paid for the mask. The shopkeeper wrapped her purchase.

"For carnival?"

"Carnival? Oh, no. I'm only here for a few days."

"*Ostreghèta!* You do not know? Tomorrow, tomorrow!" He threw up his hands indicating the city was now alive with pre-carnival festivities.

It was true. She didn't know how she didn't notice. That explained the dwarves. And the bright colors. She clapped a hand to her forehead.

"I've been preoccupied."

He looked at her quizzically. She handed him twenty Euro and he gave her the bag.

It was early afternoon, and couples strode by hand in hand as she crossed the bridge to the hotel. She paused at the center of the bridge, looking out at the water and over the Grand Canal. Yes, she was certain she was on the right track.

Surprisingly, Luisa Vernetti was happy to see her. Alice had expected a disgruntled bureaucrat. Instead, she encountered a pleasant and more than a little excited woman who wanted nothing more than to talk about the history of Venice.

The tiny office was crammed with papers and books that had no discernible order.

"You know," began Alice. "The smell of this room reminds of an old library. When I was young I used to stick my nose in my favorite books and breathe in that old book smell. Deep. It was soothing."

Luisa laughed, a light tinkling sound that reminded Alice of springtime warblers.

"Yes, the smell of history. It is comforting at times. And, I must also admit, sometimes it is stultifying. All this history...and only me and one other archivist in charge of it all."

"Your English is impeccable," Alice blushed. "I'm sorry," she quickly retracted. "That's sounds very condescending."

"No worries," Luisa laughed again. "I studied in England."

"Maybe you understand the nature of my request, then?"

"In all my time of working here, and it has been fifteen years now, I have never gotten such a request. In fact, I don't think anyone has asked for such records. Surprisingly."

"Perhaps the task is too daunting. I mean, miles of shelving. That's a lot of history." said Alice.

"Yes, it is. And you need to know where to look. But come, I want to show you something."

They left the tiny office and entered the main hall, a seemingly endless parade of shelves containing books and folders. The thin sun entered through a side window illuminating the dust in the air. Luisa waved her hand, throwing millions of particles into a gyrating frenzy. "And all of it turning slowly to dust."

Alice sneezed.

"Bless you. I don't have time to dust this thousand-year history. Just parts of it." She turned the corner and pulled a book from the shelf. " But here, this is what I wanted to show you." Alice set the large book on a table. "Turn to the marked place." she said.

She flipped to the letter G. "I think I recognize this book, or I mean, I've heard of it."

"This is the Book of Gold." Said Vernetti. "In it are all the famous patrician Venetian families."

Alice looked through the columns of G's.

"They're all here," said Vernetti. "Every noble who was somebody; everyone who managed to get his family name listed in this book. And some of them went to pretty drastic lengths to be listed in this book. If you made it into this book, you were somebody."

"A popularity contest of sorts?"

"Yes, you could say that. You were guaranteed all the special privileges of the realm if you made it. The best courtesans; the best banking relationships. You name it, you had it. Do you recognize anyone in particular?"

Alice traced her finger down the page and stopped at a name. "Gonzaga?"

"Yes!" Vernetti's eyes lit up. "Now, after I found that name, I did a little more searching. Come."

Vernetti led Alice through the maze of books. After walking what seemed to Alice the entire thirty-six miles of shelving, she turned, "It's right over here." She walked towards a section that looked as if it hadn't seen the light of day in many years. Vernetti flipped a switch and a soft light flickered overhead. "I had almost forgotten about this section, but when I saw the name Gonzaga, a light when on." She glanced above them at the old flickering bulb. "So to speak."

Plucking a volume off the shelf she set it on a nearby table. Sitting down, she motioned for Alice to sit next to her.

She turned to a page and pointed to a passage. "It is here I found some very interesting information that I think you will be interested in. And I'm so happy the patrician decided to write in Italian instead of Latin. Because I would have had trouble with the translation."

"What is it?" said Alice.

"It is the Gonzaga family chronicles of a particle period. In this instance, the time period that you were looking for was the summer of 1593. Would you like to hear it?"

"Please."

"In the flowering summer heat," Vernetti began, "we received a poet and playwright from England. He wishes to study the *comedie d'arte*. After some deliberation, we decided to give him asylum. He goes by the name of Christopher Marlowe." She paused and looked at Alice. "Is this the information you seek?"

Alice could only nod.

"Here is your scapegoated, maligned, and banished intellectual. Congratulations, you found him."

"No, you found him. I thank you. I thought it impossible."

"Maybe it is the spirit of *carnavale*. Perhaps it is a thinning of the two worlds where all things meet." She shrugged. "I have never found such a fantastical discovery. And yet, come to think of it. I did get a request once." She glanced out the window, a faraway look in her eye. Long ago, when I first started working. He was an American, too."

"Someone else searching for Christopher Marlowe in Venice?"

"No, he said he was looking for Shakespeare. Smelling, Snelling...Schelling. Yes, Jim Schelling, that was his name."

Alice blanched. "You're sure?"

"Yes, quite. I remember now. Are you alright? You don't look well. "

Chapter 52

Alice stumbled into the narrow street. The night air was filled with smoke, and the sounds of drunkenness and merriment were everywhere.

Her spirits rose and then crashed again. The fact that she had found him alive, here in Venice, was one half of the puzzle. Now the Shakespeare critics could not so easily dismiss Marlowe as a possibile writer of the plays and sonnets.

She thought of Jim Schelling making his way to Venice to find Marlowe in the Book of Gold. Why would he venture all the way to the patrician archives to hunt Marlowe down? Was he trying to get rid of the evidence? The paper trail? He had always been quick to dismiss Marlowe as Shakespeare, and had made fun of her, calling her a Marlovian.

Luisa Vernetti said that she had refused his request of taking the Book of Gold with him. She said the archival repository was in no way a library, but she would be more than happy to make a copy of any documents he would like. She said he then became angry with her. He stated that he knew people in high places and they would make her life very uncomfortable when they found out she had refused his request. Vernetti told him she was a simple bureaucrat, and not many people would care to be bothered with her. When he realized no amount of wheedling or conniving would get him what he wanted he had left.

Alice imagined her tinkling laughter trailing after him as he descended the stone stairs that led to the top floor of the archives.

Vernetti had begged off enjoying a celebratory drink in the spirit of *carnvale*. She had said the *carnavale* had worn on her over the years and all she wanted to do was get back to the mainland and her family. Venice now was a city for tourists and *carnavale* was a festival of fantasies. "As I grow old I am too much rooted in the present." She had said.

Alice pulled the mask from her bag after being jostled on the street for not partaking in the illusion. She was reminded of the masques of the Renaissance staged in England. A favorite of Ben Jonson, Kit Marlowe had not written any. Just one, he had told her during the night of the quill pen, for a nobleman. He would not tell her who. "There is such a device, as you would not believe. A very honeyed thing 'tis. Come to. I shall show thee."

A display of fireworks rose overhead, turning into a cascading rainbow of color. Alice turned towards San Marco square, pausing at a column. A line of masked merrymakers held hands and wove themselves through the line of columns. When they got to Alice they playfully pushed her forward. She fell into the square and was helped upright by a masked man clad in black. Through the smokey maze of the square there was a small stage.

The haze cleared but the smell of incense and marijuana lingered. Punch and Judy strode about on the stage and the crowd laughed uproariously. Alice crept closer, listening to what the characters said. It was a mixture of old Italian and Latin, and she could not understand a word of it. The audience stared in rapt attention.

An orange flash caught her eye, and to the right of the stage a small band of dwarves appeared. Alice recognized them from the train station. Much to the consternation of the actors, they formed a ring around the stage and circled round. The audience laughed even harder at their antics. Once the dwarves realized they had stolen the show, they disbanded and moved towards the spectators. In a dreamlike haze, a dwarf motioned to Alice. She stared at him a moment then moved towards him.

"Alvis?"

He turned the corner and disappeared around a column. She followed so as not to lose sight of him. The spacious square turned into a passage along a narrow canal. The canal thinned of people and became dark and deserted.

"Wait!" Alice hurried to keep up as the dwarf turned into what looked like an entrance to a deserted shop. The entrance led to an alleyway, and as she turned to look for the dwarf, someone grabbed her from behind and shoved something hard against her hip.

She screamed and a man dragged her further into the alley into a shop entrance.

"Tell me where it is and I'll let you go." His breath smelled of stale wine and cigarettes and she gagged as he pressed his face close to hers.

"I don't know what you mean." Her heart pounding, she desperately tried to imagine what the man wanted.

"Don't play stupid. You've seen the bookseller and have the document."

The man pushed her into the corner and pulled away from her, cornering her next to the door. She recognized him from the Paddington Station hotel as the man who had been following her. He pointed the gun at her head.

"If you won't tell me where I can find it, I'll kill you." His eyes trained on her and Alice saw the cold steel the hotel maid spoken of.

"Please, I—" A muted thumping noise hit the man and a piece of his head blew off and hit the wall.

Alice screamed and sank to the ground. Another man came towards her and she clawed at the wall trying to right herself.

"Alice." His voice was gentle as he held out a hand. "It's Neville Cruise."

"What?!" she screamed. "Why should I believe—"

The street lamp illuminated his face, and she realized he was telling the truth.

He bent over and pulled the man's wallet from his jacket. She could barely look at the bloody mess.

"Come quickly." He began walking. "They'll be watching us and we need to leave." Neville moved swiftly away from the scene and Alice stared after him.

"C'mon!" He ran back and grabbed her arm, pulling her after him.

"We need to talk to the police. The authorities."

He laughed. "Right."

"What are you doing?"

"I work for the British Secret Service. MI6."

"What?"

"Rather like your CIA. Except better." He smirked.

"How can you joke about this?"

He frowned. "Alice, please. If we don't leave now there will be a whole lot more trouble to follow."

"Why should I believe you? You could be a psycho and working with this guy. A whole lot stranger things have—"

"He believes you've seen the London bookseller."

"How would you know that?"

"There are a whole lot of things I know about."

"Yeah? Like?"

"The Shakespeare connection."

She followed him.

"How did you know about the London bookseller?"

Cruise pulled out his mobile. "It's secure. Yes, I had to,…yeah. There was no other way. Okay, sure." He laughed. "Right. Bond." He slipped the phone back into his pocket."

"What was that about?"

"Had to tell the boss I pulled a proper James Bond."

"And now we'll sleep together." she said.

"Right." He said, grinning.

They moved into San Marco Square where the smoke and fireworks became overpowering, where the stares were intrusive. Alice donned her mask as faces appeared from all around her— staring.

"I'd like to know what's really going on," she said.

A man dressed as Punch walked the square on stilts. He had two bags with him, one containing brightly colored orange and pink candies, which he handed to people freely who smiled and spoke to him, another was filled with balls of gelato, which he dumped on the heads of those he deemed not adequately participating in the festivities. Alice steered them towards a mask vendor when she saw he was making his way towards them.

"I would think that you would want me to take my mask off instead of put it on." he said.

"If you don't put this on we will be unmercifully harassed."

"Yes. And that is why I'm here, so you won't be harassed. To protect you. You see, I've been assigned your case."

"When?"

"You do remember Hatfield House?"

"How could I forget? That arrogant bastard Cecil. I'm sure he had Celeste murdered."

"He did seem to be extorting monies from prominent nobles—lords and ladies of the realm—many of whom were connected to Shakespeare at one time or another."

"So you were investigating the Shakespeare connection?"

"Yes, I can't give out all the details, but that's why I was there, in Hatfield House."

The street narrowed and the crowds thinned. The smell of smoke dissipated, while bursts of fireworks flared in the distance.

They stood before her hotel, and Alice took off her mask. She took a deep breath of air. "I can finally breath."

"You'll be leaving for London tomorrow then?"

"Yes."

"I'll fly back with you."

"Why not? Apparently it will be hard to shake you."

He flipped open his mobile. "Yes, tomorrow. One moment." He held the phone away from his face and turned to Alice. "What flight?"

"Twenty nine. Ryanair."

He flipped the phone shut. "Good to go. I'll see you tomorrow then. An early one, it is. Good night." He nodded and stepped quickly into the night.

Alice stood holding his mask, wondering if she should yell after him.

***

She peered out her window into the early morning. The city was quiet and the water was still and gray in the canal. Alice waited for him, but he did not appear. She lay her key on the table and walked out the door.

When she boarded the flight, he still had not arrived. Alice wondered if it all wasn't a vague, badly rehearsed dream. The kind that would never make it on stage. She felt slightly paranoid. Perhaps it was a matter of slipping back into the madness?

Staring out the window she concentrated on the workers dressed in orange ready to usher the plane down the runway. He ran through the gate and out towards the plane, waving as he went by the workers, who laughed as he ran by. Bounding up the steps he spotted her at the end of the aisle and plunked down next to her.

"Whoo! Almost didn't make it."

Alice looked out the window, trying to hide her smile. She didn't want him to see the relief on her face.

"Fashionably late?" she said.

"No, it's what you Yanks would call sleeping in. Last night took it out of me."

The plane taxied down the runway and Alice braced herself for take-off.

"Alright? You look a bit stressed." Neville said.

"I hate this part of flying."

The engines whined and the plane pulled itself into the air. Buffeted by wind, it shook.

He put his hand over hers. "No worries. You have me and my parachute."

She squeezed her eyes shut, listening to the engine and clenching her muscles against the plane's agonized lurching towards the open sky.

"If you think this is bad wait until we get over the Alps. Looks as if there is a bit of weather coming through."

"Thanks."

As the plane leveled once it reached cruising altitude, she opened her eyes. A flight attendant stood before them.

"Would you care for a drink or anything to eat?" she said.

"Bloody Mary. Stoli." He said.

"Isn't a little early?" Alice said.

"Of course not. We British agents need our cocktails."

"Nothing for me."

The attendant smiled and moved behind them.

"Truth is, they know who I am." He winked. "How do you think I got on this flight?"

"Not impressed, Cruise."

The flight attendant brought him his drink. "Thanks, love." He took a sip. "Ahh, now that's what a drink is all about. You should have one. It seriously will help with your nerves."

She glared at him. "I was almost murdered. I'd rather keep my wits about me."

"I don't take it lightly, Alice. Speaking of which—" He flipped his mobile open. "Yes, on the way. See you soon." He flipped the mobile closed and pocketed it. "Sorry. Had to tell the boss about my whereabouts."

"You mean he doesn't instantly know? C'mon Cruise, with all these high tech gadgets? I'm sure he can zero in on you via satellite or something."

"Well, actually he can, but it might blow up the plane."

"I'm starting to think you're a nut."

"Alright, Alice. Enough banter. I understand your situation and that you want answers."

"That might be a start."

"It is a matter of the national trust. In England and America. There are a few people who would love to keep this matter silent."

"Wait, wait, wait." She held up her hand. "What matter are we talking about exactly? We need to start on the same page."

"The Shakespeare connection."

"So you think Marlowe is Shakespeare?"

"It is not a matter of what I think. It's a matter of what I know. There is a lack of hard evidence proving Marlowe is Shakespeare, but on the other hand there are volumes of evidence pointing to the fact that he probably is."

"So?"

"My point being, there a few powerful people who can, and will, keep this silent. Why? Because the man who was Shakespeare knew quite a bit about powerful people, people who would rather keep certain things quiet. Certain things in the closet."

"And how do you know this?"

"I do know a bit about my fellow, albeit past, spies. Walsingham was the man who developed modern espionage."

"What kind of secrets are you talking about, Cruise?"

"Very important secrets. Secrets that involve the national trust. See, the thing is, Alice, this is a lot like a tapestry. And once you start pulling on a thread, the whole thing could unravel." He sipped his drink, then took a large swallow. "These people from the past, these nobles, of course all knew one another. They each knew, or wanted to know, what the other ones were up to. And if you pull the Shakespeare connection apart, the whole house of cards it rests on will come crashing down. People start snooping in places that they wouldn't have thought to look before."

She sat quietly looking out the window. "I get it."

"Do you? In a way, all of English history rests on this sordid little fact of Shakespearean controversy. Can you just picture it?"

"What?"

He put his hand to his face in mock disbelief. "Oh my, if Shakespeare is not Shakespeare, then what else was going on during that time? What was your ancestor doing to my ancestor? What! You took away my noble privileges. How dare you!"

She laughed.

"It's no trivial matter. Everyone believes that horrid looking man in the frontispiece of the first folio is actually William Shakespeare. It's all based on a charade, isn't it?"

"It is." she said.

"And before you know it, the monarchy will be questioned, and who is the rightful title to it all. It will all come crashing down."

"It might."

"And," He swallowed the rest of his drink. "It's all because of you, my dear. You upset the proverbial apple cart."

"I didn't start the whole thing, Cruise. There have been plenty of Marlovians before me."

"Yes, but they didn't have the evidence, now did they? And..." He leaned close, and whispered in her ear, "they didn't go back in time."

His breath tickled.

"Don't poke fun."

"I'm not. I believe you."

"Do you?" She looked at him, searching his eyes.

"Yes." He looked back. Level and uncomplicated. "So listen to me now, Alice. The bookseller in London checks out. A bit eccentric, you'll see. But an honest gent. But there is someone else in your life I'm concerned with."

"Who?"

"The professor. Jim Schelling."

"I know about his dirty dealings with me, Cruise. He is trying to take my theatre away from me. Which, by the way, I contacted an attorney about, and it looks as if he won't after all. I'm surprised you don't know about that."

"Just be careful, Alice. I worry about you."

"What? Are you trying to tell me you care?"

He turned to her, and cupped her chin in his hand. "Yes, I am." His lips touched hers, and surprised, she kissed him. The feeling was warm and whole and she didn't question it. But she pulled back.

"I can't."

"You can. But you don't want to."

"I can't right now."

"Alice, look at me."

"There's too much going on."

"You're still in love with a ghost. Aren't you?"

"Of course not."

The plane descended, lowering itself by degrees. The captain announced they would be in London shortly and to please fasten their seat belts.

Chapter 53

In love with a ghost. The thought haunted her. *How dare he!*

If she let Kit go, it would all be a dream. She did not want to let go. It had meant so much. They had been through so much. Hadn't they? How could she possibly let that memory go? If she let it go a sacred piece of history would slip through her hands. It would absolve into the void, into meaninglessness, into nothingness.

Alice understood that Cruise knew this.

Irritated, she pushed open the heavy glass doors of the hotel. It was a cheap hotel she had booked at the last moment in Venice. Located on the Bankside, it was near the Rose Theatre.

She clanked up the stairs with her suitcase and walked the tattered and tired carpet to her room. Fumbling with the key in the lock, she finally managed to push open the door. She threw the suitcase in without even looking at the room. Slamming the door she moved down the stairs and out the door.

Time had passed in London. Instead of the old timber frame, Tudor-style houses, there now were high rises and modern glass buildings. Where once there were cobbled streets and the steady clop of horse's hooves, there now was pavement and the rushing movement of automobiles. Alice felt disoriented and checked her watch.

She found herself drifting towards the Rose. She remembered that its foundations had been unearthed in a routine archaeological excavation in 1989. Would there be nothing but bricks? Bones? She consulted her map. Yes, here it would be, right around the corner.

The building confronting her was all bright glass lined in metal mirroring the sidewalks, cars, and buses sweeping by. Alice was rooted to the spot, uncomprehending the scene. The marquee sign largely and loudly proclaimed "Rose Theatre."

Alice felt nothing and tried to remember the stage. Tried to remember Kit putting his arms around her and whispering in her ear. Tried to remember his velvet doublet against her skin. She stood in the busy sidewalk and felt empty. Unfolding her hand in front of her. There was no other hand. No other vision.

A man bumped into her, a tourist, and like an automaton, she turned towards the London Bridge.

***

The bookstalls at Saint Paul's Churchyard was where one would go for the best and brightest of the Elizabethan age. But that was long ago.

The bookstore she sought was called Gnosis, and as she walked, she kept an eye out for it.

"If you go looking for mystery, aye Alice, you will not find it. 'Tis everywhere. Unravel the thread." Kit said.

"Leave me." She whispered.

The map she held in her hand was crumpled from much use. She consulted it again, and found the correct street, turned left.

A small placard hung over the shop, which was wedged between a bakery and a print shop. The sign merely said Gnosis. A large stone gargoyle sat over the sign.

She pulled on the door handle, but it was locked. Noticing a buzzer, she pushed it. Nervous, Alice wiped her hand across the back of her neck. She turned towards the street. A pigeon flew overhead.

Her heart was pounding when a voice came over a small intercom. "Yes?"

"Hello? This is Alice. Alice Petrovka?"

"Oh yes. Come up, please."

There was a buzzing, followed by a break and release on the door handle. Alice pushed the door open. An old stairs went to the second floor, and she walked upward, keeping a hand on the side rail.

The door opened and the silhouette of a man with white hair appeared.

"Hello? Alice, is it?"

"Yes."

She smelled old building, books and must.

"Come, come."

He ushered her into the sanctuary. Surrounded by books and dust, Alice tried to get her bearings.

"Mr. Cotten?"

"Oh, aye. Yes."

She grabbed his hand and shook it.

"You'll be in need of some tea?"

"That would be most kind."

He hurried to an electric kettle that would boil water in a matter of seconds. Alice wondered why the English still didn't rule the world with this invention.

He emerged with the tea. "Best thing since digestives."

She sat in a padded chair with the tea. Nibbling on a biscuit, she began. "According to a very famous actor, Sir Laurence Olivier, we are now in the second Renaissance." She looked towards a small window of light. "And you know, I believe him."

He nodded and smiled. Alice continued. "I don't think Kit would want anything less than to be proclaimed the real Shakespeare."

He laughed. "Of course, dear Alice. The looking glass is upon us." He hurried amongst his shelves and came forward with a manuscript. "At long last." He handed her a much-used and fingered first quarto.

She rested it on her lap before opening it. Sipping her tea she noticed her fingers trembled.

"So, this is it?"

"'Tis." Alexander Cotton had laughing blue eyes.

"Mr. Cotton, there are—"

"Please call me Alex."

"Yes, Alex. You know, I quite expected you to be an old, boring, English snob. Or a snooty eccentric."

"I've been called an eccentric, yes. Not everyone understands my passion for Gnosis. You know in the Greek it means knowledge."

"Of course." she said.

"We do move in the same circles, Alice. You knew Celeste Cecil, and she told me to contact you if anything turned up. Well, it did, and here it is on your lap."

"The play?"

"There is a message in the margins. In *Hamlet.*"

She flipped to the tragedy. "Where? What lines?"

"I believe he starts at act three, scene two. Line 233."

Alice scanned the page, there, starting at line 233, wedged carefully in the margin, was a small script:

As you ask,
Come find me here, and be my love
You shalt find me here, up above.
No longer bootless, but without a soul
Your other half.
Christopher Marlowe
In the end...

"He's talking about Northern Italy. Here, where it says "No longer bootless." Italy is shaped like a boot. "Up above" refers to northern Italy and where he is staying. With Gonzaga." She placed her finger on the words. "He is specifically making reference to the noble family he stayed with."

"A coded message." he said.

"In the end." What does that—" She quickly flipped to the end of the book. At the end of the last play was the line:

All plays herein by the poet and playmaker,
Christopher Marlowe

Alice stared at the words.

"He did it." Setting the folio aside she looked out the window. Everything had changed and everything was the same. She set aside the book.

"You have no idea how much this means to me." she said.

"There is much work for you to do, Alice."

"What do you mean?"

"They'll all come out of the wood work now. The evidence is definitely on your side—this is a first edition folio, printed in 1623. Shakespeare was supposed to have died in 1616, and of course Marlowe was stabbed in Deptford in 1593 and thrown in a plague pit in the churchyard there. Or so the story goes."

She sighed and slumped in the chair. "You're right, Alex. The Shakespeare industry will hit me full force with its foot soldiers. Bombers." A large pigeon flew on top of the gargoyle's head in front of the shop. "But does it matter? I have what I want. I have the evidence."

He patted her on the back and picked up her tea cup. "Time will tell, love. Time will tell."

Chapter 54

The porch swing creaked quietly as she listened to the cicadas in the trees. They droned on in their hazy, late summer way.

Alice felt that the end of summer always had a quiet, dying quality to it. The sun had reached its zenith, and everything green and vegetative exploded in ripeness. But that was it. Nothing was growing anymore.

She pushed the hair from her forehead. The warmth of the late afternoon sun hung in the trees.

Joannie pushed through the screen door with their drinks.

"What's wrong with you, Petrovka? I leave you for two minutes and you get all morose on me."

"I'm fine. Just thinking of the upcoming meeting with Jim. You don't think I'm losing it do you?"

"No. If you recall I was one of the few people in your corner when you did lose it. Apparently this Cruise guy is, too. Very good looking, I might add." Joannie winked. "Love the dark hair and blazing blue eyes. What a great combo. Too bad he's not a she." She laughed. "Does he have a sister?"

Alice took a sip of her lemonade and winced. "I can always count on you, Bryant, for cutting edge humor and drinks. Holy moley. What is the ratio of vodka to lemonade in this?"

"Oh, probably like one to one. As you know my math skills never fail me, even though I no longer have a job where I can use them." She took a sip of her drink. "Ahh...just right. So back to this Cruise guy. I must say I was totally floored when he contacted me."

"I'm sure he was very nosy."

"To say the least. But that's the thing. I finally said, after tip-toeing around with his secret agent thing for a while, "You like her, don't you?" He tried to play it off, then decided he would have to come over and speak to me in person. Man, those British guys really like their tipple, don't they?"

"I suppose. What did he say?"

"Well, he brought over the Moet and Chandon. Can you believe it? Champagne!" Joannie clinked her glass against Alice's. "Cheers. He said we needed to toast a job well done, so we put back a few."

"Bryant, please. Cut to the chase already."

"He said he could tell a true psychic because he was a bit psychic himself so he never doubted you. But he said he would chalk up the heavy duty feelings for you due to saving you from that psycho...big adrenaline rush and all. So he'd just leave it be."

"Hmm. Is that it?"

"Pretty much. Awfully nice man, at first I thought— oh no, another British guy." She frowned. "You know what I mean?"

"I think I've had my fair share of all things British."

"Yeah, I know what you mean. But, I could tell, Petrovka. He was really sincere."

"Sincerely nosy is what he is."

"Sure, it amazes me what he knows." said Joannie. "But there's more to it than that. And I do think he cares." She finished the rest of her drink. "Time for another. Need a refresher?"

"No. Still working on this."

Alice silently moved the swing, watching as young couple walked by. She thought of Renita and Dion and wondered how they were. With a pang she realized she left no forwarding address for them.

Joannie banged the screen behind as she sat down with her drink. The swing creaked.

"The thing is Petrovka. We're free."

"Yes. Free from Albert, that nasty job, and—"

"Hire me as an actor. I'm ready to try my hand." Joannie said.

Alice laughed. "There is that. My theatre. Which, of course, I have to speak to Jim about." She wrinkled her nose. "I'm really not looking forward to that."

"Do you think he'll give you a hard time?"

"I don't think it will be too bad. Maybe I'm making too much of it. Really, it will be a bunch of paperwork. He's stepping off the board and signing off. At least I won't be bothered with *that* anymore."

"Yeah, what a numbskull." Joannie said. "I can't even believe he pulled that. Right when you were down and out. What a major jerk!"

"He's got a few issues." said Alice. "You find out who your friends are." She jiggled the ice cubes in her drink. "Truthfully, there are some things I'm not sure I know how to be free of, or even if I want to be free of them."

"Such as?"

"You will never know, no one will ever know, what I experienced. I don't know if want to be free from Kit." She stared down the street. She could no longer see the young couple.

"You're right. I don't know what you experienced. That'll be tough. But you're in the here and now, Petrovka. *The here and now.*"

"I hear you."

"So what's the alternative?"

"I don't know. I just…don't know."

Chapter 55

She couldn't resist because she still had a key. And although she wasn't scheduled to meet with him for a few weeks, she found herself back in the place where the ritual could be completed.

Alice was determined. After speaking with Bernie again about linking the past and the present with ritual, she felt it could be her last chance.

Kit had been haunting her. Night after night she had dreams of him reaching to her, begging her to come to him.

At first she had gone for long walks. She had eaten good food, avoided stress, and stayed away from all things Shakespearean. She began studying twentieth century theatre. Anything that hinted at the Renaissance was avoided.

But it was useless. She was plagued with a deep longing that could not be quenched. She went to meetings, out to lunch with friends and co-workers, and kept her apartment tidy.

And that's when the dreams started. At first she had gotten up, rinsed her face with water, and went back to bed. When that didn't work, she stayed up late reading novels. When that didn't work she read the plays. And then the sonnets. One sonnet in particular had caught her eye:

What is your substance, whereof are you made,
That millions of strange shadows on you tend?

Since everyone hath, everyone, one shade,
And you, but one, can every shadow lend.

She found the words rolling through her mind like a carriage through a grassy field. And like the carriage, she was carried away. The fuzzy parameters that held her in check gave way and she remembered, quite clearly, the road to the palace with Francis Walsingham.

Alice now clutched the sonnet in her hand. She had written it down and pocketed the paper. At odd times she took it out. Waiting in line at the grocery store, or for a teller at the bank, she read the lines. The lines that seemed immortal, speaking of shadows within shadows.

Now, at the Lion, she glanced at her watch and noticed it had stopped. *Time had stopped.*

Clutching the sonnet in her hand she whispered the words.

She saw him too, whispering words. His words were different, and she struggled to understand what he was saying. *Alice?*

The world around her gave way, fading and receding in an intangible tangle of evidence that no longer supported it. She saw him in a candlelit room.

Alice, come back to me, come back, come back…

Alone in the room, he reached for her.

"I'm here!" Alice looked around the theatre, the stage. She reached out her hand and the sonnet slipped from her fingers, falling to the ground.

The door creaked, and he appeared on the threshold. He wore the red slashed doublet. The door shut behind him. He walked down the aisle, towards her, towards the stage.

She held up her hand, blocking the spotlight, trying to get a better view of him.

He laughed. "Alice, Alice, Alice. You've always been caught in fantasy. Haven't you."

Shocked, her stomach gave way, free-falling as if in an elevator. She put out her hand in a protective gesture.

"Jim! What are you doing here?"

Schelling hopped up on the stage. "I guess I could ask you the same thing. Our meeting isn't 'till next week."

"This is my theatre, Jim. I want you to leave."

"Leave?" He laughed. There was a glint in his eye and he pulled a knife from a sheaf at his side. "Let's do a bit of *Hamlet*, shall we? Why waste the afternoon?"

Alice swallowed hard as fear tore through her veins. "Not in the mood."

"Then tell me, are you in the mood to give up the first folio? Or shed a little blood?"

"You're crazy."

"Me? Crazy? Tsk, tsk, my dear. You are the crazy one. Everyone knows it."

"I don't have the folio here."

"Don't lie to me. I know it's in the safe in your office. You're so predictable." He grabbed her arm, then twisted her around with the knife at her throat. "Now, my love," he whispered in her ear, "pretend I'm Marlowe and let's do a little playmaking. *Othello*, I think."

"He would never do this to me!"

"Wouldn't he? He was trying to save his precious skin."

"Elizabeth was saving his precious skin. Let me go, Jim. Everyone will know it was you. Everyone knows I have the folio."

"You and the bookseller. That's it."

"There's someone else."

He laughed. "Who? Your British spy? I made sure he will never know. Ah, we have a jealous muse, my Alice. But you and I know Marlowe cannot be claimed as our beloved bard Shakespeare. Just won't work."

"Who's paying you Jim?"

"Are you going to get me the folio, Alice? Or do you want to finish your suicide?"

"Suicide?"

"That's what this is my dear."

There was a blinding shock of light as the door flew open. Alice gasped and Schelling squinted his eyes. "A little playmaking here!" he said. "We'll be done in a minute."

"We're done with the play, Schelling. Let her go."

Confused, Alice watched the woman advance. "Bryant?"

Joannie trained the gun in front of her. "Sorry, I don't have time to explain, Petrovka. Second career you could say."

Schelling moved Alice protectively in front of him.

"A little two step, Petrovka! You know what I mean."

Alice moved her legs to give Joannie a clear shot at Schelling. Schelling dragged her off the stage.

The shot rang out and Schelling was flung away from her. He screamed and hit the ground. Joannie ran up and kicked the knife away from him.

The door opened again and a man walked towards them. "Bloody hell, Bryant, you don't mess around, do you?"

"You taught me well." Joannie holstered her gun.

"Amazed." said Alice.

"Yes," said Cruise. "This is the end scene, Alice. And as Olivia says in Twelfth Night: 'Most wonderful.'"

"Help me!" yelled Schelling. "You people are lunatics."

Joannie hoisted him to his feet after she handcuffed him. "Right."

"You shot me in the arm! I need help!" Schelling stumbled forward.

"That I did, Schelling, and there are people waiting outside for you. And, if you're lucky, an ambulance."

"I'm bleeding to death!"

"C'mon. Enough with the theatrics, it's just a slight superficial. You should be happy I'm such a good shot." She pushed him forward and he reluctantly moved down the stairs and up the aisle.

Joannie looked over her shoulder. "I'll see you two in a few?"

"Yes." said Cruise.

A plainclothes officer stuck his head around the door. "Debriefing?"

"Yeah!" Joannie waved him outside as she pushed Schelling out the door.

"Debriefing?" said Alice.

"Yes. That's what it's called in the intelligence world. But I think we both know what happened here." He looked down at the pink and white rose at her feet. Tentatively, he took her hand, saying:

If we shadows have offended,
Think but this, and all is mended—
That you have but slumbered here
While these visions did appear.
And this weak and idle theme,
No more yielding but a dream.

"No." whispered Alice. "It was more than a dream."

"I know." said Cruise. "But perhaps…" He picked up the rose at her feet and held it out to her. "Can you learn how to love in the present?"

She looked at the rose in his hand but did not take it. "I don't know."

He studied her face a long moment, then walked off the stage and up the aisle.

Alice saw a darkened room lit by a candle. A lone figure labored over a piece of parchment with a quill and an inkpot. She saw the ink-stained hand pause, and then the figure rose from the table and went to the window and stood, gazing out.

"So this is how it is to be." she said. She turned towards Cruise.

"Wait!"

Cruise turned.

"I can try." she said.

He smiled. And waited for her.

323

AUTHOR'S NOTE

I consulted many sources when writing this novel. It is not meant to be read as a historical timeline in regards to Christopher Marlowe's murder. As a work of fiction, I took many historically inaccurate liberties. For example, Sir Francis Walsingham was dead when Alice Petrovka goes back in time to meet with Marlowe, and the Duke of Valois is modeled on the Duke of Anjou and Henri III of France. Queen Elizabeth was well past the days of being courted by any French nobleman when Alice speaks with her. Those of my readers well-versed in Shakespearean authorship studies will recognize many other inconsistencies in historical events involving Christopher Marlowe. Historical fiction is just that. Fiction. History is used by the writer to tell a story that will hopefully inspire and entertain, much like Marlowe and Elizabethan England did and still does for me. If you are interested, I have included a partial bibliography of sources which proved important in telling the story. Please visit www.theshakespearean.com for further information on Christopher Marlowe, the authorship controversy, and teacher resources.

BIBLIOGRAPHY

Budiansky, Stephen. *Her Majesty's Spymaster: Elizabeth I, Sir Francis Walsingham, and the birth of Modern Espionage.* New York: Viking, 2005.

Clegg, Cyndia Susan. *Press Censorship in Elizabethan England.* United Kingdom: Cambridge University Press, 1997.

Cressy, David. *Literacy and the Social Order: Reading and Writing in Tudor and Stuart England.* New York: Cambridge University Press, 2006.

Diagnostic and Statistical Manual of Mental Disorders DSM-IV-TR Fourth Edition. American Psychiatric Association, 2000.

Gurr, Andrew. *Playgoing in Shakespeare's London.* New York: Cambridge University Press, 2004.

Hoffman, Calvin. *The Murder of the Man Who Was Shakespeare.* New York: Grosset and Dunlap, 1955.

Kendall, Roy. *Christopher Marlowe and Richard Baines: Journeys through the Elizabethan Underground.* London: Fairleigh Dickinson University Press, 2003.

Lanyer, Aemilia "The Poems of Aemlia Lanyer: Salve Deus Rex Judaeorum." In *Women Writers in English 1350-1850.* Edited by Susanne Woods. New York: Oxford University Press, 1993.

Marlowe, Christopher. "Lucan's First Book." In *Complete Poems*. Edited by Drew Silver. New York: Dover, 2003.

Marlowe, Christopher. "The Jew of Malta." In *The Complete Plays*. Edited by Mark Thornton Burnett. London: Orion House, 1999.

Mears, Natalie. "Courts, Courtiers and Culture in Tudor England." The Historical Journal 46 (3) (2003): doi: 10.1017/S0018246X03003212

Nicholl, Charles. *The Reckoning*. New York: Harcourt, Brace & Company, 1992.

Read, Conyers. *The Government of England Under Elizabeth*. The Folger Shakespeare Library, 1960.

Rowse, A.L. *The Case Books of Simon Forman: Sex and Society in Shakespeare's Age*. London: Picador, 1974.

Rowse, A.L. *The Poems of Shakespeare's Dark Lady*. London: Jonathon Cape Ltd, 1978.

Salgado, Gamini. *The Elizabethan Underworld*. London: The Folio Society, 2006.

Shakespeare, William. *The Complete Pelican Shakespeare*. Edited by Stephen Orgel, and A.R. Braunmuller. New York: Penguin Group, 2002.

Shakespeare, William. *Shakespeare's Sonnets*. Folger Shakespeare Library. Edited by Barbara A. Mowat and Paul Werstine. New York: Washington Square Press, 2004.

Tucker, C.F. Brooke and Nathaniel Burton Paradise, eds., *English Drama 1580 – 1642*. Massachusetts: D.C. Heath and Company, 1933.

Wraight, A.D. *In Search of Christopher Marlowe*. London: Macdonald & Co, 1965.

Weil, Judith. *Christopher Marlowe: Merlin's Prophet*. Cambridge: Cambridge University Press, 1977.

Woods, Susanne. Lanyer: *A Renaissance Woman Poet*. New York: Oxford University Press, 1999.

Yates, Frances A. *The Rosicrucian Enlightenment*. London: Routledge and Kegan Paul, 1972.